Burning Lies

Helene Young lives in Trinity Beach, on the edge of the Great Barrier Reef in North Queensland. Her work as a senior captain with a major regional airline takes her all over the east coast of Australia. She was voted most popular romantic suspense author by the Australian Romance Readers of Australia (ARRA) in 2010 and 2011, and her recent novel *Wings of Fear* won the Romance Writers of Australia (RWA) Romantic Book of the Year Award in 2011.

heleneyoung.com

HELENE YOUNG

Burning Lies

MICHAEL JOSEPH
an imprint of
PENGUIN BOOKS

MICHAEL JOSEPH

Published by the Penguin Group
Penguin Group (Australia)
250 Camberwell Road, Camberwell, Victoria 3124, Australia
(a division of Pearson Australia Group Pty Ltd)
Penguin Group (USA) Inc.
375 Hudson Street, New York, New York 10014, USA
Penguin Group (Canada)
90 Eglinton Avenue East, Suite 700, Toronto, Canada ON M4P 2Y3
(a division of Pearson Penguin Canada Inc.)
Penguin Books Ltd
80 Strand, London WC2R 0RL England
Penguin Ireland
25 St Stephen's Green, Dublin 2, Ireland
(a division of Penguin Books Ltd)
Penguin Books India Pvt Ltd
11 Community Centre, Panchsheel Park, New Delhi – 110 017, India
Penguin Group (NZ)
67 Apollo Drive, Rosedale, North Shore 0632, New Zealand
(a division of Pearson New Zealand Ltd)
Penguin Books (South Africa) (Pty) Ltd
24 Sturdee Avenue, Rosebank, Johannesburg 2196, South Africa
Penguin (Beijing) Ltd
7F, Tower B, Jiaming Center, 27 East Third Ring Road North,
Chaoyang District, Beijing 100020, China

Penguin Books Ltd, Registered Offices: 80 Strand, London WC2R 0RL, England

First published by Penguin Group (Australia), 2012

1 3 5 7 9 10 8 6 4 2

Design by Cathy Larsen © Penguin Group (Australia)
Cover photographs © Woman: Rebecca Parker/Trevillion Images;
Burning land: Cuellar/Getty Images; Palm trees: Shutterstock
Typeset in 11/17pt Sabon
Printed and bound in Australia by McPherson's Printing Group, Maryborough, Victoria

National Library of Australia
Cataloguing-in-Publication data:

Young, Helene.
Burning lies / Helene Young.
9781921901225 (pbk.)

A823.4

penguin.com.au

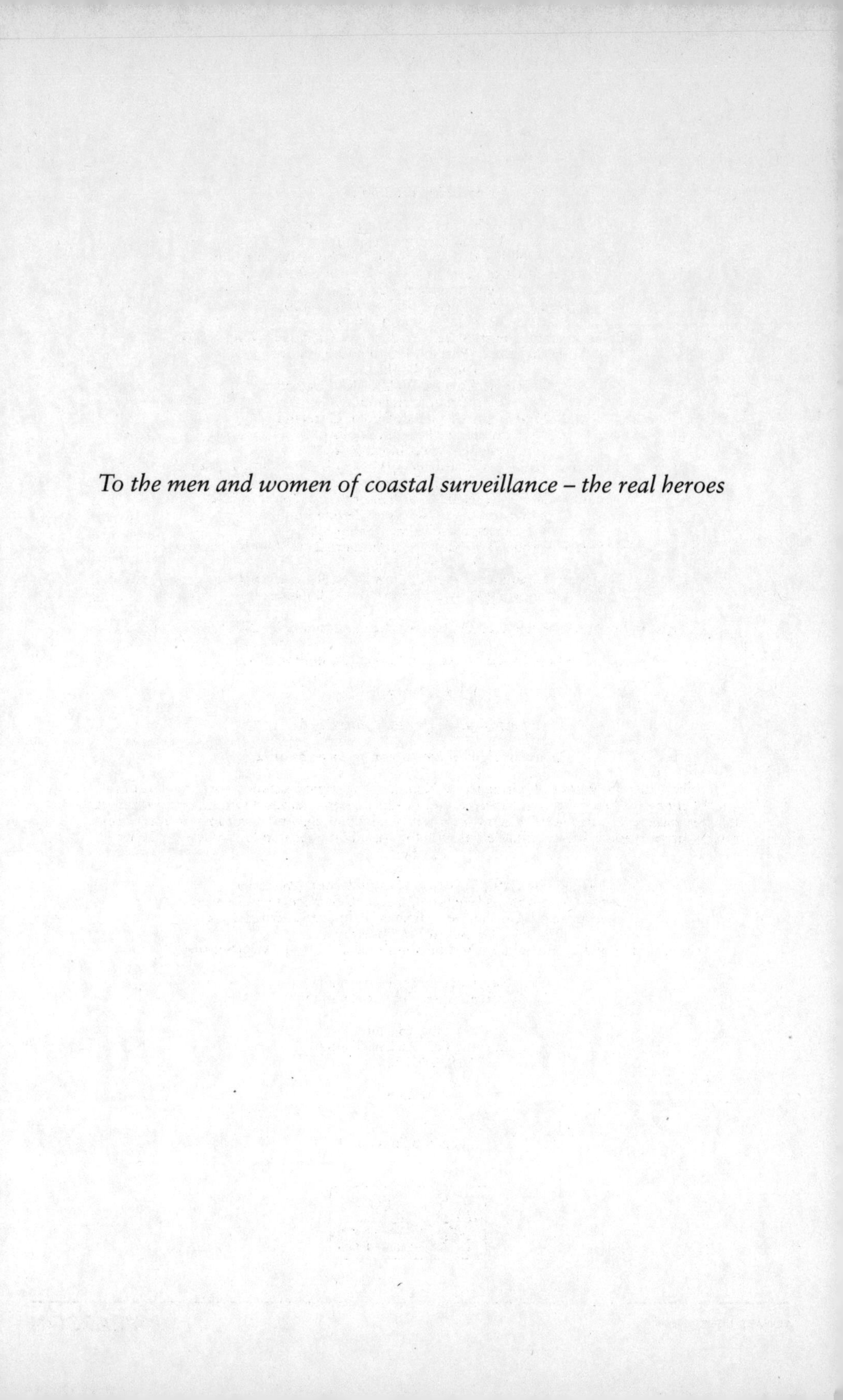

To the men and women of coastal surveillance – the real heroes

Prologue

Canberra, ACT, Australia

THE aircraft bucked in the swirling heat. Flames shot up through the plumes of dense smoke, flaring and leaping as though trying to scorch the paint from the fuselage.

Kaitlyn's five-point harness pressed into her, jabbing the sharp plastic edge of the Border Watch visitors pass into her chest. After a week in the air she still found the unpredictable movement of the Dash 8 alarming. The smoke had seeped through the air conditioning, biting at the crew's throats and stinging their eyes. The two Border Watch crewmen, who sat at consoles that wouldn't have looked out of place on a NASA space shuttle, appeared unconcerned. This was just another day at the office for the surveillance crew. On the other side of the aisle the Australian Federal Police senior constable had filled another sick bag. Trying to ignore the smell, Kaitlyn clutched her own sick bag in one hand and leant over the Forward Looking Infrared screen.

For a disconnected moment she felt as though she was a child again, watching her parents' black and white television and feeling ill after too many of her mother's homemade sweets. If only it were that simple.

'There he is again.' The mission commander next to her stabbed his finger at the FLIR screen.

Swallowing, Kaitlyn forced her throat to relax. 'It looks like the same man we were tracking before. Even without being able to see his face clearly.' She felt way out of her depth, but they were depending on her to read this man and his intentions. She summoned her confidence. 'The way he's holding the cigarette and leaning against the car with his ankles crossed says he's enjoying watching the havoc he's created. He's relaxed, at ease with what he's done. Same stance, same baseball cap – same guy as earlier in the week.' The resolution of the image on the surveillance equipment was crystal-clear, but the man's face was hidden by the square brim of his cap.

'You're absolutely sure?' the mission commander asked, leaning closer to the screen. She could smell sweat overpowering his sharp aftershave and she raised her hand to her nose, trying to breathe normally.

'Yes, I'm positive.' She looked up at the commander as he started punching buttons on the satellite phone.

'Right,' he said. 'We call it in. Do you think you can identify him?'

'Not yet. With the sunglasses and cap . . .' She hesitated. 'He looks familiar.'

'Okay, keep watching. I'll zoom it up. Maybe he'll remove them at some stage and we'll get a better look at him. If not, no matter – the cops can pick him up anyway. We've got the registration and footage of his car. Fuckin' arsonists. Capital punishment's too good for them.'

Kait had been so focused on the car they'd been tracking that she hadn't been paying attention to the landscape. They were now flying over another fire front, further to the west of their original track. It was disorienting to see the country from above. The hills lost their shape and height. Roads twisted in unpredictable ways.

The familiar roof and fence line of her neighbourhood's primary school became clear in the jumble below. She froze.

'Wait! Where are we?'

'That's Narangba Drive, off the Monaro Highway,' the mission commander replied tersely, before returning to his conversation on the phone.

'No! ' Kaitlyn stuffed her hand in her mouth. 'It can't be!' The blood drained to her feet, leaving her cheeks cold. The sick bag crumpled in her fist.

The mission commander finally registered her distress as he ended his phone call. 'You okay, love?' he asked.

'My house,' she croaked. 'I live on Narangba Road.'

'Shit. You live down there?'

Kait's fingers slid over the keyboard, taking the vision wider. She had no way of stopping the moan that started low in her chest. It couldn't be. She didn't want to believe the picture was real. As the aircraft flew on, she spotted her house. It was engulfed in flames, the corrugated-iron roof curling in the heat like the blackened petals of a flower opening on a glowing red heart. Worse still, she saw two familiar cars in the driveway, with flames already consuming them. What was her father doing there? Why was her husband home from work? He should be out fighting the fires. The fear, the pain, squeezed her lungs.

'*Noooo!*' She didn't realise the wail of grief was hers until a strong arm wrapped around her, taking her weight as she slumped forwards.

Chapter 1

Five years later

KAITLYN Scott's skin felt hot, stretched tight across her cheekbones. After a complex, six-month operation involving the full gamut of Australian Border Protection agencies, the end was literally in sight. As the aircraft turned for another run over the dramatic scene below, she adjusted the range on her equipment with delicate touches that belied her tension. The FLIR was trained on four vessels.

Cocooned in the aircraft, adrenalin poured through Kait's body. She knew the crew of the Australian Navy Patrol Boat, HMAS *Childers*, would be feeling the same heated rush as they powered along behind the large motor launch. Two rigid-hull inflatables, full of armed Navy personnel, flanked the cruiser. On their current track they would plow into one of the Ribbon reefs. That would be fatal, not to mention an environmental disaster.

With the nape of Kait's neck prickling with nerves, she keyed her microphone. 'Warship *Childers*, this is Border Watch one-five-three. Be aware there is a section of reef two miles ahead at twelve o'clock, over.' Her voice was calm, but her words held urgency. She felt sure the crew of the patrol boat would be well aware of the danger, but she was compelled to double-check.

'Border Watch one-five-three, roger that. *Childers* out.'

Almost instantly, the left-hand inflatable closed on the cruiser.

The one to the right swerved towards the stern of the vessel. She relaxed an inch. Time to finish it. She and her crew had been part of a tag team of aircraft shadowing the motor cruiser since it re-entered Australian waters in the Torres Strait four days ago. They now had video footage that proved the vessel had been running guns into Papua New Guinea and drugs back into Australia.

Stray bullets hitting the water around the inflatables kicked up fountains of spray. She saw pieces of fibreglass fly off the side of the motorboat as the servicemen returned fire. She flinched. HMAS *Childers* bore down on the three smaller vessels as Navy personnel swarmed over the cruiser. The churing white water from the big twin diesels died to a simmering whirlpool.

It was over. Six crewmen lined the back deck, hands on their heads, with a row of guns trained on them. Almost an anticlimax. Kaitlyn took a couple of deep breaths, knowing the others would all be doing the same thing, and ran her hand down her throat. It wasn't possible to remain detached.

'We're reaching our latest divert time,' Morgan cautioned from the flight deck. Kaitlyn knew she could depend on the captain to keep them on task as long as was safely possible. If Morgan said it was time to leave, then it was.

'Okay, well done, guys,' Kait said. 'Let's head home and relax. Customs is very happy with our work.' She clicked her seat back on its track and stretched her cramped legs up the aisle. The adrenalin, the apprehension, would take a few minutes to ease. Waggling her toes in her black boots, she avoided knocking the two long-range fuel tanks positioned between her and the flight deck. Being tall had its disadvantages.

As the Border Watch mission commander, she sat halfway down the length of the Dash 8 aircraft, in front of her console. On the other side of the aisle her young observer, Matt, moved his chair back from a similar console. The Border Watch fleet circled the coastline of Australia like an airborne electronic eye, which gave them a unique office with very little room to move.

The high-wing aircraft rolled out of the turn and Kait allowed herself to be distracted by the view. Time to unwind and come back to earth, literally.

'Spectacular. The colours are amazing,' she said. The other three crewmembers murmured in agreement. At 1500 feet, the ocean stretched from horizon to horizon, the build up of thunderstorms ahead the only indication that the Australian coastline was just out of sight. The outer Great Barrier Reef was like a series of giant freshwater pearls, strung together in a rope and resting on French navy satin. In the late afternoon, with the sea breeze fading, the breaking waves of the Coral Sea added a white ruffle to the eastern side of the reefs.

'Dan'll be happy to see you, Kait.' Morgan spoke from the flight deck.

'And I'll be happy to see him and his cheeky grin,' Kait replied with a twinge of guilt. Being a single mum had major drawbacks, and leaving her seven-year-old son with her mother, Julia, was the most painful. When she was away for work the deep ache in her heart kept her awake long past midnight in her silent hotel room.

'How's Julia doing?' her friend inquired.

'She's thriving. Finally. I think she's decided to embrace the Tablelands' country lifestyle instead of comparing it to a big city. Last week she took up clogging. The week before she signed up for a quilting course.'

'Clogging? What on earth is that?'

'Not quite sure. Irish dancing for the modern matron?' Kaitlyn laughed. 'She's trying to convince me I need to go too. I think she's decided to organise my social life as well. As if I've got time for one.'

'You should make more time for you,' Morgan insisted. 'I have no idea how you juggle such a busy life and that huge drive home after work.'

'Like you're in a position to lecture,' Kait replied with a smile, knowing Morgan had her own family pressures to deal with. 'But you're right, it does have its moments.'

Happy Jack Valley, just outside Atherton, offered safety in anonymity for her family. Having her mother living with them made the arrangement possible. Despite Julia's low-level guerrilla tactics aimed at convincing her to find work closer to home, Kaitlyn knew she needed this job, needed to do something vital, something meaningful, to stay sane. It kept the guilt at bay. It let her love her little boy without having to remember his father. It helped to fill some of the void her own father's death had left.

Kaitlyn squashed that thought before it could grow. It was good to be part of a team, to feel responsible, to belong. It would be even better once she was home again with Dan and Julia.

The coastline was now in sight, with a line of ominous thunderstorms looming over the Great Dividing Range and Cairns Airport. She sighed. It might take a little longer to get back on the ground and start driving up the winding road to her home, high on the hill.

Matt interrupted her thoughts. 'Hell of a storm season. The lightning coming out of those cells is wicked.'

Kaitlyn nodded. 'It's such a shame it's so dry. I've never seen so many storms fail to deliver. They build, they thunder, they die. No rain.'

'Yeah, I'm not keen on getting up close and personal with one of them.'

'You and me both.'

'As if I'd fly through that lot,' Morgan interjected. 'But we will have to divert to the west and come in over the Tablelands.'

'Great,' Kait said. 'What's another ten minutes between friends?'

The others laughed, but Kait had to force her smile as she resettled her headset over her ears. It had been a long day and the earphones felt like they were compressing her skull.

'Border Watch one-five-three, due to traffic delays you're cleared to hold at Biboohra, all turns to the right. Expect a set course time of zero-seven-two-zero. And you can expect the ILS runway one five.'

Kaitlyn heard Morgan sigh as Tim, the first officer, read the details back to the air traffic controller. An Instrument Landing System approach meant that visibility at the airfield was poor. It looked like the weather was going to persist right through to touchdown, adding more time to their flight.

'Sorry, guys, there's smoke haze at the airfield so we're on instrument approaches as well as dodging storms,' Morgan said. The aircraft slowed as she reconfigured it to give them maximum endurance. 'Seems fires have started up on the range again while we've been away.'

Kaitlyn's top lip beaded with sweat. The thought of fires always did that. She squeezed her eyes shut, fumbling for her sunglasses in her jacket pocket, and swallowed, trying to control the surge of fear. It didn't quite work. The acrid burn of smoke had been sucked into the aircraft air conditioning and in an instant she was back in Canberra. For a split second the memories paralysed her before she wrestled them under control. Her nerves were at snapping point.

'Kait? Kaitlyn?' Matt's voice broke through, but it took a moment to quarantine the horrific images.

'Sorry, must have nodded off for an instant.' Her observer didn't seem to notice the mammoth effort she'd made to pull herself together.

'Have there been any fires out near your place yet?' From the tone of his voice, Matt had already asked the question.

'Not close to us,' she managed to reply as she smoothed her hand down her auburn plait.

Tim joined the conversation. 'Dad says there've been a stack of fires on the Tablelands already this season. He can't believe Mother Nature gets all the blame.'

'Your dad's right. There have been more than usual. Only a couple of them have been hazard reduction burns that got away.'

Kaitlyn had joined the Oakey Creek Rural Fire Brigade, a volunteer organisation that provided backup for the professional firefighters, as soon as she and her family moved into the area. It was the least she could do, even though it ate into precious family time. Mostly the RFB were called out about once a week for grass-fires. This last month felt like it had been continuous. It was taking its toll on Kait and her family, as well as the rest of the team, but she had no choice. She couldn't say no. The guilt wouldn't let her.

'How's the brigade holding up?' Morgan asked.

'Doing it tough. We're spread thin on the ground. I just wish . . .' Her voice petered out. No words could explain the deep-seated frustration, the anger, at having to fight deliberately lit fires. With a father who was an arson investigator, she'd grown up with a crystal-clear understanding of the power and the horror of fire.

The aircraft made a gentle turn to the right as they reached their designated holding point. Kait could see the plumes of smoke rising from at least three fire fronts. The old memories surged back at her and she clenched her jaw, her feet, her hands against them, willing them away. It was always like this at the start of the fire season. All her insecurities, all her fears surfaced. She'd lost more than just her father, her husband and her house in those dreadful Canberra fires. She'd lost her ability to trust.

Kait knew she had to distract herself, keep busy. She reached out with a slightly shaking hand and turned her FLIR on again. The black and white image stayed clear even when the lurching aircraft flew through a thick cloud of smoke. Matt coughed at the strong smell of burning eucalypts. 'That's a bit rough. Can't we hold in the other direction?'

'Smoke's worse over there,' Tim retorted.

'Have a look at this, Matt,' Kait said. 'Have you seen fire on the FLIR before?'

The young man shook his head and slid his seat sideways to look at the screen. 'That's so cool. You can see everything.'

'Tell me what you're seeing,' Kaitlyn said. 'Cars, fire, people? Can you tell the difference?'

He frowned, then jabbed at the screen. 'That's a line of fire. And I reckon there's a couple of vehicles over there.'

'And what about this?' Kait pointed at a section to the left of the screen that was rapidly becoming the centre as the aircraft turned inbound again in the holding pattern.

'I'm not sure.'

'It's someone using a drip torch,' Kait said. She decreased the range on the FLIR and enlarged the image. 'See, they're laying a line of fire, some sort of back-burn.'

'Wow, I had no idea we could use the FLIR for this.'

'We don't often have a need to.' She zoomed in further. The vehicle was a Rural Fire Brigade truck. Whoever was driving it had finished their work and was heading back towards Mareeba. She widened the image again and stopped in surprise. 'What the hell?' The containment line was in the wrong place. 'What's the wind doing?' she asked.

Morgan answered. 'It's a south-easterly. Not much in it at the airport, probably a bit stronger on the Tablelands. Why?'

'I think there's fire heading towards a group of firefighters.'

'Seriously?' Matt asked. 'How can you tell?'

'See which side the vehicles are on?'

'The left?'

'Yep. And they'll be fighting the fire with the wind on their backs.'

'Right. So the fire there, the one that's just starting, will burn towards them?'

'That's what it looks like to me. I hope to God they know what they're doing.'

Matt eyed her. 'How come you know so much about this?'

'I had some experience a few years ago.' It was a monumental understatement. Even with the stranglehold she had on her emotions she knew she couldn't talk about it. Hadn't talked about it in five years.

'Do you want me to request a change to the holding pattern?' Morgan asked.

'Let's just see what it looks like on the second pass. We must be due to turn again shortly?' she queried.

'In ten seconds,' Morgan answered.

'Okay. That'll be fine.' Kait adjusted the range again. They weren't technically on task at the moment, but if she wanted to divert the aircraft for a closer look she could.

Matt hovered over her shoulder as they turned outbound again.

'See?' She pointed. 'I think it's moved closer already. It's growing fast.'

'So, what do we do?'

'We call it in. We still have another ten minutes of holding, don't we, Morgan?'

'A bit less and we don't have much fuel left after that.'

'Okay, thanks.' Kait dialled out on the satellite phone, reaching the Border Protection Command in Canberra. They took the details, but it didn't sound like they appreciated the seriousness of the situation.

Frustrated, she pulled out her iPhone and called another number.

'This is the Atherton Fire and Rescue Service. If this is an emergency, hang up and dial triple-0 now.'

She disconnected. 'Damn.'

'No joy?' Morgan asked.

'No, BPC don't normally handle this sort of thing. And the fire station's diverting to voicemail. Can we stay another ten minutes?'

'I'll request it.'

Kaitlyn tried other phone numbers. No luck. Either the phones were down or the people she was trying to call were fighting the fire.

Morgan had no luck with air traffic control either. If she didn't take their approach slot in five minutes they'd be waiting another forty minutes, and they didn't have enough fuel for that.

'Could you be reading this wrong?' Matt asked with a shrug, looking embarrassed.

'It's possible; it's been a while, but . . .' Kait focused on the screen and felt relief flow through her. Her shoulders eased down. 'They're moving. Maybe BPC did get through. The trucks are on the move.'

Matt leant in again. 'That second fire looks awfully close.'

'It is, but they should be right if they don't mess around.'

'We're starting descent now, will that be a problem?' Morgan asked.

'No. It should give me better definition.' They ploughed back into the smoke again. She heard the warning tone as the autopilot disconnected in the rough and tumble of the turbulence.

'Border Watch, you're cleared to track Biboohra, Codie, descend 6000.' Air traffic control gave them onwards clearance via the approach waypoints.

Morgan read the instructions back and, as they turned, Kaitlyn could see that the men and equipment below had cleared the fire zone. The fire front was enormous and she doubted they'd be able to control it. She kept the FLIR focused on it. Matt was still beside her.

'So what's happening now?' she asked, wanting to see how much he'd learnt.

'They've shifted the trucks clear. The one that lit the fire seems to have stopped a few miles away.'

'Good, spot on. Zoom in, maybe we can see the driver.'

Matt centred the image. 'There. He's got his back to us, though.'

'I must know him if he's with the RFB.' Kait looked for a distinguishing feature, but the aircraft was now heading away and descending, so the area would soon be off the screen. They reached the limit of the FLIR's range just as the man finally turned around. She couldn't quite make out his features.

'Damn.' Could he simply have lit it in the wrong place? It didn't seem possible that the RFB would get that wrong. They were too professional. Kait felt her stomach tighten. Weren't they?

The foreboding, coupled with the earlier vivid flashback, was making her feel sick. She turned the FLIR off. Maybe she was just too damn suspicious for her own good. Was she going to see arsonists in every fire she witnessed for the rest of her life?

They were established in the approach now and the calm voice of air traffic control transferred them to the tower frequency. Kaitlyn gazed out the window. Earl Hill was alight with orange and red. High up in the house line she could see the flashing lights of emergency vehicles. Seeing that battle made her desperate to get her feet back on the ground and fight, tooth and nail, to protect her land, her home, her family.

It made her desperate to scoop her boy up in her arms and keep him safe – not just from the future, but from the past.

Chapter 2

THE acrid black smoke poured out of the gaps in the doorframe. Through the visor on his self-contained breathing apparatus Ryan could feel the heat. He shifted his shoulders under the heavy coat. Perspiration ran down his spine, soaking his T-shirt and waistband.

Air hissed in his ears as he inched forward, loud even against the background of roaring fire. He tested the door for heat with the back of his gloved hand. He'd heard the warnings, understood the theory, but this was a whole lot more confronting than a burning mock-up. This was the ultimate test, and everything about it was more vicious, more fierce, more dangerous than the training.

The fire hose, rigid with water pressure, weighed down his shoulder, dragging at an old injury. He gritted his teeth and hoped like hell the muscles in his arm were as strong as he thought they were. The fire commander's voice crackled in his earpiece.

'Ready, Ryan. Frank.' It wasn't a question.

'Affirmative,' he rasped, hearing his partner respond as well. His tongue slid over his lips. Saliva was already hard to come by. It was only going to get worse.

'Go, go, go.' Frank's voice was steady but urgent.

The pressure on the door was immense from the heat trapped inside the house. The only thing holding the door closed was the flimsy lock. Ryan leant against the timber, feeling the weight of the hose shift as Frank took the strain. The latch let go and the door slammed him back a couple of steps before his boots gripped and he closed the gap. The heat was unbearable. His eyes watered despite the protective equipment. Ryan aimed the jet of water into the wall of orange and red. The only visible effect was a curtain of steam that rose as the water vaporised. It shot the temperature even higher.

Pumping 2000 litres of water a minute, the hose kicked and bucked in their hands. Using all their strength they hung on, directing the jet into the raging inferno. Ryan's earpiece crackled again.

'Truck's almost exhausted. Pull back to reconnect.' The hose started to sag as it ran out of water.

'We need friggin' mains pressure if we're going to beat this,' Frank growled. Ryan had no response. Neither did the fire commander. The next team squeezed past them before they were even clear.

The small, chaotic street looked like a carnival with its crowd of onlookers. Neighbours always came to watch. Fire tenders rubbed shoulders with ambulances and police patrol cars. Beside Ryan, Frank cursed as he pulled his helmet off and slid the breathing apparatus over his head. Perspiration poured down his face, staining the neck of his blue T-shirt black in the vee of the bright yellow jacket.

Ryan eased his own helmet and breathing equipment off, feeling the air in a cooling rush down his back. Even thirty degrees felt cold after the furnace of a house fire. The rumble of the fire drawing air sounded like a freight train in a subway.

Water had never tasted so good, he thought, feeling some run down his chin as he sucked from a bottle. The water washed some of the taint from his throat, but his nostrils were still full of the stench of burning house.

'Go, go!' The pump man by the truck was pointing up the street. 'They've got the hoses coupled to the mains. Not sure the whole family's out yet.'

Frank swore again as he and Ryan headed to the other yellow-clad figures, who were hauling a hose across the grass. They both had their helmets back on and checks completed by the time the hose was in position.

'Too hot for anyone to survive in that,' Frank said.

Ryan could only agree. He'd never felt anything like it. Surely no one inside could be alive.

With a snap, a main beam in the roof cracked. What happened next felt like slow motion to Ryan. The already distorted iron seemed to hesitate, puff up and outwards and then, with a wrenching groan, it collapsed, showering sparks skyward like fireworks. It hit the storey below. Heat and flames shot out empty windows, debris raining down in a 50-metre radius.

Voices crackled in his earpiece. 'Assistance required around the back. There's someone injured. Someone down.' It was the first crew on the scene calling for help.

'Frank, Ryan. You get that.' The fire commander had tabs on all his crew.

'On our way.'

The crew in the backyard had their hose trained on the shattered upper storey of the home.

Ryan reached the body first. It was a boy, lying on the remains of the fallen back door. His face was blackened and raw, the skin round his nose and mouth crusted with soot. The hair on his head was shrivelled and patchy. Ryan could see the knees on the boy's jeans had burnt through from crawling through the fire to escape.

'I've got you, buddy. I've got you.' The boy's eyes were closed, his lashes singed back to the lids, eyebrows gone. Ryan cradled him close, again feeling the twinge in his shoulder. He struggled to keep his footing on the rubble as he stood up. 'I've got you.' Had the lad been trapped on the other side of the door? Had the roof's collapse literally blown him outside? Ryan didn't know, but he guessed it was probably too late anyway.

The child was feather-light. Picking his way through the broken shards of the boy's home that were littering the yard, Ryan strode around the side of the house. The little bundle in his arms gagged and retched. All Ryan could do was shift his position and give the lad a clearer airway. He knew that damage from fire was often secondary, hidden. Lungs destroyed by inhaling smoke and heat didn't heal. Skin so badly burnt the nerve endings no longer felt pain couldn't fight off infections.

The paramedics had the stretcher and drip ready to go as Ryan eased the boy down onto the crisp white sheet. He could see the focus on their faces as they went about their job, the words between them short, sharp bursts of sound that meant nothing to him. Codes, acronyms.

'Ryan, they need us to take over the hose at the front. One of ours is down with smoke.' Frank clasped his shoulder. 'You okay?'

'Yeah. Let's go.' Ryan pushed the image of the now inert child aside. Nobody knew if anyone else was still inside.

They'd barely got to the front fence when the house exploded, knocking them both off their feet and tossing the team ahead of them aside like rag dolls. The boom seemed to echo and roll across the suburb for several seconds. Then the sharp patter of falling wreckage as it showered down around them.

'Frank?' Ryan rolled over onto his knees next to the older man. 'Frank!'

His partner groaned then coughed, shaking his head. 'I'm okay. The others.'

It was pandemonium now, with uninjured workers rushing to help those closest to the blast. The house had ceased to exist. The danger now was from spot fires started by the scattered shrapnel. The hoses were already being redeployed to the new danger zones. It was going to be a long afternoon.

Four hours later they had a semblance of control again. Ryan didn't think he'd ever been so exhausted in his life. He sat on the step of the truck, glugging straight from a two-litre bottle of water. There was so much sweat trickling down his knees that he could feel it squishing inside his boots. Two litres wasn't going to make a dint in his thirst.

Frank, fifteen years older and at least 30 kilos heavier, didn't look fazed. He took a sip from his bottle and clapped a hard hand on Ryan's shoulder. 'You get used to it, mate. Do it long enough and you stop noticing the heat, you stop craving water. '

'Yeah, right. Tell that to the camels in the Sahara.'

Frank laughed as he took another swig. 'You stringy blokes feel it in your bones. Me?' He patted his substantial girth. 'I've got plenty of cover.'

'How'd you reckon the young one will go?' Ryan regretted the question as soon as he asked it, his throat tight with an emotion that was all too familiar of late. He knew it wasn't possible to take this stuff personally and stay sane. He knew you shouldn't, couldn't ask these questions.

'Not good. Maybe if his mum and sister had survived it would have helped. If the neighbours are right about hearing yet another domestic before the house went up, chances are his old man's either shot through or died in the fire as well.'

'Arson?'

Frank shrugged. 'Leave that to the experts. The explosion could have been something as simple as an LPG car in the garage. Could have been something else.'

'Right. The official line.' Ryan took another gulp of water. His eyes were trained on Frank's face, willing him to answer. 'And if you were a betting man?'

His partner looked away. 'Once a wife-beater, always a wife-beater.'

Ryan could only nod, the bottle dangling from his fingers as he felt his lungs squeeze.

'Hey, Frank?' The fire commander beckoned him over. The big man went, hitching at his pants and snapping his braces.

Ryan stayed where he was, his chest painfully tight. This was supposed to be his final training run before he headed back to his world as an undercover cop in the Australian Federal Police. This was conditioning him for a new role as a volunteer firefighter at Oakey Creek, on the Atherton Tablelands. It was supposed to be low-key, from an undercover perspective. His masters had deemed him burnt out after his last two-year assignment, buried deep in the Nemesis outlaw motorcycle gang.

Low-key? He looked down at his hands, recalling the stillness of the child. He felt the slow burn of anger.

Could a father do that to his own family? There may have been times growing up when Ryan had hated his father, but for all his faults his old man would never have laid a hand on his family.

How out of control could a person become? How did life become so cheap, so bloody inconsequential, that it could be snuffed out so carelessly?

And then the truth hit him.

He was guilty of the same callous disregard for life. A good man had paid the ultimate price when Ryan's last undercover operation went south. Who was most guilty? The president of a bikie gang giving orders to kill, the hit man pulling the trigger, or he, Ryan, for not intervening to save the man?

Who?

And who the hell was Ryan, anyway? Which Ryan was responsible? He had no idea who he was any more. No idea if he ever would again.

His anger fell away and before he could control the freefall, he felt a snap, an almost physical break inside. Water spilt from the bottle, splashing his boots.

He tried to breathe, but his lungs wouldn't fill. The day narrowed into a grey fog. The bottle dropped from his grasp. When Frank's heavy hand landed on his shoulder he felt nothing.

All the lies, the cheating, the double-dealings of his past operations had finally caught up with him. He couldn't do this any more. He wanted out. He wanted . . .

'Buddy?' The pressure in Frank's hand increased as he shook Ryan. It broke through the mist and he sucked in smoky air. His lungs hurt with the sudden pressure, but it brought his sight back. He still couldn't speak.

'Drink some more. You're dehydrated.' Frank thrust the bottle back into his hand and crouched down next to him. 'First one's hardest. Gets easier from here on in.'

'Yeah, right.' The words croaked in Ryan's throat and he raised the bottle to drink. If only it was the first tragedy he'd witnessed. He tried to speak again. 'Right. I should have drunk more.' He avoided Frank's candid gaze. A man of Frank's experience would recognise his reaction for what it was.

Ryan didn't need his pity. He'd get through it. He had before. One more time he had to reinvent himself.

He had a job to do. Catch an arsonist before he killed again.

Find the truth.

Tell more lies.

Chapter 3

THE drip torch spluttered, flared erratically, then hissed as the wick took. In the early morning light the amber flame looked gentle and benign. Chris Jackson pocketed the cigarette lighter. Liquid gold ran in a stream from the torch's curled spout. The pile of twisted paper on the ground blackened and crackled as the fire took hold. No smoke yet; the heat was too intense. Tiny firelighters glowed blue among the twigs and leaves as they took life. With a *woof* the pile ignited, a column of grey smoke shot into the air and died in a swift rush. The flames leapt higher.

He walked a hundred metres, waving the wand at patches of dried grass and leaving a glowing trail behind him. The spiky vegetation transformed into vibrant, living sculptures. The heat was growing with each step.

With his free hand, he tugged his collar higher and adjusted his cap low over his eyes. 'That'll do it,' he muttered, stepping back from the growing inferno, feeling the wind ruffling his hair around his ears. A good stiff breeze, a steep hill and a load of fuel. Only be a matter of minutes before a fire front a couple of hundred metres wide would begin its inexorable march through the trees.

His ute was parked far enough away for safety, but not so far that he couldn't get to it in a hurry. He'd laid the embryonic fire in the right place. Not like that idiot last night who'd almost trapped him and the crew with his piss-poor efforts at laying a containment line. Chris spat on the ground. The bloke should have known better; he'd been doing it long enough.

No mistakes like that for Chris. He could afford to saunter back and lean on the bonnet, enjoying the life in the leaping flames. They danced and shimmered, forming eddies of orange tipped with white heat. Streaks of chartreuse and indigo swirled through the fire as the different barks and leaf oils ignited. There was nothing more beautiful than fire. It mesmerised him, just as it had almost forty years ago. Back then, they were tiny fires, contained in a barbeque pit and closely supervised.

Now? Now fire was his to command.

Time to go. He had things to do before he could start the day. He straightened up reluctantly and forced himself into the car. The bitter smoke irritated his throat as he inhaled a deep lungful of air. Something about burning eucalypts gave him a heady rush. Worth the discomfort of its antiseptic overtones.

The car radio crackled into life as he turned the ignition. The man from the bureau of meteorology was halfway through the morning weather report. He turned it off. No need to listen to him saying there was a complete fire ban due to the predicted increasing winds in the afternoon. He'd known that this morning when he got out of bed and looked at the sky. The fine, high cirrus cloud, turning vibrant pink with the sunrise, spelt a change of weather. It never lied.

His phone rang and he squinted at the pad, angling it so he could read the screen against the glare. 'Fuckin' hell,' he grunted before answering. 'G'day.'

'What the hell are you doing?'

'Just finishing up some back-burning.'

'You're crazy. Your trail of destruction has even made it into the *Sydney Morning Herald*. Don't think I'm not capable of going to the police. I am. This is my company now.'

'Easy to say, harder to do, mate. It won't look good. I've got records too.'

For a moment there was only static down the phone line. When the caller spoke again he sounded resigned. 'Stop pissing about and get down to the Sydney office, Jackson. I will not negotiate over the phone.'

'You'll negotiate where and when I decide to.'

Chris hung up and dropped the phone onto the seat next to him, feeling the anger roil in his gut. He eased down on the accelerator and drove sedately along the track. The leaping, trembling fire helped to settle him. The scrub at the base of the trees rustled as small animals fled from the heat and smoke. He felt a twinge of guilt. Something always died with fire. Something always lost out.

Sometimes that was tragic.

Sometimes there was no other way.

Chapter 4

'ENOUGH. I want this resolved now.' Grant McCormack was oblivious to the sweeping views over Sydney Harbour Bridge from the top floor of the McCormack Mines building. He strode back to the table and slapped his mobile phone down on the polished top in front of his company lawyer and fellow director, Don Adler. 'Get rid of Jackson. We'll find another way.'

Having newly taken the helm of the family mining company, Grant was struggling to cut away some of the dead wood. And that was literal as well as metaphorical. He couldn't see the need to hang on to anything that wasn't a core exploration business. Greentrees Plantations and their swathes of pines had no place in a mining company. Their only value was in what lay in the soil beneath their roots. They were an acquisition his father should never have made but burning them down was not an option. Grant had no stomach for arson.

Adler waved the outburst away. 'Give him time and he'll deliver. He has in the past.'

'And if someone dies because of it?' Grant fired back, pushing his cuffs up his wrists. 'Instead of negotiating with the landowners in good faith we burn them out? Keep paying a psychotic firebug hush money for the rest of his natural life?'

The silence dragged on as the two men eyeballed each other. This time Grant was not backing down.

'So, what would you have me do? Kill him? Dispose of his body?' Adler queried, his sarcastic smile not reaching his pale grey eyes. He was twice the age of the younger man, employed by Grant's father as a newly qualified lawyer when McCormack Mines was a fledgling company grubbing around in the dirt looking for tin.

Grant could only shake his head, his nostrils pinching with disgust. 'There will be no killing.' On each word he leant a little further across the polished mahogany. Adler held his stare then shrugged dismissively.

'Keeping Chris Jackson on a retainer for five years has been a small price to pay. We'll recoup it in the lower price of the land purchases.'

'It's criminal.'

'Your father didn't think so.'

'My father's not running the company any more.'

'No, he's not.' Adler managed to make the words sound like an insult.

Grant ignored the slap-down. His old man was in a secure facility with advanced Alzheimer's. His rapid decline had given Grant the chance to radically change the direction of the business. Those changes were bearing fruit and he did not want the company tainted by a connection with a convicted arsonist.

Stripping McCormack Mines back to its core business of digging minerals out of the earth relied on mining permits. Governments tended to refuse permits to companies that weren't seen to be aboveboard. Grant had had enough of Adler's Machiavellian ways, but for now he had to keep him on side, and in the company. Adler knew too many secrets.

'We're going round in circles,' Grant said, breaking the silence. 'Secure the parcels on either side. Get an exploration permit for them and we have a stranglehold on the other block. Once the dust settles we buy it back from the receivers who are dismantling Greentrees.'

'We've already tried that.' Adler sounded like he was lecturing a toddler and it grated. But Grant didn't bite. 'The widow won't sell and the deceased estate is still going through probate.'

'The widow won't sell for the figure she's been offered. Give her more money.'

'Then it's unviable.' Adler turned up his elegant palms.

The condescension was almost Grant's undoing. It took a great deal of effort to keep the anger from his face. Instead, he rolled his toes tight inside his shoes. 'If you and my father had been smart you would have transferred the deeds for the block at Happy Jack Valley from Greentrees to MCM before you started burning the other GT pine plantations in New South Wales and Victoria. Anyway, you don't expect me to believe you didn't get a tax advantage out of it by writing the timber off the books.'

'Tax advantage or not, we're still bleeding money.'

Grant continued to push Adler. 'Write it off the balance sheet and move on. There's enough happening in Western Australia around Kalgoorlie, and potentially up in North Queensland.'

Adler shook his head. 'Give Jackson another week. If he hasn't done the burn-off by then we can reassess.' He was on his feet now, straightening the lapels of his bespoke suit.

Grant wasn't surrendering. 'Next week we're flying to Cairns to meet Mr Jackson in person. Set it up.'

'That's not necessary.'

'Either you set it up or I'll tell my brother exactly who's sleeping in our father's bed now.'

Grant got a great deal of satisfaction from the fury in Don Adler's face. He kept his hands flat on the table, fighting the urge to do some damage to the aquiline nose opposite him. His jaw ached with the effort of controlling his temper.

Adler swung away, buttoning his coat before reaching for the door handle. He stopped with the door half open, venom in his voice and hatred in his eyes. 'Your mother is never going to vote with you.'

The click of the latch closing set Grant's muscles free and he ran his hand through his thick blond hair. 'No, she won't,' he said into the empty room. 'Not while you're screwing her senseless.'

Chapter 5

'DANIEL, you're being unreasonable. We don't have time for a horse.' Kaitlyn pushed her wet hair behind her ears, thankful the sweet cinnamon of her shampoo had replaced the smell of smoke.

'*You* don't have time, you mean.' Dan's normally cheerful face was screwed up in disgust. She stifled a sigh. By now she thought her son understood that her switch from Dan to Daniel meant it was time to back down. Apparently not.

'If I don't have time, then neither do you.' Kaitlyn dropped the cooler bag she was packing onto the granite bench with a small thud. 'When was the last time you cleaned your room, put your bike away or bothered to do your chores?'

He glared back at her, his brown eyes starting to sheen with the threat of tears. Even his freckles seemed defiant, stubborn reminders that the milky-white skin both Dan and Kait shared didn't suit the hot burn of the north Australian sun.

'You're mean, you're mean! That's why I don't have a dad. You're too mean.' He whirled away as the tears welled, his grubby training shoes sliding on the tiled floor as he shot out the screen door. It slammed behind him, but didn't rattle the wide, solid windows next to it.

Kaitlyn leant against the kitchen bench. His words hurt. She knew he didn't understand the full effect of them. How could he? Her little boy needed a father, and she was incapable of providing one for him. The guilt ate into her, twisting like a knife in her stomach.

'He doesn't mean it.' The quiet words from behind were meant to soothe her, but they didn't. Her mother rested her hand on top of Kaitlyn's. The length, the shape, was identical; only the surface had changed with the years.

Kaitlyn let her hand lie for a moment before she straightened up and pulled away. She didn't have time for self-pity any more than she had time for a horse. Saturdays should be for family, not heading down the range for an overtime shift. She should have refused to do it.

'I know, I know. There's no point in wishing things were different. They can't be.' She forced a smile. 'He'll cope.' Just like he's had to cope with so many other disappointments, she added silently.

'Maybe we can find someone interested in Dan exercising their horse.' Julia was nothing if not persistent.

Kaitlyn snorted. 'Then you'll be tied up driving him to that as well as swimming, Scouts and whatever other sport's in season.'

'Hmm.' Her mother was scheming. Her schemes usually involved Kaitlyn being caught up in something she had no intention of finishing. This time Kait wasn't going to be ambushed.

'That's a no, Julia. A big, fat no.'

'Of course, my darling.' Her mother patted her hand one more time before she went back to the stove and her simmering pot. 'You know best. I've put your overalls in the wash already. I hope you don't mind, but the smell was quite intense.'

Kaitlyn tried to ignore the tiny niggle of annoyance. Julia took cleanliness to a new level. In this case it was probably justified, but sometimes Kait felt as though she lived in an advertisement for washing powder. She also knew she'd just been diverted from the real issue. Deflection was Julia's specialty.

'Thanks for that,' she replied with a small forced smile. 'It was only a grassfire, but there must have been something dead in the paddock. The stench was pretty rough.' Her RFB pager had dragged her from sleep. A grassfire was threatening houses along the Dimbulah road. Probably a careless smoker flicking a butt out the window. It made her angry all the same. Courtesy of the early call out she was now pushing to leave for work on time.

She picked up the cooler bag just as the chime of incoming emails threatened to distract her again. Great, the internet was back up after forty-eight hours offline. She half turned to the laptop, then stopped.

First things first.

Daniel was taking his frustration out on the yard. She couldn't see him behind the giant girth of the rose gum, but the blizzard of silvery-green leaves swirling in the air wasn't happening by itself. The eucalypt's pale limbs stretched up to the deep blue sky. In the distance, the McAllister Ranges lay low and long, shimmering in the heat haze as they poked through the smoke. Normally the view lifted some of her angst. Today the blanket of smoke reminded her of the dangerous fire rating and the spate of fires they seemed to be endlessly battling.

Outside, the storm of petulance abated. Dan shuffled along the fence line, his hands jammed in his pockets, shoes scuffing the earth as he continued to kick at the leaves. He made his way over to the black bike propped against the shed. It was almost too small for him now, but she refused to buy him a new one until Christmas. He'd just have to ride with his knees up around his ears a little longer. At the rate he was growing she'd be buying a new bike every year.

She checked the clock again. Running out of time. In ten minutes she'd have to be out the door. Leaving arguments unfinished was a cardinal sin she'd never commit again.

The screen door swung back on its hinges and she swatted away the fly that immediately homed in on her face. 'Dan? Honey, can we talk, please? I need to leave for work in a minute. '

He grunted, fiddling with his bike as she walked towards him. The determination on his face always tugged at her, even more so when she was about to leave him for six days. She resisted the temptation to run her hand through the coppery waves curling round his ears. A seven-year-old is not a mummy's boy, but she loved the slippery feel of his hair over her fingers.

'Dan, you know if I could I would gladly give you a horse.' She paused, making him shift his eyes until they met hers. 'You know I'd do anything for you, but this . . .' She rolled her palm up. 'This is just not possible. Julia can't help with a horse. She's nowhere near strong enough and she's almost seventy-seven. You know that. Riding lessons during school holidays are as good as it gets, kiddo.'

His gaze dropped to the floor and his mouth turned down, but she saw resignation rather than hostility in the lowered shoulders. 'I know, but it's not fair.'

'Neither is it unfair. It's just the way it is.' Whether he liked it or not, he knew that was the truth, just as she did. 'You be good for Julia. I'll be back in six days.'

'Yeah.' He bent over the bike again, but not before she'd seen a tear roll down his cheek. God, it hurt.

She raised her chin, willing her own eyes to stay dry. 'Hug.' She reached out and gathered him close, smelling the sweet fragrance of shampoo, the tart spice of gingernut biscuits and the overlaying bite of the eucalyptus leaves. He melted against her, turning his cheek to rest on her white T-shirt. She felt the sob catch before he released it. 'I know, baby, I know. I'll be back soon.' She let him go the instant he straightened away. The rare hug was a concession she treasured and never took for granted.

Ten minutes later, Kait shrugged into her green jacket with its Border Watch logo, her temper simmering. Why the hell had she accepted an extra duty on a day off? She dragged her auburn hair into a tight plait to restrain the curls. Four-day trips were bad enough. A six-day duty was way too long.

But she was their last option. They needed more crew, but government regulations made the training long and intensive. They couldn't just hire someone off the street. Knowing all that didn't ease her resentment. Usually she could summon a smile when she went to work. Not today.

Tinted sunscreen was about as much make-up as she had time for, and eye drops meant there were no traces of her private tears. She stopped just long enough to check her reflection in the full-length mirror. She was once more the consummate professional heading to work, protecting the Australian coastline.

She swung by the computer. Forty-three emails. One was from the Department of Immigration. Something to do with the application for Daniel's passport. When they moved to North Queensland she'd reverted to her maiden name and changed Daniel's surname to Scott as well. It made it easier to leave the hurt and pain behind.

She read the first line, then re-read it, her frustration escalating into the red zone. They'd rejected the application.

'Bloody bureaucracy.' Apparently she was missing a signature: Dan's father's. She wanted to stamp her foot at the stupidity of it. It was a bit hard to get a dead man to sign a damn form.

Her sigh emptied her lungs. When would it end? Five years

after that devastating fire and still he made her life difficult. She closed the computer. Too late to worry about it now. She'd work it out when she got home.

Julia and Dan were nowhere to be seen as she drove out the front gate. She ignored the dart of disappointment and pulled up at the T-junction with the main road. The car seemed to veer to the left, but she made it another 500 metres down the road before the thudding noise made her stop. The way the car dipped as she hit the hard shoulder told its own story.

'Damn it.' She gave in and kicked the bloody flat tyre, knowing that wasn't going to fix it. The road was empty and, at this time on a Saturday, she'd be lucky to get the RACQ out to help in less than an hour.

She bit back another curse and shrugged out of her jacket, slinging it into the car. Changing a tyre was no great challenge, except that she'd be late for work and hot and sweaty by the time she finished.

It took about ten minutes to get the car jacked up and the offending tyre off. In that time only three vehicles passed by. The two with women drivers slowed, offered sympathy and understandably carried on. The third one tooted and kept driving right on by, with a very masculine yell of approval out the window.

Kait was still fuming over that little number when a white four-wheel drive coming the other way slid to halt next to her. Red dust shrouded its shiny paint. The dark window rolled down. A young guy with a cap, wrap-around sunglasses and a beard leant out.

'Need a hand there?'

Chapter 6

RYAN did what he always did when he took on a new identity. He got a haircut.

He'd driven into Cairns the night before and camped out in a private room at a backpacker's hostel on Grafton St. Some trendy place with cashed-up grunge travellers. The girl behind the counter had cast an appraising eye over him, hitched her short skirt a little higher and pulled her plunging neckline a little lower. Damn fine cleavage too, but sex wasn't on his agenda.

With a rueful shake of his head he'd lifted the keys from her glossy fingertips, slung his backpack over his shoulder and asked for directions to the fire stairs. 'Know your exits' was basic stuff.

The designer walls of his room had closed in on him, so he tucked his gun in its ankle holster, locked his papers in the safe and headed down the fire stairs again, staying well clear of reception.

He walked for three hours, burning restless energy and taking in the glitzy waterfront along the Esplanade. At one end, the wooden boardwalks and bike paths meandered past spreading fig trees. They skirted along the rock wall that kept the Coral Sea at bay as it swelled in over sandy mudflats, glistening in the reflected lights.

At the other end drunken revellers sprawled around barbeques by the giant lagoon pool. Standing at its apex he could see that the designers had nailed the shape of Queensland. To the west, the high-rise apartments and hotels were glittering towers of light against the dark backdrop of soaring mountains, which were more felt than seen.

Families played tag under park lights; couples in the first flush of love ambled along, sharing secrets and passionate kisses. It washed over him, through him, past him. It didn't help his frame of mind.

At one in the morning he crawled into bed. The noises from the room next door left nothing to his imagination. He kind of wished he'd taken up the receptionist's earlier offer. At least now he would be stretched out asleep, rather than rock-hard and lonely.

Breakfast was a welcome distraction from himself. The waitress stopped for a chat, her demure white T-shirt covering a fit body. She had none of the overt sexuality of yesterday's offering, and a hell of a lot more appeal. He laughed at her jokes, enjoying her quick wit and shy intelligence. She was about fifteen years too young, and safe from him. Maybe she knew that. Trying out her fledging sexuality on a target that didn't scream 'danger'.

An hour later he was comfortably nestled against a motherly shelf, as an amiable older woman styled his hair and gossiped. It was one of those delicious moments that only a man could enjoy. She chatted to the rhythmic click of her scissors, the rasp and slide of the cut-throat as she shaved his neck smooth. Then the fluffy brush drifted across his skin like a caress.

He caught the speculative look the hairdresser shot at him as she angled the mirror so he could see the back of his head.

'Good-looking guy like you should have no problem finding a date in Cairns,' she said with a quick flick of her wrist, the cape swirling around him. 'Mind you, I don't think beards are all the rage. Maybe you could lose that.'

He grinned. 'Who said I'm looking for a date?'

'I know a man who's been on rations when I see one. Try the Pier Tavern. It's better than the nightclubs. Different kind of girl. You Navy or a miner?'

He shook his head. 'Neither. Just here on holidays.'

'Right.' She smiled at him. No malice, just curiosity. 'My husband got shot once. Left a crease on his head too. The hair never did grow back.' Her heels clacked across the floor, her hips swaying. 'Twenty, thanks.'

As she rang it up he checked out his new haircut in the mirror. She was right, he did need to lose the beard, but he'd do that in private when no one would see. The haircut hid the scar on his head, but the hair around it had grown back silver. Most hairdressers had no idea what it was. The occasional barber would pick it.

He drove out of Cairns, his elbow resting on the windowsill, his shirt stuck to him. The city sprawl had reached the sugar cane. Hopscotch fields, most cut already and neatly replanted, a few waving high stalks with fluffy tails of flower spikes, lay cheek by jowl with houses and shopping centres. He passed the turn-off into the estate where Jack Coglan had once rented a house. The guilt, the regret, sat heavily.

Jack Coglan, retired soldier, bush-tucker expert, devoted father and husband who'd fallen in with the wrong crowd. Jack had mortgaged his soul to hell to pay for his wife's cancer treatments and lost her in the end anyway.

Ryan had met him during the two years he was undercover inside the Nemesis outlaw motorcycle gang, doing things no sane man should do. Jack had looked out for him in a way no one else ever had. Sure, Jack might have been up to his neck in the gang's filth, but he was different. Ryan had already worked out how to get the older man out with minimal jail time.

Instead, the hard men of Nemesis had shot Jack's dog, and then in a hail of bullets they'd taken Jack's life. Ryan hadn't been able to do a damn thing. If he'd intervened to save Jack it would have blown two years of hard work out of the water. Not just Ryan's hard work, but that of the team who supported him.

He knew he'd done the right thing by his masters, but he doubted the sense of having betrayed a friend would ever leave him. He wasn't sure he wanted it to. A man needed to be reminded that the difference between good and evil could be a matter of who employed you.

An hour and a half later, still lost in his thoughts, he was going too fast as he came around a bend. A silver sedan was parked on the side of the road, hazard lights flashing, and a curvy woman was in the process of rolling a tyre into position. He stamped on the brakes and rolled down his window.

'Need a hand there?'

The woman straightened up. She looked pissed off. 'Almost done, but thanks for the offer.' Her voice was crisp, educated, used to giving orders.

'Looks like the hard part's still to come.' He flicked on his vehicle's hazard lights. 'I'm not going anywhere in a hurry.'

He didn't miss the flash of relief in her eyes as she lowered her gaze to the tyre. Pretty eyes they were too, and he bet she had a great smile when she wasn't frowning. Humming a tune, he parked the car and walked down the dusty road. Crusoe, his partner in the AFP, would be proud of his rescuing a damsel in distress. And what better way to fit into a community, he decided. He could do this. Being undercover was the easy part.

'Ryan,' he said, holding out one hand and removing his sunglasses with the other. 'Brad Ryan, but everyone calls me Ryan.'

And so it always began. A new name, a new undercover role. Which Ryan this time? he thought, as he gripped the woman's long slender hand and smiled directly into her brown eyes.

Chapter 7

IT was impossible not to smile back at him. A good-looking guy, a bit younger than her, wearing faded denims and a T-shirt that fitted in all the right places was hard to go past.

'Kaitlyn.' She found her hand in a warm clasp that made her conscious of her own dirty, sweaty grip. 'Sorry.' She wiped her hands down her pants. 'I'm a bit mucky.'

'Understandable. You've done well.' He sat down next to the axle, without any regard for his clothes, and looked up from under dark lashes. 'In fact, better than well. I'd give you ten out of ten so far.'

Kait felt warmth flood up from her toes, a tingling rush at his compliment. 'Thanks,' was all she managed to say as he turned back to the task.

In what seemed like seconds he had the wheel positioned on the studs and the first nut in place. She almost groaned. It would have taken her a hell of a lot longer. She had to say something, but his masculine competence made her feel like a star-struck teenager.

'Thanks for stopping to help. You're going to end up covered in dust as well.'

'Hey, my pleasure. Can't have a lady who looks like she's on her way to work changing tyres in the dirt. Live near here?'

He had a low drawl that was easy on the ear, and he was

exceptionally easy on the eye, even with the scruffy beard. His dark brown hair wasn't quite long enough to curl at the back of his cap. She caught the tail end of his gaze as it wandered over her and didn't miss the lazy grin of approval. She knew she'd gone pink, and with her pale skin it would be obvious. It wasn't every day an attractive guy with friendly hazel eyes sat at her feet checking her out.

'Up the road a bit. I probably should have turned around instead of stopping here.'

'No, it's never safe to drive on a flat. It could roll off the rim.'

'I guess so. And you? You live around here?'

He laughed. 'First time back in over twenty years. I've moved up from Sydney. I'm renting up the road for a bit until I get a feel for the place and work out where I want to buy.'

'Really? Bit of a change of pace from Sydney. You've brought work with you? Not much around apart from fruit picking at this time of year.' She looked across at his car. She'd missed the New South Wales registration plates when he pulled up.

'Sort of. Taking some time out for a while.' He didn't elaborate, but his eyebrows lowered for an instant. She knew what it was like to keep secrets. Ryan was entitled to his. In a country area like this she knew how easy it was to reinvent yourself and your history. Who you were in the community was more important than who you used to be.

He carried on threading nuts onto studs. 'Can you reach the wheel wrench?'

She handed it over and for a split second wished she wasn't still wearing her wedding band. The moment of vanity almost made her laugh. Ridiculous woman. He wouldn't even notice.

'Social life's a bit limited around here.' Kaitlyn didn't want to pry, but she was intrigued enough to wonder if there was a wife and associated children.

'That wasn't on the list of desirable attributes I gave the real estate agent.' A hint of laughter touched his voice.

Kait felt the heat in her cheeks again. He made renting a house sound sexy. She tried for offhand again. 'Plenty of bushwalks in the area and some great bird-watching hides. The limestone caves out at Chillagoe are spectacular and then there's always Tinaroo Dam if you're into water sports.'

'I'm sure I'll find plenty to do.' He slotted the final nut on the wheel and cocked his head in inquiry. 'A bit rough, working on a Saturday.'

'Yes, it is, but duty calls, apparently. For me, anyway.'

'So, how far have you got to go?'

'I'm headed down to Cairns.' She looked at her watch and grimaced. 'Do you mind if I make a quick call while you do that? I should let them know I'll be late.'

Tanned forearms flexed as he rotated the wheel brace, giving each nut an extra nip. He glanced up at her with those cat eyes and a nod of his head. 'Go for it. I've almost finished. You'd done most of the work.'

By the time she'd made the call he had the car off the jack and everything stowed in the boot.

He dusted off his hands as she rejoined him. 'Good to go. Get them to check the nuts when you take the tyre in. Just in case. I couldn't find anything obviously wrong, but maybe you've got a faulty valve.'

'Thanks for your help. I really appreciate it, Ryan.'

'No worries. Happy to help in any way I can, Kaitie.' He cracked another grin and Kaitlyn felt her heart skitter. I bet he is, she thought. He'd be happy to help any number of women, from the look of all that charm.

'Safe drive.' He held out his hand again and this time she took it in both of hers. His skin was smooth under her fingers. No calluses pressed into her palm. His nails were square, neatly cut. Not used to manual labour, she decided, risking a direct smile.

'And you. See you round.'

Ryan held her gaze for a fraction of a second then grinned at her. 'You can be sure of that.' He loped across the road to his car and didn't look back as he drove away.

She sat for a moment once she'd buckled up. In the rear-vision mirror she saw Ryan's four-wheel drive indicate for a right turn just before it vanished around the bend.

She frowned. Ryan was headed up Happy Jack Road? It was a dead-end, 12 kilometres of barely sealed dirt with the grass verge creeping closer every week. There was nowhere to go down that road, just her house and old Jerry O'Donnell's place, right around the other side of the rim.

Was he renting the high-set house? Jerry had been packed off to a nursing home nine months ago, but she knew it was still full of the elderly man's possessions. She checked on it occasionally and ran the ride-on mower over the grounds.

She did have a contact number somewhere for Jerry's son, or maybe he was the son-in-law. Hard to remember – his self-important grandstanding had kind of scared her off. He was some bigwig in Defence. She'd left several messages inquiring about Jerry's health and never got a reply. Perhaps she should try again. They all missed their elderly neighbour, Dan particularly. She shied away from examining just why the thought of Ryan living up the street had sent a shiver through her body. It would be good not to have to worry about mowing his block in future.

The highway skirted around her property, then dropped past the forestry block. She eased off the accelerator, risking a glance at the low, undulating structure that appeared to float in the distance. It wasn't for sale at any price. The real estate agents could knock on her door all day and she still wouldn't accept their increasingly generous offers. Maybe she was the only one who thought it was beautiful, but she knew its beauty was in its clever design and immense strength. It would withstand severe weather like cyclones and, more importantly, firestorms.

Built to rigorous standards, she trusted it to protect her family. Never again would she lose her house to the violence of nature. She swallowed, forcing the edge of nausea back down as the old grief, the visceral fear, welled up and threatened to swamp her.

Never again would she be complacent or trusting of anyone.

Chapter 8

RYAN hummed an old Billy Joel song as he drove – the one that went 'if that's moving up, then I'm moving out'. It suited his optimistic mood. Who knew changing a tyre could lift his spirits like that? He needed to get out more. The sexy married lady with the flat tyre had the sort of colouring that belonged in an English rose garden, not up in North Queensland. The logo on her shirt said she worked for Border Watch.

He searched through his memory for what he knew about the organisation. He'd worked with them on the last operation. If he remembered correctly, there were two flight crew on every flight, plus an observer and a mission commander. Which one was she?

Up ahead he could see the first house on the road. He left the window rolled down. A whiff of something rich and spicy tangled with his tastebuds. He slowed to get a better look.

They'd torn down the shack and built a new house since his last visit. City folk, he'd bet. No one else would put up such an ugly cement and corrugated-iron monstrosity. At least they'd had the good sense to face the fantastic view from their perch, high on the edge of the escarpment. Of course that meant Jerry's house and theirs were looking at each other like a couple of prize-fighters, all pumped up and ready to brawl. Jerry's was the old timer in bovver boots. The other was the brash new kid on the block with designer sneakers.

For the next five kilometres the road followed the ridgeline. There was nothing but sloping grass and open forest to Ryan's right and a steep drop down to an old plantation on his left. The road was starting to show sign of neglect. He had no idea who was responsible for it. Main Roads or Council? If it got much worse he'd need to find out.

Finally he got a good look at the old place. Someone had mowed the grass – straight lines, neatly overlapping. It looked like a country cricket ground. He crossed mowing off his long to-do list.

Ryan was pretty sure his father wouldn't have organised it. His dad was too ticked off about the contents of Jerry's will to do anything useful with the house. Unfortunate that Rear Admiral O'Donnell had taken early retirement from the Navy. Meant he had too much time to stick his nose into his son's business. Bit late for paternal pride now, Ryan thought, pulling the keys from the ignition. It was not a case of better late than never. Never suited Ryan fine.

He eased himself out of the car, stretching his shoulders back as the full force of the warmth hit him. The house was smaller than he remembered. High-set colonial with boxy verandas, crazy crooked stump caps and wide weatherboards begging for a coat of paint. Great Uncle Jerry had been a retired train driver. The pile of scrap metal, spare parts and scavenged goods stretching along the back fence seemed to have grown to match the size of the old fella's heart. He must have been collecting right up until they carted him off in an ambulance.

Had Jerry laughed out loud when he signed his will, handing everything bar the house over to a charity for homeless boys? Ryan was wryly amused. Jerry's comment, perhaps, on the lack of parenting in Ryan's life? The old man had never hidden his contempt for Ryan's parents.

Jerry had left the house to Ryan with a string of conditions requiring him to work with the charity to turn it into a facility to house some of those boys. Perhaps that was an attempt to prod Ryan into doing something else for a career. Fat chance. Policing was Ryan's life and he had no intention of taking on a charity for juvenile males in any capacity.

Fortuitously, though, Jerry's will gave Ryan somewhere to stay without too many questions to be answered. Ryan had had no intention of staying in the house again, but when this job investigating an arsonist on the Tablelands had come up it was the logical solution. A fictitious real estate agent was easy for the Feds to organise. All inquiries would be answered appropriately and the details of anyone poking around would be recorded. Ryan was just a single man renting a house in the country.

He squinted across the valley, measuring the distance between the two houses. If he could see them, they could see him. He pulled his binoculars out of their case and homed in on his neighbour's place. The trees had been cleared up to a couple of hundred metres out. One lonely, imposing gum had survived the chainsaws, holding its crown high above the landscape. The gardens surrounding the house looked cared for, although lightly planted.

The striped pattern on the lawn opposite was familiar. Must be the neighbour who was mowing Jerry's block as well. He stopped himself. Technically it wasn't Jerry's place any more, but the fading name on the letterbox would stay.

He pulled the house keys from his pocket. They were worn smooth and felt as though they still held some warmth from their former owner. The wind lifted a pile of leaves under one corner of the house. For a moment Ryan thought he heard a ragged sigh. He whipped around, automatically fingering the cold metal tucked into his waistband. Nothing moved. It took a moment for his muscles to relax again.

'Christ, mate,' he chided himself, 'you're losing it. Too jumpy.' Maybe the bloody shrink was right. The thought of Leila, the youthful police psychologist, brought a wolfish edge to his smile. 'Lamb to the slaughter,' he'd told Crusoe. 'Do you think lovely Leila really understands that undercover cops lie for survival? If the crims can't tell fact from fiction, how the hell is she supposed to know if I'm telling her the truth?

His partner, Craig 'Crusoe' Robinson, had just shaken his head as Ryan headed off for his psych assessment. Ultimately the sweet-faced babe had seen things his way and returned him to active duty. Although she'd managed to sneak in the caveat that he should be removed from undercover ops before the end of the year.

He turned a lazy circle, scanning the trees and sheds on the property.

Silent.

Empty.

Alone.

Dust drifted from his steps as he ambled across to the house, putting thoughts of Sydney and his last assignment behind him. This was his here and now. No one but his boss knew he was here. Yet.

He stopped at the bottom step, ran a hand over the railing. Jerry's father had built this house with his own hands for his bride. The railings were still held in place by the same wire nails. The family had raised eight boys here.

Funny that Jerry had gone the other way and never even married. Ryan could relate. Hell of a lot easier that way. If a man travelled light, he couldn't be tied down.

And, a darker corner of his mind acknowledged, if a man had no family, then no one could exact revenge on them for the sins of their father. He didn't bother trying to push that thought away. It kept him strong. It kept him vigilant. Just because he was out of Sydney, working something low-key, didn't mean that danger and violence wouldn't follow him north. The Nemesis bikies and their drug lord partners had long reaches, even from behind bars.

The stairs creaked as he took them two at a time. He scraped his nails over the smooth beard on his chin then slotted the key in the lock and turned it. As the door swung open he felt the musty air escape around him with a rush. The hallway was dark, the ceilings high. He hesitated in the light before he stepped over the threshold and back into his childhood.

He hadn't counted on the memories being this strong, and he gave himself a mental shake. First things first. A shave, a beer and a shower, in that order.

He took his time shaving the beard off. It always stung when he hadn't used a razor in a while. He looked ten years younger with it gone. The silver patch in his hair was the only sign that he was now midway between thirty and forty. The beer was cool on his lips as he took another long pull.

With the towel slung around his hips he could see the U-shaped scar on his triceps. He tightened his left hand into a fist involuntarily. The tendons still weren't as strong as they had been before a machete sliced into his arm. He'd been attacked onboard a ship involved in a smuggling operation. That had been the beginning of the downhill slide in the last case. It had ended with a bullet creasing his skull shortly after Jack Coglan was shot dead.

The shrink would be alarmed to know he'd contemplated suicide. He'd never do it, but he'd run the numbers just the same.

Another form of risk assessment. Before Nemesis he'd have dismissed that approach as a coward's way, but after Jack's death it had come to seem a valid way to go if the circumstances required it. That was as close as he came to acknowledging that the last operation had left him vulnerable.

Leila had insisted he needed to accept he'd been traumatised, dismember the experience and then put it back together with a realistic, positive angle. He was polite enough not to laugh. The way he saw it, spending two years of his life undercover with Nemesis had meant he'd blurred the edges of his mind, his identity, his reality. There was no way to undo some of the things he'd done.

Sure, he'd busted the whole gang wide open, along with its links to an international crime syndicate. Yes, they'd cleaned out a corrupt cell of New South Wales police drug squad, but it didn't change the fact he did not like the person he'd become. Lying was second nature now. Cold, ruthless, calculating.

He swallowed the rest of the beer and stepped into the shower. Water helped in a ritualistic cleansing way, but it didn't last. Today would be no different.

He'd become Bradley Ryan, Ryan to his mates, a fireman from Sydney looking to get over a broken marriage by hanging out in North Queensland. Tomorrow a new operation to catch an arsonist would take its first tentative steps. Get it right and he might stop tragedy on the Tablelands.

Get those early steps wrong?

Then he might die. Somehow that wasn't such an uncomfortable thought.

Chapter 9

'SORRY I'm late,' Kaitlyn said, hurrying into the Border Watch briefing room in Cairns. Her bag hit the floor next to one of the computer consoles. 'I got a flat tyre five minutes from home.'

'You should have flagged down a truck,' her colleague Lauren said with a toss of her blond hair as she stacked flight plans, weather forecasts and paperwork into a pile. 'I would have. A girl could break nails changing a tyre.'

'Then I'd still be standing on the side of the road, Lauren. I don't have your star power. Anyway, a guy did eventually stop and help out. Better late than never, I guess.'

'It's no problem,' Lauren replied before amending it with an apologetic shrug. 'Not with me, anyway, but the boss is back from Canberra and wants to see you.'

'Really?' Kaitlyn finished entering her sign-on details into the computer. 'What's Tony doing here on a Saturday?'

'Don't know. Unhappy home life?'

'He's annoyed?'

'Well.' Lauren leant back in the black office chair, stretching her hands above her head. 'Let's just say he wasn't happy, but the man never is. You ask me, he doesn't get enough sex, so women are on his hit list. You, me and Morgan are his personal crosses to bear. Don't let it get to you. Just smile that enigmatic little number you do and he'll forget what it is he wants you for.'

Kaitlyn managed a laugh. 'Lauren, you do rabbit on.'

'I know. Cal keeps telling me that too.'

Kaitlyn headed for the corridor, still smiling. She knew what the young captain was doing and appreciated it. Unfortunately her apprehension hadn't diminished by the time she walked through the largely deserted offices and rapped on Tony's door.

He pulled his glasses off and rested them on the folder in the middle of the giant blotter that filled his desk. The downlights reflected off his almost bald head. Some men looked sexy as hell without hair. Tony wasn't one of them.

While waiting for him to speak Kaitlyn couldn't stop her gaze going to the photo behind him of an F-111, afterburner blazing like a comet as it arrowed into a black sky. Maybe it was hard for a retired RAAF top gun to find himself heading up a base of surveillance pilots flying turbo-prop aircraft. Maybe that's why he was such an uptight, authoritarian jerk most days. Then again, maybe Lauren was right. Tony's wife never looked happy either.

'Kaitlyn, I understand you called in a bushfire at the end of your last shift.'

She relaxed a touch. So that's what this was about. She'd checked with the boys from the Oakey Creek RFB. It seemed a containment burn had gone the wrong way, lit by someone from one of the other brigades. Dimbulah, Wondecla and Oakey Creek all helped out if required. They'd said someone had misjudged it. Kaitlyn didn't quite see it like that, but she wasn't going to argue with the guys on the ground. She filled the silence now.

'Yes, I did. We were in a holding pattern and I could see a firefighting team in a danger zone. I was going to talk to you about it during the week. I didn't expect to find you here on a weekend.'

He nodded and his flinty grey eyes met hers. 'You were out of line doing that, but you may well have saved lives.' His gaze was unwavering. 'Because of that we've had a request for assistance from the government. I need some input from you before we decide how to approach it.'

That would have cost him dearly, asking for help. She bit her tongue as he continued. 'The fire authorities believe there's at least one arsonist operating on the Atherton Tablelands.'

There it was: the truth she'd already suspected. The frisson of alarm rippled through her, heated her skin.

'I see.' And she did, but she didn't want to be in this position. It had taken a huge toll on her, using the FLIR the other day. But refusing to help wasn't an option.

'Someone mentioned you were there in the Canberra fires. I looked up your record. You flew many of the missions with our crews.'

Swallowing, she forced her voice to work. 'I did.'

'Great. You're the only one left with any experience of this. The pilots have all left for airline jobs. When you finish this mission you'll be on office duties for a week so we can put together a case plan for the operation. It will need costings, crewing numbers and training requirements.'

'I didn't work for Border Watch then. I was with the Federal Police.' She didn't want this, didn't want the burden, but even as she protested she knew she'd have to go through it again. 'I was only helping to interpret the FLIR images.'

'I know that. It says here you were seconded from the AFP because of your skills as an identity specialist.'

'They thought I was good at reading faces, body language.' The words croaked in her throat and he peered over his silver frames at her. She swallowed and continued. 'No one had used the airborne technology like that before. It was experimental. I was only one member of the team. I didn't do it alone.'

'They caught two of the perpetrators because of you.'

She could only nod mutely. Only two. The final one was never caught.

Clearly, her record didn't show any of her personal tragedy, and Tony wasn't the kind of manager to engage his staff in small talk. He didn't care if they had a life outside of work. He mightn't even care that she'd lost her husband and father in those fires, along with her house, her peace of mind and nearly her sanity.

'Right. Good. Next week you'll be working with me to come up with a proposal. You can go now.'

He was scribbling notes on his blotter and for an instant she wanted to rage at him, pound her fists on the desk, make him see her as a person. But she knew that would be futile. It wasn't his way, nor did she want or need his sympathy.

She would find the strength to discuss that Canberra operation. Yes, they could have done things better, quicker. They may have saved more lives. She'd learnt so many lessons, but the most powerful one was to stop the fire before it spread. Catching the arsonist was vital too, but fight the fire first.

Kaitlyn walked through to the quiet of the briefing room, the walls papered in maps showing the extent of their watch area. Its familiarity steadied her, eased the uneven thud of her heart and the thrumming in her temples. She could feel the blood in her cheeks returning to normal. She knew firsthand the anguish, the suffering that fires caused, especially those deliberately lit. Healing took years. Only the scars on the outside showed.

It wasn't possible to be the same person. Everything changed. Everything had to be rebuilt, not just the houses. She wouldn't be here in North Queensland if it weren't for Gary, the mission commander on that horrific day. Gary had tracked her down after the inquest. Suggested a fresh start would help and nudged her in the direction of Border Watch. Told her she had skills that could help save lives, keep people safe. It was what she needed to hear at the time. She owed him a great deal.

The new start, new job and new house had made it possible to go on living.

And now she needed to use the aircraft and her skills to hunt an arsonist again. She had no choice.

But this time she'd find the arsonist before he killed someone.

Chapter 10

THE school children were as rowdy as ever as they jostled each other getting onto the bus. The older ones took over the back row. The pecking order flowed from there to the nerdy ones at the front.

'Belts on,' Speedy yelled as the door hissed closed. 'No exceptions, missy.' He glared at the teenager with wild bleached hair in the back row who poked her tongue out him, the silver stud in the middle of it adding to his annoyance. 'Get off if you don't like it,' he called, buckles clinking against seats as the children around him did as directed. He opened the back door. 'Off?'

'All right, all right,' the teenager snarled back at him, clicking her seatbelt into the keeper.

He knew she'd undo it as soon as she thought he wasn't looking, but he'd done his best to keep them safe. It made him sick to think there were drivers who didn't bother. You take on this job then you do it right. Kids had no idea about safety.

The bright red hair of the young lad in the middle of the bus caught his attention. Daniel Scott. He'd told Speedy his mum's birthday was coming up soon. Dan's mother was a good-looking woman who always had a friendly word for Speedy. He knew there was no Mr Scott.

One of the advantages about being a driver, everyone looked right through you. You were invisible, part of the furniture. It was why Speedy had taken the job. He could go places no one else could. He learnt things from listening to the conversations around him. He knew stuff because no one looked twice at him.

It made him feel safe, made him feel a part of something. He could still remember the slick sweat of relief when his blue card, the state government permit allowing him to work with children, came through without incident. You knew your identity was clean when it got through that test.

The first drop-off was a good fifteen-minute journey and he drove sedately. Speedy. That's what everyone called him. It used to be Blue, but his red hair had paled to brown and silver long before he moved here. Now they called him Speedy because he never drove fast. Not the school bus, not the rural fire truck, not his ute. Speedy suited him just fine. Even his orange firefighter overalls and pale blue bus-driver shirt were embroidered with Speedy.

Forty minutes later, he arrived at the top of Happy Jack Road. The bus was empty but for Dan. He hesitated for a split second.

'I'll drop you to the gate, mate,' he said over his shoulder. Dan had moved to the seat behind the driver.

'Thanks, Speedy,' he mumbled, looking embarrassed.

'I won't tell if you don't, eh?'

'All right.' The kid looked down at his Nintendo, his hair flopping over his forehead.

'Your mum home?'

'Nah, just Nana. Mum's away at work.'

'Right. When's she back?'

'Why?' There was suspicion in Dan's bright eyes and the angle of his head.

'Just asking.'

'Oh. Day after tomorrow.' Dan bent forwards again and Speedy squinted ahead as a vehicle came around the corner. He edged the bus over towards the verge, but the driver of the oncoming car flashed his lights and pulled onto the hard shoulder to let the bus through. Speedy raised a hand in thank you as he eased past. The other driver raised two fingers off the steering wheel.

Speedy didn't recognise him. Out-of-towner. 'Know him?' he asked the boy.

Dan shook his head. 'Nah, I think he's looking at Jerry's place. Saw him yesterday and the day before. He waved.'

'Is that right? You don't go talking to strangers.' There was no question in his words. 'You be careful. You hear me?'

He realised he was being overly concerned, but he couldn't stop himself. Dan looked down again, but not before Speedy had seen the frown on his face. Speedy knew all about dangers that this boy couldn't even dream of. He pulled to a stop in Dan's driveway and waited for the boy to unload his bag. The bus vibrated as it sat idle, rattling the loose change in Speedy's pocket. Before he could stop it, he remembered his stepfather jiggling his pockets as he stood at the bedroom door. The briefest flash of memory before he caught it and slammed it away.

'See you tomorrow, Speedy,' Dan called, retrieving his bike from the bike cage and bumping it down the stairs.

'Sure thing,' he muttered. He closed the door and threw the bus into reverse, manoeuvring it through a three-point turn. 'Sure thing.'

Whoever the guy was in the flash four-wheel drive, at least he understood country protocols. But who the hell would want to live in old Jerry's place? It was a dump. It had to be over a hundred years old. Even the water tanks looked ancient. He'd ask around tonight at the pub. Small town, someone would know what the go was.

His thoughts kept him company on the drive back to the bowls club where he picked up the group of retirees. It took a little longer to load them into the bus than the kids, but the noise levels were the same as he drove them back to the Rose Gum aged care home. They bantered with him, cupping their ears to hear him better.

His shoulder was slapped a dozen times as they filed out. A couple of the women gave him motherly smiles as he helped them down the last small step. The younger of the two carers stopped next to him, smoothing her glossy hair. He could smell her perfume and the faint musk of a woman. She was an attractive divorcee and he wasn't immune to her charms.

'Thanks, Speedy. You're so patient with them all. They much prefer you in charge of the wheel. They think the world of you.' She leant in a little. 'And do so I. See you next time.' She hit him with a wide smile that seemed all the brighter for the shiny lip gloss.

'See you later, Lorraine.'

'See you, Speedy.'

The older carer was the last to leave. 'Catch you next time.' The glance she gave him was shrewd. It didn't need to be. He knew better than to take Lorraine up on any perceived offer. The company didn't like the drivers fraternising with the customers. Of course that didn't stop him fantasising about what it would be like to lie with a woman without money changing hands and without the spectre of failure looming in the dark.

He shifted in his seat, feeling his body burn with sudden desire. He lifted his foot off the brake and the bus moved forward. Time to visit the house in Parramatta Park down in Cairns again. The women were clean and the prices reasonable. Better to service the need than become consumed by it.

Chapter 11

SORTING through Jerry's junk was taking longer than Ryan had expected, but he had nowhere else to be. Ferreting around in someone else's life had always fascinated him. Perhaps that was part of the reason he'd become a copper. You were legally allowed to root around and uncover other people's secrets. In fact, it was your duty. In a weird way he'd always been reassured by the strangeness of those lives. It made his seem a whole lot less dysfunctional.

A phone rang and he reached up to the table from where he sat on the floor. It was his undercover phone, his 'hello' phone.

'Hello.'

'Ryan.' It was pure gravel.

'Hello?' He straightened up, not recognising the voice.

'Don't think there won't be payback.'

'Mate, think you've got the wrong number. Who're you looking for?' He didn't hang up, hoping they might trace it. The caller at the other end laughed, a mirthless bark. Ryan tried again. 'Sorry, who is this?'

'You've got no idea what we're capable of doing to you. No fuckin' idea.'

The phone went dead and Ryan dialled out. 'Trace required.' He read out his phone's details. He didn't think he'd held the caller on the line long enough. 'Getting soft, mate,' he chided himself. 'Keep 'em talking. Basic stuff.'

He shifted onto his knees and reached out to drag the last suitcase towards him. The top journal shook a touch as he lifted it out. He glared at his hands. What the hell? No scumbag bikie was going to rattle him.

His other mobile phone rang. This number he knew. He still paused before he answered, sighing as he slumped onto the floor in resignation. 'Marion, hello.' He tried to put some welcome into the words.

'Ryan, darling, how are you? You haven't rung in weeks. Where are you?' His mother's voice was one of her best features, low, husky and warm. It bore no relationship to the woman.

'Busy working.' He knew she hated his job, and that was without having any idea what it really entailed. All she knew was that he'd denied her the kudos of being the mother of a naval officer. She'd loved being able to boast about him when he was dux of his class at officer training, when he won the inter-services swimming trophy, when he was chosen above classmates to speak at functions.

A federal policeman was a long way down the ladder on her status list. Knowing he was an undercover operative might have added some drama for her, but her lips were legendary for being loose. He'd played on that when he wanted something spread far and wide. He'd been callous enough to dump a girlfriend that way. Even now, that memory made him squirm. Thankfully, he'd come a long way from that level of immaturity. Now he just stayed away from commitment full stop. And told his mother nothing.

He realised she'd asked him a question. 'Sorry, you were drowned out by the noise outside. Say again?'

The click of her tongue was unmistakable. 'You're as bad as your father. He doesn't listen either.'

No surprises there. Ryan held his laugh.

'I asked if you were going to be here for your father's sixtieth birthday party. It's in four weeks' time and I need to let the caterer know numbers. We'd both appreciate you being here. You *are* our only child.'

Inwardly he groaned. This might be a duty he couldn't escape. 'I'll see what I can do.'

'Will you bring a partner or can I invite one for you?'

'No, no. I'll bring a partner. No need to go fishing for me.' She'd spent her whole life fixing him up, starting with his tenth birthday party when she'd had to have even numbers. It hadn't got any better with time.

'Fiona's divorce is through and she'll be there.'

'Thanks, but no.' He was firm this time. Fiona was far too nice and far too damaged for him. He had nothing to offer her but more pain. The work phone rang and he eyed it off as it vibrated towards the edge of the table. 'I'll call you back.'

'But darling —'

He cut her off and reached for the other phone as it tipped over the edge. 'Hello.'

'Mate, you busy?' It was Crusoe.

'No, you?'

'Some interesting chatter around. Check out the score.'

The phone went dead and Ryan pushed to his feet, dusting the seat of his jeans as he walked over to the computer. He still had his own phone in his other hand and he placed the two side by side. The work phone was state-of-the-art technology. His own was a Nokia brick from the era when phones enabled you to talk to someone, not tweet, Facebook, take photos or surf the web. It also never missed a beat.

The email from Crusoe was a detailed run of surveillance on two of the Nemesis boys who'd been released on bail early in the case. It looked like they were getting serious about trying to find Ryan.

The Nemesis network had been wrapped up, along with the business interests of an international criminal, Rashid Mahoud. Rashid's books alone were enough to incriminate the club. The trial would succeed even without Ryan's testimony. The bikies had nothing to gain by killing him, except a longer prison term. And revenge.

They'd even been rash enough to approach one of the New South Wales police undercovers for a possible hit. Couldn't be better for collating more charges to hang on them. Conspiring to kill a federal policeman held significant penalties.

Ryan started to dial his mother's number again, knowing that if he didn't she'd be offended for weeks to come and make his life hell. He was about to hit call when he heard a noise outside and shot to his feet, reaching for his gun.

He hadn't heard a car approaching so it might be someone on foot, or maybe on horseback. Around these parts plenty of people had horses. He edged closer to the long windows in time to see a bright flash of auburn hair. His shoulders dropped. The kid from the bunker next door, fiddling with something on the carry rack of a pushbike.

Ryan tucked the gun into the waist of his jeans and pulled his shirt down over it. Damn. He'd have to discourage this. There was no place in an undercover operation for a stray. A child caught in the crossfire if things got ugly didn't bear thinking about. He didn't need that on his conscience. Jack Coglan was enough guilt for a lifetime. He felt the familiar lurch of his stomach. Just another memory to punch aside. Footsteps scraped the bottom stairs and the sound nudged him into action.

He opened the front door and strode to the edge of the veranda, hands on his hips.

'G'day.' He went for unfriendly and saw the recognition of it in the young lad's face. The tin in his hands shook for an instant.

'Hi.' The boy swallowed. 'Nan said it was okay to ride round and see you.'

'Did she.' Ryan gave the lad full marks for standing still. He looked like he wanted to bolt.

'Yep, she said it wasn't polite to ignore you. She sent a cake.' He held out the tin.

'Right.'

'I'm Dan.' He inched up the stairs and held out his hand, the cake still clutched in the other. Someone had taught the kid manners.

'Ryan.' He reached down and made sure not to engulf the young hand completely, but he needn't have bothered. For a youngster Dan had a firm grip and long fingers. He also looked Ryan straight in the eye. Despite himself, Ryan cracked a grin.

'Good handshake there.'

'Thanks.' Dan blushed crimson. 'Here.' The lad thrust the cake at him and Ryan took it.

He tried again, remembering how hard it was at that age to speak to adults. 'You want some cake? Some water?' The heat of the day was still intense and the afternoon breeze hadn't materialised. Sweat stained Dan's neck and armpits. His fair skin didn't sit well in the tropics.

'No.' Dan shook his head then seemed to remember those manners. 'Thanks. I've had some already and Nan doesn't let me out without water.'

No mention of a dad. Interesting. 'So, how was school?'

'Good.' No sign of resentment or complaint. 'Swimming today so that's cool.'

'I bet.'

'I'm home early.'

'Yeah?'

'The bus driver drove me all the way. That's why I've got time to ride now.'

'Homework?'

This time the straight nose screwed up. 'Yeah, lots. And piano.'

'Right.'

'My nan teaches me, and Mum sometimes.'

Okay, so there was a mother.

'Your dad?'

'No, I don't have a dad.'

'I see.' And suddenly he did. The kid was lonely and in need of a father-figure. He couldn't do that. He had no idea how. 'Well, nice to meet you, but I better get back to work. Do you need a lift home or are you right to ride?'

'I'm right.' He looked crestfallen. It niggled at Ryan.

'You want to poke around the yard?'

'Can I? Jerry used to let me sort stuff.'

Of course. Jerry would have loved having a young person to talk to. It made sense.

'You go and sort to your heart's content, then. Yell if you need me. I'll be inside.' Jerry had let Ryan ferret through the piles of junk when he was about Dan's age. Every once in while Jerry would join him and they'd unearth some fascinating piece of machinery just waiting to be reconditioned. Ryan had learnt more in the school holidays up here than he had the rest of the year.

The 'hello' phone rang again inside and he nodded at Dan. 'Fill your boots, mate.'

The quick grin Dan shot him was pure delight, but Ryan walked back inside feeling like a jerk. The kid wanted company, not a licence to fossick.

'Hello.' He placed the tin on the table and pried the lid off as he answered. The sharp citrus tang hit his tastebuds. A fine-looking orange cake.

'I've got a deal going down. George St, near the bus station.'

'Not interested today. Maybe next month.'

'No, you don't understand. I need this.' Ryan recognised the voice of one of his old informants who he'd kept in contact with long after that particular operation was over.

'Yeah, sorry, mate, but I'm not in a position to buy.'

'I need to see you.' The man was sounding desperate. Ryan tuned into the background noise. Someone else was talking.

'That's not possible.'

'Where are you? No one's seen you.'

In that instant Ryan knew what was happening. 'I'm in WA on business. I'll be in touch when I get back.'

'Okay. You'll ring me, right?'

'Yep, sure. The crack over here is crap. I'll be in need of some good stuff when I get back.'

'Right. Ring me.'

'I'll do that.'

He disconnected, feeling sorry for the rentboy. Life was hell when you'd hit the streets at sixteen without protection. Pedro had no future, but Ryan sure as hell didn't want to read about the man's death in the papers.

He called the trace unit and left the details of the second call.

Unfortunately, all that was likely to tell them was that Pedro had called and some unnamed scumbag in the background was telling him which questions to ask. All things being equal, they'd rough Pedro up a bit then leave him alone.

Outside he heard a length of what sounded like iron being pulled free. Hope the kid doesn't hurt himself, he thought.

He looked at his other phone, where his mother's number waited to be used. It was not cowardice that held him back, he tried to console himself; it was self-preservation. She made him slip out of his undercover role quicker than anyone else.

Right now he felt like he was juggling two personalities and two operations. The sooner they got Nemesis off his back, the sooner he could concentrate on the arson attacks.

The one saving grace was that an out-of-town bikie was going to stand out like dog's balls in this neighbourhood. Should he have that discussion with Dan just in case – tell the kid he could only be here if Ryan was home? From the sound of metal scraping over metal, the boy had found something to investigate. The phone rang again before Ryan could make up his mind.

'Marion, sorry about that. I was just about to call you back.' One more lie wasn't going to kill him.

Chapter 12

THE tyres stopped rumbling as they hit the smooth driveway. Kait could feel the stress of the last six days drain out of her toes.

She frowned. This time of the afternoon Julia normally played the piano. Long sweeping passages of music would fill the house as her mother's supple fingers roamed across the keys. Today? Nothing.

Odd. If Julia wasn't playing music, she was cooking. But there was no sound and no smell, other than a smoky overtone from the bushfires. Kaitlyn stabbed at the remote control, a frisson of alarm lifting the fine hairs on the nape of her neck. Impatiently, she waited for the door to rise on the garage.

No car. Julia wasn't here.

Kaitlyn felt her skin tighten further, a tiny rash of goosebumps spreading across her arms. 'Stop it,' she muttered. 'You're being ridiculous.'

She left her overnight bag in the boot of the car and unlocked the heavy door to the main house, fumbling the keys in her haste.

'Mum? Dan?' The silence pressed down on Kaitlyn. The rapid tattoo of her heart echoed in her ears. 'Julia? Dan?' She dropped her keys on the benchtop and hovered her hand over the stove. No residual warmth.

'Dan?' She strode through to her son's bedroom. No school bag discarded on the floor. Nothing in the laundry basket either. Back to the kitchen, this time bumping her thigh on the doorframe as she whirled through.

With fingers splayed between her breasts she came to a stop in front of the fridge. 'Damn.' She pulled the piece of paper free from under the magnet and read the words aloud.

'*Kait, had to pick Daniel up from school. The bus broke down. Tried to call, but the phones seem to be down again. Love, Julia.*'

Kaitlyn rocked back on her heels and reached for the counter to steady herself. These panic attacks still struck in the odd, unguarded moment. The sense of impending loss was irrational, but overpowering. Would there ever be a time when she was free of it?

'You're an overprotective worrier of a mother,' she muttered. 'Get your bag out of the car and calm down before they get home.'

She heard a vehicle coming up the road. Curiosity won. She opened the door in time to see a white four-wheel drive trailing a cloud of dust towards Jerry's place. Ryan's car. It seemed her good-looking rescuer was indeed renting Jerry's house. And that shouldn't have made her smile, but it did.

She'd managed to haul her bag to her room before she heard the familiar note of Julia's car. She even resisted the urge to meet them at the door to the garage. That would be a giveaway. Julia would guess she'd worried.

'Mum, Mum, I'm home!' She heard Dan's footsteps clattering towards her. 'And you should have seen the grasshoppers at school today.'

Kaitlyn breathed in through her mouth, held it for a second, then out through her nose. Her voice was steady. 'Really?' she called out. 'What class were the grasshoppers in? Sports class doing high jumps?'

'Oh, Mum!' She heard his giggle before he barrelled through the doorway. It eased the knot in her stomach. He launched himself at her, wrapping his arms and legs around her like a clinging koala. She swung him high, loving the feel of him. It wouldn't be long before he'd be too big for this, she thought, depositing him on his feet. He plonked himself on her bed and picked up her work jacket, tracing the logo with his fingers.

'Science,' he said. 'The grasshoppers were in science.'

'Oh?' She went for mock horror and could tell from his goofy grin he knew he was being teased. 'You didn't kill them, did you?'

'No, Miss Kelly did that before class. We just had to name their bits, like wings and legs and mandibles.' He got the last word out after two attempts, tapping his fingers together as though they were jaws moving. 'They were so cool. And Jo got into trouble for chasing Wolfie, and . . .'

His stories ran into each other, cramming six days into a ten-minute ramble. He trailed behind her as she slipped back into the routine of home.

'How was swimming?' Kait shoved her work shirts into the washing machine and turned the dial.

'Good.' He beamed. 'I'm number two in the relay team.'

'That's great,' she gave his arm a gentle tap. 'Build these up some more.'

That launched him on another tangent. Skype chats kept her sane and connected to her family while she was away, but there was no substitute for the real thing. Watching Dan worry a loose tooth with his tongue as he talked reminded her how fast he was growing up.

'Cake time?' she asked.

'Yum. Nan made a chocolate one last night.'

'Bet I know who licked the beaters.' Kaitlyn bumped him with her hip as they walked through to the kitchen, making Dan giggle again.

'Hi, Mum,' Kaitlyn gave her mother a hug, feeling the fineness of Julia's bones under the light cotton shirt she wore. Julia barely reached Kaitlyn's chin now. Her soft cloud of hair had faded to an elegant grey; no sign left of the fiery red she'd passed on to her daughter and grandson.

'Good to see you, darling.'

'Good to be home.' She smiled down at Dan, who was hopping from foot to foot. 'Did you lick the bowl too?'

'Yep, but Nan wouldn't let me taste the cake hot.'

The older woman handed over a slice of chocolate cake. 'Things taste better when they've rested.'

'Ha.' Dan fell silent as he licked the icing off the slice of cake.

'Good drive home? I hope you didn't worry. The phone's still down.' Julia shot a quick glance at her daughter. 'I rang Telstra to report it again. They said someone would come tomorrow, or maybe the day after. You know what they're like. The mobile was playing up as well so maybe it's the whole district.'

Kaitlyn nodded as she reached into the fridge and snagged the cold water. 'Typical. I found your note. What happened to the bus?'

'The school said it broke down, but it seems they were short a driver. Speedy had been called out to fight a fire that was bigger than expected so he couldn't get away. The bus company couldn't find a replacement in time so the school principal thought it best to get parents to ferry the children home.'

'And you should see all the smoke in town. The fire trucks were busy.' Dan's eyes were bright. There was nothing like a fire truck to bring a gleam to a small boy's eyes. Dan had no idea they had the opposite effect on his mother. He was too young to remember that day in Canberra.

'Really?' Kaitlyn brushed some icing off her son's cheek. The warm surge of love for this little being, her little man, was almost overpowering. She itched to hug him close and bury her nose in his silky hair. He leant away, trying to get more cake in his mouth before he spoke again. Kaitlyn ignored it, not prepared to reprimand so soon.

'Yeah, and I think Speedy waved at me, too. He was in the beat-up old truck that rattles.'

'Was he speeding?' Kaitlyn couldn't resist.

'Nah, nothing fast about Speedy.'

She laughed and swatted him across the top of his head as he grinned at the familiar joke.

'Homework?'

'Yeah.' It always fascinated her how clearly the inflection in his voice could do disdain.

'Hop to it, then. Bring it in here so we can do it together.'

He slid off the stool and raced for his room. There was a moment of quiet in the kitchen.

'How was your trip?' asked Julia.

'Good. Long. Lauren was the captain, so that's always a riot.'

'What's happening next week?'

Kaitlyn grimaced. 'Office. All week. That means driving down and back every day.'

'Oh dear.' Julia put some garlic into a pan and the aroma filled the kitchen. Kaitlyn sniffed appreciatively. She didn't tell her mother about the new project. Julia would be upset, worried about her. It wasn't worth it.

'At least I've got four days off now. So, what have you been up to?'

'A little trip to Cairns.' Julia reached down beside her and deposited a familiar brown shopping bag on the bench. 'Here.'

'More clothes? Kaitlyn laughed, peeling the golden heart sticker off and seeing white tissue paper.

'I think you'll look gorgeous in them.'

'For me?'

'Just a little something.' Julia turned back to the stove.

'Thank you.' Kaitlyn knew there was no point in arguing. Accept gracefully and ignore the feeling of being a charitable cause. Julia did have impeccable taste and a healthy bank balance.

'I'll try them on after I've had a shower.'

'Here, Mum.' Dan slid back onto the seat and dropped his books next to her elbow. 'Maths?'

'Hmm . . .' A shower could wait. 'What else have you got?'

'There's reading. He didn't appreciate my choice,' Julia chimed in.

'It was baby stuff, Nana.'

'Nothing baby about *The Hobbit*.'

'But it's not real.'

'And Zac Powers is?' Kait knew Julia battled to get Dan reading.

'*Muuum*.'

'Well?'

'He's cool.'

'Ah, I see.' She rolled her eyes at Julia, who turned back to the stove with a matching eye-roll. 'So, maybe you can read me a Zac story, then we can read a chapter of *The Hobbit* together.'

'Maths first?'

Kait saw the stiffness in Julia's shoulders. 'Reading first.' Julia did so many of the hard yards, the least Kait could do was support her.

'Okay,' Dan huffed as he pulled a book from the bottom of the toppling pile. The tiny moment of tension that had raised its head was gone. Kait settled further onto the stool. Five minutes later she was absorbed in the latest adventure herself.

The background noise of Julia shaking the pan to loosen the crispy bacon blended with the hiss of the taps and the rhythmic chopping of vegetables. The three of them slipped back into a routine easily. Julia and Kaitlyn had been close before the fire. And afterwards? With so much they couldn't share with outsiders, they'd turned to each other for comfort. They were more than mother and daughter, and Dan cemented them even closer.

An hour later he'd finished his homework and escaped to the yard.

'I sent Daniel over to introduce himself to our new neighbour.' Julia waved a spoon as Kaitlyn looked up sharply. 'I sent a cake over. It's the neighbourly thing to do.'

'I think he might be the guy who stopped and helped me with the flat tyre last week.'

'Really?' Julia looked visibly brighter. 'It's good to know your neighbours.'

'Well, yes, but *we* haven't officially met him yet.'

'Ryan. His name's Ryan.'

'It is my roadside rescuer. Still, we should have both met him before we let Dan go and annoy him.'

Kaitlyn's pager beeped before Julia could argue.

'How do these things work without phone lines? Maybe the mobile network is up again,' she said, walking over to retrieve the pager. 'Damn, they need me,' she said, checking the message from the RFB. Before she could reach for her mobile it rang. 'Hi, Kaitlyn speaking.'

The voice at the other end was familiar. The dispatcher from the RFB. She listened with a frown.

'Kait, I'm glad I got through. The bloody phones are down all over the place. Can you suit up and help out tonight? We've got a fire burning towards the houses up from Rocky Creek on the other side of the highway. We've had crews out all day and we need numbers. I can't get hold of most people.'

She sighed, dragging a hand through her hair. 'Sure, sure. I can be ready in half an hour. Where do you want me? At the base?'

'No, Speedy's got the old truck. He's just been to refill so he'll stop by. I'll radio him.'

'Okay. Give me thirty minutes.' She disconnected with a deep sigh. Dan was going to be devastated when he realised she wouldn't be home for dinner. But there was nothing she could do. She couldn't walk away from the threat of fire. She couldn't.

'Trouble?' Julia asked.

'Yep. Looks like the phones are down, so they're short-staffed. And there's been way too many fires for this time of year.' Kaitlyn chewed the inside of her lip. 'I think there's someone behind all this.'

'Arsonist?'

'It's too early for schoolkids larking about. It usually takes them a couple of weeks of school holidays to get up to that much mischief, and then they're only small fires. Holidays don't start for three weeks.'

'Have some food before you go.' Julia was already scooping pasta into a bowl.

'I'll get changed first.'

Kaitlyn mulled it over as she pulled on woollen socks and long underwear. The bright orange rural firies' overalls might be fire-retardant, but she wanted more protection than that. Some of the recent fires were harmless, just hazard reductions that got away. Others, like this, were too close to populated areas to be allowed to burn out. Too coincidental. Arsonists liked an audience.

Kait had firsthand experience with arsonists. She knew it could be the innocent-looking boy next door. It could be a man with golden hair, green eyes and a shy smile. It could even be a serving fireman, one of the men entrusted to stop fire spreading, destroying and killing.

She knew because the last arsonist she'd met had been her husband, killed by a fire he was accused of lighting, a fire that burnt out hundreds of kilometres of plantation pines, two outer suburbs of Canberra, and took the lives of five other people, including that of her father, Stephen.

Chapter 13

SPEEDY turned into Happy Jack Road, smiling. His lucky night. Kaitlyn Scott was going to fight fires with him. She'd joined the rural firies about three, going on four, years ago, and in all that time he'd never once had the pleasure of being alone with her in the truck.

'How lucky can a guy get?' he asked out loud. He changed the radio station to some easy-listening music and cranked up the air-con. Through the trees he could see glimpses of light. Not everyone appreciated the design of Kaitlyn's ugly house, but he did. He could see why she'd built what she'd built. She was thumbing her nose at the fire. More power to her. The lady had guts and brains. And she was a bit of a looker, underneath the plain clothes and trademark plait. Plus she had a nice laugh and she wasn't afraid to share it.

No snobbery in her, unlike some of the other prats around. And Daniel was a good kid. He kept a special eye on Dan. No harm was going to come to that one. The radio crackled with chatter between some of the other crews. A bloody busy day. Fires on three fronts. Nothing too serious, but enough to keep them busy. Of course, the conditions were forecast to deteriorate in the next few days. The fire warning was already at 'extreme'. There was only 'catastrophic' to go.

The front door was open and he drove up to the garage. 'Nice,' he murmured, looking around at the sparse but elegant garden. Kaitlyn was backlit as she came out to meet him. Speedy could see her mother hovering behind her. Now there was a beautiful woman, despite her age. She must have been a hell of a looker when she was younger. And her daughter had the same smile.

He leant across and pushed open the passenger door. 'Kait, nice to see you,' he said, extending his hand. Her skin was cool, the fingers long and strong. He made sure not to hold them too long.

'Hi, Speedy. Sounds like a busy night.' She clicked the seatbelt in as she finished talking and he was back on the road before he replied.

'Been a busy day, too.' He didn't bother keeping the note of fatigue from his voice. 'Let's hope it's not too late a night.'

'Lucky I'm not working tomorrow, I guess,' she said with an easy smile. There was no hint of complaint, but he knew she hadn't been home long. He'd seen her car go past when he was leaving Rocky Creek to refuel.

'Lucky you, then. I've got the school run tomorrow morning.'

'Yeah, heard you missed it today.'

'Sorry about that. The fire was getting away from us and there were a couple of newbies out there. We need more crew.'

'Hard to get good people, I guess, when we all have such busy lives.'

Speedy grunted. 'I hear there's at least one new guy joining. He's living out in Jerry's place, near you. A Sydney metropolitan firey who's on sick leave. Hope it's not bloody stress leave.'

Kaitlyn half laughed, the sound almost throaty. 'Ryan. He stopped and helped me change a flat tyre the other day. At least you'll save on pick-ups if we're both available.'

'Just great.'

'Cheer up, he'll run rings around people like me. Maybe we can all learn something.'

'Or he'll get his crew injured, or worse, 'cos he doesn't understand wildfires.' Speedy knew he'd been too harsh when Kaitlyn didn't reply. 'Sorry. But I've seen too many heroes in my time who don't know what they're doing.'

'Guess we'll wait and see,' she replied. 'So far I've only seen professionals up here.'

'Yeah, most are, but there are always nutcases around. Seems to me there're too many fires at the moment.'

This time she didn't look across at him. Shocked? Angry? Nope, she was considering his words and he'd bet a fiver she agreed. He warmed to the topic.

'I've done twenty-seven call outs since mid-October. That's almost one a day. I know I've only lived here for five years, but I've never seen anything like it.'

'I know.' She sounded thoughtful. 'We've only been here five as well, but maybe I haven't paid enough attention in past years.'

'At least most of these fires are in areas where they don't do too much damage. Then every once in a while you get one like this.'

They were approaching the top of the long descent to Rocky Creek and they could see the smoke billowing in the darkening sky. Flames were leaping from eucalypt to eucalypt, devouring the tall timbers in a blazing shower. This one was a long way from being controlled.

Speedy swung the tanker off onto the verge and pulled it to a stop. An instant later their doors slammed in unison. With helmets and safety gear in place, they had the hose out and running in less than three minutes. Speedy heard the relief in the voices over the radio. Three trucks might just pull this one back.

He and Kaitlyn worked side by side, gradually pushing the fire back on itself, over already blackened earth. Gain three feet, lose two. Most of the large trees through this section had been shattered by Cyclone Larry a couple of years earlier. Those trunks were now dried-out hulks, deadly time bombs waiting to explode as the fire engulfed them. All the weary firefighters could do was keep battling and hope the shrapnel didn't find them.

One of the few saving graces was that the wind was at their backs and dropping as the sun sank behind the Great Dividing Range. Speedy coughed, feeling the burn in his throat reach irritation level. He'd need a drink soon. The roar of the fire had subsided to a rumble. Still sounded like a freight train, but not so close any more. Smoke made his eyes water, but he resisted the temptation to wipe them. Nature did a better job than his filthy gloves. He yelled to Kait, his voice hoarse.

'Drink! We need water.' He saw her nod, but turn back to the line she was working on. Stubborn, too. He added that to her other good points.

His kit was in the cab along with hers and he dug around to find her camel pack. Her jacket carried a whiff of perfume. He could almost taste it on his tongue. Then his fingers found the straps to the water bag.

'Here!' he yelled and waved it at her. This time she came towards him. They both gulped greedily from their bags. Out the corner of his eye he saw a tiny rush of water on her chin. It was unbearably erotic and he turned away.

'Reckon we've got it this time.' He spoke to distract himself.

'Hmm.' She wiped her mouth with the back of her sleeve, leaving a smear of charcoal across her cheek. 'Provided the wind doesn't get into it tomorrow.'

'Forecast for a wind change, so it should be easier.'

'I see no sign of rain on its way.'

'Nah. Won't see anything significant until January at the earliest.'

'Hope the forecasters have got it wrong then. The countryside is tinder-dry.' She dropped her pack back into the front of the truck. 'How much longer before we run out of water?'

Speedy checked the gauge on the side of the tank. 'Another half-hour, max.'

He could see the other crews working the adjacent flank of the fire. That meant they'd not only pushed it back, but narrowed it as well. The houses further up the hill behind him would have a sleepless night, but they'd be safe.

One crew checked in on the radio. They'd run their water tank dry and were heading home. Exhausted from a long day, they weren't coming back. Five minutes later, they stopped by.

Max was the leader. 'Can't understand it. This bloody thing was all but out, then it flared up again. I've reported it to the police. It didn't do that by itself. It had some help.' He spat on the ground. 'Some bastard's out there watching us run round like ants and laughing at us. He's going to get someone killed soon.'

Kaitlyn was silent after they drove away. She looked worried, but Speedy had no comfort for her. The second crew called in to say they were going to refill and they'd be back.

Speedy clipped the radio back on his belt. 'Just us for a while.'

Kait nodded. 'Any point in laying a trail further back so there's a bigger fire break?'

He looked where she was pointing and considered the slope of the land. She was right. If they took that parcel out as well there'd be a good 500 metres of burnt ground before the start of the residential blocks. A hell of a lot easier to defend. She went up another notch in his estimation.

'Better do that while we've still got water to control it.'

'I'll keep the hose then,' she said, with a half-smile he could only just make out. 'I'm not overly fond of the torches.'

'No worries, love. I'll handle that. Necessary evil.'

The drip torch was a vital piece of equipment. It laid a trail of fire from its glowing wick that could shape the burn. Speedy enjoyed using it. At the same time he also fully understood its power.

The temperature had dropped with sunset, but the heavy protective clothing that kept the fire out also kept the heat in. Underneath the coat he could feel his armpits were wet with sweat.

Kait was already stowing the hose so they could move the truck. He liked how methodical she was. She almost looked slow, but she did it right first time. Hare and the tortoise, he thought, priming the torch.

'Good to go?'

'Certainly.' She buckled up again, even though they were driving a relatively short distance and not on a road. Safety-conscious all the way.

For the next half an hour they worked in companionable silence, pushing a line of fire up towards the area they'd only an hour ago fought so hard to extinguish. He knew to the untrained it didn't make a lot of sense, but firebreaks were standard containment measures. The fire crackled now, its roar muted. Flames snaked along the ground with only an occasional flare-up.

By the time the second team returned Speedy and Kait's tank was almost dry. The pair took their leave. The others would fill the graveyard shift if needed. Kaitlyn slumped against the door as they drove up the hill.

'You okay?'

'Yep,' she sighed, pushing herself upright. 'I just hope this isn't the work of an arsonist, or someone's going to get hurt before the wet season.'

'Let's hope you're right. If the police catch him there are some who'd turn up to lynch him.'

She grimaced and ran a hand over her face, pushing back damp hair. 'That would make them just as bad as the arsonist.'

'Maybe he'd deserve it.'

She was silent for a minute. 'Except that sometimes things aren't always as they seem. That's what our justice system's all about: innocent until proven guilty.'

Irrationally, it made him angry. He turned into her driveway a little too fast and hit the brakes. 'Sometimes it takes a strong man to right a wrong.'

'Or a strong man to make a mistake,' she said with a weary smile. 'No offence, Speedy. It's been good working with you tonight. I learnt a lot. Thank you.' Her touch on his arm was fleeting. Then she gathered her bag and coat and got out of the truck.

Her touch had stopped him dead. 'No worries,' he called through the window. 'I'll see your kid in the morning.'

Driving away, he watched her outside light go out in his rear-vision mirror. She was going to bed, and that thought made his body tighten with want. Even without her history she was desirable. With that history she was damn near irresistible.

Chapter 14

'HERE'S your uniform and your ID. Final assessment will take a week or two to organise and you'll be buddied up with someone at Oakey Creek meanwhile. It's a newish team out there, but they're committed.'

Ryan nodded, holding the bright orange overalls under one arm, thankful his induction had been straightforward.

'Welcome to the team.' The training officer on the other side of the desk held out his hand. 'It's not often we get seasoned fire-fighters joining us. Hope you stick around.'

'I plan on it,' Ryan said. 'Pace of life in the big city got a bit too much to handle.'

'Know what you mean,' the man replied, coming around to open the door for Ryan. 'It's a quiet place up on the Tablelands. Not a lot happens. You'll get called in for car accidents if the full-time guys at Atherton or Mareeba are tied up. That can be hard, but I guess you've seen that all before.'

'Yeah, done a bit of that.'

'Hopefully not too much more then.'

Ryan added a silent prayer for that, then thanked the training officer and headed for his car. The furnace-like heat almost knocked him backwards as he opened the driver's-side door. His pocket vibrated. He slung the gear on the back seat and dragged his phone out.

'Hello.'

'Ryan.'

'G'day.'

'Where are you, buddy?'

He didn't recognise the voice. 'Out and about. You?'

There was laughter. 'We're watching you. Just remember that.'

The phone went dead in his hands and Ryan shrugged, kept talking as though it hadn't. He leant back against the vehicle, forcing a laugh, and ran his hand through his hair, eyes scanning behind his glasses. Nothing, no movement anywhere.

He opened the rear door of the four-wheel drive, pulled a bag out and took it around to the passenger side, still with the phone glued to his ear in animated conversation. There was no sign of anyone, but that didn't mean they weren't in one of the surrounding buildings, biding their time.

On days like today he had to leave the gun hidden in the car, and he felt naked and exposed without it. The trial of the Nemesis members had commenced today in Sydney. Was this call connected to that?

Finally, satisfied he'd done all he could, he lowered the phone. It could just be someone messing with his head.

As he drove out of the car park and turned left to head south out of Cairns, he dialled.

'Ryan.' He rattled off a code number. 'Another trace.' Again he gave them the number, rapid-fire. 'Let me know.'

The traffic was heavy until he cleared Edmonton, then the road opened up. Cane fields still flanked the highway. Ahead, a pyramid-shaped hill jutted through the rich green fields. Walsh's Pyramid. This time last year, when Ryan had found himself stuck in Cairns in the aftermath of the Nemesis mess, he'd hiked up the Pyramid.

His phone beeped with an incoming text. Sitting at a red light he thumbed through it. As he suspected, they had nothing on his mystery caller. The problem with technology was that over-the-counter gadgetry was often years ahead of the government's procurement process.

He turned off before Gordonvale, heading up into the hills. The Gillies Range was part of the Great Dividing Range, a weathered spine running the length of Queensland. To the east lay fertile coastal plains. To the west lay the drier lands. Atherton sat at almost 800 metres' elevation: nights chilly, the days pleasant. Ryan appreciated that every time he drove back up the range. What he didn't appreciate was the winding, twisting road to get there. Lucky he didn't get carsick.

As he rounded another hairpin bend, back in second gear, it struck him this would be the perfect place for an ambush. He'd need to be vigilant. In the rear-vision mirror he saw a ute, closing on him fast. He checked that his gun was in the side pocket of the door. The next overtaking lane was 500 metres ahead. He upped the pace, trying to see into the other car. The tinted windows made it impossible. He memorised the registration number.

A truck roared past, going downhill, compression brakes hammering against the incline. Ryan almost flinched. Without realising it, he had the gun in his hand as he pushed down on the accelerator. He wanted maximum torque if this got ugly.

Yellow signs warned of the next sharp bend. He pulled left into the passing lane, easing his foot off the pedal and letting the car decelerate rapidly. The ute swerved out and surged past him. A laconic wave from the passenger said thanks as the vehicle hurtled up the hill.

Sweat trickled down the middle of Ryan's back. He shook his head, trying to shake the adrenalin clear. 'Damn it,' he muttered.

'You're seeing shadows.' The phone call had unsettled him more than he cared to admit.

The rest of the drive was uneventful. He swung through the pretty hamlet of Yungaburra at the top of the range. The ute from earlier, with its twin wide-diameter exhaust, was parked outside the pub. The sticker across its rear window proclaimed 'JetPilot'. Two young men wearing jeans, tight T-shirts and wrap-around sunglasses were drinking beers under a white market umbrella. They didn't raise any alerts on Ryan's radar. And neither of them showed any interest in him.

His phone chirped again as he neared the main roundabout in Atherton.

Incoming message. Crusoe. *Check your mail.*

He needed his encrypted line. It could wait until he got home. He pulled into the shopping centre at the back of Atherton's main street. Thirty minutes later he turned into Happy Jack Road, loaded up with groceries.

He'd found himself reassessing the new house every time he drove past. It'd grown on him. At dawn and dusk it changed colour, glowing pink in the soft light like a modern-day Taj Mahal.

Dan wasn't hanging off the fence this time. Ryan ignored a twinge of regret. He'd always claimed to be allergic to kids, but Dan was disarming.

According to Dan, his mother, Kaitlyn Scott – she of the flat tyre – was a mission commander for Border Watch so spent a lot of time away from home. There was definitely no Mr Scott. No need to question why that made Ryan smile.

Driving around the ridge, he admired the views. Even with smoke in the air he could see all the way to Mareeba and the end of Lake Tinaroo. Beyond was shrouded in haze as the wind swirled and eddied around the mountains.

It took him two trips to get all the shopping plus the firefighting gear upstairs and his left arm was aching by the time he'd finished. Reaching into the fridge he snagged a cold beer and twisted off the top. After a deep drink that sent a cooling rush through his stomach, he lifted his computer out of its case and onto the table. It took a few minutes for it to load and find a connection. He dragged a chair over and swung it round, resting his arms on the back as two emails arrived. The first one was the urgent information.

Dave Tyson was now the third member of Nemesis to be released on bail, pending some legal argument. The club still had clout. Dave 'Weasel' Tyson was not one of the hard men of the gang, nor one of the brightest. A risk, rather than a threat. Ryan figured he'd see him coming a mile off. Even if Weasel shaved off the handlebar moustache and changed his haircut from a mullet, the lightning bolt tattoo up the side of his neck was going to be hard to hide.

The other information Crusoe had provided was more interesting. He'd been busy in the Feds' database. Apparently Derek Barton, one of the main suspects in the earlier fires at the Greentrees plantations in Victoria and New South Wales, changed names like most people changed cars. He'd been christened Derek Barton, but when his mother remarried he'd been given her new husband's surname. Jackson, Derek Jackson. Sometime later he'd reverted to his birth name of Barton. His prison record listed him as John Derek Barton. That record showed he was released five years ago, after serving three years for an arson attack. He was now forty-two.

Mr Barton had plenty of supporters. His crime had been to burn down the house of a known paedophile. That made him a hero to some people. The prison psychologists had been very happy with his rehabilitation and his interactions with other prisoners. That fact alone made Ryan uneasy. He knew firsthand you could lie to a psych.

After his early release, Derek disappeared. Nothing, no trace for two years. He then made a brief appearance, before vanishing again. No bank accounts accessed, no Centrelink payments claimed, no tax returns lodged. His mug shot from jail was typically bland. Change his hairstyle, gain or lose some weight, grow a beard, and he'd be a different man. Ryan knew it wasn't hard to alter appearances.

Crusoe had dug up some other possible photos of Derek. They were three years old and lifted from CCTV footage at a petrol station. The police had confiscated the footage at the time of the last Greentrees plantation fire. The images were distant and grainy, showing a slim man with a ponytail, wearing a cap and sunglasses. Could be anyone. The police investigating the arson on the plantations had made hard work of fingering any suspects back then. The only reason Derek Barton's name had even cropped up was because a local barmaid had given them such a good identikit photo that the computer had tagged Barton as a match. The barmaid had then identified him from the prison mug shot, but before they could pull him in for questioning he'd vanished. The trail was now three years cold. Derek Barton had stayed off the radar.

One theory said he'd picked up a new identity. Or he'd been caught in one of his fires. Ryan suspected it was the former. In the age of computers it was relatively easy to reinvent yourself. A man like Mr Barton, with contacts from jail, wasn't going to find it hard at all.

If he was here on the Tablelands, then the most likely way for Ryan to find him was to visually identify him.

Ryan added the latest photos to his phone gallery. 'Derek Barton, I'm going to find you before you do any more harm.' He stretched his arms above his head, feeling the stiffness in his shoulders. Needed a good run to loosen up. Give him a chance to scout out the neighbours some more. First thing tomorrow.

Something landed on the roof with a thump and Ryan was on the floor with his gun out before he could identify the noise. The sun had set while he'd been trawling through Derek's files. At least the only light in the house was now the glow from his computer. Of course, that also pinpointed where he was.

He lay on the floor, straining to hear the direction of movement. Nothing. He took a shallow sip of air, breathed out and rolled over to sit up. Still nothing.

Getting to his feet, he edged towards the sound. This time, when it started to move, he was ready, tracking it to the rear of the house. When the noise changed from a thump to a long slide, he stopped walking and shook his head.

'Bloody hell,' he muttered, tucking his gun into his waistband again. The noise reached the guttering at the back. Ryan grabbed the torch and headed to the veranda.

He spotted the odd shape hanging down from the roof as soon as he opened the door. A brush-tailed possum with impossibly large eyes peered at him, unblinking, in the beam of light. It sparked a memory of Jerry teaching him to feed possums.

'Okay, my little beauty, I'm not going to hurt you.' It didn't move.

'What do you think, little one? An apple? Strawberry?' The possum just hung over the edge, looking inquisitive. Ryan left the door open and went to rummage in his fridge.

When he returned, the furry marsupial was sitting at the top of the stairs. It looked nervous but defiant, like it was bolstering its courage. That amused Ryan. He applauded the bravado. An undercover used it every day he, or she, went to work.

'Here you go.' Keeping his movements slow he slid a piece of apple and a strawberry across the wooden floor. He stepped back to the doorway and watched as the animal's nose quivered, scenting the air. If Ryan could smell the sweet fruit then the possum definitely could. It inched over and delicately grasped the strawberry, then backed away. Rocking back onto its hind legs it held the fruit in both paws and proceeded to devour it with tiny nibbles.

Ryan smiled. He'd done this before in a time of innocence. The memory was strong. Some of the day's tension eased. He should stop being so jumpy. Nemesis was a long way away from North Queensland.

Chapter 15

'ARE you sure you didn't just leave it at school?' Kaitlyn tried to keep her voice patient. She could hear Julia playing scales on the piano as she walked into the house. Dan followed, dragging his heels.

'I rode it home. How could I have left it at school?' He looked mutinous, not guilty. 'Someone stole it.'

'Did you see anyone around?'

'Yes. Ryan, the guy from over there.' He flung his arm, pointing across the valley. 'The big white car.'

'He's been here at the house?' She couldn't believe this. Surely Dan didn't mean their neighbour had stolen the bike?

'No. He waves when he drives by.' Dan shuffled his feet. 'But someone stole it. They must of.'

'Must *have*,' she corrected him automatically. 'Just let me put my bag away and get out of my uniform.'

The music stopped and her mother's subtle perfume drifted into the room a second before she did. 'I've already looked everywhere I could think to, Kait.' She pressed her cheek to her daughter's in welcome and patted her shoulder. 'It's vanished.'

Kaitlyn resisted the urge to rub her temples. This week it felt like everything was turning into a disaster. The daily drive up and down the range was taking its toll on her. Tony was being a pain in the arse and interfering, even though he had no experience at all with fires. By his own admission he'd never even been close to one. Thank goodness for Morgan and Lauren or Kait would probably have told him he was an incompetent, micro-managing boss who should trust people instead of spreadsheets. She pushed all that aside. She was home now. 'Give me time to change. We'll find it.'

Even walking into her bedroom, her sanctuary, with its floor-to-ceiling view of the McAllister Ranges, didn't soothe her today. She screwed her work shirt into a ball and aimed it at the laundry basket, temper in the toss. She felt bitchy as all hell and just for once didn't want to have to deal with everyone else's problems. For two days she'd been playing phone tag with Immigration, still trying to sort out Dan's passport issue.

She caught sight of herself in the full-length mirror as she hopped from one foot to the other, dragging on a baggy pair of shorts. That stopped her. Her skin was more pale than usual, her jaw tight and jutting, the frown lines between her straight brows furrowed deep. Anger and frustration radiated from every curvy inch of her. Not a good look. She straightened up, fastening the shorts and trying to organise her logic.

Was Dan was capable of lying about this? Or had he been careless with locking the bike up and knew he'd be in trouble? But who would take his bike? Borrowed, stolen, trashed? If she reported it to the police, the chances were nothing would happen. Insurance was next to useless. The excess always seemed to equal the amount they paid out.

Leaning closer to the mirror, she patted her cheeks and unlocked her muscles. He's seven, she reminded herself, and fatherless. Go easy.

She shrugged into a gardening shirt missing half its buttons. The old, long-sleeved corporate number was a leftover from her days in Canberra, before the fires, when an air-conditioned office was her workstation, not the endless blue of a northern sky. It hung on her more than it used to.

Dan was eating biscuits in the kitchen, his feet hitting the kitchen cupboard as he swung them back and forth.

Julia, immaculate as ever in a loose, buttoned dress, leant on the counter, leafing through a newsletter from the clogging society she'd joined. She looked up at Kait and smiled. 'A wine?' The glasses were already lined up, waiting. The smell of roasting meat filled the room.

'No thanks, Julia. Best we go and do some detective work. Come on, kiddo. Let's see what we can deduce.'

Dan's stool rocked as he jumped down. He scooped the remaining biscuits into his hands and silently followed her outside.

The day still had some heat to it and she swatted away a couple of flies. Mid-November and the dry ground was baked hard. They'd had late September rain after a wet winter. Consequently the native grasses were tall and thick on the other side of the fence. Snakes she could live with, but the fire risk made her uneasy.

On days like this she questioned her motives for moving her family to a rural area. Defiant pride wasn't an admirable character trait, but in the aftermath of the coronial inquiry into the Canberra fires she'd been angry and bitter, guilty and sad. Defiance had saved her from depression. The knowledge that her husband's actions had torn other families apart, as well as her own, was a burden she'd thought would destroy her. It hadn't. It had made her stronger, tougher, at least on the outside, but she could never forget it. She didn't want to forget it.

'I left it there after school.' Daniel scampered up next to her, pointing. 'By the gate.'

'And then you went inside? And next time you looked for it the bike had gone.' Kaitlyn scanned the yard. Maybe someone had hidden it as a joke, although that seemed as likely as someone stealing it. 'That was this afternoon?'

'Yesterday.' He looked down. 'Nana said you had enough problems and we'd find it today.'

'You didn't tell me yesterday?' She knew her words had been sharp the instant his bottom lip wobbled. Sharp enough to make twin trails of tears run down his cheeks. With little fists he scrubbed them away, standing his ground.

'It's not my fault.'

It killed her to ignore the tears, but she knew she had to be firm until she got to the bottom of this. 'Okay.' Kait moderated her voice. She was ticked off that her son and her mother had kept it from her for a day. She always had time for them, didn't she? Guilt reared its head again and she struggled to ignore it.

'Let's check the other side of the fences. Maybe someone dumped it in the scrub.'

She grabbed the yard broom from beside the door. Dan shuffled along behind her as she walked out the gate and along the boundary. Swishing the broom in front of her to flatten the grass and scare any snakes, she worked her way along the fence, Daniel two paces behind in his sneakers. The grass ahead moved in a distinctive ripple and she put out a hand to stop him.

'You go back inside, Dan. Get the keys and we'll check the shed as soon as I'm done here.'

Without a word he turned and stomped back to the gate, each heavy footstep saying more than words. She shaded her eyes against the glare of the dropping sun, surveying the thick tangle of grass. 'Damn it. This is silly,' she said to herself. 'Get the mower before you stand on a whole nest of snakes.'

Half an hour later she'd searched everywhere and come to the conclusion that Daniel was right.

'Looks like someone did take it, Dan. Let's hope their need was greater than ours.' She sighed, running an exasperated hand through her hair. 'I'm sorry I didn't believe you.'

He gave a jerk of his shoulder and looked a little less dispirited.

'I guess we'll have to get you another one, then. Did Julia take you to the bus stop today?'

He nodded without replying – still sulking, from the set of his shoulders.

Kait sighed. 'We'll go and see what we can find on the weekend. One of us will run you to the bus stop in the morning.'

'Speedy said he'd pick me up.'

'Really?' She looked down at him. 'It's out of his way.' The school bus route did an amazing job of winding its way through the rural housing estates outside of Atherton, but as Daniel was the only one on Happy Jack Road, it stopped at the main highway. That gave Dan a bike ride of almost three kilometres.

'He said it was okay, just to let him know tomorrow morning.'

'Okay, that would be easier. We'll still have to get a new bike for you.'

Daniel brightened at the mention of a new one, no doubt scheming about what gadgets he could sweet-talk her into buying for it.

'But you need to lock the next one up. You know the rules.' And that's why there'll be no horse, she thought. It would matter a whole lot more if a horse went missing.

'Yeah, yeah, I know.' He tried a tentative smile and a different tack. 'Can you help me with my homework tonight?'

'Sure. First I need to knock this grass back down, though, so you go and get started on your maths. Give me an hour and we'll tackle reading. And go tell Julia I'm going to mow.'

She knew there was no point in ringing Immigration in Canberra now. They were an hour ahead at this time of year. Maybe she could ring before work tomorrow.

Once she'd run the ride-on mower over the cleared area around the house, she drove out through the front gate. The council tractors didn't get out here often enough and she mowed more of the verge each time. She'd almost finished when she caught a flash of white through the trees. Ryan on his way home. Would she get to meet the elusive neighbour again? A stealthy warmth snuck through her body. Ridiculous woman, she cautioned, you'll look like a desperate single mother if you start blushing again. And that's if he bothers to stop.

To avoid the very real danger of throwing rocks with the mower blades she slowed to a stop, and angled towards the road. The white vehicle was almost past before the brake lights came on and it stopped in a slide of gravel.

The door opened and a worn boot stuck out, holding it back. She could hear his deep voice. Probably on a mobile phone, she surmised.

When the rest of the denim-clad leg followed the boot and he stood up, she had to fight not to stare. Without the cap and scruffy beard, the neighbour was good-looking in that messy, country-boy way, hair tousled, a shadow of new growth on his jaw. His legs seemed to go on forever. He was busy jamming the tail of his button-up shirt into low-slung jeans. It wasn't working and that made him look even more fetching as he walked towards her. Losing the beard had taken a couple of years off him.

'Hi.' She leant forward on the steering wheel of the mower. 'Welcome to the neighbourhood, Ryan.'

'Thanks, great to be here.' When his eyes flicked over her for an instant then snapped back to her face, she sat up and extended her hand. Great. She'd forgotten about the missing buttons on her shirt. There was nothing left to his imagination now. He had the good grace to look a little embarrassed.

'Thanks again for your help the other day. I didn't realise you were our new neighbour.'

'My absolute pleasure, Kaitlyn.' His handshake was like the rest of him: firm, a little rough around the edges. He didn't look like her idea of a city fireman.

'Nice house,' he said, nodding at it.

She smiled. 'Thanks. No need to be polite. I know it's not pretty, but it's safe.'

'It does look indestructible,' he said with a quick grin. 'Kind of like a citadel that's thumbing its nose at Mother Nature.'

She laughed, surprised by his insightfulness. 'I guess you'd be right about that. Dan says you've moved into Jerry's place? How's he doing in the nursing home?'

For an instant there was wariness in his eyes, then he shrugged. 'I don't know. I found the place on the internet. The agent mentioned the old fella who owned it had recently been packed off to a nursing home. Left a lot of furniture behind. Suits me. Think I'll get my own bed, but the rest is good to go.'

'How are you finding it?'

'So far so good. The locals are friendly, although I mustn't be dressing right. They all pick me for a city guy.' He looked down at his clothes, his lips softening with the hint of humour. 'Am I that obvious?'

'The lads up here tend to drive utes. And they don't wear Jag jeans. You got the R.M. boots just about right, though maybe they need a few more scratches.' She smiled to take away any criticism. 'And never, ever wear a baseball cap. You need a hat, preferably battered and torn with a couple of holes through the brim.'

'Like yours?' The laughter made it to his eyes this time.

'No.' She settled it more firmly on her head. 'Mine's a city girl's hat and I'm proud of it.'

'Guess you or your husband have been keeping the grass down at Jerry's place. Thanks for that.'

Kaitlyn shook her head. 'No thanks required. It's purely selfish on my part. I like to keep the grass cut to give us the best possible chance if bushfires come through. With the wind from the north, any fire over at Jerry's is going to roar down through that valley of pines and up the ridge to here.' She patted the mower. 'Only takes a little over an hour to knock it over. Let me know if you want to borrow it.'

'Think I might need some lessons on how to handle it first.' His easy grin said he was flirting, but she dismissed the thought. He wasn't as young as she'd first thought. There was a maturity to him, a thickening of muscle, that belied his youthful looks, but he still had to be a couple of years younger than her. So far out of her league that she felt safe smiling back at him.

'I'm sure a guy like yourself knows his way around. Just drop by and ask. Better finish this before the light goes.'

'Sure. Say hi to Dan.'

'Will do. Julia said she'd sent him over with a cake. I hope he behaved himself.'

'Yeah, he's been around a couple of times. I think he wanted to scrounge around in all that junk.'

Kaitlyn laughed. 'Jerry and he used to spend hours doing something in that yard. I never did understand the attraction. Hey . . .' She hesitated. 'I don't suppose you've come across Dan's pushbike? It's a black Huffy Revenge bike. It's vanished into thin air.'

'Maybe the alien spaceship took it.' His expression was earnest and for a startled second she thought he was serious. Then he laughed. 'Sorry. I used that excuse as a kid and it got me such a hiding. I figured every young boy must have tried it at some time.'

'Not Dan,' she retorted. 'And please don't give him any ideas. His imagination is vivid enough.'

'I'll refrain.'

'I'd appreciate that,' she said, trying to look serious and knowing she'd failed.

'And no, I've only seen his bike when he's been on it. Anyway, I'll let you get on with the mowing. See you round.'

She nodded a smile as she started the motor and pushed it into reverse, not waiting to see him go. Her smile stuck. A neighbour with a sense of humour who was not averse to flirting? Pity she wasn't home more often. But then, she was rusty, out of practice at talking to men, laughing with them in a social setting. She hardly remembered the delicate dance of the dating game. After so long being a mum she thought she had the 'invisible woman' routine down pat. Now? Ryan had sparked a tiny flame she was foolish enough to imagine fanning into life. The laugh escaped before she could stop it. *Ridiculous, Kait.* He probably talked to every woman like that.

A thwacking noise from the blade and a vibration that shook her seat forced her to stop just before she finished the last stretch of grass by her boundary. Exasperated, she peered underneath the mower. Fabric seemed to be wrapped round the centre bar but there wasn't quite enough light to see clearly. With the blades disengaged, she drove the mower into the shed and flicked the light on. The machine was too heavy for her to roll on its side so she lay down and tugged at the material.

'What the hell?' She knew before she'd freed it completely that it was one of her few lacy camisoles. Somewhere buried in a drawer was a matching pair of equally fancy knickers. 'How on earth did that get out there?'

The rational explanation for this would be clothes blown off the washing line, but it didn't work. She hadn't worn this particular item for many years; it was a reminder of a younger Kaitlyn, in the early years of a marriage.

She sat up and rested her arms on her bent knees, contemplating the destroyed garment. Was it attention-seeking behaviour from Dan? Was he going off the rails because she wasn't home enough, leaving Julia to shoulder too much responsibility? Julia never complained about essentially becoming a mother again so late in life, but Kait had noticed she tired more easily than she had a year ago.

Kait sat up straight, stretching her ribs up and out, trying to still the disquiet inside. Going off half-cocked wasn't going to be productive, but somehow she had to get to the bottom of this.

By the time she went in Dan was bent over his book, finger tracing each line as he read to his grandmother. Kaitlyn smothered her guilt before it got the better of her.

'Hey, guys, anyone know how this ended up on the outside of our fence?' Kait waved the mangled garment from two fingers.

Dan frowned and screwed up his nose. 'What is it?' There was no recognition, no remorse in his face, nothing remotely untoward. Kaitlyn hoped her rush of relief didn't show.

Julia held out her hand and stretched the damaged fabric over her fingers. 'I don't think I've ever seen it before.' She raised questioning eyes to her daughter. 'Is it yours?'

'Yep. I haven't worn it since the fire.' The spasm of pain across Julia's face jabbed at Kait. 'I can't work it out.'

'Well, I don't know either, but dinner is ready when you are.' Julia was frowning as she turned and deposited the offending item in the rubbish bin. Kait had the uneasy feeling her mother wasn't being entirely honest. She had no idea why.

'I'll have a shower. Be five minutes.' Better to leave it alone, Kait decided. If Julia knew something, she might have chosen not to say anything in front of Dan. There'd be time for the two of them to discuss it later, when he was in bed.

The shower revived her, although none of the afternoon's optimism returned. Dan's bike was more important than her silly camisole, but were the two things connected in some way? Surely they would have noticed if someone had broken into the house?

Wouldn't they?

Chapter 16

RYAN followed as Speedy ambled through the sparse building. 'This is where you stow your gear. You can put a padlock on it if you want to, but no one ever does.'

Ryan took note. Rule number one: do as the others do.

'There's a tearoom over there. General housekeeping. Keep it tidy, leave it as you find it. If something's running out let Trudy know and she'll top it up. Showers are through there, same deal as the kitchen. Most people don't wash up here; they go home.' The stern look he bestowed on Ryan was also noted. Ryan felt like sighing. This could be a very long couple of days. Speedy was making it clear that he had no time for city slickers who thought they knew fires.

The sad part was, Speedy was right to be wary of Ryan's ability. The least his boss could have done was organise someone laidback to buddy him.

'We've had a really bad run this year. Call out after call out. Did you say you have a regular job?'

'No.' It was the first word Ryan had said in several minutes. 'Still looking for something.'

'Right. That's good.' Speedy looked marginally happier, then he scowled again. 'Of course, you can only go out with a trainer until you're checked out.'

'I know.' Ryan was used to hostility from criminals, but this was different. This felt like a straight personality clash and he'd have to be careful to keep a lid on it. 'I appreciate I have a lot to learn about this sort of firefighting. I'm conscious you guys know your terrain and your equipment a hell of a lot better than I do, but I learn fast. Happy to be told.'

'Yeah, right.' Speedy seemed slightly mollified. 'We'd better run through the equipment. The oldest truck is the only one here today. The new one's out, but it's easy to manage anyway.'

For two hours Speedy grilled Ryan. It was almost as intense as the Fire and Rescue division. Thankfully, Ryan managed to fumble through without too many slip-ups. It occurred to him as he stowed the hose that the years he'd spent in the Navy had laid good foundations for just this sort of situation. You took orders and got on with it.

The three years in undercover ops with the AFP were the absolute reverse. There, he had to think on his feet, second-guess his boss and put up with the heat from above if he screwed up. He'd rarely taken orders from anyone.

Speedy was more your 'yes, no' kind of guy. They'd moved onto the paperwork when the phone rang.

'Speedy.'

Ryan could see from the expression on his face that it was a call out. Time to see if the training came close to reality.

He didn't wait for Speedy to finish the call. The truck was ready to go. He just needed his gear. By the time he'd retrieved it from the locker room, Speedy was waiting.

'You drive,' he said to Ryan. 'Wanna see how you handle the truck.'

'Sure.' The keys were in the ignition and Ryan drove it out. 'Which way?'

'Turn right. We're headed up Carrington way. The urban firies are busy with a road accident on the Gillies highway. Someone's reported a fire up in the hills behind Carrington Road. A lot of new homes in that area. Silly fools subdivide their acreage and put slab homes in unsuitable places, right among the trees and at the foot of the bloody hills. Should be laws against them.'

Ryan grunted, not wanting to venture an opinion.

'You're up Happy Jack Road, aren't you?'

'Right.'

'Near the Scotts'. You in Jerry's place?'

'Yep.'

'At least the old man did one thing right and cleared most of the trees around his house. You'll need to keep the grass down. Kait's got the right idea. You have met your neighbour, haven't you?' There was an edge to his voice.

'Of course. Kait. And her son, Dan. He's been around a couple of times.' Ryan shrugged. 'Seems like a nice kid.'

'He is.' Speedy looked riled. 'He's a good kid.'

Now what was the problem? He was supposed to talk to his neighbours, but not the kid?

'He's got no father. He's impressionable,' Speedy said with a glare across the cabin.

'Seems pretty balanced to me,' Ryan replied.

'Yeah.' Speedy was not happy.

Ryan tried another tack. 'Kait well-liked, locally?'

'Yes. She's a volunteer with the Rural Fire Brigade as well as the SES. Bloody good worker. Methodical.'

Ryan could only nod. From the look of the straight lines she ran with her ride-on mower, she was all of that and more.

Speedy seemed to realise he should be giving directions, and that kept him busy right up to the turning down Carrington Road. The smoke was rising ahead and once they passed a cattery they could see the blaze.

'Fuckin' hell. The wind's already got it.'

Ryan had noticed the trees starting to toss in the stiffening breeze. Up the hill it would be even stronger. 'Are we going to need reinforcements?'

'Yep.' Speedy was already on the radio, calling it in.

As they approached, Ryan could see landowners with hoses and mops, putting out embers that attacked in glittering showers. Many had neatly mown blocks, but several in the danger zone were nestled into the trees. Everywhere he looked, the ground was parched and dry. Long grass on public land fanned forward under the wind. The hill slopes had a thick covering of dry vegetation.

Too late to do a hazard reduction burn now. All they could do was set up containment lines. Speedy pointed to a turning coming up and Ryan drove in through a gate, braking beside a dishevelled older man.

'Mate, glad you're here. It came out of nowhere.' The man pushed a broad-brimmed hat back from his lined face, his mouth pinched and tight. Ryan slammed the truck door and clapped him on the shoulder, feeling the smoke already irritating his lungs.

'We've got reinforcements on their way. Looks like you've done good work.'

The man shook his head, drawing his thick coat tighter around him. 'Not enough. I've sent my wife and the dogs into town with a friend. She can't walk. I can't have her here.'

Ryan felt the other man's fear and grief. 'Good decision.'

Speedy called him. Ryan flashed what he hoped was a reassuring smile at the homeowner and strode around the truck.

'Get the hose going. Start wetting down the area round the house. We'll need to back-burn this lot.' Speedy gestured to the land from the house to the boundary. 'Starve the bloody thing out.'

Half an hour was a long time with a fire, Ryan thought as he got to work with the water. Nothing to do but their best.

Once Speedy was satisfied they could control it, he started a slow walk with the drip torch. Ryan had to admit he was impressed. The line looked spot-on. The fire raced away in glowing rivers, barely visible in the bright sunlight, headed on an oblique angle for the fire front proper. It spread from the grass into the shrubs and licked the trunks of larger trees, curling the bark and causing leaves to drop in blackened flakes. But its lower intensity kept it from reaching the highest branches.

Rationally, Ryan knew it was the wind rising from the flames that made the trees toss, but they looked as though they were writhing in agony, desperately trying to shake the devouring monster clear. Playing the water along the line, he could see how mesmerising fire could be. Hypnotic. The beauty in the flames as the colours danced and spun like swirling ribbons was undeniable.

A loud bang up the hillside made him start and half crouch, instinctively reaching behind him. No comfort there today. The overalls had no place for a weapon.

He searched for the source of sound and found a trail of falling embers. A giant tree had exploded, and burning particles now showered down around them. The older man scurried forwards with his wet mop and dabbed at them, extinguishing as many as he could.

Speedy barely seemed to notice as he walked back to the truck. He picked up a beater and joined the man putting out spot fires. By now the fire trail he'd laid was closing in on the main burn. He spiralled his finger in the air. 'Wind it up. We need to move to the next one.'

Ryan reeled the hose in and stopped beside the homeowner. 'You call again if it threatens you. The road should stay open anyway, so you can always evacuate to where your wife is.'

'Thanks, but I'm staying. This is all I've got.'

And that, Ryan found, was a common thread through the day. People didn't want to lose their homes so they stayed, putting themselves at great risk, determined to tough it out. By six o'clock he was shattered, feeling the pain in his arm slowing him down. 'You'll do,' was all Speedy said as they parted ways at the RFB base.

Ryan guessed that was as good as it was going to get.

Lights were on in the Taj as he drove past. No sign of the kid outside, nor super-mum. He was kind of looking forward to seeing Kaitlyn again.

The last thing he remembered to do before he collapsed into bed was put the gun and car key under his pillow. The state he was in, he'd take some waking. He'd need any advantage he could get if he had to leave in a hurry.

Chapter 17

KAITLYN swapped the phone to her other ear and spoke slowly. The receiver felt like it was scorching her skin.

'I can't provide my husband's signature. He's dead. I don't have a death certificate because in cases where there's no body, it can take seven years for the issue of such a certificate. It's coming up on five years now. I did fill in the B-9 form that explained all that.' Kaitlyn was trying not to lose her temper with the woman from the Immigration Department.

'But if you'd just let me explain,' the woman replied. 'It's not the lack of proof or incorrect forms. Our records show that Chris Jackson is still alive.'

Her voice was heavily accented and Kaitlyn had to remind herself to be patient. This might just be a language problem. She pinched the bridge of her nose between her fingers and exhaled. Phone conversations always lost the subtle nuances.

'Look, buried in your database is the fact Christopher Jackson died in a Canberra fire five years ago on Wednesday the third of December. His body was never found, but he was presumed dead as there was very little left of the house.' Or my father, or my life, she thought, the silence stretching out.

'I see.' But it was clear the woman didn't see. 'I'll need to check with my supervisor. What number is best to contact you?'

'I'll hold, thanks,' Kaitlyn replied, knowing full well that if she waited for them to ring her back it might take days. The squeaky wheel was the only way to get results, and clogging up the phone line made her a squeaky.

'Just one moment, madam.'

The hold recording droned on, and on, and on. The way this was going, Julia would be back from dropping Dan at school before she was off the phone, and Kait would be late for work. Again.

She tapped her fingers on the benchtop, a monotonous drumming keeping time to the words. Two more years and she'd have the damn piece of paper saying Chris was dead.

Her fingers stopped and she looked down at them. Would there ever be a time when her blood didn't heat in anger, her skin tighten with humiliation, and her eyes burn with the loss, the grief?

She missed her father, not her husband. If the fire hadn't got Chris she doubted they would still have been together. The inescapable truth was that they should never have married in the first place. An unexpected child was no reason to tie two very different people together.

'Hello?'

'Yes, I'm still here.'

'Thank you for holding; we appreciate your patience.'

Kaitlyn didn't say anything. Like she had a choice.

'I'm afraid this is more complicated than your application indicated. You'll need to provide additional information. Our records definitely show that Christopher Jackson is alive and well.'

'He can't be!' Kait wanted to shout down the phone as the knot in her stomach grew. 'It's a mistake. Can you check his details again?' She recited his date of birth and their previous address in Canberra, and heard fingers tapping on a keyboard.

'I'm afraid it's not a mistake,' the woman said.

'Where? What address? I'll go and get him to sign the bloody thing.' She was shaking now, blood roaring in her ears.

'I'm not at liberty to disclose that information.'

'You have to, otherwise how the hell am I supposed to get the form signed?'

The pause lasted for what felt like minutes. 'Kairi, Queensland.' The words were clipped. 'He's been living at the address for two years. That's all I can give you. I shouldn't even be giving you that.'

'Kairi? K-A-I-R-I?'

'Yes.'

Her head throbbed. Just up the road, half an hour away? How could that be? Surely if he'd survived the fire he would have been in contact? Goosebumps spread down the backs of her arms and she gripped the receiver with both hands, feeling it rattle against her ear. Surely they were wrong? They had to be wrong.

'Are you there, Ms Scott? Hello?'

Kaitlyn swallowed, trying to find enough saliva to wet her lips. 'Thanks for your time,' she croaked, and hung up.

She stood up, pushing the stool back with her foot. Where the hell did she go from here? The police?

'I've no damn idea,' she muttered, striding out onto her long, wide veranda. Across the way she could see early sunlight glinting off the windows of Jerry's place. The air held a faint taint of smoke. Left over from the night.

She stomped the full length of the house. How could it be? Was she supposed to believe that her husband had faked his death to escape prosecution and now lived close enough to make contact with his son, but hadn't bothered to do so? She wanted to scream, throw something, rant, but it was not her nature to be impulsive. The one time she'd acted on impulse she'd been rewarded with an unexpected pregnancy, then a beautiful son. She closed her eyes against the strength of the memory and slumped against a post.

Chris had been a local fireman who her father, Stephen, had befriended at a fire scene. The younger man had shown an interest in the intricacies of arson investigation and Stephen was always keen to share his knowledge. Kait had been introduced not long after. She'd been flattered by the golden-haired man with calm green eyes who showed her such respect. They'd gone on a date to the movies, then several times to dinner. She liked him, he made her laugh, but there was no fire, no passion – more the comfortable fit of a friend. But he was persistent.

She succumbed to his gentle charm two months after they met, never dreaming one shy encounter might lead to something more permanent. By the time she realised she was pregnant an abortion was out of the question. Secretly, she'd been glad. To make a choice would have been heartbreaking. Daniel was born healthy, late and very much wanted by his mother. His father was a different matter.

In hindsight, Chris had married her out of respect for her father. Stephen and Julia were from a generation for whom the stigma of an illegitimate child was still strong. They were appalled to find their serious, studious daughter was pregnant out of wedlock. But they'd supported her.

A shift of breeze brought a stronger smell of smoke in from the west and Kait scanned the horizon. No sign of telltale build-ups or columns of smoke. She straightened up. She'd never believed the accusation that Chris had lit the fires. That was as likely as accusing her father of lighting them. The two men were professionals who understood the fascination and the power of fire. Stephen had always maintained that there was a little pyromaniac in all of us, but most of us were too scared to do anything silly.

Just why Stephen had gone to his daughter's house that day, no one knew. Nor could anyone explain why Chris's ute had been stacked with full fuel drums if he'd been the one responsible for starting the spot fires that had destroyed the Greentrees plantations. Surely to God he would have known better than to torch the trees bordering his own property. Being a fireman, he would have known the chances of that fire getting away. The frantic phone calls he made from the property calling for assistance didn't make sense if he was the arsonist. She'd heard them all. The police had insisted she identify his voice. Unfortunately, she'd been able to do just that. Her father's badly burnt body was found partly covered by roofing iron. He'd suffered a head wound but the autopsy indicated he'd been unconscious when the fire roared through. That only served to point the finger more directly at Chris, and yet . . .

And yet she would have bet her life on the man. He may not have been husband material, or even father material, but he was no more an arsonist than she was.

His gutted ute, scraps of his clothes, and his twisted and melted mobile phone were all they recovered from the fire. That, along with some human remains that were a match for his DNA, was deemed to be proof that he'd died in the fire he was accused of lighting. At the fire station where he worked, his locker was found empty of any personal items. That contributed to the theory that he was planning to die that day, that he'd deliberately cleaned out any evidence before he'd torched his own home.

For Kaitlyn, it had always raised the spectre that Chris was planning on leaving her. So why did she find this latest twist with Immigration so shocking? Hadn't she always wondered if there was another explanation? Did someone murder him? Or was he still alive? If he was, why had he lit the fire? Too many questions.

She stopped pacing and stared across the valley, seeing the tops of the trees shiver in a shift of wind. When she'd bought this land the native plantation in the valley was owned by Greentrees. At the time, their safety record in North Queensland was enviable, but now they were in receivership and the plantation was untended.

Maybe Julia had a point. Maybe Kait had chosen to thumb her nose at the gods of fire and build something strong, impregnable, on the very precipice of an inferno.

And why? Because you wanted to prove you'd put the shame, the fear, the anger behind you. Maybe that shame and anger had followed you and your family after all.

'No,' she said into the stillness. 'No, Chris. This will not destroy us. If you are alive, I'll hunt you down and make you pay for what you've done. If there's another explanation, another answer, then I'll find it this time. And if you've been wronged, then I'll lay you to rest.'

She strode back inside, anger still heating her skin.

For a fruitless thirty minutes she trawled the online phone directory, Google, Facebook, several other sites, and even the Australian archives. There were the death and funeral notices she knew all too well and a few matches on Facebook that she quickly discounted. She hadn't really expected to find anything. If a man was going to fake his own death and then disappear, he was unlikely to shout his activities from the rooftops.

The chair seemed to sigh as she stretched back in it. For a long moment she hesitated, then sat forward in a rush. What use were contacts if they couldn't provide information when you needed it?

The number she dialled wasn't listed, but she knew it off by heart. The answer was a distracted mumble.

'Martin?'

'Speaking, speaking.'

'Martin, it's Kaitlyn, Stephen Scott's daughter. I'm sorry to trouble you at work.'

'Kaitlyn? How lovely to hear your voice, a welcome distraction. How's Julia and your lad?' The voice was creaky, but she knew the brain behind it was still sharp. Martin Farrell would in all probability be carted out of his office in a body bag. His job as an arson investigator had always been consuming, but once Maggie, his wife of forty years, had died, it became his life. He didn't even have a pet any more. The scruffy little mutt who'd been part of his family for so long hadn't survived Maggie by many weeks.

Kaitlyn doubted that Martin ate anything at home and, if his secretary hadn't taken it upon herself to feed him lunch, he would be even more skeletal than he was.

'Doing well, thanks, Martin. The pace is pretty slow up here. Having a yarn seems more important than getting the job done. I think it suits Julia. She's even playing the piano again. And Dan?' She laughed. 'Dan's most pressing problem is his recent and burning desire for a horse, which his mean and improbably hard mother won't buy for him.'

Martin laughed. 'I'm glad Julia's playing again. Your father would have liked that.'

'You're right. Dad would have been sad if that beautiful piano had stayed silent.'

'And you? You always played so well.'

Kaitlyn shook her head. 'I don't play like Julia. I was only ever adequate.'

'No, no. Maybe you didn't play as brilliantly as Julia, but maybe you didn't apply yourself, either. If you had, who knows?' Kaitlyn could almost see him shrug, gangly shoulders rising up to meet ears that stood out from his long head. 'But you didn't ring for a lecture. What can I help you with?'

'I'm sorry, Martin, it's complicated. Is now a good time or are you busy?'

'Complicated is good and I have all the time in the world for you.'

'Thanks.' Kaitlyn hesitated, paranoia raising its ugly head. 'Julia wants to go back to England for a visit. She wants to take Stephen's ashes back to the village where they met as children and wants us to go with her. Dan's never been. So I applied for a passport for Daniel and there's been a hitch. It seems there's a problem with the paperwork. It's a long shot, but I have no one else to ask.'

'You need a reference? A title search?'

'Not that easy, Martin. I wish it were.' She tried to steady herself, but her words came out in a rush. 'They're saying Chris is still alive, that I need to get him to sign the forms before they can issue a passport. I don't know where to begin. I thought I'd dealt with all this and put it behind us.' She knew her voice had a catch in it, but there was nothing she could do.

'I see,' Martin replied. 'That's a big call. It's been five years now. I guess they haven't issued a death certificate either?'

'No, they haven't.'

There was a pause as Martin thought it through. 'So, you need to prove he did indeed die or, if he's alive, find him.'

'Yep. In a nutshell, that's it. I can try to follow up the identity side of things, but the possibility that he did survive the fire? I have no idea how to do that.'

'But I do, and I have your father's case notes prior to that final fire. What about the police?'

'I haven't even discussed this with Julia yet. I haven't decided what to do. Everyone up here knows us as the Scotts. It was the best I could do for Dan. If I go to the police I'll have to explain everything. A small place like this . . . it could get out. I don't want my son to have to bear the stigma of being an arsonist's son.'

'Of course you don't. Did Immigration give you any other information?'

'They said Chris is allegedly living quite close, in Kairi, but they didn't give me an address.'

'You've tried using all the usual sources?'

'Yes. There's no one by that name listed anywhere in North Queensland. A couple I found on Facebook matched up with phone listings in other states and they are way too young for Chris anyway.'

'Right.' It sounded like he'd sat up straight, his words decisive. 'I'll need to get back to you, review the notes again. Is this the best number to contact you on?'

'No, can you phone my mobile?' She rattled off the number and he repeated it back before she continued. 'I don't want Julia to find out about this until I know one way or the other.'

'Of course, of course. Nor Dan. You know . . .' He trailed off before he started again. 'I know you always had concerns, as did I, that something was wrong with that crime scene. Did someone else want us to think Chris lit the fire? Or did he really start it so he could disappear, but the plan went wrong?'

'He may have wanted out, Martin, but I can't believe he would torch an entire neighbourhood just to free himself from a burdensome wife and child. He loved Stephen, even if he didn't love us. I can't accept that he would have killed Dad first, then set a fire that would cause so much devastation. I just can't. He was scared of commitment, but that's not a crime.'

'No, it's not. Stephen loved Chris as a son, and your father was a very astute man. He wouldn't have welcomed him into the family if he thought he was a danger.'

'I know. And as to someone else lighting the fire? You and I both know we never caught the arsonist I was tracking that day in the aircraft. I'll never stop wondering if he was the one really responsible. If he could have started both fires.' She couldn't stop a deep sigh from escaping. 'One day soon I'll have to tell Dan the truth about his father's death.'

'The truth might never be found. The rest is conjecture.'

'Maybe. With this latest development, maybe not.'

'If I play the devil's advocate and say Immigration's right, then Chris living up near you is perfectly within the profile of an arsonist. Look for him as a park ranger or a firefighter, maybe SES. Whoever lit that fire in Canberra knew what they were doing. They lit it with the breeze in the worst quadrant and in an area that was hard to access. They knew full well what would happen.'

Kaitlyn was nodding as Martin spoke. She knew all that. She'd pored over the evidence in the months that led up to the coronial inquest. She'd seen the evidence her lawyers had been given. It all pointed to the same conclusion. The fire was the work of an arsonist who understood fire. The injuries to Stephen showed little or no struggle took place. He'd know his assailant. He'd been murdered.

'Thanks, Martin. I don't want to tell Julia just yet. I'll try the softly, softly approach and see what I can turn up.'

'Do that. I'll be in touch. Give my regards to Julia and say hi to Daniel. And Kaitlyn? Try not to worry too much. This might just be a clerical error.'

'Thanks. I hope so.'

The phone dangled from her hand, buzzing with the disconnect signal as she stared out the window. 'I hope so, for all our sakes.'

'Kaitlyn? What's going on? What don't you want to tell me?'

Kait swung around. Julia had parked the car in the driveway and Kait hadn't heard her slip through the front door. Her mother was ashen-faced, her hand spread like a protective star between her breasts. Kait could see the rapid rise and fall of her chest. She had no choice but to tell her.

'Sit down, Mum.' She held out her hand and squeezed her mother's fingers tight against the tremors. 'It's complicated.' Julia moved to one of the upright chairs, relinquishing Kait's fingers.

'Try me.' Julia sat with her spine straight and her chin up. Kait thought of it as her concert pianist posture.

Though her cheeks flushed pink, Julia's face remained composed as Kait told her what the Immigration Department had said.

'So if Immigration are right, Chris is alive and well, living in Kairi,' Kait finished up with a shake of her head.

'But we would know. We would have seen him. They're mistaken.' Julia was trying for businesslike now, sorting, analysing, discarding. 'What did Martin say?'

'Hello to you, for starters. He's delighted you're playing again.' Kaitlyn managed a tiny smile.

'Oh.' For an instant Julia looked girlish and flustered before she gathered herself. 'And what else?'

'He's going to take another look at the findings of the inquest.'

'Damn investigators didn't look hard enough.' The use of language was uncharacteristic.

'Martin always did speculate that Chris may have been framed, or even caught in the fire accidentally. Either way, he should be able to get an address for the current Chris Jackson. Where to from there?' Kait shrugged. 'I don't know.'

'Could . . .' Julia stopped, pressing her lips together. 'Do you think . . .' She tried again. The words came out in a rush. 'Is it possible, after all this time, to find the truth?' She wanted reassurance, but Kait couldn't give it unreservedly.

'I don't know, Mum. In my heart I don't believe Chris did it. He loved Stephen and you.' She paused. 'I don't believe he could have killed Dad, not like that.'

'And he loved you and Dan too.' Julia always could read her daughter. 'I know you don't believe me, but he was only guilty of being scared. Scared of being a poor parent, of letting you down, letting Dan down. He told Stephen he hated his own father. I don't know what the trouble was – for Stephen, what was talked about in confidence stayed in confidence. But whatever it was, it made Chris doubt his ability to be a father. He would have come round eventually. How could he not have, when we were all so close?'

'Oh, Mum, you can't say that.' Kait didn't want to hear any of this. It was easier believing she and Chris never had a future anyway, than to grieve all over again for what might have been. All she'd ever wanted for Dan was the same loving, supportive childhood she herself had had. This soul-searching didn't bring her son's father back, didn't give Dan a hard chest to hug tight, a role model to learn from, or footsteps to follow.

'I can. Your father believed it. You must never doubt Chris's love for you and Dan.' Julia's voice quavered on the last word. Tears glistened in her eyes, spilling over her lashes.

'Mum, I'm so sorry.' Kaitlyn wrapped her arms around Julia, needing to give her comfort even while she craved it herself. 'That's why I didn't want to tell you. I didn't want you worried or upset.'

'You have nothing to be sorry for. None of this is your fault.' Julia's voice was thick, her cheek pressed tight to Kait's. 'You've kept us safe.'

But Kait knew it would always feel like it was her fault. Julia had lost the love of her life. No matter the calm veneer she wore as a shield, Kait had watched her mother age dramatically after the fire. Some of the spark was back now, but the real joy, the laughter, hadn't fully returned.

How could it, when she'd lost so much?

Chapter 18

TRINITY Inlet stretched away to the hills of False Cape and Second Beach, heat shimmering over the grey-green flanks. The hotel's air conditioning kept the temperature down, but the atmosphere in the room was heated.

'Neither the insurance company nor the Australian Federal Police have any new evidence. They can't connect McCormack Mines to a bushfire that happened five years ago on a property in Canberra under the management of Greentrees,' Chris Jackson said, happy that he looked out of place in the opulent hotel suite. 'And I didn't meet your old man until after that fire, anyway.'

By the wide window, Grant McCormack sat forward. 'They will still be looking for patterns, and four Greentrees plantations burnt to the ground in five years will give them one. There are other ways. You've been paid enough for the jobs you've done. I want to end this relationship between you and MCM now.' The last word was directed at Don Adler, who was reclining on the couch with a bored expression. The lawyer didn't bother to answer, just moved his shoulders under his expensive suit jacket.

Chris lounged back in his chair by the desk, rocking it against the springs. It squeaked annoyingly well. 'But *I'm* not ready to end this relationship.' He rolled the last word around his tongue, the insinuation clear. 'They can't prove anything. Bushfires happen. Australia's renowned for them. Your father had an agreement with me. A lifetime agreement.'

McCormack glared across the room at him. 'My father no longer runs this company.'

'Yeah, but neither do you, laddie.' Chris knew that would rile the young McCormack, but he was surprised by just how much.

'You're wrong, you're fucking wrong and you're underestimating me.' The venom in McCormack's voice matched the hatred in his eyes. For the first time, Chris saw some of old man McCormack's fire in the pup.

Chris didn't hold back with his smile, knowing it would goad the young man further. He had the ace. He had the proof of their business agreement. 'Why would they think a fire in North Queensland was suspicious? Two blazes in Victoria and one in New South Wales, at a time when carbon credits were big news and plantations were failing, were easier to pin on an arsonist. But there's no way they'll connect this to you. You've paid me to do a job and I've laid all the groundwork. The Happy Valley plantation will be caught up in a spate of fires plaguing the district. You'll be pure as the proverbial snow.'

'I keep telling you, no one can connect us to another fire at Greentrees,' Adler interjected with an impatient shake of his head. Chris knew that Don Adler had presided over the company when it survived class actions brought by villages claiming environmental degradation from the mine's tailings dam in PNG. He'd played hardball then; he would again.

Adler understood that fires were convenient disasters that eased the way for mining by reducing the need for environmental impact studies. A fire-damaged parcel of land was a hell of a lot easier to exploit. And the lawyer was up to his eyeballs in corruption. Chris trod carefully around him. Adler had always been harder than the old man to deal with. And he wasn't the pushover Grant McCormack was. The younger man was soft, a fuckin' bleeding heart, ready to do deals with greenies. Time to finish this conversation, Chris decided.

'Don's right,' he said, 'but we need to be very careful about how we proceed. I've got a fall guy lined up. Just need to position him. City guy who'll have no supporters around here. Just give me a little more time.'

Adler spoke again. 'Yes, but time is the one thing we don't have in abundance. We need to know if this is viable land or not. One of the big multinationals is snapping at our heels, along with several junior miners from Western Australia. We need to move now. The sampling we did up Malanda way two years ago came back negative, but it still got the major players interested. The geologists are positive this area is much more promising. If we sample, we show our hands before we've secured the land.'

'Yeah, I understand that. They found gold back in the early-settler days. Alluvial in the valleys. Every chance there'd be some in the hills. It must have washed down from somewhere.' Chris made the chair squeak again.

'So, it comes back to you and your skill, Mr Jackson.' Adler had taken over the conversation. McCormack was glowering from the window. 'How soon can we expect to have the job finished?'

The bloody lawyer was smooth. Had to give him that. Chris turned his hands over, palms up, and shrugged. 'You want it to be identified as suspicious, then I can do it tomorrow. You want to make it look like just another bushfire gone wild? Then let me do it in my own sweet time.'

McCormack stood up, the chair shooting back behind him. 'You've had an interesting life, Mr Jackson, or is it Derek Barton?'

He lowered his voice, forcing Chris to lean in. 'Three name changes – that I know about, anyway – a prison term for arson, special mentions for impersonating a fireman, and illegal possession of firearms.'

Chris pursed his lips, trying to slow his racing pulse. How the hell? He shook his head decisively. 'No. Sorry, mate, you've got me mixed up with someone else. Pity the poor bastard who's got all that hanging over his head. What'd you say his name was?' He knew his identity was watertight. It had to be. There was no way these arseholes could have found out anything about his past. Not without him hearing about it first.

One thing jail time did was give you good contacts. Counterfeiters, drug runners, forgers, even a couple of big-time boys with connections to international crime syndicates and a motorcycle gang.

The silence dragged on and he let it. First one who broke was the chicken. Right on cue, McCormack caved in. 'This is bullshit. Find another way. We'll kill someone with this madness. Take your payout and I won't go to the police.'

'You won't go to the police?' Chris pushed to his feet with a harsh laugh, the anger a raging burn now. For fuck's sake, the man was stupid. He had no idea of the consequences. 'I don't have time for this shit. You've paid me to do a job. You don't want me to finish it? Fine.'

He kept his footsteps measured as he crossed the glossy tiles, expecting them to stop him. Opening the door halfway, he hesitated and turned. 'Of course, I'll expect payment for my services to date and the usual yearly retainer.' He left them with a polite nod. 'Gentlemen.'

'Fuckin' morons,' he fumed as he shot down fourteen floors to the hotel lobby. Why the fuck interfere now? Why couldn't they just leave him to do the job they were paying him to do, the same way old man McCormack had trusted him last time?

He'd laid a careful cover and found the perfect fall guy. Maybe he needed to put the wind up him, make him look edgy, suspicious, leave nothing to chance.

No way was Chris blowing this identity. It suited him. The money set him up for life. Not a flash lifestyle, but a comfortable one with plenty for a rainy day. There was enough salted away that if it all went to hell in a handbasket, he could change identity at short notice.

But that wasn't his plan. This time he wanted to stay. He had friends, a purpose, and he had a side benefit. If he played his cards right, he just might get a family of his own – one that was almost flesh and blood.

Chapter 19

'WE'RE done. We find another option. He's mad, unbalanced, and a blatant fucking liar.' Grant hardly waited for the door to close.

'Where the fuck did you dig up that dirt?' Adler sounded incredulous. He rarely swore, so Grant knew he had him rattled.

'Why? Didn't you research him before you used him last time?'

'Your father found him. I didn't ask questions.'

'Bullshit.' Grant was gratified to see that the older man looked pale. 'You have files on everyone and you're not going to use a man like that without collating every last detail of his life, just in case you need leverage.'

'He was a convicted arsonist with a jail term. He'd burnt down the house of a known paedophile. He needed money. That was all we needed to know. He was released from jail as Derek Barton, turned into Chris Jackson. Of course he'd changed his name. It would be hard to get on in life with a prison sentence on your record.'

'You should have looked harder,' Grant snapped. 'I did my own investigation after our last conversation. Did you read the transcript of the court case?'

Adler shook his head and Grant snorted in disbelief. 'Find that hard to believe since you're the lawyer, but just in case you're not lying, he claimed to have been the victim of a paedophile ring as a boy. He claimed his stepfather was the ringleader. Damn shame that fine man was already dead, along with Jackson's own mother, so he couldn't defend himself. Your man's only living relative, his younger half-brother, refused to give supporting evidence at the trial. Seems they'd been estranged for a long time. The half-brother never even came to the trial, let alone visited him in jail. I can't believe it's a coincidence that the same brother died in a fire shortly after Derek – or Chris, or whatever the fuck his name is today – was released. You know what else is remarkable?' He didn't expect an answer and didn't get one. 'The last identity switch Derek Barton made was to take over his dead half-brother's name, Chris Jackson. And the real Chris Jackson? He died in a fire that also killed his father-in-law and burnt his family home to the ground, along with several Canberra suburbs and the first of the Greentrees plantations. Reckon Derek Barton might have had something to do with that one too? He's not a sane man.'

From the look on Adler's face, Grant decided he really hadn't known the truth about Derek Barton's history. He didn't give him time to argue.

'So, we pay him off. Find another way. You're going back to Sydney this afternoon. I'm going up to Oakey Creek to have a look at this land for myself.'

'That won't achieve anything.' Adler was regrouping.

'My peace of mind.'

'Pointless.'

'To you, maybe. Your ticket's booked. So is my car. I'll see you in the office when I get back.'

'If you go digging around up there you're likely to stir up a hornet's nest.'

'No one knows who the hell I am. They won't give a rat's arse about me.'

'I won't see you take this company down.' Adler was back on song.

'You're damn right you won't. I have no intention of doing anything that will destroy what my father worked so hard to build. That's exactly why this madness stops now. I'm not being blackmailed by an unhinged psychopath.'

Grant went through to the bedroom to collect his bag, not acknowledging the protests from Adler. He was out of there. 'See you next week.'

The taxi rank had one lone maxi idling in it. A quiet Monday in the Cairns CBD. Grant sat up the front with the driver. 'Avis car rental, thanks.'

Twenty minutes later, armed with sat nav and a bottle of water, he turned onto Mulgrave Road. The rental guy had said it was a straightforward trip. He hoped so, because he was dropping with exhaustion.

'Too damn long coming,' he muttered, his anger still boiling. Don Adler had been a thorn in his side for his entire life. A manipulative, scheming lawyer, who constantly played both ends off against the middle. Grant found it almost impossible to believe Adler hadn't known the truth about Barton. Adler usually left nothing to chance.

The only reason Grant had uncovered anything was because he'd hired a very thorough private investigator, who'd turned up Derek Barton's possible involvement in the Canberra fires.

The coronial inquiry had determined that the young half-brother, Chris Jackson, was the arsonist. The private detective had drawn only one conclusion: the court had accused, and convicted in absence, the wrong man. It was easy to see how, with the public baying for answers, they may have taken the convenient option and pinned it on a man who couldn't defend himself. The man's wife and son had left Canberra not long after. Who could blame them, with all that hatred around?

But how to stop Barton now? Could he confront him again and convince him to give up? Was it better to go to the police and lay the evidence out for them? The Federal Police? The chances were there'd be major repercussions for the company. Arson and fraud made great headlines. If Grant turned witness he'd probably get away with some fines for not coming forward sooner. Maybe it was time to activate the shelf company he had ticking away. It would mean starting from the bottom again, but anything had to be better than living with blackmail. Or was there another way?

Chapter 20

RYAN decided it was time to explore further afield, get his bearings on the Tablelands. He'd spent the day driving to all the main state-forest campsites. Most of them were empty except for day visitors. In a few more weeks, once school was out for summer, they'd be bursting at the seams.

The Herberton Range Conservation Park was the last one on his list. He left his car in the empty parking lot and hiked up Mt Baldy. The view over Atherton stretched away below him. To the north and east were the McAllister Ranges. The vantage point gave him a chance to get the lie of the land sorted in his head.

Dense green plantations stood out from the silver and greys of the native trees and the patchwork of agricultural land. He could see where Happy Jack Road curved along the rim of the range. The Greentrees plantation took up a good chunk of land, but with its slope he guessed it wouldn't have been a great block for cattle, and it certainly didn't suit crops. Jerry's place was a white dot on the edge.

The Scotts' house was tucked in a little further. He could only see the cleared land that ran to the edge of the escarpment. There were a couple of forestry trails running through the plantation, one giving access to Happy Jack Road. The others came in from the bottom and dissected the block into manageable chunks. He'd checked out the gates on the plantation trails and they were all padlocked. Be good to know who had the keys.

For now, his day was finished. Nothing worth noting. The smoke haze on the horizon was residual. There were no new fires, no arsonists lurking in campgrounds, and no sign of the elusive Derek Barton, not that he'd expected there would be.

The wind had whipped in from the north-east, blowing the smoke west. The sky was a seamless blue. A couple of thunder-heads were growing on the ranges to the east. Twelve months ago, he'd been watching a cyclone swirl down the coast, wondering if he was going to get out in time. This year the rain had come early and then disappeared. It was shaping up to be a trying fire season. He hoped the analysts came up with more information so they could catch the mongrel arsonist before someone died.

He was sweating by the time he got back to his car, and wished he'd been smart enough to find a house with a swimming pool or, at the very least, air conditioning. Maybe he could be neigh-bourly and drop by the Scotts'. He'd seen air conditioners banked along one wall. Would the delightful Kaitlyn be home? A yummy mummy – that's what Crusoe would call her. His partner had a track record with older women. Ryan had always tended to go out with the younger ones. They were easier to brush off when the need arose, and most of them weren't into commitment any more than he was.

But Kaitlyn?

Interesting that a curvy woman perched on a ride-on mower, wearing gardening clothes and an outrageous hat, could possibly pique his interest. But she had. Truth be told, he'd been interested when he helped fix her tyre, although the wedding band had warned him off. Since there was no man about the house he figured the guy had probably died. It would be unusual to wear a wedding band after a divorce. Damn shame working undercover didn't run to casual relationships while he was on the job. Still, no harm in flirting, and if that got him a dinner invite, that was just fine too.

He was still smiling when he turned into the Scotts' driveway. Their double-front door looked to be made of heavy timber, with a spy hole recessed into it. No glass to break. Piano music poured from the house, soaring and trembling and sobbing with emotion. He stood, transfixed. Classical music was not his taste, but this was amazing. He hesitated before pressing the intercom button. Doubtful anyone would hear it over the music.

He stepped back and looked around, admiring the curve of the walls. The house looked impregnable. No cracks for fire or wind or water to penetrate. He followed the pebble path to the left and couldn't resist rapping on the solid garage doors. The end of the house had no windows. It faced west, so there was sound logic in that. The path continued to the front of the house – or was it the back?

The wide windows there stood open, which explained the volume of sound. He didn't get two paces before the music stopped and there was movement inside.

'Can I help you?' A smiling older woman leant through a doorway.

'Hi, wonderful music, sorry to disturb you. I'm Ryan. I've moved in up the road.'

She came to meet him as he talked. 'Of course you have. You've waved a few times. Julia, Dan's nana. So lovely to meet you. And thank you for helping Kaitlyn with the tyre. She's so independent.' She gave a little laugh. 'I thought you were the police. Apparently, someone found Dan's bike out in the scrub near Herberton. It went missing over a week ago.'

'That's a long way from here. A friend of Dan's borrow it?'

'No, we don't know anyone living over at Herberton.' A tiny frown drew delicately arched brows down over her eyes. 'It's all very odd. I don't know . . .'

He saw her visibly rally herself, even though her hands ran up and down her arms, smoothing, soothing.

'I guess the main thing is that they've found it.' He smiled, wanting to lessen some of her tension. 'And thanks for the cake you sent over with Dan. It was truly delicious. Very kind of you.'

She still looked unhappy, but managed a polite smile. 'I'm glad you enjoyed it. How rude of me to leave you in the hot sun – would you like a cool drink or a coffee? I have some blueberry muffins almost ready to come out of the oven.'

He checked his watch and went with a boyish grin. 'If you're sure I'm not intruding? Freshly baked muffins sound too good to be true. Haven't had those since I left home.' That was a lie – his mother didn't bake anything except herself, by the pool in a bikini. But unless he'd misread it, there was something upsetting Julia. Best way of getting answers? Talking.

'What was that music?' he asked, following her inside.

'Chopin. "Fantasie Impromptu."'

'It was amazing. Who's the performer?'

She smiled, but didn't answer. He looked around. The beauty of the interior was in sharp contrast to the exterior of the house. A grand piano dominated the room. Its highly polished black timber glowed in the sunlight streaming in through the windows opposite.

'It's the piano.' She waved her hand at it. 'It has wonderful tone and I like to play while I wait.'

He was perplexed. 'You were playing that? While you waited?'

She laughed this time. 'For the baking to finish.'

'Naturally, doesn't everyone play Chopin while they bake?' He couldn't help teasing. 'You play beautifully.'

'I used to. My fingers are less supple these days. Daniel plays too. It's a wonder you haven't heard scales most afternoons. Jerry used to say if the wind was from the south, he could hear us.'

'Now you mention it, I have heard some tinkling a couple of times. I didn't think too much about it.'

He slanted his head as he answered, taking in the tiny details that made up a home, a family. The pale timber panelling, white walls and strong colours in the floor rug were stylish. Photos in plain frames and different sizes formed a patchwork along one wall. He would have loved to take a closer look, but Julia led the way through to the kitchen where a solid granite bench faced more windows. He didn't miss the shutters that guarded all that glass. The smell filling the air made his mouth water. Blueberry muffins.

'Coffee, tea?'

'Coffee would be great, thanks. Your house is beautiful.'

'Yes, isn't it.' Julia smiled at him. 'I have a very clever daughter.'

'And she plays the piano too?'

'Of course.' A slight hesitation. 'Kait has the real talent.'

'Not everyone has a baby grand in their house.'

'It's no baby.' Her smile took away any offence. 'And no, most people don't, but I was a professional pianist once. Now I really only play for myself.'

She handed him a steaming mug. 'Sugar? Milk?'

'All of the above,' he replied. He spooned two teaspoons into his cup. 'And you?'

'Neither, thanks.'

'Sweet enough, as they say.' He flashed a grin at her and knew he'd got away with the corny line when she laughed and turned to the oven.

The aroma as she opened the door was heady. He doubted he'd ever smelt muffins straight from the oven. With deft flicks of her wrist she transferred them, one by one, onto a wire rack.

'Here, don't burn your fingers and please don't tell Daniel if he gets home before you leave. I never let him have them straight from the oven.'

'Our secret.' And any others you'd care to share, he thought, biting into the soft cake. It melted on his tongue, crisp on the outside, buttery-soft inside. And it burnt the hell out of the roof of his mouth. The pain was worth it. 'Mmm, this is great. You must have no trouble bribing Dan with these.'

'He's a good boy.'

'Apart from losing his bike.'

'Yes, but he didn't. That's the point. And I can't help wondering. You see . . .' She stopped again. 'No, I shouldn't gossip.' She turned away.

'Don't think of it as gossiping, think of it as sharing.' She didn't answer, so he tried again with a chuckle. 'A trouble shared is a trouble halved?'

'Oh, you're good, you're very good.' She half turned, this time with a smile. 'Sometimes, living this far out I wonder how safe we are. You know about Kaitlyn's flat tyre the other day. They didn't find anything wrong with it when she took it in to be repaired – no puncture or anything. Then she found . . .' Was Julia blushing? It looked like it. 'Well, she found an item of her clothes outside. In the grass on the other side of the fence.'

'Right.' He wasn't sure where this was headed.

'You see, this house is like Fort Knox. The doors and windows all have deadlocks. We have a security alarm. Her car is never parked outside, so how did the tyre go down? And her clothes. She hadn't worn that particular item for years.'

'Someone broke in?' He reached for another muffin. Good delaying tactics, he convinced himself. Nothing to do with how great they tasted.

'I don't see any other answer. I haven't told Kaitlyn, but twice I've found the door unlocked when I came home. I assumed it was my fault, blamed it on old age.'

'It happens.' He shrugged, trying to allay her concerns while his own had just gone to red alert. 'The tyre could have had a faulty valve? Maybe Dan borrowed his mum's clothes for a fancy dress and forgot to return them.'

'Did you borrow your mother's clothes when you were seven?' she asked.

'Ah, no, I didn't, but then, my mother's clothes were hung in colour-coordinated lines and she knew if anything was out of place. But I had friends who did raid their mothers' wardrobes.'

She looked amused for a moment. 'Well, that's not something I can see Daniel doing. And the bike disappearance baffled me.'

Hearing the litany of things that had gone wrong baffled Ryan too, but he wasn't going to upset this gracious lady unnecessarily. He could see where Kaitlyn's fine features and long hands had come from. Those hands were currently wringing each other in an anxious little tussle.

Julia would have been a very beautiful woman when she was younger. He had trouble pinning an age on her. Anything from mid-sixties to late seventies. Right now she had furrows on her smooth forehead and pinched lines around her mouth. He'd bet there was more to it than this, but she wasn't about to share everything with a stranger.

'Kaitlyn says you're a Sydney firefighter.' She changed the topic and smiled, welcoming again, but there was a lingering sadness in her eyes.

'I was. I'm not sure that I'm ever going back to that.'

'It must be very stressful. And the shift work. My husband was an arson investigator.'

'Really?' Now that surprised him. There weren't many of them around.

'Yes. He was very good at what he did. Solved a lot of cases.'

'He's retired now?'

'No. He passed away a few years ago.' She looked as though she wanted to back away from the conversation. He saw a flicker of strong emotion before she controlled it.

'I'm sorry for your loss. It must have been very hard.'

'Yes, it was, and I'm a silly old woman bringing it up like this.' She patted his hand as it lay on the benchtop. 'So, what brings you to the Tablelands?'

'I'm off on stress leave.' He slipped into his cover. 'The doctors recommended twelve months off. I'll see how it goes, but I think I need a change.'

'It would be difficult, especially the ones you can't save.'

She'd hit that raw nerve he tried so desperately to ignore. 'Yeah, it is.' He knew his vocal cords had tightened and he deliberately set the cup down on the counter to stop his hands clamping around it. 'Nothing the other guys don't have to deal with as well.' He tried to reinstate his mental swagger, but it wasn't working. There was something compelling in the sympathy radiating from this woman, this stranger. It felt like a confessional.

'We're all affected in different ways by loss. Look at Kait. She's squared her shoulders and carried on, knowing Daniel and I both depend on her. I love her for that, for her strength, but I know she's hurting just as much as I am.'

'For losing her father?' Ryan asked, wanting to know more about Kaitlyn, her family, her life.

'Yes, and . . .' Julia stopped again. 'And other things, things that aren't mine to talk about. Would you like to stay for dinner?' She'd visibly regrouped and Ryan felt the strong urge to say yes. Instead, he shook his head, alarmed at the ease with which she disarmed him, had him fighting to stay in role.

'No, thanks. I've imposed enough.' He was on his feet and moving before he could change his mind. Everything about this place was seductive. The earthiness, the beauty, the smell – everything made him want to stay. At the same time, his instincts were screaming at him to run, run, run, as fast as his R.M. boots would take him. He needed to go before he got involved. The coffee and the muffins were a bad idea. He didn't need the gentle mothering. Kaitlyn was a bad idea.

Julia walked him through to the front door and watched as he drove off. It took a truckload of effort not to plant his foot on the accelerator and roar away in a cloud of dust. She wasn't to know she'd gone straight to the heart of his fears. Maybe pretending to be on stress leave was a bad idea too. Maybe his body was starting to believe it.

Chapter 21

KAITLYN knew there were those at the public meeting who thought she was an interfering greenie from the city who'd built her ugly house to show them how smart she was. She also knew there were many more who did understand fire and who shared her views.

The man on stage at the moment was one of those. As head of the Atherton Tablelands Geographic Information Services, or ATGIS, he was responsible for the North Queensland Wildfire Mitigation Project. He'd been in local government for many years. He'd run the local State Emergency Service when it was still a newly formed rabble of enthusiasts. He was now the head of an organisation that brought together all the local resources and gave them the tools to manage their communities and minimise the fire risk.

A series of PowerPoint graphs about fuel loads were being beamed up onto a large screen. He was deciphering them for the one hundred–strong crowd that was crammed into the CWA hall. Hazard reduction burns were the main topic after such a hot start to summer and the long, wet winter.

She heard the squeak of the side door and turned her head. Well, well, she thought, it was the delectable Brad Ryan coming in from the dark night. He was checking out the group, and many of them were checking him out in return. She knew the curiosity wasn't just about his previous occupation. Eligible men were thin on the ground in Atherton, let alone attractive ones.

She focused back on the speaker just in time to see him nod a welcome to Ryan. He knew him already? Ryan certainly got around.

The presenter took another half an hour before he called for questions. Kaitlyn shifted in her seat. Now came the interesting part.

The first question was one dear to her heart.

'So, what's your opinion of "stay and defend"?' It was one of the bolshie Taylor clan from out in the hills near Herberton, renowned for their opposition to evacuating. The problem was that their houses were located high on hills, surrounded by trees. The greater the slope, the faster the fire potentially spread. The deeper the fuel load on the forest floor, the more devastating the intensity and the more chance of fireballs bouncing through the crowns of the highly flammable eucalypts. The Taylors all lived in prime country for the 'early evacuation' plan.

The ATGIS chief shook his head. 'You know my opinion, Jacko. If you've cleared your property of excess fuel, installed some decent water pumps and secured a guaranteed water supply, then an able-bodied person should be able to defend against a normal-sized bushfire. If, however, you live on an escarpment with steep inclines and uncontrolled slopes below you, then defending is not an option. But —' He held up his hand against the howls of protest that broke out from around the room. 'But, it's your call. We don't have a forcible evacuation policy in Queensland. We can only warn you when the risk is high, and send out texts in the event we deem an evacuation to be necessary. I can't make you leave. I can only strongly suggest it.'

'Installing pumps costs money. We don't all have truckloads of money to pay for that sort of shit.' The older Taylor threw a spiteful glare at Kaitlyn.

She stared back, keeping her face impassive. He was never going to get a rise out her. No one else needed to know it was Julia's money that had paid for the beautiful house. The insurance on Kait's house in Canberra hadn't been worth the paper it was written on. With her own husband accused of lighting the fire, the insurance company hadn't paid her a cent.

Jacko had come out to give her a quote on the installation of the rainwater tanks and two big pumps. He'd told her then, in no uncertain terms, that she was throwing her money away. She and her pumps would never work.

Obviously, he hadn't got the job. Nor had he been civil since. It didn't bother her. Among the sea of faces she could see a cluster of fellow rural firies, about half of all the teams in the area. There were a couple of faces she didn't recognise. A clean-cut guy about her age, who looked like he'd lost his suit jacket in an effort to go casual, was taking notes. Government department, she guessed. Several new couples. Probably bought acreage and were now wondering what the hell to do in the event of a fire. Hope they were paying close attention.

Then there were the Taylors, who simply turned up to be belligerent. And the Taylors had a habit of holding the floor . . .

She managed to stifle a yawn. She had an early start tomorrow. The lady next to her, who happened to be Dan's teacher, sent her a sympathetic look. 'They do go on, don't they?' she whispered. 'Why bother coming if you're going to argue black is white? Silly people should know everyone thinks they're troublemakers.'

Kait smiled at her. 'You'll have an early start tomorrow too, I guess.'

'Yeah. Thank God the end of the term is only a couple of weeks away. Mind you, that means the report cards all have to be done.

Your Dan's a good boy, a real pleasure to have in class. I'll be sorry to lose him next year.'

'You only teach Grade Two?'

'Yeah, they start getting more difficult once they turn eight. I like the babies. More fun.' She smiled at Kait. 'You wouldn't know he came from a single family. You and Julia have done a great job.'

Kait was a little embarrassed. 'I always worry he's a mummy's boy. He can be soft at times. And I'm away from home so much, I also worry he's going a little wild.'

The woman smiled again. 'No danger of that; he has beautiful manners. You'll turn out fine husband material for some lucky girl. Have you had him tested for the gifted program?'

'No.' Kait shook her head. 'We'll see how he goes. No pressure yet. He's very good musically. Julia used to be a piano teacher. Probably the only kid with a concert grand as his first piano.'

'I didn't know that. You should consider testing him. I can give you some books and games he can practise on. He's very bright. Oh, thank God.' The room had broken out in polite clapping, and people were starting to move. 'I'll see you at the last P&T night for the year?'

'Yep. I'll make sure I'm there,' Kaitlyn replied, swinging her bag over her shoulder and following the teacher to the back of the line trailing out of the hall.

Kaitlyn saw Ryan threading through the chairs towards her.

'Hey, neighbour,' he said, grinning. 'We should have carpooled.'

She had to smile back at him, knowing her heart had skipped a beat. His easy charm smoothed her prickly edges. Insane. 'I had no idea you'd be here.'

'No, why would you? I used to work for the Sydney Metropolitan

Fire Services. Thought I'd better put my hand up for the rural brigade. Had a chat with the boss of ATGIS today. Seems like a good bloke.'

'Yes,' Kaitlyn said, pushing her hair back behind her ears, conscious that for once it was a loose cloud around her shoulders and Ryan's eyes kept straying to it. She must look like a wild hillbilly with flaming hair. Days like this she wished she bothered to get a good cut. 'He's very proactive and well respected.' She wrinkled her nose and slanted her head towards the Taylor clan, who were now gathering as a group near the front door. 'Of course, there are always those who disagree, but it makes life more interesting.'

'Can I get you a drink?'

'Oh.' She was surprised. 'A cuppa would be lovely.'

'Tea?' He looked shocked and she couldn't stop her laugh.

'I don't think the CWA catering contingent runs to alcohol. And I don't drink coffee this late at night.'

He glanced at his watch. 'I don't call eight late, but hey, if the lady would like a cup of tea, I can manage that.'

'White, no sugar, thanks,' she called after him as he headed towards the tiny kitchen. He charmed his way around the women in the queue. The guys might not be so friendly, but those boyish good looks worked on the females. He even cadged a biscuit out of them.

'There you go.'

'Thanks. You're not having anything?'

'Ah, no, I don't drink instant coffee and tea is a bit wishy-washy for me. I'll have a beer when I get home.'

'Oh, well, a double thanks then.' She was embarrassed at having let him get her a drink.

'Sit outside? It's a bit warm in here.'

She smiled up at him. 'And there I was, thinking I was having a hot flush.'

'You are definitely not old enough to be having a flush.' His fingers curled round her elbow as he steered her through the people. His touch made her almost spill the liquid in the cup. She hoped he hadn't noticed.

'So, how's Dan?'

'Fine, thanks.'

'At home with your husband?'

'I should have explained. There is no husband. It's just Dan, my mother, Julia, and me.'

'Sorry. I just thought.' He nodded at the silver band on her left hand.

'He died. Five years ago. I see no reason to take it off. He's Dan's dad.'

'And it keeps strangers at bay.'

'Not all of them.'

'No,' he acknowledged her dig with a grin. 'But then, I'm not strange, just new to the place.'

She had to laugh outright. 'Are you sure you don't sell used cars? You have the glibbest lines I've ever heard.'

'You bring out the gentleman in me.'

'Oh, please.' She almost choked on her tea. 'How long can you keep this up?' She regretted the words as soon as she saw the gleam in his eyes.

'No one's ever accused me of lacking stamina.'

'Okay, okay, too much information.' She put her free hand over her ear and changed the subject. 'So, how's it working out in Jerry's house? Julia said you dropped around yesterday afternoon.'

'It's great, although I do have one complaint. I think there's a master chef camping out somewhere near your house. Every night I get this amazing aroma of cooking, then I'm left staring at my Lean Cuisine or spag bol, wondering who it is that's feasting in heaven.'

'Ha, well, your flattery is wasted this time. That's Julia. I work away a lot, usually for four to six days at a time. My mother is an awesome chef. She took the job of feeding her family to art-form status. She did a cooking course that lasted three years and was the equivalent of an apprenticeship. Some of my most vivid memories involve wrestling with homework at the kitchen bench, classical music filling the house, and Julia waving herbs under my nose saying, 'What do think this one goes with?' It's a wonder I passed anything at school. Food in our house is to be worshipped.'

'A woman I could fall in love with. She fed me blueberry muffins yesterday. I'm afraid she thinks I have no manners. I just about inhaled them.'

Kaitlyn finished her tea in a quick swallow and stood up. Time to go. He was far too easy to talk to. She'd let her guard down. Dangerous. 'Thanks for that. I'd better get going. You'll have to drop around again. Julia loves to feed an appreciative audience. Dan and I get a bit blasé about it all.' She held out her hand to shake his, but he took it in both hands and smiled into her eyes.

'I'd like that. Get to know you more.'

'Right.' She pulled away. Bet he was that friendly with everyone.

He didn't look ready to leave. 'Good to hear Dan's bike turned up.'

'A true godsend. I have no idea how it made its way to Herberton, though.'

'Seems a little strange. Police have any idea?'

'No, they simply returned it, glad to have been of help.'

'Hmm.'

He looked like he was about to speak again so she cut in. 'Nice to see you again. Better get going.'

'And you. See you round.'

She could feel him watching her as she headed off to her car, dropping the paper cup in the bin as she passed.

Driving home, she couldn't help letting her imagination off its leash for just a moment. What would it be like to share her bed with a man again? To wake up next to the warmth of an adult male, not a wriggling, kicking worm of a sleepy seven-year-old who'd snuck into bed for a quick cuddle and then gone to sleep? What would it feel like to have those slightly roughened hands run down her body and cup her breasts?

She groaned out loud. 'That's as likely to happen as hell freezing over, so don't go there. He's got to be at least a couple of years too young, you old cougar.'

Besides, she reminded herself as her thoughts darkened, she still had to track down her allegedly alive husband. Not only was she potentially still married, she was potentially still married to an arsonist. That dampened her mood. No place for a new man in her life.

Her father's old colleague, Martin, was yet to get back to her, but she was working on her own angles. Was there a connection between her suddenly resurrected husband living up the road, so to speak, and the arsonist at work on the Tablelands? Was she drawing too long a bow?

She'd charted up Chris's history, trying to look for patterns in his behaviour that might point to the truth. She felt like all she needed was time, but time could mean more fires, or worse.

Julia's forced cheerfulness for the last two days was telling.

They both needed an answer to this one, and soon.

Turning into Happy Jack Road, she saw an erratic light over at Jerry's place. It looked to be moving around in the yard. How could that be? She'd left Ryan at the meeting, and no one had overtaken her. She stopped the car at her front gateway and turned the lights off. Now what?

There it was again. A faint, bobbing light, like someone walking with a torch. That couldn't be good. She got out of the car. The TV was on, so she knew her mother was still up.

'Hi Julia, I'm home,' she called as she opened the door.

'Kait.' Her mother sounded drowsy. She was nodding off more and more in front of the TV these days. 'How was it?'

'Oh, the usual nonsense from the Taylors.' She rolled her eyes. 'Have you heard any cars go by? I can see a light around in Jerry's yard.'

'No, no, I haven't.' Her mother looked embarrassed. 'But I may have dozed off a couple of times. Maybe it's Ryan, out spotting possums.'

'Nope. I left him at the meeting.'

'Oh, he was there? That's nice. Did you say hello?'

'Thanks, Mum, yes, I was polite. He is our neighbour.'

'That's good.' Julia had brightened. 'Daniel says he always stops to say hello when he drives past. He's a very handsome man.'

'I'm surprised you noticed.' Kaitlyn shook her head. Her mother's matchmaking gene was nearly as evolved as her cooking gene. 'Anyway, I'll just drive around and check. It seems a bit strange.'

'Do you want me to come too?'

'No, no. You stay with Dan. I've got my phone. I'll ring the police if it looks suspicious.'

Being neighbourly was ingrained. As an adolescent, Kait had

spent hours hosing Canberra gardens in the middle of hot summers when the occupants were away on holidays. She'd fallen in love with too many cats and dogs that had boarded with her family during those same long breaks. Being in the country made it even more important.

She passed the top of the fire trail and wondered if someone had come through there. Possible, but it would be a hard slog, even in a low-range four-wheel drive.

With about a kilometre to go, she saw dim lights heading up the road towards her. Whoever it was only had their sidelights on. They looked like they were travelling at speed. She pulled onto the hard shoulder, staying well back from a sharp bend ahead, conscious there was a significant drop-off beside her. Better to give them room.

Without the pressure of driving, she watched the glow of the other vehicle coming towards her. They were caning it, dust billowing around them in the low light. She couldn't see enough to recognise the vehicle, although it looked big – a ute, maybe.

As it came around the corner, its headlights flashed on, along with a bank of spotties high on the roof. Blinded, Kait threw her hand up in front of her face to shield her eyes. Bloody hell! She couldn't see a darn thing. She thought she heard the slide of locked brakes, then an instant later the vehicle hit her. It was only a glancing blow, but that was enough to drop her rear offside wheel deep into soft dirt. Her car tilted, and the banking started to crumble under its weight.

Kaitlyn screamed.

Chapter 22

LEAVING the community hall took longer than Ryan had anticipated. Grant McCormack collared him, saying he was with the receivers for Greentrees. Had heard Ryan had moved into the property at the top of their plantation. Ryan knew all about Mr McCormack already. His comprehensive file was sitting on Ryan's hard drive. Receivers my arse, Ryan thought with a polite smile. His company was half the reason Ryan was here in North Queensland.

In person, the CEO seemed like a reasonable man. Ryan knew he'd worked in PNG for the family gold mine before things fell in a heap up there. He wasn't at the helm when they started diversifying and buying failing assets in Australia – his father was. The old man loved shelf companies. They covered a multitude of sins. He clearly didn't realise that the computer age had brought greater cooperation between the Australian Crime Commission, Federal Police and the Taxation Office.

Greentrees had been in trouble after fires destroyed large swathes of its plantations of mature pines. A forensic accountant pointed out the pines were worth more burnt as insurance money than alive, pulped or even used as carbon credits. The fact that at least one plantation turned out to be sitting on a coal seam was a stroke of good luck, wasn't it? Ryan chuckled. People had no idea how much information was available on the web, if they only knew where to look.

He pressed the remote as he walked to his car, surprised when the lights didn't flash. He tried again as he got closer, then hit the lock button. The lights flashed that time. 'You moron,' he chided himself. He'd been running late, but that didn't excuse forgetting to lock the car. He slid into the front seat and checked the ashtray. Still full of loose change, so no one had broken in. The engine started with a little more of a rev than necessary and he eased his foot off the accelerator. No point in getting angry, but he wasn't as sharp as he should be. He wasn't in the habit of putting himself at risk.

His thoughts shifted back to Greentrees and the plantations. Originally, they'd been set up as a tax-avoidance scheme for high-income earners. Superannuation when you weren't really in superannuation. As start-up plantations they'd attracted tax-free investments that would take twenty years to mature, and then technically they could be rolled into a new plantation for another block of time. By the time an investor got their money back they would be retired, having paid little or no tax. Oddly enough, the ATO had clamped down pretty hard on that loophole and a swag of high-flyers lost their dough. The following year, the trees started burning.

And that, thought Ryan as he drove out of the centre of Atherton and up the hill towards the Tolga scrub, was why he was in the top of Queensland, pretending to rent a house he'd unexpectedly inherited and playing at being a fireman.

The pattern suggested to the Australian Crime Commission that this was in fact grudge arson, rather than insurance fraud as the first investigation assumed. An investor who'd lost their money, taking it out on the trees. The team in the AFP thought otherwise, and they'd gone to considerable trouble to unravel the web of connections. Sitting right in the middle of that web was Mr Grant McCormack and McCormack Mines lawyer, Don Adler. Another undercover AFP operative was in place in the south-west corner of Western Australia, where Greentrees had two more plantations.

Just before the turning for Happy Jack Road, a large four-wheel drive ute rocketed out of the intersection ahead of him. The car's high beams dazzled Ryan, so he didn't get a good look at it. All he saw was a bank of spotlights, a gun rack on the bullbar and the side of a metal trayback as it shot past.

'Jesus Christ,' he growled, looking in his rear-vision mirror. They'd almost mowed him down. The unease he'd felt at his unlocked car reared its head. Someone looking for him? He'd be pretty pissed off if his cover was already blown.

He drove past the Scotts' place. Kaitlyn was still up, he noted. The outside light cast a golden glow across the driveway and he could see lights over the lawn on the escarpment side. It was oddly comforting, knowing they were facing each other across the valley.

You crazy man. She didn't quite make beautiful with that wild mass of copper hair, but . . . He tried to define what it was about her that drew him in, that made her so appealing. Was it her wry humour? Her laughter, that seemed to bubble up, making it impossible not to smile in return? Or her porcelain skin and liquid brown eyes. Maybe it was the intelligence he saw in those eyes. She was smart, way smarter than him probably. What sort of woman designed her own home and worked for an organisation like Border Watch? With those smarts, the chances were she saw him as some sort of lame-brain fireman who'd run away from Sydney in the middle of a nervous breakdown. That didn't sit comfortably.

Sure, she didn't know the real him, but then, neither did he. Which meant he could carry on being Brad Ryan, who flirted rather obviously with good-looking women.

He whistled as he drove, tapping the wheel in time to the tune on the radio and suddenly feeling more optimistic. Not far to go and he had a cold beer waiting for him.

'Holy hell.' He slammed on the brakes, feeling them lock before he eased up. He was out of the door in an instant and racing up the road towards a familiar car, which was tipped precariously on the edge of the escarpment. 'Kaitlyn!' he yelled. 'Kait? Are you all right?'

She appeared from the left of the car. In the glare of his headlights he could see dirt on her hands and smears on her face.

'I hope to Christ they weren't friends of yours, because if I catch them, I'll get the book thrown at them.' There was no mistaking the anger in her voice.

He added it up in a split second. 'Big trayback ute with a gun rack and spotlights?'

'I don't know. They blinded me with their lights. I couldn't see anything. You know them?' She stomped round to stand in front of him, her hands on her hips. He stared. This woman had problems with her buttons, but now was probably not a good time to tell her she had a couple too many undone, plus dirt on her face.

'No, I don't know them. They almost wiped me out. What were you doing down here? Didn't I pass your place a couple of kilometres back?' He was trying to lighten the tone because he sensed fear as well as anger in her. God, she was sexy.

'More fool me for being a good neighbour,' she said, rubbing her neck and spreading more smudges. 'I saw what looked like a torch bobbing around at Jerry's place – sorry, your place. So I went to take a look. Figured all I had to do was drive in and drive out, and that would scare them away.' She snorted and shifted her weight from one foot to the other. She was trying too hard to appear nonchalant.

'A light at my place?' Ryan didn't like the sound of that.

'Yes. Next thing I know a vehicle is barrelling at me. I pulled to one side to let it through. Lucky I did because they still managed to clip me, and then they kept driving.' She shuddered and this time crossed her arms over her breasts. 'I thought I was going over the edge.'

Her voice cracked on the last word and her legs looked like they might buckle. Ryan had a dozen questions he wanted to ask, but he did what any man would have done: reached over and put an arm around her shoulder. What surprised him was the instant reaction from his body. Without thinking, he put his other arm around her and pulled her close. She rested against him and he was lost in the soft, womanly curves of her. Her hair smelt of shampoo, her skin of a warm perfume with a hint of cinnamon. Despite the fact she was shaking, there were no tears. She was tough beneath the softness.

They stood like that for maybe a minute, until he felt her straighten. He forced himself to ease away, resisting the urge to rub his chin across her hair and feel the slippery slide of it.

'Sorry about that,' she muttered.

'Don't apologise. Since it was my place you were rescuing, the least I can do is tow you out. Then maybe you'll let me get you a proper drink.'

She managed a shaky laugh and looked down at the ground, catching sight of her cleavage. Her fingers fumbled to fasten the errant buttons. 'Thanks, I'd appreciate that. I'd better let Julia know I'll be late. She'll start to worry if I don't reappear soon.' All brisk and businesslike, she turned away from him, but he couldn't help noticing that she avoided his gaze.

He would not allow himself to overstep the mark with his neighbour, especially not while he was on the job. Odd that she'd snuck under his radar and become a persistent little itch he wanted to scratch. Best to keep busy and it would disappear. And if not, well, he would disappear soon enough.

A quick inspection of her vehicle showed it was relatively stable. Its left rear wheel was hanging in space, but the chassis and driveshaft had settled onto a ridge of solid ground. While she couldn't drive the car out, it didn't look like it would move any further down the slope either. Through the open window he could see the park brake was on and the car was in gear. Good.

He loped back down to his car. It would take a bit of manoeuvering to get his car into position with the winch, but that would be a whole lot quicker and cheaper than waiting for a tow truck to come out from Atherton at this time of night.

He could hear her on the phone as he climbed back out of his vehicle. The headlights gave him enough light to work by.

'No, I'm fine. I'll report it as a hit and run and the insurance will cover it. I'll go into the station and fill in the forms tomorrow.' She paced up and down, her hand massaging her neck.

She wasn't mucking around, he thought, as he ran the hook and cable off the drum. Sliding under the front of her car, he found the fixed eyelet and secured the hook to it.

As he crawled out and stood up she finished the phone conversation and came over to him. He could smell her scent across the gap. There you go again, he thought with dismay as his heart picked up a beat. She's a mother, for Christ's sake. Behave. He knew none of his unwise thoughts would show on his face. He spoke for distraction.

'I'll need to get the brake off and the car into neutral, then we'll be good to go. Just let me take the strain before I hop in.'

She shook her head. 'Put the tension on it and I'll get the car set.' There was a hint of a lopsided smile. 'I think I'm lighter than you, or at the very least I know the car.'

He turned back to his winch with a wry chuckle. 'I'd say you're definitely lighter than me.' The sound of the small motor stopped any further conversation. Her words seemed more an acknowledgement that she was statuesque than an attempt at gaining a compliment. It just piqued his interest even more. Appearance seemed to matter little to her, yet her easy grace transcended the practical clothes and the wild hair.

'Right.' He stopped the winch. 'She's safe for now.'

Kaitlyn gingerly climbed into the car, put it into neutral and released the brake. Her car lights dimmed for an instant. Before he could yell a warning she was out, shutting the door softly behind her. He didn't quite close his mouth in time.

'It's power steering. Without the ignition on the wheels would have been pointing the wrong way. Harder to tow that way.' She smiled. 'Thought you were going bite my head off.'

His mouth snapped shut. 'Smart woman. I should have thought of that. Probably not a good time to admit I've never recovered a car without a driver in it before.'

'That's all right. Neither have I. Virgins together.'

He almost choked. Was she being deliberately provocative? She'd already headed for the passenger side of his vehicle and was in before he was.

With his hand on the key, he looked across at her in the light of the dash. 'Ready?'

'Yep.' Her hands were steady in her lap. That sort of composure after what she'd just been through surprised him.

Her car made a grinding noise and resisted for a moment, but then came free with a rush. He stopped the winch as soon as it was on level ground.

'It's less than 500 metres to my place. Drive it there and I can check out underneath before we take you home.'

Her saw her suck in her cheeks for an instant, weighing up the options. 'You're probably right. I don't need to discover the brakes or steering are damaged as I'm taking one of those bends. Sorry to put you to so much trouble.'

'Can't leave my neighbour stuck in the dark,' he replied. 'Especially when you were looking after me.'

It took another couple of minutes before they were ready to travel in a little convoy up the road. He made her go first in case something did fail on the car – although what he'd be able to do he didn't really know. Not for the first time he lamented the fact that his upbringing had not been a practical one. His skills were stretched changing a tap washer proficiently. Political debate or sport had been more important at his father's dinner table, and he suspected his mother had enjoyed having tradesmen in the house when his father was away. And that was a whole can of worms he was never going to examine too closely.

Old Jerry had been the only one who showed any interest in him, but the visits had stopped abruptly when Ryan was twelve. He had no idea why and, at that age, he'd known better than to ask. The summer holidays spent roaming these hills became distant memories. Six years later, he'd moved out of home and joined the Navy.

Kaitlyn drove into the yard and stopped past the front stairs. He parked in front of her so his headlights could provide some visibility.

'I'll get my torch and see what we can see. How did it feel?' he asked.

She waggled her head from side to side. 'Steering was fine and so were the brakes, but there was a bit of rumbling from the back.'

The scrape up the side of the car was obvious now. It was more than just a glancing blow. The house and yard were silent. He hesitated a fraction before he walked up the stairs. Could he be certain the intruder had left? The scurrying rush of the possum across the roof reassured him.

Kaitlyn looked up, alarmed. 'What was that?'

'Tame possum,' he explained as they reached the veranda.

'Right.' She sounded edgy.

'Excuse the mess,' he said, before pushing open the door and flicking the light switch. She ran into him as he stopped dead, and his hand flashed out to grip her arm.

'Holy hell. Stop right there.'

Chapter 23

THERE was no way anyone was this untidy, not even a guy. The place had been trashed, ransacked. Obvious why the people who'd sideswiped Kaitlyn had been in such a hurry to get away.

Ryan left her in the doorway, picking his way across to the light switch on the other wall. She could see that it was more of the same in the next room.

'You should call the police. This isn't kids messing about.'

'Certainly isn't.' His voice was curt, taut. He was moving cautiously. As he turned to flick on another light she caught a hint of a bulge in the small of his back. He was carrying a weapon. She hadn't noticed that on the roadside. It ramped up her concern. What was going on here? Had she misjudged him? Blinded by his good looks?

'I can call them,' she offered, her voice steady. 'They know me. You're new in town.'

He blinked at her this time, as though he'd finally registered her words. 'I don't think anything's missing, so there's no point. I'll let the real estate agent know tomorrow. Some of this stuff is the previous owner's.'

That made Kaitlyn annoyed as well as uneasy. Why didn't he want the police involved? What was he hiding? 'If it's Jerry's stuff, he'd expect you go to the police.'

'Yeah, right.' He turned around. 'Look, I'm sorry, but I can't do that drink right now.' He waved a distracted hand at the mess. 'I'll check your car over then follow you home.' He looked more angry than upset as he walked towards her, his movements rigid with control.

'Sure.' She didn't know what else to say. While the fact he carried a gun made her alert, there was nothing in his demeanour to suggest he was dangerous to her. Of course, she'd been wrong before, she reminded herself, but in her experience with the AFP, drug dealers and crims did not rescue women with flat tyres, volunteer for rural fire brigades, or chat to seven-year-old boys who lived next door.

It took him a couple of minutes to locate a serious-sized torch in all the mess. He led the way back down the stairs. After five minutes of crawling around in the dust he decided the car was okay. Nothing was leaking.

'I'll still follow you home. Peace of mind.'

'Okay . . .' Now she was even more confused. Did he want to make sure she didn't hang around? 'You've got a truckload of cleaning up to do in there. I could help. I know where Jerry kept most things.'

'I'll be right, thanks.'

It suddenly struck her. He was being too careless with the house. 'Jerry's dead, isn't he. The real estate agent must have told you something about Jerry.'

He looked cornered. She stayed silent, waiting, not letting him off the hook. Ryan caved in. 'He passed away a few months ago, apparently. That's all the real estate lady said. When I realised you didn't know, I didn't want to be the one to tell you. None of my business.'

'Oh.' She'd been half expecting it, but still her eyes filled with tears and she turned away, sucking in air. What a prick of a night. 'He was a good neighbour. A good friend. I did wonder, when I couldn't find him in any of the nursing homes close by.' She brushed the tears from her cheeks, willing her voice to steady. 'Sorry. Bit emotional tonight. Embarrassing, really.' She tilted her head back. *Don't think about Jerry yet.* 'Better get going.'

He didn't move to touch her, just opened the driver's door. The air around him felt warm as she brushed past. She'd bet ten bucks that calm exterior was hiding a burning rage right now, but she gave him full marks for staying civilised.

As she watched him prowl back to his own vehicle, scanning the area around the house as he went, the random pieces of information she was sifting through clicked into place. What if he was some kind of undercover cop? Might even make sense if he was with the arson squad. Her fingers itched to get to her computer. She hadn't spent ten years unravelling false identities with the Feds for nothing. Brad Ryan must have some history, and if she couldn't find it then he didn't exist.

She waited for him to start his vehicle before she headed down the track ahead of him. He stayed close, but not so close as to be intimidating. She flicked her headlights to high beam and added the side fog lights as well.

Her palms went slick as she drove past the spot where she'd been run off the road. Too damn close for comfort. Unlikely she'd ever drive this road again without a little tweak of alarm. Glimpses of the lights of her house started to appear through the trees. Welcoming. Safe.

She pulled into the drive, expecting Ryan to do a U-turn and head home. Instead, he pulled in behind her and got out.

'Sorry about that.' With his hands thrust into his pockets he looked less sure of himself. 'Back at the house. It was insensitive of me to tell you Jerry was dead after what's just happened.' He was a man with a burden, the laughter gone from his eyes.

'It's okay.' Kaitlyn managed a tired dismissal, sensing he didn't need her anger or her grief right now. Goodness knows what was really going on in his life. 'I kind of guessed Jerry wasn't coming back. Dan will miss him. I'll tell him on the weekend. Maybe we can come and say goodbye to him.' She knew she was in danger of crying. She pushed the tip of her tongue into the roof of her mouth. Sure-fire way of stopping the tears. It had worked for the last five years. 'And thanks for all your help tonight.'

'I think I owe you the thanks. Can we talk later in the week? Dinner?' His words sounded gruff, almost as though he'd said something he regretted. 'I owe you that at least. Probably an explanation as well.'

'No explaining required. We're neighbours; we don't have to know your business.'

'I'll drop round.'

He was gone before she could reply. The warm, charming flirt from the CWA hall had morphed into a worried man with a gun. She had no idea why someone would ransack his house, or run her off the road, but she was going to find out.

Chapter 24

RYAN crouched at the spot where Kaitlyn's car had been shunted so close to the edge. The slide marks from the car's chassis ended millimetres from the drop. His torch illuminated the tree line some 50, 60 metres down the steep embankment. For a vivid instant he could see the car rolling, tumbling, sliding and slamming into the trees before the flames lit the sky in a blinding flash. She might have survived, but probably not.

His stomach tightened. He'd seen enough accidents to know you had to stay detached. No room for emotion. How the hell had the sexy neighbour got under his guard? He rocked back on his heels and played the light over the road. Most of the tracks had been obliterated by his efforts to tow her out. There was a hint of skid marks, raised dirt, but he couldn't be sure. No clues left.

Nemesis was the most likely culprit, but there were inconsistencies. If they knew where he lived, then the chances were they'd know the vehicle he was driving. They would have known they'd run the wrong one off the road. But then they'd roared past him without a second glance, as far as he could tell. Panicked, maybe? Or just an inopportune accident?

He chewed on his lip. Could it be the arsonist? Always possible someone had got wind of his investigation, even though only the regional commander was supposed to know.

The dust shifted as he stood up. So dry, too dry. The place was like a tinderbox. A worse car accident would have taken all this out: Jerry's place, the forestry, and maybe even Kait's house.

Lucky.

But then, he didn't believe in luck.

He dusted off his pants as he climbed back into his car. The sooner he rang this in, the better. He wanted some answers. And backup.

With all the lights on, it looked like a party was in full swing at Jerry's. The gun in Ryan's hand didn't waver as he walked up the stairs. Broken furniture and scattered possessions were all that greeted him. No unexpected visitors were waiting, no obvious sign of a booby trap. He was angry with himself for exposing Kait to the danger. He should never have suggested driving back to his house. He surveyed the main living room, tucking the gun away. Too late to worry about that now. Where the bloody hell did he start?

He sent a text to Crusoe. Short, succinct. *Nemesis may be here.* The phone clunked onto the sideboard, the only upright furniture in the room. 'See how much sleep you get now, Crusoe,' he said into the silence, knowing his partner would be soon be scouring surveillance tapes for the surrounding areas, looking for possible sightings of the bikies.

Half an hour later, his arms aching, sweat pouring off him, he had the furniture roughly back in place. It would take an upholsterer to get the stuffing back into the chairs. The kitchen he chose to ignore. That would need plastic bags, lots of hot water and some heavy-duty cleaning products. And he'd need to go shopping for food again.

The main bedroom was the most untouched, but they'd ripped the back out of the wardrobe and the wooden planks now covered his mattress as it lay half off the frame. Old papers were scattered across the floor. Ryan knelt to bundle them up. He freed a soft-covered book from underneath the mattress, the writing in it spidery and deliberate. And familiar.

He turned a page and the date caught his eye: 12 December 1943. Jerry's diary. He frowned as he read the entry.

Hard day today. We are all cross-eyed from committing so many ranks to memory. Our trainer is a tough man. He needs to be, I suppose. 'Undisciplined rabble from Australia with no respect for authority,' he keeps calling us. He's right. No Australian is going to put up with that stiff upper lip carry-on.

Ryan turned the page. More observations of the men in his group and their British commanders. Apparently it was pretty chilly in England in the depths of winter. He knew Jerry had been in the Second World War, but the old man had rarely talked about it. Neither did the family. In fact, Ryan's father hadn't liked the old man at all. Ryan had realised later that the only reason he'd been allowed to spend school holidays up on Happy Jack Road with his great uncle was because it suited his parents not to have to deal with their son.

Once those visits stopped so abruptly, his only contact with Jerry was by mail. A Christmas present reliably arrived every year, normally a book, an adventure story. Letters turned up more frequently as Ryan got older.

He searched his memory for what he did know. Jerry used to march on Anzac Day, along with his dwindling band of cohorts. He stayed home on 11 November and observed a minute's silence at the eleventh hour. He abhorred war and had protested over Vietnam and both the Iraq campaigns. Ryan remembered the police arresting Jerry for a sit-in somewhere in the late eighties. At the time, Ryan had been in the Navy, first foot on the ladder of success, and was angered by the protests, embarrassed by his relative. Later, his opinion had changed.

He still had the letter Jerry had sent when he heard Ryan had signed up for the Navy. Same fluid handwriting as this. Ryan had been full of self-importance and the burning desire to follow in his father's footsteps, and had dismissed his great uncle's words of caution. What the hell would he know? he remembered thinking. Old man had driven trains all his life.

The reality was, of course, that before the trains, Jerry had survived the war, like the rest of his generation. Turns out he knew a hell of a lot more than Ryan.

Ryan closed the worn covers. He'd make time to read it, but first he had to get some sleep. That wasn't going to be easy tonight, with adrenalin still simmering in his blood and his senses on full alert.

If tonight's break-in was Nemesis then he'd unwittingly involved Kaitlyn Scott and her family. If that was the case, he had two options: stick like glue or distance himself completely. Either option held its own dangers.

Tomorrow. He'd work it out tomorrow.

Chapter 25

'ARE you all right, darling?' Julia hadn't budged from her armchair, fabric from her latest half-made quilt still draped across her lap. Kaitlyn hesitated as she locked the front door. She knew that the minute her mother saw her face she'd go into interrogation mode.

'Kaitie?'

'You're still up.'

'The show's just finishing.'

'Right.' Kait dropped onto the wide leather arm on her mother's chair. How much to tell her? The full details of the car accident could wait.

'So, do you have any idea who ran into you?' Julia wasn't going to be fobbed off.

'No idea at all.' Kait could only shrug. 'A random accident.'

'Was someone there? At Jerry's place?'

'Yes.' Kait sighed this time. There was no easy way. 'And they've left Ryan with a hell of a mess to clean up. The place has been ransacked.'

'No! I really didn't hear anyone go by.' Julia pushed herself to the edge of the seat, peering up at Kait as she slipped her reading glasses back on. 'How dreadful.'

'Yeah. I think a lot of Jerry's things have been trashed. Hard to see under all the mess. It's going to take Ryan a while to sort it out.'

'I can give the poor man a hand tomorrow. What a terrible thing to have happen in our neighbourhood. Did you call the police?' Julia didn't quite meet Kait's eyes and she didn't wait for an answer. 'Poor Ryan. And poor Jerry. He'll be so upset if anything's damaged. We'll have to let him know.'

'Mum . . .' She intertwined her fingers through her mother's, trying to prevent them trembling. 'That isn't going to be possible. The real estate agent told Ryan that Jerry . . .' The words were so hard to get out. She tried again, watching the colour fade from Julia's face and the tears fill her eyes.

She could only nod in response to the mute question, squeezing her mother's hand tight. 'I'm sorry. Jerry's gone. He passed away earlier this year. Ryan didn't know any more details.' Her voice broke. Jerry's death felt like one loss too many. It cracked open a tiny fault line in the dam wall of her self-control. The flood of tears she'd resolutely locked away five years ago burst through and poured down her cheeks. She struggled to stem the flow and bring them back under control, but they dripped off her chin.

Julia took little sharp sips of air, trying to speak as she shook her head in denial. 'I don't . . . I can't . . . No . . .' she hiccupped. 'Why didn't Jerry's family contact us?' Her voice barely made it above a whisper.

'I don't know, I don't know. Oh, Mum.' Kaitlyn slid all the way into the chair next to her mother and pulled her close. Julia's whole body shook with her sobs as Kait rubbed a calming hand over her back. Five years ago it had been the other way around.

So much sorrow. It felt too heavy to carry, too hard to face. Coming on top of the allegations about Chris, Kaitlyn felt as though she was slipping beneath a tidal wave of emotion. She needed a lifeline and there was none to be found. She had to flounder on and be strong.

'Mum, Nana, what's wrong?'

Kaitlyn almost swore. Standing in the doorway in his Spiderman pyjamas, Dan looked so solemn. Julia leant away as she dug for her handkerchief and pushed to the edge of the seat. Kait swiped her palms down her cheeks, knowing it wouldn't help much.

'Dan, you should be asleep, honey.' She reached out and tugged him down onto the arm of the chair. She was struggling to regroup. 'We're just being silly, it's okay.' She slid an arm around his shoulder.

He shook his head, tears magnifying his eyes as his gaze darted between the two women. 'No, you're crying. I heard you talking to Ryan outside.'

Kaitlyn glanced at her mother, who was now standing up. Too late to try deflecting. 'Honey, we can talk about this in the morning.'

'No,' he said, raising his voice. His tears burst over his lashes, leaving twin trails down his cheeks. 'What's wrong?'

Kaitlyn pulled him down on top of her, the two of them squashed into the armchair. 'Dan, you know where Dad and Grandpa have gone?'

'Yeah.' He looked suspicious, as though he expected her to fob him off. ' They're in heaven.'

'Well, Jerry's gone to catch up with them too, say g'day.'

'Jerry? But what about his house? And Ryan?' His chin and bottom lip wobbled.

'Jerry was very old.' Kait took her time looking for the words. 'It was time for him to have a rest. The house and the big yard? It took up a lot of energy, even with you helping him.'

'So, he's not coming home?' The tears had dried up as he tried to process it.

'No, Dan, he's not coming home. Jerry passed away earlier this year and I've only just found out.'

'Is Ryan going to look after his house, then?'

'For now, yes.'

'So, Jerry's with Dad and Grandpa?'

'Yes.' Kait continued to run her hand up and down the knobbly studs of her son's spine, feeling the tension turn to acceptance. Death was something he was exposed to every time he looked at a family photo. He was taking it way better than she'd expected.

'Can I still visit his house?'

'As long as it's all right with Ryan.'

'Okay.' Dan rested against her, pulling a loose thread on his cuff. His breathing was fast, shallow. Who knew how he'd take this tomorrow?

Kait could hear kitchen doors opening and closing as Julia fussed. It was a rhythm she remembered from her own childhood. Lying in bed, drowsy with sleep, hearing her mother stow the final things away, then the lights would go out one by one. The last light was always the delicate lamp on Kaitlyn's dressing table. Julia would press gentle lips to her daughter's temple, then the darkness would cocoon Kait as she slid back into childhood dreams. Tonight, listening to it held the same comfort.

Dan stirred in her arms. 'Can I sleep in your bed?'

'Sure. For tonight.' Better that she be there if the truth hit him during the night.

Julia came back to the chair, her arms folded around her. Kait shot her a questioning look and her mother managed a tremulous smile.

'We'll talk in the morning,' Julia said. 'Good night.' She leant in for a final hug and a kiss. For a moment the three of them rested there, together, safe.

Kait wished she could keep them like that forever.

Her eyes were gritty from lack of sleep, her mouth grim. The computer's clock said it was just past two in the morning. She could hear Dan's snores fluttering through slack lips behind her.

'Nothing,' Kait murmured, her fingers resting on the keyboard. It had taken her a long couple of hours to decide there was nothing substantial on Bradley Ryan in any of the usual sites.

Did that make him an undercover cop? Or could he be someone who'd been resettled, given a new identity? That could also explain the gun, and the lack of history. Happened far more often than people realised. She'd bet he wasn't a killer, but maybe a corporate criminal? She didn't know how she felt about that, but for now she let it go. Make some more inquiries tomorrow.

She knew she wouldn't sleep, knew she'd lie there awake but she slid into bed anyway. Dan snuffled and wriggled closer.

Martin still hadn't got back to her about Chris, but then, he wouldn't until he could tell her something. One way or the other. Maybe tomorrow.

Her neck was sore and she shifted, trying to get comfortable. It didn't help. Probably whiplash from the sideswipe on the way to Jerry's. That moment felt like it had been days ago, instead of merely hours.

Jerry. Gone.

In her oversized bed, with tears dampening the pillow beneath her, she remembered Jerry and his kindly ways. It must have been hard coming out as a gay man in a small town where everyone knew your business. To be vilified by a minority because your life partner was another man, taken by cancer the year Kait moved her family next door.

Even harder to know that people kept their children away from you because you might infect them. She'd seen the very real joy on Jerry's face when he described the time he'd had with his great-nephew. She'd also seen the very real pain when he talked about the lad's bigoted father realising his uncle was gay and banning him from all contact. In the way of elderly memories, the first half of Jerry's life was more vivid than the second.

He'd adored Dan, the grandson he'd never had, and that had been reciprocated. Dan would miss him more than he realised right now.

Rolling onto her stomach, she wrapped her arms around the pillow and buried her face. Tomorrow she'd have to be strong for all of them. Tonight she could cry for all that she'd lost.

Chapter 26

CAR lights shone through the gap between the faded curtains. Just a flash that slid across the crazed paint of the weatherboards, but it was enough to wake him fully. Chris Jackson hadn't slept soundly since he was a boy. It was a hazardous habit to let your guard down.

Funny thing was, that habit had kept him safe in jail. A light sleeper heard trouble before it found him.

He lay in his narrow bed and listened, watching the lights swing past again. They glinted off the rusting ceiling fan that was idling above his head. Someone had definitely done a drive-by at five a.m. A new car, not a diesel, probably mid-sized as the engine was just ticking over. It sounded stationary now.

The bed squeaked as he swung his feet to the floor, the old lino cool under his soles. He smoothed his moustache down. McCormack? Or someone sent by McCormack?

There were no streetlights down this end of the road. He'd seen to that when he moved in. Wasn't hard to keep them broken. He was the only one likely to complain. Derelict house up the end was waiting for demolition. One on the left was still vacant. He slid his hand behind the curtain and moved it a millimetre. The vehicle was just out of sight. He shuffled across to the other side, but it had moved further along by then. It was inching down the street, lights off now.

He sucked in air through the gaps in his teeth. Patrol car, maybe?

Had there been another breakout from Lotus Glen, the maximum-security prison up towards Dimbulah?

Maybe it was a coincidence, someone lost. He made it to the next room, the floorboards creaking under his weight, and sidled up to the window as the engine noise increased. It was already up the street.

'Shit.' The downside of a darkened street. He couldn't make out any details except that it was a late-model sedan.

Definitely not a cop car.

Wide awake now, he padded into the kitchen and filled the kettle, hearing the water hammer in the pipes for the first couple of seconds. He leant against the laminated benchtop as the water came to the boil. The click of the kettle was unnaturally loud. Lost in thought, he almost jumped. Sun would be up soon enough. He might as well get going with the day. The cupboard door needed an extra tap with his foot to close it after he'd replaced the box of teabags. He rinsed the teaspoon under running water and dropped it into the tannin-stained sink.

With a fresh mug of tea in his hand he waited as his computer sprang to life. Three years in jail had provided many opportunities. They called it networking, in the business world. You met people inside you hoped died long and horrible deaths. Others you became friends with and never saw again. Then there were those you bonded with so tightly you never let go of them. Probably part of what made it so friggin' hard to stay straight once you got out.

He logged in and clicked on the 'Return of the Drones' icon. How the hell did the authorities think they could control prisoners when they gave them computers and internet connections? Half the fuckin' drug deals in Australia were set up using online games like this one.

If the authorities followed the link, what could they prove? Everything was conducted in code.

Yesterday he'd sent off some names. He wanted the latest on Grant McCormack, Don Adler and the McCormack empire. Late last night he'd added Bradley Ryan. Trudy said the hotshot firey had been talking to Kaitlyn Scott at the meeting last night. No way was he going to allow Ryan to cosy up to Kait and her family. He'd waited too long to get this close. She just needed nudging in his direction.

The game opened and he checked his inbox. He had two replies, which he read in chronological order. McCormack was up here on the Tablelands. Seems he'd driven from Cairns and checked into a hotel at Yungaburra. Chris couldn't believe the dickhead would come all the way from Sydney to create trouble. Old man McCormack would never have got his hands dirty. MCM had always used hired help.

It made him snigger. You don't mess with me, laddie. You were barely shaving when I killed my first man. You don't have a fuckin' hope.

The next one from a tame prison guard was more worrisome. John Derek Barton's file had been requested from corrective services. Was this to do with McCormack? Did he have a longer reach than Chris realised? Was that how he'd found the connection between his two identities?

The sun was well up now, pouring in through the windows despite their grimy patina. The heat of the day was on the rise. He had a shower and shrugged into his neatly pressed uniform. Another side benefit of prison. All that laundry duty taught a man how to crease straight.

He looked at the clock radio. Seven-fifteen. Time to go. An

instant before he logged out of the game he saw a message had come through from a contact in Canberra.

'What the fuck?' The chair scraped across the floor as he pulled it to him and sat down heavily, scanning the information.

Bradley Ryan, the metropolitan fireman from Sydney, had a fabricated history. In other words, he didn't exist. But another ex-fireman called Ryan Braddon did, and he'd been released from prison a year ago after doing seven years for kiddie-fiddling. Braddon had now vanished. Chris's prison source thought he'd been relocated up north.

Chris hawked the taste from the back of his throat. Fuckin' paedophiles. They did their time and then the government went to great lengths to give them new identities so they could resettle them. Scum, filthy fuckin' scum, who preyed on the vulnerable and betrayed the most basic trust in the world.

Worse than robbers and drug dealers, they were. Right on the top of his hate list, alongside rapists. Castrate the lot of them and bugger the chemical method; go for the rusty knife. There were plenty who came out of jail minus some of their moving parts. He'd assisted in the showers a couple of times.

There was a phone number, but he didn't have time to call. Later. He sent off another message. He needed more information before he acted, but he'd be watching. Daniel was too precious to him. No one would be allowed to get near him. McCormack's problem suddenly seemed like a great opportunity. Instead of setting Ryan up to take the fall, Chris could kill him as well. He just had to be careful not to destroy the Scotts' house. It would take careful planning and the right wind, but it was nothing he couldn't manage.

The anger flared in him, heating his blood. He knew what

would ease it, what would bring him some peace, but today was shaping up to be catastrophic on the fire front. There'd be enough to do today. He just had to wait for the pager to go off. And it would.

Patience. His fingers tapped the tabletop. Who are you really, Bradley Ryan? Whoever you are, I'm coming after you and you won't know what hit you.

Time to pay a visit.

Chapter 27

'CROISSANTS for brekkie?' Kaitlyn closed the front door. They were Dan's favourite and usually a weekend-only treat. This morning needed all the help it could get.

'Morning, my love.' Julia had gone to some trouble with her make-up, but there were still shadows under her eyes and hollows in her cheeks.

'Get any sleep?' Kaitlyn dropped the paper bag on the benchtop and gave her mother a hug that lasted longer than usual.

Julia shook her head. 'Not much. And you were out early?'

'Yeah, I hope you don't mind me borrowing your car, but I'd rather get the mechanic to check the damage on mine before we drive it again. And . . .'

Julia waved Kait's apology aside. 'Of course, of course. And what?'

Kaitlyn hadn't intended to mention her dawn investigations to Julia, but now she felt compelled to share. 'Martin found an address. Sent it through this morning. I checked it out.'

Julia's knuckles went white as she picked up a china cup. 'And?'

'I don't know.' Waves of adrenalin were still heating Kait's body, an hour after her drive-by. But her hands were finally steady. Playing cops and robbers had not been in her childhood repertoire.

'Where was it?'

Kait glanced around. 'Dan?'

'In the shower still.'

'How is he?'

'Okay, I think. He looks like he got more sleep than either of us.'

'Good. He snored all night.' Kait managed a tiny smile.

'So?' Julia pushed again.

'The address is in Kairi, up an unsealed dead-end road. It's a low-set weatherboard on a basic housing block. The place on the right looks like it's going to fall down in the next cyclone. The one on the left has a 'For Rent' sign hiding in long grass.'

'Do we know anyone in the street?'

Kait shook her head. 'A Toyota ute was parked nose-first in the carport. It had spotties on the roof rack. I've got the rego. I'll send it off to Martin. Unfortunately, half the population of the Tablelands drives something similar.'

The bathroom door slammed, followed a second later by running feet.

'Mum!'

'Hi, darling.'

He slid to a stop in front of her, hands on his hips. 'Where'd you go?'

'Thought you might be hungry.' She opened the bag so he could see the buttery pastries.

'Yum. But it's not Saturday.'

'A treat.'

'Great.' He had the fridge open and the strawberry jam out before Julia could get plates on the bench.

'Easy, tiger, that's enough jam for a football team,' Kait warned as he spooned a pile of sticky pink fruit onto the plate.

He grinned at her and shoved the spoon in his mouth,

smacking his lips around it. 'I'll share with you,' he said, teeth and tongue now stained red.

'Thanks, I'll get my own.' Did he remember last night's storm of emotion? Or had it all rolled into a dream for him?

'One for you, Julia?'

'I'm not hungry yet. I'll have one later.'

Julia turned away, but not before Kait saw the hint of tears in her mother's eyes. Jerry's death had hit her hardest. Understandable, since they'd had so much in common.

Kaitlyn didn't push her. They'd each find their own way through this latest loss. It did mean she wasn't going to share the rest of Martin's email with Julia just yet.

She left Julia and Dan debating the merits of extra butter on croissants, and re-read the email as the electric toothbrush vibrated in her mouth.

The bottom line was that Martin still believed Stephen and Chris had died in the fire. What he also believed, and always had, was that someone else had lit the fire and then escaped. Was it the arsonist Kait had been tracking in the aircraft?

Martin had no new answers. Her father was still dead and there was still someone out there claiming to be Chris Jackson. She took small comfort from Martin's strong belief that her husband was no arsonist. The flip side of that was the knowledge Chris and Stephen had probably been murdered. It made no sense. Why would anyone want to murder them? Who was using Chris's identity?

What the hell was going on?

After a long day in the office she was no closer to an explanation. Her head throbbed. At least the training program was finally finished. She and Morgan had checked and rechecked to make sure they had all bases covered. Lauren had swung by on her way home after a four-day trip. The three of them spent half an hour swapping news in the car park. As a child, Kaitlyn only ever had one or two best friends. That habit hadn't changed. She didn't need a busy social circle; family had always been her focus. Walking to Julia's car in the late afternoon heat, Kaitlyn contemplated the differences between herself and her two friends. Morgan, happy and pregnant, was going home to her man. Lauren had skipped out of the office and back to Callam.

Kait was going home to her mother and her son.

For a fleeting moment she allowed herself to consider what it would be like to have a pair of strong arms around her, a partner to share her day with, a man to laugh with. She gave herself a mental shake.

She'd had strong arms around her last night and it had felt like heaven, just before she'd spotted a weapon at his waist and realised she knew nothing about him. Forget it, girl. Undeniably, his was the sexiest pair of arms she'd ever had wrapped around her. Add to that his body – lean, muscled and inescapably male. The tang of aftershave and —

No, stop.

Think of something else.

She checked in with Julia and wrote down a list of things her mother wanted from the shops. Now all she had to do was drive for an hour and fifteen minutes with just her thoughts for company.

The radio was full of talkback tonight. She changed to CD, knowing it would be lucky dip. Dan's taste was evolving and Julia only played classical when she was in the car alone. Dan won. It was Jessica Mauboy and she let the rhythm and blues roll over her, her thoughts in freefall.

Chris Jackson, Brad Ryan, and an arsonist. They rolled around and around as she examined them from every angle. Another option surfaced. If Martin was right and Chris had been murdered in the fire in Canberra, had the arsonist then deliberately taken Chris's identity?

If this man was living at Kairi, did that mean he was the cause of the recent wave of fires on the Tablelands? Could it be that she'd met him already? Had she worked with him, shared a beer with him in the Barron Valley pub? Was he using another name here as well? It was possible, but maybe too far-fetched. Maybe she was reading more into this than was there . . .

And Ryan. It seemed too coincidental that he'd moved here at a time like this, with a background in firefighting, and a gun at the ready. She didn't believe in coincidences.

Undercover? Or something more sinister? She opted for undercover. He was too clean-cut for a criminal.

By the time she reached the Walkamin jump-up and the last long stretch of road towards Atherton, she still had no answers. She'd just have to wait until tonight for more information. Too many other things needed her attention.

In Atherton, she had to cruise around the supermarket car park until she found a spot. Everyone was doing their mid-week shopping.

Engrossed in the ingredients on a jar of strawberry jam, she almost dropped it when a deep voice spoke in her ear. 'Go with the blueberry, it's wicked.'

And so was the grin on Ryan's face. 'Ryan.' She knew she looked off-balance and there wasn't a damn thing she could do about it. No matter her suspicions about this man, he made her blood sing in a way that had her cheeks burning. 'Buying cleaning products, or did you get that sorted?' She probably sounded shrewish, but it was the best she could manage on the spur of the moment.

'All done. Finished it this morning. Place is shipshape again. I think Jerry would be proud.' His look softened. 'How much did you know about him?'

'Why?' Kait kept her voice neutral, not wanting to risk any more tears. Just let him say one bad thing about Jerry and she'd freeze him dead on the spot.

'I found his journals. He'd hidden them in the wardrobe and the idiots last night pulled the back out of it.

'Is that right? I didn't know he was a writer.' She was intrigued despite herself.

'Second World War. I think he was a spy.'

'Really?' She could believe that. 'Who for?'

'The Brits. Seems he had an aptitude for languages. They used him in Germany. Makes fascinating reading. I can drop them round.'

'Oh, no, that wouldn't be right.' She backed up a step.

'I don't think he'd mind you reading them. He had later journals too. I'd already found them. You guys were his family. The closest thing he had to a daughter and a grandson. I think he may have been half in love with Julia.'

'Oh?' Kait couldn't help but smile. 'That would be the food. She loved feeding him, even though I always suspected he couldn't possibly eat all the leftovers she sent him home with.'

'It was the whole package. But I guess she was the wrong gender.'

'Hmm.' She glanced up at him from under her lashes. So he knew Jerry was gay and didn't seem to have a redneck reaction. Points to him. 'They were good friends. She was devastated last night when I told her. She's been missing him. They both loved classical music.' Her throat tightened and she did that trick with her tongue again, hoping it would stave off any tears. Ryan didn't seem to notice.

'Maybe Julia would like to read them.'

'Maybe.' She could manage one word at a time.

'And Dan. It might help Dan deal with losing him.' He shrugged, suddenly looking uncomfortable, awkward. 'If he knew some more about him, maybe it would give him stronger memories of Jerry.'

His thoughtfulness surprised her. 'Maybe you're right.'

'I'll drop them round and you decide. Once you've finished with them I'll give them to the estate agent. They'll know who to send them to. They didn't seem too worried about the break-in, provided I wasn't.'

'So you rang them?'

'Sure. Nothing was stolen so I didn't bother the cops. They're busy enough.'

'Right. Well, I'd better get going. Julia's waiting for me and the dinner ingredients.'

'See you later, then.'

Next aisle up she ran into Speedy. It was one of those days. 'Hey, Speedy, how are you?'

'Fine.' He didn't look happy.

'Everything okay?'

'Yeah, sure. Why?' He didn't meet her eyes, his glance directed over her shoulder.

She turned her head and caught a brief glimpse of Ryan at the check-out. A testosterone thing between the old guard and the new kid on the block? 'You look tired, but I guess with all these fires it's no wonder. You're just about single-handedly managing them all.'

'Just doing my job. Just like you do yours,' he replied, his stance relaxing. 'Good thing Dan's bike turned up, then.'

'Yeah, very glad about that. Appreciate you dropping him home a couple of times. It made it so much easier for Julia.'

'Anytime. And Kait, Kaitlyn?' He stumbled over her name and the colour rose in his face. 'Happy birthday for Saturday.'

'Aw, thanks, Speedy. Did Dan tell you?' She was touched that the bus driver took an interest in her family. No wonder they said such good things about him.

'He's made a present for you and he showed it to me on the bus. You'll love it.' It took her by surprise when he leant in and gave her a kiss on the cheek. It wasn't a peck, he lingered too long for that, but she took it in the spirit she judged it had been given.

'Thanks. You're lovely.' She patted his shoulder. 'Better run, though. I'm already late.'

'Off you go. Enjoy Saturday, eh?'

Ten minutes later she hit the road and headed for home. She judged her equilibrium to be almost back in balance. Ryan had a way of appearing when she least expected it. And every time he rattled her composure. Without fail. Ridiculous.

And then Speedy? If she'd read that right he didn't look happy to see Ryan. A competitive thing? She'd only heard good reports about Ryan's ability with the team, but he'd been out with Speedy so maybe Speedy knew more than everyone else.

Looks, as they say, could be deceiving.

Chapter 28

GRANT McCormack had been sniffing around the area for three days. He was glad he'd hired a large car with enough power to keep him out of trouble – not that he was expecting trouble, exactly, but he didn't trust Chris Jackson. He'd been disappointed not to come face to face with him at the community hall meeting. Still, it was probably best they didn't meet in public.

Twice today he'd seen Jackson from a distance, togged up in his orange overalls and driving a fire truck like a respected member of the community. What a perfect cover for an arsonist. Nirvana for someone fire-obsessed, and Jackson was obsessed as well as mad.

Grant remembered his father shooting a rabid dog in their house in New Guinea, years ago. The animal was half crazed with the disease and nothing was going to stand between it and freedom. Grant could still recall the snarl of terror and hate on the animal's face as it made its final lunge at them. He got the same impression from Chris Jackson. The arsonist was going to go down fighting.

The first house up Happy Jack Road was the Scotts' place. He admired the clean lines, the tidy gardens and the clever use of position. It had been designed for this spot and this spot only. At the meeting the other night he'd heard that Kaitlyn Scott was a smart and determined lady. He'd added top-end attractive to that.

She'd gone before he had a chance to talk to her. There was no missing her bright hair as she left the hall with a sway of her hips. He'd always had a thing for redheads.

Brad Ryan was an interesting character. Lucky he was just renting, because Grant got the impression he'd be a tough bastard to negotiate with. He was sure a hell of a lot was going on behind the amiable smile.

It was hard enough trying to deal with the lawyers for the bloke who'd inherited the place. The will might have been finalised, but the new owner wasn't negotiating.

The Scotts' house was closed up. No one answered the door. He wandered around the side, tried the wide doors on that side. Nothing. No one home and nothing unlocked. He peered through the glass and whistled. A grand piano. The place had a homely, comfortable look. Very nice. Ms Scott had good taste and obviously some cash to burn.

He kept walking around the house until he came back to the front. If she was cashed up, then it made it harder to bargain. Financial need had a powerful way of making people ignore the fine print.

He got back in his car and drove on towards the deceased estate, admiring the sweeping views and the swathe of plantation to his left. It would be a shame to see all those trees cleared, but gold mining necessitated land clearing. Easy to see why the geologists thought there might be gold here. He'd spent enough time with the WA operation to know the signs himself. If his father had listened to him, Grant would have gone to university and done geology. But his father never listened.

There was a ute out on the grass verge. It had a big bank of spotlights and a gun rack. Ryan must like to shoot. Grant hadn't picked up that vibe the other night. He parked behind the ute and laid a hand on the bonnet as he walked by. Hot. Hadn't been parked long.

'Anyone home?' he called. No one appeared. 'Hello, Mr Ryan? It's Grant McCormack. We met the other night. I'm with the Greentrees receivers.'

His foot was on the bottom stair when the door burst open and a bullet tugged at his sleeve before burying itself in the dirt behind him. He threw himself sideways and kept on tumbling and rolling towards his car. What the fuck was going on? Another bullet zinged past him and embedded itself in the car door.

'Holy fucking hell.' He yanked open the door and hauled himself inside. The side window shattered around him as the engine roared, his foot flat on the accelerator. He created a cloud of dust as he spun the car through ninety degrees, the steering wheel slippery in his hands.

He swore again as he fishtailed down the road. What the hell was Chris Jackson doing at Brad Ryan's house?

Chapter 29

RYAN had been in the Atherton library for most of the day. Not only cool and quiet, it was full of information. Leafing through back issues of *The Tablelander* had given him an even clearer picture of the rising number of fires. He reckoned it had started last season. Time to head home and log on.

He was halfway across the wide pavement when he saw Dan get out of a parked car and run down the street. Julia was driving Kaitlyn's car, with its bruised and scraped side. Ever the opportunist, he strolled over. The window slid down as he approached.

'Ryan, how are you?'

'Julia, lovely to see you.' He bent down and leant on the door. 'Dan's in a hurry.'

'He has to buy a birthday card for Kaitlyn. It's this Saturday. He's made her a jewellery box, but needs a card.'

'Having a party? I do love cake.' He didn't need to force his smile.

'Are you angling for an invite?'

'It's possible.'

'Then you must join us. You'll be very welcome. Seven o'clock for seven-thirty.'

'I'll bring some wine.'

'No need for that. You'll be our guest.'

'Okay.' He gave in, knowing he'd take something regardless.

They chatted for another five minutes. Ryan needed no pretence to be charming. The Scott women were very easy to spend time with.

'Ryan?'

He turned around as Dan scampered back up the street, clutching a brown paper bag.

'Find a good card?'

'Yeah. One with a puppy on it.'

'A puppy? That sounds cute.'

'Did Nana tell you what we're giving Mum?'

'A jewellery box?'

'Yeah, but something else as well?' Dan was hopping from foot to foot with excitement.

Ryan glanced at the paper bag in his hands. 'Wild guess but . . . a puppy?'

'Yeah! How cool? A puppy.'

Ryan had never been allowed a pet of any kind as a child so he could understand Dan's excitement. And the kid's joy was infectious.

'A Heinz 57 from the pound, or is she more a purebred type?'

Julia laughed as Daniel puzzled over the reference. 'It's a he,' she corrected. 'A stray from the Mareeba dog home. I think he's a staffy-cross. All black and very cute. You'll meet him Saturday. Jump in, Daniel. Your mum will be home soon.'

The car door slammed and Julia waited for Dan to buckle up.

'What has baked beans got to do with a dog?' he said with a frown.

Julia patted his knee. 'I'll explain on the way home. Seven o'clock, Ryan. See you then.' The last was directed out the window.

'Done. See you Saturday.' Ryan tapped the door as he straightened. The window slid up and he stood for another minute to watch her reverse out and drive away. Daniel waved distractedly.

He looked up and down the street and spotted the shop he was looking for. The bell rattled as he pushed open the door. A woman with a phone pressed to her ear and a harried expression screwed up her face in apology.

'No, no, take your time. I'm not in any hurry,' he said and she shot him a tight smile before continuing the conversation. Ryan tuned out.

He had a good view across the road to the front door of the Barron Valley pub. It was knock-off time for the average worker, so a steady trickle of predominantly male drinkers was wandering through the front doors. A cold beer would go down just fine right now. That and one of the giant steaks they served up. His kitchen cupboards were still looking pretty bare so it might be an easy option for dinner. Cleaning the place up had been enough of a chore. Shopping was not Ryan's forte.

'Sorry about that, love,' the woman interrupted his thoughts. 'What can I do for you?'

'I'm after a bunch of flowers. Something bright.'

'Sure. You want to take it with you now or order it?'

He didn't miss the pointed glance at the clock on the wall. 'Collect on Saturday?'

'Right. Good. Roses, perennials, lilies?'

'Not roses. Something tropical, maybe?'

'Tropical's good.' The phone rang again and she excused herself to answer it.

'Sorry,' she said, finally hanging up. 'Trudy's been called out again. She's firefighting with the rural guys. Bloody fires are getting out of hand. Makes me short-staffed.' She pulled the order pad towards her. 'Pick up Saturday?'

'That's the plan.'

'How much do you want to spend?'

Ryan cast an eye over the forty-dollar price tag on the arrangements sitting forlornly on an iron stand.

'Will sixty get me something better than those?'

She grinned. 'Those are reduced to sell, but sixty will get you a nice bunch. What's it for?'

'A friend's birthday.'

'You want to impress? Seventy would be better.'

'Done.' He handed over his credit card. 'Bit smoky out. Usually this many fires around in November?'

'No,' she said, looking up sharply. 'Last year wasn't good, either, but this is ridiculous. You ask me it's got something to do with those developers. Government changed the guidelines for land clearing so now they just burn out what they want then get a permit to do whatever the hell they like.'

'You think the fires are deliberately lit?'

'Can't see any other explanation.' She leant on the counter as she slid the machine across for his PIN. 'You're new around here.'

'I am. Just moved up from Sydney a couple of weeks ago. I might know your missing florist. I've joined the Rural Fire Brigade.'

She glanced at the name on the card this time. 'Ryan. Trudy said there was a new guy. You're the firey from Sydney.'

'Yeah, that's me. I don't think I've met Trudy.'

She laughed. 'If you'd met her, you'd remember. She'll be fixing your arrangement. You might meet her Saturday, if she's not called out again. There you go.' She handed over his receipt and card.

'Town like Atherton, I guess most people know each other. I like that.'

'Depends whether you want most people having an opinion about you or not, I guess. You'll work it out fast enough. Plenty of single ladies looking for a man. 'Specially one who buys flowers. That gets around and they'll be lining up.'

Ryan shook his head, trying for soulful. 'Not looking for a serious partner. Just here to regroup, really. I had a friend who moved up this way. Used to tell me how much he loved it. I lost contact when me and my wife split up. Must track him down again.'

'What's his name?'

'Derek, Derek Barton, although he called himself John as well.'

She frowned, then shook her head. 'Can't think of anyone by that name. He moved to Atherton?'

'Near here. Used to tell me about the crumbed steak at the BV.' He jerked his head at the pub over the road.

The florist laughed again. 'Well, he definitely lived in these parts if he knows the BV. Ask around over there; they'll know him if he's still around.'

'Thanks, I'll do that. See you Saturday morning.'

'Not me. Trudy. Enjoy that.'

He was still smiling as she shut and locked the door behind him.

In his experience, women had the best memories for names. Maybe Trudy would help.

He paused outside for a leisurely scan of the street. All clear. Shoving his hands into the pockets of his jeans, Ryan sauntered across the road and into the dark foyer of the Barron Valley. Funny how all pubs smelt the same. It didn't matter whether they were newly renovated or – in the case of the BV – an old, tried and true small-town pub. Beer soaked into the carpet, smoke leeched into the upholstery and the smell of hot chips and fried onions permeated every architrave, exhaust fan and menu.

The sounds of laughter, the clink of glasses and the occasional tinkle of a pokie machine spitting out its bounty were familiar, all backed by bass-heavy music in sync with writhing bodies on a widescreen TV in the front bar.

Ryan's nostrils flared with craving as he headed through to the sports bar. He'd started smoking when he infiltrated Nemesis. It had taken four long months to kick the habit. He'd been clean for eight months now and he had no intention of picking it up again. He was sure he'd shaved a few years off his life, but it was either smoke or get tattoos. Smoking at least was reversible.

He nodded to the old boys propping up the bar. They were the characters in a small town Ryan had learnt to cultivate at the start of any operation. These two were called Pete and Baz. He'd got their life histories on his first afternoon in town: one was a retired bank manager, the other a retired Supreme Court judge from Melbourne. They liked their afternoon drink in the air conditioning, were happy to have a chat, and just as happy to be left to their own conversation. The cricket was playing on TV, a test match between the South Africans and the Aussies. The lads were glued to it. There was national pride at stake.

Ryan made his way through to the back bar. Several of the Oakey Creek team had just arrived. He recognised Speedy and a couple of others. The buxom blonde in the middle was new. Trudy?

Ryan nodded at the barman and waved his finger in a circle. The man took the notes he left on the bar. Two minutes later Ryan balanced a tray of full beer glasses as he threaded his way to their table.

Speedy rather reluctantly introduced him to the two he didn't know, the woman included. Ryan pulled up a chair and sat down next to her. Trudy was indeed unforgettable. Ryan turned on the charm.

'Busy day, huh?'

'Just the one crew,' she replied, flashing a bit more cleavage. 'Me and Stan. A grassfire on the Dimbulah road. Lots of smoke. We needed to manage the traffic as well as keeping an eye on the fire.' She looked flushed. It would have been bloody hot out today, but Ryan thought there might be another reason her cheeks were pink.

He went with sympathetic. 'Hot to be standing on the road all day.'

'It certainly was. So, you're from Sydney.'

Her wide blue eyes were fixed on his mouth as he answered. In the past he would have happily used that attraction to get her into bed. Information was all too easy to gather in the languid aftermath of sex, but he wasn't going down that line here. And he refused to acknowledge that Kaitlyn Scott might be the reason.

Instead, he carried on making small talk, observing the others at the table. They were a close-knit team. Stan was next to Trudy. Ryan instinctively warmed to the older man, whose belly shook with each laugh. A cheerful asset to the operation. Speedy was at the far end, holding court, and Ryan saw the man's gaze sliding away from his too many times.

The topics ranged across everything from fires to cricket to politics. Funny how people from the city, himself included, could forget that people from the bush were just the same as them – they spoke the same language, discussed similar things and worked hard to put food on the table.

Dinners started to be delivered to tables around them. 'I think I'll have a steak before I go home. Anyone else eating?' Ryan asked.

The others all shook their heads.

'Don't get the crumbed one or you'll end up looking like Stan,' Trudy joked, poking her elbow into the rounded stomach next to her.

They all laughed and it served as a cue to leave, chairs scraping as they stood up.

'See you later.' Ryan acknowledged their goodbyes with a wave of his hand. He'd do some more digging with Trudy on Saturday.

He ordered his meal and stood by the bar, watching the national news. The lead story was an out-of-control bushfire in Victoria's Gippsland that had already destroyed thousands of acres of farming land. Now it was encroaching on towns. The police were sure it was the work of arsonists.

'Arseholes,' Ryan muttered to no one in particular.

'They should be given harsher sentences.' Baz had moved from the front bar and was holding his knife and fork, still wrapped in their paper napkin. 'Tougher justice. You can't rehabilitate pyromaniacs.'

Ryan grunted. He kind of agreed, but he also knew the jails were full to overflowing. It was only when an arsonist killed someone that the law seemed to come down on them. If it was just property destruction it almost didn't seem to count.

That annoyed Ryan. If it was your property that had just been razed to the ground, your stock that had been barbequed or your house that had just ignited in a fireball, he reckoned you were entitled to see it very differently and demand a harsher penalty.

'Too many fires around here at the moment,' Baz continued. 'They should be investigating. I told the police.'

'You reckon there's an arsonist up here?'

'One of the last cases I heard on the Victorian bench was arson fraud. Ever heard of Greentrees plantations?'

'Don't think so.' Ryan was alert now.

'Never mind. Four years ago, Greentrees were found to have made misleading claims regarding insurance payments for two burnt-out plantations in Victoria. Fraud. The details don't matter, except that they have another plantation up here. Still have a couple in Western Australia, too.' Baz put his cutlery down on the bar. 'I saw the evidence. Before the plantations finally went up in smoke there'd been a run of blazes. Property losses, no lives. It was the work of an arsonist. This is the same pattern. I've been watching.'

'So, are the police investigating?'

'Not quick enough. The conditions are so treacherous. The fool will kill someone.'

'I guess all we can do is be vigilant.'

Baz grunted and collected his cutlery again as the barman came through with a plate.

'Do you know someone called Derek Barton?' Ryan asked, not wanting to waste the opportunity.

Stopping, Baz squinted. 'Name rings a bell. Who is he?'

'A friend of mine who moved up here. Trying to track him down.'

'Another copper?'

'Sorry?' Ryan hoped he sounded puzzled.

'Another Fed, like you?'

Ryan laughed. 'No, another fireman, like me. I'm not a Fed.'

'Right.' Baz tapped his nose. 'My memory's shot. Dinner's ready. When I remember where I've seen him I'll let you know.' He walked off to his usual table.

Chapter 30

'OKAY, I get why we might have invited him to a party, but this is a family affair. Dinner, not a party.' Kait was determined not to get into an argument with Julia again. Both their tempers had been ratty since finding out Jerry was gone. But neither Julia nor Dan had bothered to mention Ryan's impending arrival until moments before he was due. And now it was too late to do anything more than ditch her baggy trackpants and T-shirt, find a bra, and dig out something that didn't need ironing. She and Dan had barely been home half an hour from an afternoon party for one of his friends that had run later than expected.

And her hair? For Christ's sake, she fumed, how the hell could she do anything with her hair with five minutes to spare?

'Take your time. You've got that lovely new dress I bought two weeks ago. You haven't even tried it on yet.'

'Right. I should have known there was a reason for it.' Kait knew she was being rude.

'And Ryan gets to meet Nero, too,' Dan chimed in from the floor, where he and the wriggling puppy were playing with a rope toy.

'Great, whose side are you on, big fella?' She scowled at her son, unable to put any real feeling into it. Dan grinned at her, a dark gap showing where his latest tooth had fallen out.

'Nana feeds me cake.'

'Traitor.' She had to laugh at him now.

'*Smart* traitor.'

'That too, and not the same smart you think you are.' His giggles followed her into her bedroom.

How could she possibly stay angry with a scheming grandmother and a small boy? So what if she looked like a mum? She was a mum. Kait rummaged in her drawers, debating. She told herself off for being vain and ridiculous. Ryan wouldn't notice what she was wearing, much less whether it was ironed. She held up a couple of outfits before shaking the wraparound dress Julia had bought out of its tissue paper.

She cursed as she heard a car pull up outside. Nero started barking, territorial already.

The dress would have to do, shop creases and all. She bit through the plastic price tag. Fingers crossed Julia had the size right.

Of course she did. Kait smoothed it over her hips and adjusted the tie at the back. And thank God for Kait's favourite designer, Francine, and her fine eye for detail and even finer eye for cut.

With furious hands she dragged the brush through her hair. Once it was flat enough she twisted it into a low knot on the nape of her neck. *Forget make-up, girlfriend, go the gloss.* It was lodged in the bottom of her bag and she bent a nail digging it out. She stretched her lips and swiped the pale colour over them. There. Enough.

She heard Julia and Dan greeting Ryan at the front door, Nero's claws scrabbling as he yipped. No way was she making some sort of late appearance like the lady of the house. This would have to do. She joined them at the door.

'Ryan, what a pleasant surprise.' She held out her hand to shake, knowing she sounded like she looked: flustered.

When he raised her hands to his lips and pressed a gentle kiss on the soft skin beside her thumb she almost melted at his feet.

'A pleasant surprise indeed.' His voice was low, a hint of gravel. 'You look lovely. Not a day over twenty-one.' The look he shot her sent her heart rate off the scale, adding elevated blood pressure to wobbly knees. 'Happy birthday, Kait.'

In his other hand he held out a beautiful bunch of flowers. Grateful for a camouflage she took them and cooed, burying her face in the bright petals to hide the flush in her cheeks. What the hell was she thinking? She knew the answer, just didn't want to admit it. Lust. And it was so misplaced, so damn overpowering, it was almost debilitating. It must be hormones.

'Come through, I better check the oven.' Julia took charge and turned for the kitchen, leaving them to follow. Dan and Nero were practically doing circles around them.

Kaitlyn couldn't stop the tiny shiver that rippled from head to toe when she felt Ryan's hand on her back, just above her waist, the pressure gentle, the touch warm through the silky fabric.

If she was going to spend the whole time this hyper-aware of his nearness, it was going to be a very long evening.

'So, who's this gorgeous couple getting married?'

She stumbled and Dan cannoned into her legs. Reaching out with one hand she steadied him and turned to where Ryan was pointing. She relaxed. It wasn't her in the photo.

'Nana and Grandpa,' supplied the ever-helpful Dan.

'Julia and Stephen.' Kait elaborated. 'Aren't they beautiful?'

And they were. Married in a simple ceremony with a small gathering of friends, they were an elegant older couple. A matron of honour and a best man were the only attendants. The day was a golden haze around them, sending the light through Julia's upswept hair.

'You look so much alike.' Ryan smiled into Kait's eyes and she had to laugh it off. This was too intense.

'I don't think so.' She touched her hair, feeling stray curls already escaping around her temples. 'Mum's always been so stylish. Elegant.'

'More of the same, from where I'm standing.'

'That's because my mother still dresses me,' she replied, with a flippant flick of her fingers. 'Not something I'm proud of, but there you have it.' She needed to find level ground. Didn't care that she might look like a fool. It was better this way. Get in first.

She breezed ahead of him, leaving him to look at the photo wall with Dan. Her own wedding photo was less prominently displayed in the bottom-left corner. She could hear Dan explaining each photo in great deal.

'Drink? A beer, wine, gin and tonic?' she called, reaching for one of her mother's cut-crystal vases.

'Thanks, beer would be good. Do they put breathalysers up your road very often?'

She smiled, snipping an inch off the stems before settling the flowers in water. 'That would be a no. Waste of resources. Just don't drive off the edge.'

'Not planning to,' he replied, joining her by the bench.

'Neither was I,' she retorted, with an arch of her eyebrow.

'No,' he acknowledged. 'What did the police say?'

'Without a registration there wasn't much they could do. In the light of day the damage is more superficial. The insurance company is yet to get back to me.'

'You got it checked out?'

'Julia did. I've had her car all week. Glen from the garage came out and crawled underneath, then drove it in and put it up on the hoist. It's mechanically sound. Just needs four new panels on the driver's side.' She opened a beer, poured wine into two glasses.

'They might write it off, then.'

'Possibly, but meanwhile it's still driveable. Too far out of town to be stuck without a car.'

'Mum,' Dan interrupted. 'Look what Nero just did.' He was hugging the dog. Any reservations Kait had had about the puppy had been swept away by the instant bond between son and dog. Julia, as usual, was right.

'Oh, great. More socks.' How could you be angry at a coal-black dog with a bright red sock hanging out either side of his muzzle? 'Nero, drop!'

She didn't know who was more surprised when the dog spat out the sock. It landed on Ryan's boot.

He picked it up between thumb and finger. 'Red, pink hearts? Must be Dan's sock.'

'No way.' Her son screwed up his face. 'Mine don't have hearts on them. It's Mum's.'

Kaitlyn grabbed it out of Ryan's fingers, cutting off any discussion about her socks. 'Thank you. I'll be sure not to leave anything lying around.'

'The birthday present, huh? Who chose the name?'

Dan smiled. 'I did.'

'Big name for a small dog.'

'Mum and Nana were talking about the fires and Nana said the police were like Nero fiddling while Rome burned.'

'Right, that will do, Dan,' Kaitlyn interrupted. 'Thanks for sharing that with our guest.' Ryan at least looked amused. 'It was funny at the time.'

Dan wasn't going to be silenced that easily. 'And anyway, I wanted a horse, but Nana said we couldn't because Mum would be upset with us and then she'd tell us off.'

'Upset, huh?' Kaitlyn was not keen on having the family discussion aired with Ryan.

'Yep, you get that look on your face and you call me Daniel.' He sat up straight and screwed up his eyes in what he clearly thought was a stern look. 'And you call Nana *Ju-li-ah*.' He was a gifted mimic, syllable-perfect. And then you talk really slowly.'

Julia was trying hard not to laugh, but it wasn't working. Ryan wasn't even trying.

'And who was Brutus again, Daniel?' Kait asked her son with pursed lips.

'That would be me.' He buried his face in Nero's neck and looked up at his mother with a wicked grin.

Kaitlyn shook her head. 'It's a regular riot around here. Dan's favourite movies are comedies and Ancient Roman tragedies.'

'Really? Wouldn't have guessed that.' Ryan was poker-faced. 'And of course it is every young lad's duty to scheme. Otherwise how would they get up to mischief?'

'Ha. He can get up to mischief on your patch, then.'

Dan cut in again. 'Hey, Ryan, did you find any more of those cogs?'

'Nah, been a bit busy, mate. Maybe on the weekend.'

Kaitlyn hid her surprise at the easy connection between the two. She let Dan hold court for another couple of minutes. Ryan seemed happy enough to talk to him. Not everyone tolerated a precocious seven-year-old this well.

The beer glass had left a puddle on the gleaming benchtop by the time Ryan reached for it and took a long swallow.

'Okay, Dan,' said Kaitlyn. 'Time to put Nero down and wash your hands. Dinner's almost ready.'

For once, he went without protest, Nero trotting at his heels.

'Good-looking dog.'

'He is, isn't he? They say he won't get much bigger. I hope so.'

'Looks sturdy. Bet he has a good bark. Keep the hawkers at bay.'

'It's impressive for a dog his size,' Kait confirmed. 'Sounds pretty vicious.'

'But he'll lick you to death first,' Julia chimed in.

'Yep, and chew me out of socks if I'm not careful.'

Ryan propped his foot on one of the stools and leant on the granite top. 'That smells divine, Julia.'

'Goat's cheese soufflés for starters, coral trout for main, then a decadent chocolate cake for dessert. I hope you brought your appetite with you.'

'The smell of cooking has been tormenting me since I moved in. You've even inspired me to experiment myself.'

'Oh, really?' Kaitlyn couldn't help having a dig. 'Cheese with the baked beans?'

He laughed and she liked the way his face softened when he did. 'No, but thanks for the tip. You do that often?'

It was her turn to smile. 'It's possible I may have resorted to that a couple of times when Julia's been away.'

'She's an excellent cook,' Julia said. 'She used to follow me around the kitchen when she was young. Always had an opinion on what went with what. Do you remember when you went through your edible flowers fad?'

Kaitlyn laughed. 'Oh God, yes. Those nasturtium leaves were dreadful and I insisted we serve them to Dad's colleagues. It's a wonder I didn't poison someone. They all politely pushed them around their plates.'

'Yuk.' Dan stuck his tongue out as he returned and sidled up next to Ryan. 'She makes me eat broccoli, too.'

Kait lifted an eyebrow. 'That's not poisonous, Dan.'

'But it's a flower. Gross.'

'Technically he's right,' Julia said. 'And then there was the Christmas cake you thought needed more rum, except you didn't bother telling me that you'd added it. I still remember cutting the cake to share it around and realising it smelt too strong.'

'And meanwhile, Dad had convinced himself that you'd taken to having a tipple when he was at work, because his litre of Bundy had vanished.' They were both smiling at the memory.

'But you did improve. You're even better than me now, not that you have time any more. You used to love to cook.'

'I did. I do. And maybe I will again. So, Ryan, no call outs for the RFB recently?' She steered the conversation away before it got caught in a downward spiral. 'Seems like the fires have died down a bit.'

'They called yesterday morning when it looked like the regulars couldn't get there quick enough. By the time we were ready to go they called back and canned us. I spent some time tinkering with the gear, getting to know your set-up better. Been a busy season up here so far.'

'It has. We hope the end's in sight. Normally the wet-season rains don't come until late December, early January. If this keeps up, the whole place will have been torched by then.'

'Everyone's saying it's got to be the work of an arsonist.' Ryan leant forward as he spoke.

Kaitlyn didn't look at her mother as she weighed up the answer. 'Certainly there have been a lot of fires, but we've had a bad storm season too. More dry thunderstorms than usual. They're normally further west and south. Record numbers of lightning strikes. In this sort of country, that can start fires in the most inaccessible places.'

'Doesn't mean someone isn't giving nature a helping hand.'

'You'd know a bit about arson in your job.'

He shrugged. 'You get to learn the signs, the patterns. Makes it easier to pick what started by accident and what was callously created.'

Julia placed feathery lengths of fennel on the edge of the plates. 'You must have seen some horrendous things. I think I mentioned last time you were here that my husband was an arson investigator. He started as a fireman many years ago, but specialised in house arson. There were days he was almost speechless from what he'd seen.'

Kaitlyn saw the shift in emotion behind Ryan's polite facade. Something had hit home there. She knew how heavily her father had worn the weight of his responsibilities. Some days he'd come home from work looking shorter than when he'd left, his skin grey with fatigue. For all the flippant charm Ryan exuded, Kait sensed a more serious, maybe even troubled man hiding behind that pretence.

'Yeah, you do. I'm on stress leave.' He shifted on the stool, lowered his chin. 'Not proud of that, but the last fire I fought we lost a family.' His eyes were bleak, the tension in his jaw obvious.

She sensed that his hurt and anger went bone-deep. It explained the sadness, the weariness she'd witnessed before.

Kaitlyn reached over and touched his shoulder, feeling solid muscle under her touch. 'That would be hard, to lose anyone like that.' She knew her voice would wobble, but she had to fill the silence. 'It's not possible to save them all. No matter how good a firefighter you are.'

His face relaxed a millimetre, and she waved her hand in a sweeping gesture, moving to lighten the mood. 'Well, you're standing in my contribution to the fire-resistant building code. Maybe you've heard the stories about me and my mad designs. The guys from Oakey Creek are less polite than most. What do they call it, Dan?'

'Kait's Crazy Castle, Kait's Crazy Castle.' Dan's voice was singsong. 'But I call it Dan's Deadly Dungeon.'

Kait tossed her head, feeling more strands come loose from the knot. 'And we wear those names as a badge of honour, don't we?'

'Yep. My friends think it's awesome, especially when you let me turn the sprinklers on all around the roof.'

'Sprinklers on the roof?' Ryan asked.

'We lost our home in a bushfire in Canberra, five years ago. Suffice to say we took what we had left and headed north. And here we are.' She gestured around the house, not meeting his eyes, afraid he might see the pain she tried to hide. 'Fire suppressants, fire retardant, water sprayers, fire breaks. It's all here. Hopefully we'll never need it.'

Her mother raised her wine glass. 'And if we do, the house has everything going for it. Everything your father believed in.'

'And he knew his stuff.'

Julia smiled. 'He did.'

'You do too.' Dan's pride was obvious.

Kait winked at him. 'I love my fan club.'

'Can I have a horse?'

They all laughed and Kait waved a finger at Dan. 'Manners.' She could see the tension ease in Ryan's shoulders as he followed the shift of conversation, took a sip of his beer and smiled. He took it in another direction altogether.

'So, Julia, your husband is the good-looking guy in those wedding photos? You looked pretty special on your wedding day. He was some lucky guy.'

There, Kaitlyn thought, we've blown the sadness away for now. Julia lined up the plates, their white reflecting in the dark bench.

'I was one lucky woman . . .' Julia folded a tea towel and leant on the counter. Kait knew what was coming next. This was family folklore and she never tired of hearing it. She listened to her mother's voice take on the lilt of her hometown in England.

'We were war evacuees in 1944, Stephen and I. Just seven-year-olds, the same age as Daniel, sent to a tiny town called Ullswater in the Lake District. A wee speck on the map. They figured we'd be safe there and my mum had too many mouths to feed. Stephen's parents were already dead, killed in the blitz.'

She sipped her wine. No one interrupted, not even Dan.

'When the war was over, no one could find my family. We lived in an orphanage for two more years before they sent us to Australia. Stephen stayed with me that whole time. He was my rock, my friend, my protector. He kept me warm at night through the snow in winter. And then Australia. We were separated. I went to a family in Sydney. He went to an orphanage run by a church. And so I lost him. For thirty years, I lost him. Then he found me. I was a pianist and he saw a newspaper story and a photograph. It took him three more years to find the courage to contact me.' She pressed a hand to her cheek, her eyes bright with the memory.

'When he did, he came backstage with the most gorgeous bunch of flowers. Lilies, they were. You see . . .' She shook her head. 'Lilies grew through the snow every spring while we were in England. I didn't recognise the man he'd grown into, but his eyes . . . his eyes were the same deep, deep blue. My Stephen.'

Kaitlyn reached across and laid her hand over her mother's as she continued. 'So we married. Just as soon as he could get a licence. Kaitlyn was our miracle. Born when we were both forty-one. I miss Stephen, but I have my family, I have my memories.'

Kait didn't miss the tear that slid down her mother's cheek as she turned to the oven.

'And your music,' Ryan said. Julia nodded as she bent to retrieve trays of perfectly puffed soufflés. His perceptiveness surprised Kait. Music had saved Julia from depression after the Canberra fires.

She turned the spotlight back to him. 'So, what about you, Ryan? Family? Ex-wife? Kids?'

'An ex-wife, a mother, father and a few distant relatives.'

Another only child. Tonight the house was full of them. Kait dug some more, curious, wanting to unravel this complex man. The glimpses of softness, compassion, didn't sit with the cocky, almost arrogant side of him.

'They live in Sydney?'

'They do.'

Right . . . She drew the word out in her head. So, nothing he was going to share there. 'And you've always been a fireman?'

'No, joined the armed forces when I left school. Wanted to see the world and they promised to pay me to do that. Advertising executives have a lot to answer for.'

Kait laughed. 'And why do I sense some disappointment there? Did they not deliver on the travel?'

Her mother slid the plates across the benchtop and Kait carried two to the table, Ryan following with the other two as he replied.

'Oh, no, they delivered all right, just unfortunate that most destinations were godforsaken places torn apart by war. Not so much as a cocktail umbrella in sight, let alone a market umbrella shading a sun-lounger by a resort pool. Not my kind of adventure, really.'

Okay, they were back on flippant. 'Hmm, and the added disadvantage of being shot at, I'm guessing.'

'Absolutely. No fun there. You want to take pot shots then head to the nearest sideshow alley and pop a couple of ducks. I bet Dan would do well with one of those knock-'em-down stalls.'

Dan needed to have the whole concept explained and soon the conversation headed into the land of superheroes and games.

While the merits of the latest Thor movie were being discussed, main course came and went. Kaitlyn was charmed. No hint of condescension in Ryan. Amazing, she thought, listening to him talk roses with Julia a moment after dissecting the intricacies of Battleships, Dan's latest online game craze. He looked relaxed in a way she hadn't seen before. His guard was down and she liked the man behind the glossy veneer.

Too often she felt his eyes on her face as she laughed with her son. She didn't dare meet his gaze, in case he saw some of the hunger, the need in them. Her reflection in the long windows reminded her she was no longer a starstruck teenager.

She cleared the plates and stacked the dishwasher, the laughter from the dining room soothing her, reassuring her she'd built a good life here for her family. Safe. Her son had grown up laughing. She had learnt to smile again, joke. Maybe she would cook again. Maybe even find joy in music again.

For a moment she rested with her hands on the edge of the sink. She had no need for someone else in that mix, and yet . . . A fleeting moment on the side of a dark road had tempted her, given her a glimpse of comfort she had no right to crave.

'Can I help?' She hadn't heard him come in behind her and almost jumped, knowing she couldn't turn around just yet; her face would be too open.

'No, all good. Guests don't do the dishes in this house.'

'Then think of me as a freeloading neighbour. Bet you let Jerry do the dishes.' He came and stood beside her. There was laughter in the lines around his eyes and the soft curve of his mouth. He was teasing.

'Jerry was different.' She couldn't stop the sadness in her words.

'Okay, so he had a few years on me.' He turned as he spoke and leant against the sink. They were almost hip to hip, facing each other, but side by side. His heat bridged the tiny gap and warmed her arm. She couldn't stop the ripple of awareness, of want. The answering flare in his eyes made her nipples pebble against the soft fabric of her dress and she knew she had to step away.

Before she could move, he snagged a wayward curl with his finger and tucked it behind her ear. His touch skimmed down her neck and onto her shoulder.

'Kait . . .' he began, but she pulled back. It would be too easy to be seduced, bewitched, beguiled. Too hard to step back later.

She met his eyes, shook her head, tried to break the spell. 'No.'

'No? Or not tonight?'

'No. Not ever.'

His smile was unrepentant. 'I'm persuasive.'

'I'm sure you are. That's not the point.'

'There's someone else?'

'No. There doesn't need to be.'

'You're scared.'

'Scarred.'

'Same difference. We both are.'

'So let's leave it at that. No more scars for me.'

'You're a beautiful woman. There's no need to be alone.'

'I'm not. I have Dan and Julia. And Nero now,' she added, trying to take the situation in hand.

'Nothing wrong with a bit of baggage.'

'Don't think Julia's ever been called baggage before,' she retorted, feeling more in control.

'You know what I mean. And being glib won't deflect me.'

'It will, you know.' The chocolate cake she lifted from the fridge was a work of art. 'And if it doesn't, then this will.'

'No candles?'

'Nope, that would be giving away my age.'

'A woman in her prime.'

'Ha, there's that flattery again.'

He looked at her with his head tilted to one side. Did she detect regret, or was it just the look of a man who'd missed his chance for a night of sex? It unsettled her that she couldn't read him. He seemed so self-assured. Wounded, yes, but confident, comfortable in his skin. When he'd stopped to change her tyre he'd looked so much younger than he seemed tonight.

'You've got your hands full.'

When he placed his lips over hers she almost dropped the cake. The pressure was light, a gentle tug on her lips, the barest slide of his tongue. She didn't, couldn't, stop the tremble of her mouth and the wild race of her heart. He pressed a harder kiss to her temple and stepped back. She was lost.

'And don't you dare tell me there's no chemistry, Kaitlyn Scott.' He took the plate from her hands, the glint in his eyes roguish, disturbingly attractive. 'Let me. You might drop it.'

'As if.' She thrust her nose in the air and stalked back to the dining room, his gentle laugh making her blush.

Julia's bright eyes were almost too much and Kait's temper raised its head. Matchmaking was Julia's forte and she'd been set up tonight. But . . .

'And the ice-cream, dear.'

'Right.' Kait fled back to the kitchen, hearing Dan describe in great detail the gooey centre in the evening's cake.

The sound of Dan laughing as Ryan teased him dampened her anger. She knew it was misguided, misplaced. It was herself she was annoyed at.

And Ryan?

He was right. She was scared, too scared to try again. Too afraid of failing Julia and Dan, too certain she couldn't navigate a relationship without rocking her steady world. Too damaged to trust again.

A phone rang as Kait returned with the ice-cream. Ryan's head snapped up. 'Excuse me.' He fished the phone out of his jacket pocket. She heard him answer it.

He walked away, fumbling with the catch on the door that led to the wide veranda. If he spoke it was so softly she couldn't hear his words. Who rang someone at ten o'clock at night? Was it the RFB? Did he not have a pager? She glanced across at hers, which was lying on the sideboard next to her keys. It was silent.

She didn't want to start drawing lines between dots, but this was a man who carried a weapon, took phone calls late at night and left a trail so small on the internet as to be virtually invisible. She shut that line of thinking down. Not now.

'Mum?'

'Sorry, Dan. What was that?'

'Ice-cream?'

'Sure.' She still had the scoop in her hand. 'One or two?'

'Two?'

'Two it is, then.'

Dan had finished his dessert by the time Ryan came back through the door. Forced smile, Kait decided.

'Sorry about that. A colleague coming off a nightshift in Sydney thought he'd call.' He dropped the phone back in the pocket of his jacket. 'This looks great, Julia. Finished already, Dan?'

He was good at redirecting, Kait thought, putting her own smile in place. Lies, all lies. It didn't matter how attractive he might be; she didn't really know this man and she sensed depths that took him to dark places. He was not what he seemed, not who he claimed to be. He was living a lie and she didn't know why.

Yet.

'Time for Dan to go to bed.'

'*Muuum*,' Dan complained.

'Daniel.'

He grinned. 'See? Just like that, she says it. All right, I'm going, I'm going. Can Nero sleep with me?'

'That would be no.'

'Aw, Mum.'

Kait raised an eyebrow at him, knowing he would still find a way to smuggle in the puppy.

'All right, all right.' He held out his hand to Ryan. 'Night, Ryan. See you on the weekend?' He kissed Julia on the cheek. 'Night, Nana.' Then he sidled up to Kait. 'Night, Mum.' His hug was fierce and Kait returned it. When she opened her eyes, Ryan was watching her, his expression shuttered.

'But we haven't sung "Happy Birthday".' Julia seemed to realise the party was breaking up. 'Come on, before Dan goes to bed.'

Kait could do nothing but endure a full rendition, complete with Julia on the grand piano. Only then did Julia escort Dan to bed, leaving Kait to see Ryan out.

He gathered his jacket. 'Thanks for tonight. It was lovely. Great food, good wine, and wonderful company. Bonus having two good-looking ladies.'

His charm was back in place, a grin with the slight raise of an eyebrow that made him look sexy as hell. Chameleon.

'Hey, I brought Jerry's journals. They're in the car. Come out and grab them?'

'Must I?'

'Yeah, I think you must.' He led the way to his car and the light from the interior sent a glow of warmth over his skin as he reached across to the passenger seat.

'I'm sure you'll find them interesting. Jerry was quite a troubled man. You guys helped him find himself, find some peace.'

'Really?' Kait was perplexed. 'Apart from being vilified for being gay I didn't sense he was troubled.'

'Perhaps if you've hidden something so deep for so long, you can fool even the experts.' He looked like he wanted to say more, then changed his mind.

'Take care.' His hand skimmed her hair, cupped her chin. He pressed a kiss against her lips that felt urgent and fleeting and desperate all at once. She lifted on her toes, feather-light, unbearably touched by his need. Then the door slammed and the engine purred into life. He was gone, leaving her standing in her darkened front yard, heart hammering, body alive and tingling.

'Who are you, Ryan?'

Chapter 31

HE took his foot off the accelerator as he rounded the last bend. He'd driven like a maniac since he turned out of the Scotts' driveway. 'Fuck it,' he swore, pounding the steering wheel. 'Fuck it to hell.'

It had been the sort of evening where a man could lose his head, lose his heart. Yes, he'd set out to seduce the delectable Kaitlyn Scott, but the vulnerability, the softness underneath that motherly front of steel was almost his undoing. She looked so damn sexy in that wraparound dress that clung to her curves, moulded to her breasts and made him ache with want. She was the whole damn package. Brains, humour, looks and a fierce protector of her own.

It was exactly how Jerry had described her in his journals. Ryan hadn't set out to learn about his neighbours through Jerry's writing. Neither had he set out to find the heart of his own pain. But those diaries, spanning a lifetime of change, of challenges, were like how-to manuals for an undercover cop.

Jerry spoke of his dislocation, his inability to fit into the real world again. What was the truth? Was there a truth? Was there a way back?

Did Ryan want Kait to read them for Jerry, or for himself? Tonight, he let himself believe in a future. He let himself dream of waking up next to a woman, instead of sneaking out like a thief in the night. He'd let himself be seduced by the warmth and affection between the Scotts, treasuring it as if it were the most precious thing on earth.

And then his phone had rung.

Nemesis.

It had shattered the pretence, destroyed the mood, and underscored what a sham of a life he lived. It was more of the same: harassment, abuse, threats. He didn't expect a trace on this call either.

As he reached his front gate the headlights reflected off something shiny in the grass near the verge. He braked to a halt and left the engine running, the lights on high beam. Broken glass? He picked up a couple of pieces. Looked like glass from a car, maybe a windscreen. Where had that come from?

Was he just being paranoid again? He had his gun in his hand as he moved out of the beam of light. A lick of wind blew in from the east and lifted his collar. The stars flickered behind fast-moving clouds. Weather front approaching.

The sensor lights he'd rigged up came on as he stood, and he couldn't stop himself tensing. He'd need daylight to see anything much. It was going to be a long night.

He went inside and turned on his computer. As he waited for it to come online, he checked the doors and windows. In an operation like this he would normally have more support on the ground, but the nature of this one meant it wasn't possible. He blamed that for this compulsion, this insane need, to connect with his neighbours, even while he knew it was imperative to keep some distance. They made a good cover story, but they could also end up in harm's way and that was not what he wanted. Not at all. Now, even less so.

He slumped in the chair and scrolled through his emails. Two from Crusoe.

Possible sighting yesterday at a petrol station in Sarina, down near Mackay. Surveillance footage attached. Looks like Weasel to me and the software says the same. Headed north in a phalanx of colours.

Ryan knew there were still extensive crops of cannabis under cultivation up in North Queensland. Some of them were the high-yield hybrid crops that brought in up to 70 per cent more than the older plants. Big bucks to a club needing funds to pay lawyers. Weasel could just be checking on the vegie garden.

Ryan ran the footage. Even with a helmet and scarf muffling his appearance, it was definitely Weasel. He sat on the bike, legs thrust forward, chin jutting, hand in position on the throttle. And he had five boys in tow.

'Crazy stuff,' Ryan said out loud. If they were coming for him then they were planning on going down in a blaze of glory. There was nothing stealthy about this approach.

He watched the lights go out one by one across the escarpment. The Scotts were off to bed. Unbidden, his fingers touched his lips. She'd tasted of wine and woman, smelt of musk and cinnamon, her skin soft and smooth. The smattering of freckles, only visible when you were up so close, added a girlish charm.

He felt his body tighten. For a split second he wanted to weep – weep for the young man who had kissed so innocently for the first time at fifteen and fucked so indiscriminately at thirty-five. If he had his time again, would he retrace the path he'd chosen?

At this very instant, at this moment, he saw the answer so clearly. He'd throw it all away in a heartbeat if he could claim just a tiny portion of the love he'd been surrounded by tonight.

And that would get him killed, so he had to forget it. *Forget it, Ryan.* He was what he was: a lying, ruthless bastard who always ended up walking away.

He turned back to his screen. Sleep wasn't going to happen tonight. The least he could do was look for more answers.

An interesting snippet on Grant McCormack made Ryan sit up. Seemed McCormack was holed up at Yungaburra with a hire car in need of repairs for bullet holes, including a smashed left-hand window. Ryan gazed into space as he contemplated that. A falling out of thieves? Could it be a coincidence that he had broken glass on his front boundary?

He got to his feet and stood on one side of the front window, looking out over the dark yard. After the place had been trashed he'd debated changing the locks, but decided against it. Maybe he should do that tomorrow. Make it a priority. And rig up a remote camera for inside.

The distance from the front of the house to the boundary would be an easy shot for a handgun. Had someone been in here when he wasn't home? It all seemed implausible, but then, this wasn't the simple case he'd expected it to be.

If the glass was from McCormack's car, what the hell was the man doing out here? And who the hell had been shooting at him? Had McCormack's tame arsonist bitten back? Ryan didn't have the answer yet, but he'd have a look around the front yard tomorrow in the daylight.

He sat back down and opened the second email. It was a series of photographs, identikit specials that aged the original photo of John Derek Barton and gave him different hairstyles and facial hair. There were over twenty of them and Ryan scrolled through slowly, searching for anything that looked familiar.

Number fourteen. He kept coming back to it, apprehension stiffening his neck, raising his shoulderblades.

It was possible. Longer hair brushed back, a slim moustache, fuller in the face. He enlarged the picture and put his hand over the face's forehead as though it were the visor of a cap.

Bingo.

Chapter 32

THE beeper was almost on the floor by the time it roused Kait from sleep. She knocked it off her bedside table completely, trying to silence it.

'Damn,' she muttered. It felt like she'd had two hours' sleep. She swung her legs over the side of the bed and peered at the clock, pushing her hair out of her face. Well, look at that, she'd slept for exactly one hour and forty-five minutes. Right now, she'd give anything to roll over and pull the sheet back up, but that wasn't possible.

She dialled. Outside, the wind buffeted the house. Storm, or a change of weather?

'Hi, it's Kaitlyn. What do you need?'

'A fire's flared up with the wind. It's threatening homes out the eastern side of Mareeba. The pump on one of their trucks has packed it in so they need both of our trucks.'

'Okay. I'll be there. At the depot?'

'No, we've rung Brad Ryan too. He said he'd pick you up, if that's okay.'

'Sure.' She clipped the word. Ryan again.

Jerry's diary had kept her awake for several hours. As Ryan had predicted, it was fascinating, though perhaps not in the way he'd expected. It had sent her back to the internet and she was now quietly confident that Ryan was a federal policeman – real name

Ryan O'Donnell – who happened to be Jerry's great-nephew. Kait's friend in the AFP was on night shift and at his computer when she'd emailed him. The answers he'd supplied had raised more questions, but it was a start.

She grabbed her overalls from behind the door. Her boots were out the front. By the time she'd cleaned her teeth and emerged from the bedroom, Julia, always a light sleeper, had Kait's camel pack ready to go, along with an esky bag and thermos. Nero was snuffling at her feet.

'Thanks, Mum. Sorry about waking you. Hopefully we'll be finished before lunch. Dan will be so disappointed if I'm not back for the Ravenshoe Railway trip.'

Julia shook her head dismissively. 'We'll still go. I'd hate for him to miss it, and his friends are all going. Just let me know before twelve. We'll need to leave by then.'

'I'll call if I can make it. That might be safer in case the phones go out. I'll be here if I can.' Kait went to the front door.

'You're not driving?'

'No, apparently Ryan is.'

'Oh, right.'

'Don't go there, Mum.'

'Yes, dear.'

Kaitlyn rolled her eyes as she bent and kissed Julia's cheek. 'You are incorrigible.'

'I prefer to call it optimistic. Be safe.' The strength of Julia's hug belied the birdlike slimness of her arms. She pushed Kait towards the door. 'Say hi for me.'

'Oh, really, it's been all of five hours since you saw him.' Kait flounced out the door. A time like this and still Julia schemed?

Ryan was parked by the front gate, the passenger door ajar.

She walked towards him, glancing up at the night sky. No sign of storm, but the clouds were scudding fast so it must be the front the weatherman had predicted would roar through. It had brought wind; wild, swirling gusts that coated her throat with dusty unease. Could be nasty tonight.

She slid into the seat and jammed her bags at her feet. 'Hey.'

'Hey to you, too.' Ryan didn't look like he'd even bothered to run a hand over his hair. It stood up, tufted with sleep, and she had to physically sit on her hands to stop herself reaching across to smooth it back. There lay the road to purgatory and beyond.

'Get much sleep?'

She shook her head. 'You?'

'Couple of hours, max.'

'Coffee?'

'Really?

'Really. Julia takes catering very seriously.'

'The woman deserves a VC.' There was a flash of a smile in the dark.

She rummaged in the bag at her feet, finding the travel mugs and thermos. Ryan drove with a considered calm. Nothing rushed, nothing unnecessary.

He glanced over at her. 'Dispatch tell you anything about it?'

'Not much. The bit about the truck pump being broken.'

'Deliberately damaged, was what he told me. Smashed.'

'No way.'

'Yeah. We need to watch our backs. Look, I know you work for Border Watch. I remember hearing they did some work with fire detection a few years ago. Julia mentioned last night when you were in the kitchen that you were working on some project. Can you tell me? Is it to do with that? Catching arsonists?'

She looked across the car at him, measuring what she'd found out from her friend in the AFP, versus what she knew was fact. In for a penny, in for a pound, as Julia was fond of saying.

'The Dash 8s have some pretty amazing gear. Have you heard of FLIR? Forward Looking Infrared?'

'Sure, they use them on military aircraft and rescue choppers. They can detect heat sources. From memory, the picture looks like CCTV footage – black and white.'

'That's it. We have them on board. How about I leave it to your imagination as to what we can do with them?'

'Right.' He drew the word out. 'So, the daughter of an arson investigator must have some theories about this.'

'I do. But it's complicated.' She inclined her head. 'And right now I don't know who to trust.' She was watching his face and saw his face tighten as his eyebrows drew together. Yes, he was hiding something, knew a whole lot more than she did. But how much was he willing to share?

'Tricky, that,' was all he said. They were almost at the RFB base. The lights were on. Speedy had the two trucks out and ready. The corner of his ute was visible at the side of the shed.

'Speedy got here quickly.'

'Yes,' Kait replied as they pulled into one of the parking spaces out the front. 'He normally does. Mustn't sleep much.'

'No, seems that way.' Ryan slammed his door as Trudy pulled up behind them. Need to think about that later, Kait decided.

'Hey, guys,' Speedy called. 'Hell of a time for a fire to flare.'

Kaitlyn nodded, tucking her hair behind her ear. 'Guess the wind's built. Must be gusting up to 40 knots.'

'And increasing. I've been up for almost an hour and it's on the rise,' Speedy added.

'How many crews are on this?'

'Two of the regular crews, one rural from Dimbulah and now the two of us.' Speedy nodded at the two trucks. 'We got some of the other guys meeting us at Mareeba.'

'Water bombers at first light?'

'Yeah, the two Ag Cats from Mareeba. I think they're trying to source some helos from Cairns as well, but the rescue chopper's been called out to medevac someone off Lizard Island.'

'Right. Let's go.' Ryan had transferred their gear into one of the trucks and swung into the driver's seat. Kaitlyn joined him and they headed down the road. Ten minutes later they'd collected a sleepy Stan from Tolga and hit the highway again.

They spent the next thirty minutes discussing fires and the effects of wind. Now that she knew what she was looking for, Kait realised Ryan was very good at agreeing without offering new opinions. If he was a firey on sick leave, she was a lion-tamer. He had a lot of theoretical knowledge, even had the slang down pat, but was very light on war stories. Didn't everyone who'd fought fires, lived through the danger, have war stories? You couldn't face this raging beast and not have anecdotes of near misses, lost opportunities and moments of frightening clarity. Only way to deal with those stressful times was to talk about them.

Ahead, they could see the smoke rising in the dull glow thrown up by the lights of Mareeba. They took the turning towards Kuranda.

And there it was. The fire. Kait felt her body react as it always did. Her pulse sped up, her skin prickled. Once she started fighting the blaze, her heightened awareness was good. Right now it just made her sweat.

Flames licked and darted through the forest, spreading out

across the tall native grass. Sparks rose in billowing clouds from exploding trees.

'Freakin' hell. It's close to those freakin' houses,' Stan said. 'This'll be a bitch to contain.'

Kait called in on the radio for the GPS coordinates for the head of the fire. No town water; the mains didn't come this far. They'd need to lay a pipe and pump from a nearby creek. The other team had lost their hold on the ground, pushed back metre by metre.

'Dead man's zone.' Stan shook his head. 'They've either attacked this from the wrong side or it's jumped a containment line. What a mongrel of a night.'

'We can only do what we can.'

'And don't get caught in the freakin' zone,' Stan said, with a sidelong glance at her.

'We'll make sure we don't.'

'Sat nav says this is the spot.' Ryan turned the vehicle across the verge, heading for a fence line. He stopped at the gate.

If the plan worked, they'd back-burn between the blaze and the houses. Once the main fire front got to them, there'd be no fuel left. The wind was increasing with the impending dawn, throwing sparks high into the air in twisting spirals. There was always the danger that the back-burn could run away. Then they'd be in the dead man's zone.

'Stan, Ryan can help you lay out the water pipes. Get it pumping as fast as you can.' Kait slammed the door, adrenalin making her voice tight. 'I'll get the torch ready to go.' If Ryan was the untried novice she suspected he was, then she'd be taking extra care to keep him safe.

For two hours, they burnt and contained, shovelled and chopped, beating out spot fires that erupted as fireballs spewed from the blazing forest. The heat and smoke was intense, the noise deafening. The sharp percussion of debris raining down around them made it hard not to cringe. The crowns of the eucalypts were well alight.

She couldn't surrender.

Having lost her own house to fire, she did everything in her power to prevent it happening to someone else. Fire was personal. She hacked and hosed and harried, letting her anger give her strength. But it wasn't only anger at the fire that kept her going. There was something else, something more insidious.

Fear.

The nagging, underlying fear she might not win this time.

She kept that fear close. This was a serious fire, unpredictable and erratic. Rushing tongues of flames surged through in wind gusts and burst from the canopy, flaring across the sky and sending embers in a fiery shower to carpet the ground hundreds of metres ahead.

Each time that happened, Kaitlyn checked their escape route. If the fire front got to them before they'd finished the containment line, they could well be sheltering in their truck, wrapped in fire blankets and holding on for dear life.

Unrecognisable, dawn came and went, shrouded in smoke and heat and ash. A call came through on the radio. The police were evacuating the houses on the far side of the estate and there were elderly people needing assistance. Someone had to drive a truck over there to help out.

Kait cupped her hand and yelled into Ryan's ear. 'You go. Leave Stan and me with the pump and a couple of fire shelters. Get back when you can.'

'Bad idea. You can't outrun this if it turns,' he yelled back. 'We all go or not at all. I say we go.'

Stan was battling a spot fire that had sprung up behind them, and the stream of water was ineffective. Kaitlyn was torn. If they left this, it could mean they'd lose the houses they'd fought so hard to save. But human life took precedence. They couldn't leave the pump unattended; it was too valuable. Ryan was right.

'Pack up. We'll need to be quick.'

They were on the road in less than five minutes. The street was well alight when they got there. One house was already a roaring inferno. With the headlights on full, Kait could still only see 50 metres in front at best.

The regular fire crews were battling to contain a blaze in a big shed that was in danger of setting the houses on either side of it alight. They waved Kait and her team on down the street to a large house where six elderly residents still remained trapped. They were the last of those who'd elected to stay during the night and were now becoming increasingly distressed. A lone police motorcycle stood outside with lights flashing.

The smoke in the house was like fog. Tears streamed down everyone's faces as Kait and Ryan bundled the first three pensioners into the cab of the truck. Stan grabbed the pump from the truck before Ryan drove off, taking the pensioners to safety before coming back for the rest.

Kait coughed, her sinuses and throat swollen from the scorching smoke. Twiddling her thumbs while waiting for Ryan to return for the other three was not an option. 'Let's get the pump going, Stan.'

The house had a swimming pool, and within a matter of minutes they had a steady stream of water going. She wasn't convinced they could hold the fire off indefinitely, but it would last until Ryan came back.

Down the street a bit, the house that had been so well alight had burnt itself out in a final, shuddering collapse that sent a hail of sparks and ash scattering over the nearby houses. She could make out the circle of the sun with its halo of smoke. About eight o'clock, she decided.

The radio crackled. Water bombers were incoming. Time to get undercover. The water might be mixed with retardant, depending on where it was coming from.

Kait looked up as she heard the sound of a radial engine. Ag plane. It roared overhead, dropping its load on the frontline of the fire, laying a path that would hopefully slow its movement. She knew it wouldn't put out a fire, but it made a hell of a difference to controlling it.

Ryan hurtled back into the street, the truck lights eerie and weak. He stopped in the gateway, swung out of the cab and sprinted across the front yard. Kaitlyn almost managed a smile as he scooped the last elderly widow up in his arms and strode to the truck. He just about had to unwind her arms from his neck. Another member of the Ryan Fan Club, Kait thought, glimpsing the woman's tearful smile.

He ran over to Kait. 'I'll be back in ten,' he said. 'Pack up. That front's on the move again. The others can handle this now.'

She nodded. Smoke billowed in roiling, dense clouds shot with orange from the area they'd fought so hard to hold.

By the time they made their way back to the site, the fire had jumped their containment line. It looked impossible to stop now.

Five hours later, limbs heavy with fatigue, they handed over to another crew from Cairns. The weather front had moved through and the wind had veered. It had saved them.

The fire was corralled again, away from the housing estate. The only house lost was the one in the section they'd helped to evacuate. Not bad, according to central command, but Kaitlyn saw it differently. It wasn't just smoke making her eyes water.

She handed sports drinks, energy bars and Julia's sandwiches to Stan and Ryan, and sat on the truck's back bumper. Ryan dropped down beside her and she mustered half a smile.

'Bloody hell. That was hard work.' Ryan had ripped his overalls open down to his waist. His T-shirt was soaked. Kaitlyn knew hers was no better. Even filthy, hair flat from his helmet, and stuffing food in his face as though he'd been starved for weeks, he managed to look far too attractive – maybe more so because she'd finally seen him in action. He was the one bright spot in the whole disastrous morning.

Maybe he was still a rookie at fighting wildfires, but in the urban setting he'd come into his own. He had all the hallmarks of a trained police professional. The people they'd evacuated had responded to him. Gone was the playful flirt, replaced by a charming but firm man who cajoled and coerced without raising his voice, who got the job done with a minimum of fuss, who cooperated. He led from behind without appearing to do so. Several times she'd been on the verge of suggesting the other team change their attack when the fire was threatening to overrun them. Both times Ryan had beaten her to it, and his strategy had worked. He was instinctive, but not rash.

He'd climbed so far up in her estimation he should be dizzy with altitude sickness. She knew she was being ridiculous, but it almost brought a tired smile to her face.

Stan spoke with a mouthful of sandwich. 'Where's Speedy and Trudy?'

'They left about an hour ago,' Kait replied.

'Really?' Stan swung around to face her. 'And they didn't come around to us?'

'I think Trudy copped a branch in the face,' Ryan said, full of information. 'Not sure whether it was bad enough to need medical attention.'

'Right. Let's get going, then.' Kaitlyn squinted at her watch. She'd missed the trip with Julia and Dan. They'd be long gone. 'That pump of ours will need a bloody service. It was sucking all sorts of crap out of the river.'

The only sound as they drove back to the Oakey Creek depot was the music on the radio. An easy-listening station playing country.

There was no sign of the others at the depot. Their truck was parked inside, cleaned and ready to go again for next time.

And there would be a next time, until they caught this bastard. The Mareeba firies were sure this one had been deliberately lit. They and the police were investigating. In Kaitlyn's mind the dots were starting to connect. The first responder was worth a second look and the first responder in the Oakey Creek crew was always the same man. Was she being paranoid? Could it be coincidence?

Kaitlyn rolled her shoulders as she climbed down. 'Stan, you go. You'll be needed at the bottle shop soon for the Sunday arvo shift.'

'Yeah,' he growled, 'and I need a wash.'

'Yep, you do.' Kaitlyn patted him on the back. 'We did okay today.' She didn't need to add more.

'Yeah, but it makes me fuckin' sick to the guts that some mongrel is doing this.'

'I know.'

'I keep going over and over in my head who it could be. We must know them. It's gotta be a local. They'll fuckin' lynch him if they catch him. Speedy reckons he's got an idea, but he's not telling.' The look Stan shot at Ryan was speculative.

Kaitlyn scoffed. 'Speedy should share that with the police. It's been going on for two seasons, maybe longer for all we know, but something's caused it to escalate.'

'Yeah.' Stan shuffled his feet. 'You sure you're right with the gear?'

'Go. We'll be fine.'

Ryan waited until Stan was out of earshot. 'Didn't you have somewhere to be as well? With Dan and Julia?'

She shrugged. 'Missed that already. Once we finish cleaning up here I can at least catch up on some sleep. You look like you need some too.'

His smile was devastating, white teeth against soot-stained skin, eyes more green than hazel. 'You offering?'

'Oh, please. Do I look like I'm offering?' She didn't know whether to be amused or annoyed.

'Now you mention it, yes.'

'Ryan, give up.' She thrust the drip torch into his hand. 'Really.'

'I may be many things, but a quitter I'm not,' he countered. He walked away and starting unrolling the hose.

She steered her eyes away from the play of muscles across his back and got down to her own tasks. It would have been easier to clean up with three of them, but Stan had a wife and family to feed, and fighting fires didn't put food on the table. Selling beer to the punters did. Besides, she wanted to check the logbook to see who had arrived at the station first over the last couple of months. A long shot, but worth a look.

Ryan strode past with a hose slung over his shoulder, heading outside. He flashed her a grin. She couldn't stop her imagination heading off on a tangent. She hadn't been good at the dating game at university. She was invariably the one in the group who was matched up with someone else's best friend, a loose 'double date'. More often than not, her serious, shy conversation didn't sparkle and she never saw the guy again.

Something in Ryan disarmed her, brought out a girlish, almost flippant side to her. He made her laugh. He eased the tension in her shoulders even as he made her stomach flutter. When his gaze wandered over her, the flaring heat of desire swamped her.

She shook her head. *Stop right there.* Her life had no room for that complication. She glanced around. Ryan was still outside. The logbook was on the desk inside the office.

In four strides she was beside it, flicking the pages and running her finger down the daily sign-ons. Speedy headed the list more often than not. She heard Ryan heading back inside and closed the cover, picking up the checklist she'd been working through.

Was she being paranoid?

Or did Speedy fit the profile of an arsonist?

Chapter 33

'RIGHT. I'm done.' Ryan stretched his arms back as he walked over to Kait. Today had been a revelation. She'd driven herself past the point of exhaustion. Fighting fires was personal for Kait; he saw that clearly now.

She ticked the final item on the checklist and dropped it onto the desk with a clatter. Twisting her torso to the left then the right, she groaned. 'Me too. I can't find one more thing that needs checking. This truck is in better shape than it was when we started the day.'

'I'm certainly not.' He ached in muscles he'd forgotten he had. His head was pounding from smoke and dehydration. He needed about twelve hours' sleep. But that was all physical and fixable.

His head, his heart? That was more complicated.

In the middle of that burning maelstrom, he'd had an epiphany. He'd followed her to hell and back. They'd worked as a team, together, shoulder to shoulder in the intense heat. And he knew he'd do it all again in a heartbeat. From the look on Stan's face and those of the other crew, they too would follow her into the heart of that fiery hell. A quiet leader, who influenced rather than ordered.

It had tormented him, working so closely alone with her for the last hour. Temptation hovered within an arm's length. He'd used every witty line he knew to distract himself, enjoying the sparring, the cut and thrust of her quick humour. He'd watched her almost cry with laughter and bend double, gasping for air. He'd been mesmerised by the tiny tip of tongue that appeared between her teeth when she concentrated on a manual task. He'd seen the lines fan out from her eyes as she smiled back at him. He'd reached breaking point. No turning back. *Proceed with caution, mate.* For once he wanted to claim something intrinsically good for himself.

Kaitlyn picked up the checklist and slotted it into the wall-holder. 'And I'm not in great shape, either. I'm shattered.' She'd rolled her overalls down to her waist while she worked, and her T-shirt clung to her shoulders and back. The soot had settled like a fine veil over her translucent skin.

He brushed his thumb across her cheek and it left a smudge, a stroke of war paint. 'You don't look too bad from here.'

The smile didn't quite make it to her mouth, but he saw it glimmer in her eyes. Tendrils of curling copper stuck to her temples, the steady beat of her pulse visible under her skin. He'd never seen anything so erotic, so compelling, so utterly desirable. His blood surged. He shifted his hips against the tightening in his groin. It left him lightheaded, but that didn't stop him wanting this woman in a way he couldn't comprehend, a way he'd never experienced before, a way that stole the air from his lungs.

His brain screamed a warning. This was daunting territory, a tall waterfall plunging into raging rapids that would suck a man under, dash him against the jagged rocks and wash him up on the sand, broken and battered. He knew there could be no going back from this moment. The surge of his blood became a roar in his ears and his hand trembled as he ran the full pad of his thumb across her bottom lip.

He saw the glint of white teeth between her parted lips, lips that felt dry beneath his touch. The intensity in her dark eyes reassured him he was not facing this moment alone. It pushed him past the point of return.

'Kait,' he murmured, the edges of his voice husky. 'Do you know what you do to me?'

The shake of her head was imperceptible and her eyes didn't leave his.

'You make me . . . believe . . .' The words stuck in his throat. She made him believe he could find his way back, become a man he would respect again, but he couldn't quite say it. Not yet.

When she didn't answer he leant in and placed his lips on hers, feathered a kiss across them, so light they barely touched. He felt her quiver, smelt smoke and sunscreen and that indefinable scent that was only hers. Her breath was a gentle intake, so small he shouldn't have been able to hear it, but he did.

Afraid to see rejection – or worse, pity – in her eyes, he closed his own just as her hand touched his waist. Her fingers curled around him an instant before her lips moved, parting, letting the tip of her tongue drift across them.

His hunger exploded and he gathered her close, the groan of longing, of want, of pain, vibrating deep inside. Then she was pressed against him, one palm flat on his chest, the other stroking the muscles in his back. She gave more than she took, angling her head, drawing him deeper and easing the doubt in his heart. The heat of her mouth, the slick slide of their lips, electrified his senses. His breathing grew ragged.

The curve of her waist, the soft press of her breast and the warmth of her skin were a comfort he'd craved without knowing it. His fingers tangled in her hair and he freed it from its band, spread it over her shoulders. The smoky smell of burning pines masked the floral tang of her shampoo. He released her lips, chasing the angle of her cheekbones up to her ear, then traced the curve of her jaw down, down to her neck, exposed as she arched her head back for him, her low moan tearing into him.

His hands stroked down her sides, tracing the curve of her breast before sliding to her waist. He tugged at her T-shirt, but the cotton was sodden, clinging to her, and when it finally yielded, it lifted higher than he'd intended, baring not just her stomach but the bottom of a plain, beige bra. He'd always thought lace was his thing, but as he traced the line of underwire he changed his mind. Even Kaitlyn's underwear was subtle, simple in an uncomplicated way.

He cupped her breasts through the silky fabric, their weight and size surprising him. She was all womanly and soft against his angles and edges. It was heaven. She wriggled against him.

'Ryan,' she whispered.

'Hmm?'

'Someone's here.' She drew away from him, straightening her T-shirt, shattering the moment. Instinctively, he tried to shield her, unsure what she'd heard.

'Where, what?' Clearing his head was taking all his effort. 'Where?' he repeated.

'I just heard the outside door.' She angled her head towards the back of the building, then scrubbed her hands down her face. Ryan glanced around in time to see a flash of orange overalls disappear into the tearoom.

'Shit. Speedy,' he whispered. This was bad.

Kaitlyn groaned. 'That's going to ruin the team dynamics.'

She brushed her hair back from her face and straightened up

her shoulders. Ryan didn't miss the slow blink as she regrouped. He needed to fix this now.

'Hit me,' he breathed in her ear.

'Pardon?'

'Hit me, yell at me, then storm off to the truck.'

'No.'

He loomed over her. 'Just do it. I'll explain later. It's important.'

He saw the instant she realised what he meant, but he wasn't expecting the shove to his shoulder. It sent him sprawling across the room and into the bank of lockers with a crash that echoed off the cement floors and walls. She turned on her heel and strode from the room. He heard the door slam behind her. Smart girl.

He swore aloud, rubbing his chin for effect.

'What the hell's going on?' Speedy stood in the doorway with his hands on his hips. Ryan wondered if the older man was going to take a swing at him.

'Nothing. Just tripped over my big feet.'

'Where's Kaitlyn?'

'She went outside. Needed some fresh air.'

'I bet she did.' There was no doubt in Ryan's mind Speedy had witnessed the tail end of that kiss. He was pissed off and spoiling for a fight and Ryan was not about to oblige. Not yet.

'You can lock up. I've got to drive her home. See you round.' He brushed past the other man, half expecting him to lash out, but he didn't.

Ryan rattled the back doorframe as he left and then made a show of wrenching the door of his car open before slamming it once he was inside.

'Just keep your head turned away and ignore me.' The wheels

spun and the four-wheel drive lurched forwards with a harsh clash of gears. A ute was parked on the verge. Its big bank of spotties caught his attention as he turned past it.

'Who belongs to that ute?' he asked.

Without turning her head, Kait replied, 'Speedy.'

'Damn, I thought I'd recognised it.'

He was a fucking idiot. He'd just jeopardised everything for a kiss? How stupid could he be? Speedy didn't need any more reasons to dislike him and he didn't want Speedy offside right now.

He could see the tension in Kait's fists, which were clenched on her knees. This was going to take some sweet-talking.

The road was empty when they rejoined it, and Kaitlyn finally spoke. 'So, what are you really investigating?'

'Come again?'

The look she gave him was long, measuring, before it changed to a slow, triumphant smile. 'Bradley Ryan is a cover identity. I suspect you're with the Feds, perhaps on secondment to some other agency. It's no coincidence you're here. I'm doing extra surveillance in aircraft looking for an arsonist and the countryside is burning, courtesy of some sick bastard. Are you with an arson squad?'

'Not just a pretty face.'

'Deflecting me with charm isn't going to work.'

'I'm really just a burnt-out fireman, if you'll pardon the pun.'

She snorted. 'Did you run my name through your computers?'

He grinned, thankful she at least didn't seem angry with him. 'I prefer to get to know my neighbours the old-fashioned way.'

'Well you should have googled me. You might not have been so quick to cosy up if you had, but that's another matter.'

Two road trains roared past and she waited until they were clear. 'I used to work in a department specialising in confirming people's identities. Part of the AFP.'

He only just managed to keep his interested smile in place. This conversation had taken a turn in the wrong direction.

'I can still do some digging and I can confirm your identity is a cover. I think you are Ryan O'Donnell, a federal policeman from Sydney. Exactly what you're doing here has eluded me so far, but I will work it out if you won't tell me. And you'll just tick me off if you don't share. So?' She gestured with her hand, a beckoning motion. 'How about you tell me the truth so I can decide whether we get to lock lips again or not?'

He couldn't stop his short laugh. She'd taken him completely by surprise. 'So, if I pass your security check we can pick up where we just left off?'

'Something like that.'

'Ryan O'Donnell? Good name. Comes from a nice family, does he?' He was not going to admit anything just yet.

'Actually, I'd have to say no, he doesn't, but then it's not my place to judge. However, having an overachieving father and a social-climbing mother may not be the easiest thing for an only child. Lucky you had Great Uncle Jerry.'

The vehicle kicked as they went round the next corner. His hand had tightened involuntarily on the wheel. He corrected it, searching desperately for a way out of this minefield. He couldn't tell her the truth; too much was at stake, too many rules already broken. She was watching him with those warm brown eyes, waiting for an answer.

'So, Ryan O'Donnell, what's it going to be? The easy way or the hard way?

There was steel in her tone this time. Only one way he could go: half-truths and more lies.

'You're kind of right. I really am Brad Ryan, but there's an arson investigation into the spate of fires. You're part of it, and so am I. This time I'm involved on the grassroots side of things. I'm working with Queensland Fire and Rescue. They wanted an outsider, someone from interstate. A Sydney fireman was perfect for the job. Someone found Jerry's place, otherwise I would have rented a place in town. They thought it would give me space.' He glanced across and met her gaze. 'Not a nosey neighbour.'

She patted his knee. 'Okay, so you can't tell me everything. I can understand that for now. But don't expect me to settle for a watered-down explanation when all this is finished. No excuses then.'

'My boss would be having a coronary if he could hear this conversation.'

'He should have done his homework on your neighbour, then.'

'He did. You must have checked out fine.'

'Oh?' That stopped her in her tracks.

Was there something they'd missed, he wondered? 'Apparently your work history is exemplary.'

'Of course.' She sounded wary. He'd definitely just touched a sensitive issue. Now she attempted to deflect the conversation. 'So, suspects?'

He played along. 'Narrowed it down to one.'

'Someone I know?'

'Unfortunately, yes.'

'And you're not going to tell me?' she asked, sounding like she didn't expect him to.

'Spell it out, you mean? You're the one with the skills, you work it out, if you haven't already. This conversation is bad enough.'

'Actually, it's not a bad thing at all. I don't usually kiss my colleagues, but it's cheered me up no end to know that technically I haven't, because you're not really here. You're not real. It opens up a whole new world of possibilities.' Her touch on his temple was the lightest of caresses. She smoothed his hair back and he almost groaned.

Instead, he swallowed, kept his eyes focused on the road ahead. Was that how she saw him? A casual liaison that wasn't real? Something to amuse her?

The longing slammed into him and it hurt. He didn't want this to be a casual relationship. He wanted to be the person she believed him to be. He didn't want lies between them. But . . .

He couldn't do a damn thing. He was what he was. And he was mightily screwed up. He wished to hell he'd met her in another time and another place. Despite everything today, or perhaps because of it, he wanted to pick up where they'd left off before Speedy showed up. The Ryan who hid under so many layers of lies had a connection with this woman. It scared him. It inspired him. It made him drunk with its possibilities.

He pushed it all away and tried to retreat into his role, but he couldn't. This was too important. 'Don't make me something I'm not.'

'Don't worry, I won't.' Her voice almost sounded sad, but he didn't dare look at her, afraid of what she might see, might recognise. How did she do this to him? Her next words tipped everything on its head.

'So, the suspect. It's Speedy, isn't it?'

Chapter 34

'FUCK it,' Speedy spat, watching the car turn out onto the road. 'Silly bitch. How can she do that to Dan?' He slammed his fist into a locker, the pain sharpening his anger. She should be protecting her son, not inviting a monster into their home. How blind could women be? How fuckin' driven by their own lust that they couldn't see what was happening?

He'd fix it. It would be easy. Brad Ryan would take the fall for the arson attack on Greentrees and fuckin' well die in the blaze. The scum had preyed on a boy for the last time.

Speedy knew how to make it happen.

He'd done it before. Killing the first time is the hardest. It gets easier every time.

He could still remember puking his lunch up as his filthy step-father's blood pooled on the floor of the car. It felt like his guts were going to come right out of his body. He'd had no remorse as he bundled his unconscious mother into the passenger's seat, then steered the car off the road and towards the embankment. Once the momentum took it, he only had to watch the car bounce and roll and ricochet down the hill until it hit the bottom and ignited.

Later, his hands had shaken as he washed, and washed, and washed the blood off them. He was rubbing them together now and had to make a conscious effort to stop.

His body was consumed with old anger. He tried to walk it off, checking the depot's windows and doors, reliving that day in Canberra when he'd killed for the second time. It was still so clear in his mind, so sharply in focus, that he doubted it would ever fade.

Stephen, the almost-retired arson investigator, had worked out who was lighting the fires around Canberra. Too clever by far. The sadness in the old man's lined face when he'd found Speedy at Chris and Kaitlyn's house had almost broken Speedy's resolve. Stephen was there to warn his son-in-law, Chris, that his half-brother was out of jail and looking for him. He'd dared to offer Speedy help. Help, for God's sake!

Speedy hadn't meant to hit him, but Stephen wouldn't listen, wouldn't believe him when Speedy had said this was the only way to stop Chris from repeating the patterns of his father. The old man's eyes had accused him right up until they glazed over. Speedy had cried for that death, bawled like a baby.

Then Chris had showed up. Speedy had no choice. His half-brother wouldn't believe that his own father had been a monster, that their shared mother was complicit by her inaction. He wouldn't listen when Speedy described what he'd endured as a child at the hands of his stepfather and his cosy circle of friends. Speedy had felt nothing as the iron bar bucked in his hands and Chris fell to the floor. The fire he lit consumed his brother, purified through heat and flames. But then he'd had to light another fire to cover his trail, and that one had turned into a monster.

Then Kaitlyn had taken her son, her precious Daniel, and fled. He'd lost them for a while. She'd been clever, changed back to her maiden name, taken her mother and moved a long way away from Canberra. But he'd found them eventually. Now here they all were, and he was losing her, losing Daniel again.

He tried to stop the shaking. He was tired. For five years he'd lived his dream. He'd been inside her house, touched her clothes, her piano. He had some keepsakes. He didn't want to harm her. Not then.

But now?

The anger pushed him to his feet again.

If it was all going to end, then he was going out in a fucking blaze.

McCormack. McCormack and his friggin' demands. That's what had caused all this. His lips thinned into a tight line. After he'd shot at McCormack to scare him, when the fool had surprised him poking around in Jerry's house, he'd tracked him to Yungaburra. The car was still there, with its shattered window and bullet holes. What the fuck was McCormack doing visiting Ryan? Trying to soften him up to buy the land? Man was a friggin' idiot. Ryan was only renting.

Speedy locked the doors to the RFB building, touched the lock for luck one last time. His feet seemed to drag as he walked to his ute. The drive home felt interminable.

In his kitchen he turned the kettle on, put a teabag in the pot. Each movement was deliberate, slow.

Ten minutes later, he was logged into Return of the Drones. Money could buy you anything if you knew where to look. McCormack wouldn't see it coming.

He sat back and sipped his tea, feeling calmer now. One step at a time. Anything could be accomplished one step at time. First McCormack, then Brad Ryan.

Each time you took a man's life it was easier than the last.

Chapter 35

RYAN seemed lost for words. Kaitlyn doubted that happened very often. He hadn't answered her question about Speedy and she doubted he would. But the more she thought about it, the more she was sure she was right. The logs had confirmed that Speedy was invariably the first on the scene. He had the knowledge, the opportunity, but did he have the motivation? Ryan's reaction when Speedy caught them kissing had taken her by surprise. They weren't the actions of a man trying to keep an affair secret; they were those of a man trying to prevent a disaster. Then again, maybe it was wishful thinking to blame Speedy because it meant Chris, dead or alive, wasn't responsible for these fires. Maybe she was being foolish.

Ryan stopped at her front gate, the engine idling, and looked across the car at her. His expression was unfathomable.

'Kaitlyn, I can't tell you. You know I can't. But be very sure we're doing something about it.'

'Right.' So, she was correct about Speedy being a suspect. Ryan hadn't denied it and everything about him, from the darkened look in his hazel eyes to the stillness of his body, told her the truth. 'Don't wait too long to pick him up, then.'

'You get a photograph from that aircraft of yours and we'll have the arsonist detained before you land.'

'We're working on it.' And they were. She'd heard the Dash up in the smoke today when they'd been fighting. Maybe the crew had found something already. Lauren was in command, which gave her some hope.

'Thanks for the ride.' She smiled at him, wishing the day might have had a different ending. The man could kiss. 'See you later.' She pushed open the door and the heat of the late afternoon flooded in.

'Sorry we got sprung.' The words sounded rushed, as though he were a nervous teenager getting the words out before it was too late. The thought amused her. She didn't get the feeling Ryan had ever been nervous around a woman and yet right now he looked unsettled. All because she'd blown his cover and guessed the suspect's name? She supposed that could be unnerving.

'So am I,' she replied with a quick grin. 'Come in, if you like. Julia will have left something to eat. She and Dan are up at Ravenshoe for the afternoon. They'll be home later. She'd love to think someone other than me appreciated her cooking.'

'And you?' he asked, reaching out to wind a long curl of her hair around his finger. 'What do you want?'

The touch of his hand and the gentle backwards tug on her hair made her tingle. The pulse at the base of her throat fluttered. In an instant the tension was back between them, the awareness. She didn't hesitate.

'I'd like that,' she replied, meeting his gaze as she covered his hand with her own. She knew she hadn't imagined the heat of his kisses and the need in his strong hands. Could he really be unsure of her? It didn't seem possible and yet . . .

He pulled his hand away, her hair springing back. 'Right. How about I go home and clean up first?'

'Trust me, after a morning like the one we've had you'll crash out the minute you've had a shower. Might as well eat something here first, then head home. Come on, park by the house.'

For a moment he hesitated, then he released the brake and turned the car down the driveway.

'Over there,' she said. 'By the garden beds.'

The car doors banged and she led the way across to the house, conscious of Ryan's lean body next to hers. The smoke clung to both of them, but she could also smell sweat and aftershave in a compelling mix. Nero was yapping inside the house and shot out the door when she unlocked it, doing rapturous circles of delight.

Ryan followed Kait through to the kitchen, dropped his jacket on a chair and crouched down to mess with Nero. The pup was delighted to have a playmate.

'See?' Kait said. 'I knew she'd have left enough for an army. Lamb korma.'

A large pan sat on the stove. A pot-stand weighted down a note.

Ryan came and stood behind her. 'Kait. About before.'

She turned around to face him, surprised by his tone, then froze. He was about to apologise. Damn the man for being so honourable. She didn't want honourable right now.

She kept her voice light, teasing. 'Before Speedy turned up? Or when I guessed who you were?'

'Before Speedy.' He was frowning.

She shook her head, abruptly turning back to the stove. She didn't want to hear his apologies for something she'd been fantasising about for the last month.

'Forget it,' she said. 'We were both on a high after beating the blaze. I understand what those sorts of pressure can do. I'm just feeding you. No pressure here.'

'That's not what I meant.'

'Oh.' She shook her head, abruptly turning back to the stove and flicking the igniter. The flame flared before she turned it down to a low glow, feeling him step closer. The smell of bushfire and sweat was strong. Her body was taut, waiting. Waiting for him.

His fingers brushed the back of her neck, lifting her hair clear of it. She felt the warmth of his breath before his lips touched her. She had no hope of stopping her low moan of want, any more than she could stop her body arching, her shoulderblades brushing his chest, her bottom pressing against him.

There was no mistaking the hardness there or the intensity in his kisses as he trailed up her neck, his teeth grazing the delicate skin. His hands rested either side of her on the bench and she turned in the circle of his arms, meeting his mouth with her own need.

She'd never shared a kiss like this with anyone. It claimed her, branded her. Emptied her. He kept a small space between them and it tormented her. She wanted his arms around her, wanted to feel his arousal press against her. She needed the touch of his skin on hers, to open her body to his, to match the passion in his eyes. She slid her hands around him, tested the tension in his muscles. He didn't yield. Did he have doubts about this?

'Ryan.'

'Hmm?' His eyes were hooded as he lifted his head before slanting another kiss across her lips.

'Don't start something you're not prepared to finish.'

'I have every intention of finishing this,' he retorted, a smile crinkling his eyes. 'I just don't want to rush you.'

She lifted the bottom of his shirt and shivered as her fingers played across the hot skin of his stomach. It tightened under her touch. Was she having such an effect on him? The power was intoxicating. With a rush of desire she leant back and hauled his shirt up. 'Off, buddy. I need to see you before I die with wanting.'

'You only had to ask,' he replied, pulling the T-shirt over his head and dropping it on the floor, a smouldering look in his eyes.

While he flicked open the fasteners on the waist of his overalls, she could only stare. He was like a battle-scarred tomcat. Her fingertips sought out the marks and scars across his body. A large U-shape scar altered the angle of his left arm, but his muscles were solid under it.

He pushed his overalls past his hips and stepped out of them, dropping them on top of his shirt, then reached for her. The fitted shorts he was wearing did nothing to disguise his body's reaction. With hands that clearly knew their way around a woman's body, he had her T-shirt over her head before she realised what he was doing.

'Wait,' she said, turning the gas off on the stove. 'Not here.' She gathered the clothes from the floor with one hand and grabbed his arm with the other.

'Anywhere is fine by me,' he drawled, managing to drop a kiss on her shoulder.

'Ha. You think I'm going to risk the inquiring gaze of a seven-year-old boy?' she shot back.

'Probably not. Don't need to traumatise the kid for life.'

'And despite your good looks and charm, you could do with a shower.'

'Hmm.' Her heart missed a beat at his next words. 'A hot, wet, soapy woman. Stuff of my dreams.'

Kait couldn't stifle her groan. This was the stuff her own dreams were made of.

She pushed open her bedroom door and he stopped with a quick appreciative whistle. 'Now that's what I call a bed.'

Letting go of him, she closed the door before skirting around the centrepiece of the room with its white cover and vibrant pillows. 'Shower.'

'Where's your sense of adventure?' he said, catching up with her in a couple of quick strides and gathering her close. His skin was hot, soft, silky, and she felt the elastic spring of toned muscles. God, he was gorgeous.

'Hmm?' The sound rumbled in his throat, a deep purr. Maybe he was less tomcat and more pride-lion material, Kaitlyn thought as he nibbled across the swell of her breast, turning her belly to molten heat. Rational thought disappeared.

He fiddled with the back of her bra. 'This has got to go. Can't believe you lock these sexy girls up.' He peeled it off, tantalisingly slowly.

Goosebumps spread across her body as she reacted to his touch and the look in his eyes. No one had ever looked at her with such approval. It was arousing her as much as his touch. Her breasts rose as her back arched with reckless need. Her nipples puckered even tighter as he rolled his palm across them.

'I knew you'd be spectacular, but . . .'

She tried to concentrate on the line of silver in his hair as he bent and took her nipple in his mouth. She gasped at the heat, the blast of desire, the unbearable need, that swamped her. A shower was now the last thing on her mind. Spectacular? Her? She'd borne a child and had the marks to prove it. She had the curves of a mature woman too busy to stay fit. It was all she could do to keep her armpits shaved, and now this dangerously attractive man was calling her spectacular?

Kaitlyn arched her back as he ran his hands over her skin. Trailing fingertips brushed and teased and tested. He released her nipple with one last gentle tug.

'About that shower you reckon I need.'

'Mmm?' She brought herself back to earth. He was steering her towards the en suite.

'You should join me.' His laugh was throaty. She didn't need prompting, bumping the door open with her hip.

The en suite was roomy. Opposite the deep bath and wide shower was a mirrored wall.

'Beautiful,' he said. His eyes locked with hers. She sensed that she was seeing the real Ryan, a man stripped bare. A man with a need to touch something soft, to be himself, give himself, in a world where lies were all he had.

'Beautiful,' he said again as he slid his hands around her and turned them both towards the mirrors. He didn't take his eyes from hers as he cupped her breasts and rolled their rosy peaks again with gentle thumbs. There was no way she could stop her eyelids fluttering closed as one hand slid lower, slowly flicking the press-studs of her pants open.

His fingers dipped inside her pants and she shivered. There was no going back. He wouldn't miss how turned on she was. He had no way of knowing it had been several years since she'd had honest-to-God sex. He had no way of knowing she'd never given herself so willingly to a man. He could never know how much she craved the touch of his hands, his lips, his mouth on her body. She was stunned by the power of her need.

One hand worked her pants down, the other traced a meandering path through the soft curls between her trembling legs. As she leant back against him and her skin ignited with the contact, she knew she was lost. Forcing her eyelids up, she met his gaze in the mirror, aroused by the desire in his eyes. As he hooked the edge of her panties and slid them down, she surrendered to the heat of his hands. Tomorrow would be a different day. Tomorrow she'd worry about the morning after. Tonight he was hers.

A gust of wind showering gum leaves on the roof made her stir in the close circle of his arms. She ached, a delicious, bone-melting ache, from being thoroughly loved. And from laughing. Never had sex been funny for her before, but he'd made her giggle like a teenager, squealing as he found her ticklish spots. The next minute he'd tipped her over the top with possessive eyes and hot kisses in a shuddering climax that had left her weepy and replete.

He changed from a serious, sexy man to a boyish charmer to a 'mortal worshipping on the altar of her body' in the blink of an eye. Just how he managed to make that line sound believable she wasn't sure, but he'd mesmerised her with the tender stroke of his hands and the warmth of his lips as he discovered sensitive places she had no idea existed.

The clock radio provided the only light in the room and she could just make out his features. Relaxed in sleep, he looked boyish, untroubled, unlined. No hint of the darker depths she'd glimpsed earlier. Straight nose, broad jaw, wide, high forehead. They were classical features that the tiny scars gave character to. She touched the silver flash in his hair. Another scar. He hadn't explained the double-edged one on his arm. She hadn't asked.

She hadn't asked how old he was, either. No man in her bed for five years and suddenly she's jumping the sexiest man in the district who had to be early thirties at the most.

But his eyes were old, like a glimpse into a world where there were no happy endings. Even when he smiled, so often the humour didn't quite reach his eyes. The youthful face was a mask he wore. Tonight she'd met the man behind the boy. He was someone she could care about all too easily. Dangerous.

'You need to feed me sometime soon.' He spoke a moment before he pinned her to the bed again, rubbing his cheek across her collarbone. 'And then you'll send me home in my dirty clothes.'

'What? You want more?' She ran her hands up his back and around his neck, anchoring him to her, enjoying his weight while she still could.

'I'm thinking it's time I was going. Dan might not appreciate this.'

She met his serious look as he snagged a curl of her hair and tucked it behind her ear. 'Then you'd be thinking right. Maybe I could hide you here and no one would know?'

'Your own personal sex slave?'

'Something like that.' She smiled up at him.

'Maybe you can visit my place next time.' He planted a long, savouring kiss on her lips and as he rolled away she hugged the 'next time' to herself.

Chapter 36

RYAN stretched his hands against the curl of cramps. In the time it took to drive home from Kaitlyn's house, exhaustion had settled on him like a 40-kilo backpack. His calves ached, his back bowed beneath the weight. Seven solid hours' worth of physical labour after two hours' sleep the previous night.

He took the stairs one at a time, wondering if this was what getting old would feel like. The guilt didn't help. He'd just committed a crime against the laws of undercover operatives. He'd slept with someone who was on the periphery of his case. Undercovers didn't do that. It put innocent people in the firing line. Punishment would be swift if his boss worked it out. But he had a lightness of heart, a lift to his spirits he'd never felt before.

Maybe the shrink, Leila, had understood him better than he realised. For the first time in four years, he wanted out, wanted some normality in his life. Yet the family next door were so far removed from him and his world, the attraction of it perplexed him. How was it that what he'd always considered stifling had become warm and comforting? What he'd always considered interfering had become concerned interest?

And Kaitlyn.

He smiled as he reached into the fridge for a beer. He could see her face in his mind at the moment the passion in her had ignited. The self-contained woman with the serious smile had more tempest hidden inside her than any of the women he'd previously made love to. That list of women was considerable and varied, with some very accomplished lovers, but . . .

He flicked the beer-top into the sink and half drained the bottle. It was her almost-innocence, coupled with the blazing joy on her face as she'd come alive, that had dragged him in completely.

'Amazing,' he said, before turning to his computer.

His personal phone vibrated on the table where he'd left it in the morning. It made him realise he must have left his hello phone in the car. He looked at the number and answered it. Crusoe.

'What's up?' Ryan asked.

'Going to ask you the same thing, mate. Where've you been? Offline?'

'Working. It's fire season, in case you haven't noticed.'

'Leila's worried about you.'

Ryan dismissed that. 'Since when did you take any notice of Leila?'

'She misses you. Wants to arrange dinner for two in Palm Cove.'

'Bit busy for that.'

'We'd appreciate a visit from you in the next couple of weeks. We think we've almost got to the bottom of the garden.'

'Good to hear. Keep digging until you do. I've still got some work to do up here.'

'Think your tree change might be messing with your head, mate. Don't forget Leila's invite. She's very insistent you make the time.'

Ryan grinned despite his exasperation. So they were keeping tabs on him. He wondered how that was being managed. 'Don't sweat the small stuff. I'll be home in time for Christmas and my work will be done. It's closer than you think.'

The noise that came down the phone was half laugh, half snort.

'Get any closer and you'd be joined at the hip, mate. I'll let Leila know so she can set a time.'

The phone went dead in Ryan's hand.

'Smart-arse.' His partner's sense of humour was drier than most. It was the only way to stay sane. He remembered long nights on surveillance jobs, when they'd stayed awake with conversations that would have made the shrink's blond hair curl. He had no intention of meeting Leila up here in North Queensland.

He dropped the beer bottle into the recycling bin with a loud clunk and, despite the exhaustion, opened his laptop. It glowed and sprang to life. He left it downloading files. He needed a shower first if he was to have any chance of clearing his head.

For ten minutes he stood under the falling water, replaying the day in his head. A man couldn't be blamed for dwelling on the last couple of hours and wishing a curvy redhead was sharing the shower with him. It took some effort, but he sent his thoughts back to Derek 'Speedy' Barton and Kaitlyn's startling question. Did she know more about Speedy than she was letting on? She'd worked closely with the man for the last few years.

The rural firies were a hard-working bunch of volunteers who gave generously of their time with no reward and bugger-all thanks. They turned out for fires, for road accidents, for pet rescues and for storm damage. It would devastate them to find out that one in their midst was doing the job not for the honour, but for the sick satisfaction he gained from lighting fires.

Ryan considered what he knew. Speedy had already served time in prison for arson. Ryan was all for rehabilitating people. Sure, you could help a person turn their life around if you gave them literacy. Prisons were full of people whose poor education made their downward spiral tighter, faster and more vicious.

But if you had a person who had a history of lighting fires, a high IQ, and a seemingly normal life before he was imprisoned? Ryan figured the chances of rehab were slim. An arsonist had a compulsion that general society didn't understand and couldn't deal with.

Ryan was confident Speedy had no idea he was under surveillance. He'd done the job long enough to know when he'd been rumbled. More likely the scowl of animosity he saw in the man's face whenever they met was because Speedy considered Ryan incompetent. Although, Ryan had now added hitting on Kaitlyn to his list of transgressions.

Was Speedy's motivation fraud? Was McCormack Mines paying him? Was that why Grant McCormack was still in the area – making sure the job got done?

His best guess was that Speedy had gone rogue and was acting alone. Was Speedy targeting Greentrees because they'd called him off? The team in Sydney didn't seem to be making headway. Not fast enough for Ryan, anyway. They were missing something.

He turned off the shower and, in clean clothes, padded back to his computer, hearing the old house creak around him. He'd got used to the expansion and contraction of the old weatherboard. Sometimes he felt as though the house rumbled in agreement with his thoughts.

He scanned the files that had downloaded. Jackson had done time for torching the house of a known paedophile in a western suburb of Sydney. He'd been given a five-year jail sentence, of which he'd served three and a half. There'd been a good deal of publicity over the trial and a good deal of public support. It was easy to like a guy who'd got one back for the victims. Ryan knew the reality was different. A new crime didn't right the first one. He jotted down the name of Speedy's half-brother, Christopher Jackson, now deceased, who'd refused to give evidence at the trial on his brother's behalf.

In jail, they'd determined Speedy had an above-average IQ, with below-average education. He completed a degree in business management during his sentence. He was the perfect candidate to reinvent himself and take a new identity. His stepfather and mother were both dead, killed in a car accident when he was in his twenties.

The report then went on to mention the half-brother again. Christopher Jackson was another arsonist, but one who had died in his fire. Ryan would have laughed, except that the fires Christopher Jackson had lit cost lives as well as millions of dollars' worth of property damage in Canberra. It made a strong case for genetic criminality in that family.

Idly, Ryan scanned further, until a photograph caught his attention. He stopped with a sharp grunt. The computer flew across the desk, just stopping short of the edge before he dragged it back again, scattering papers.

'Holy fuckin' hell.'

Five years ago, Christopher Jackson had had a wife and young son. The internet connection couldn't keep up with Ryan as he searched for more information. The news articles listing the devastation from the fires that had killed Chris seemed endless. So were the stories detailing how Chris had killed his father-in-law, Stephen Scott, and burnt down his family home. He made Speedy's crimes look insignificant.

Ryan felt a punch to his gut as he read the next story, his heart hammering. For a brief second he buried his head in his hands. The photo of the bereaved wife, her small son in her arms as she walked beside her grieving mother, was stark. The expressions on the faces of the people hectoring the trio as they entered the courthouse were ugly.

Kaitlyn Scott, nee Jackson, was right in the middle of this fiasco. How did all this fit together? Was she somehow complicit in it? Did she know what Speedy was doing?

Only hours before, he'd kissed her lips and run his hands over her body, losing himself in the warmth, the welcome in her arms. The idea that she might be lying to him, might not be who she seemed, swamped him in a rising tide of disappointment and sorrow. Exhaustion finally hit. He toppled into bed.

Had he been played for a sucker after all? he thought, before his brain surrendered to sleep.

Chapter 37

'KAITLYN, love?'

She heard the words but couldn't quite raise herself out of sleep. Every muscle ached. She could have slept for another five hours.

'Ryan's jacket's here and Daniel answered his phone. Kaitlyn, wake up.'

Kait sat up so fast she nearly knocked her mother off her feet. 'What? Tell me that again.'

'Ryan's jacket. It was on the chair. The mobile phone in the pocket rang, so Dan did what we've trained him to do with the home phone. He answered it politely. The man on the other end wasn't so polite.' Julia's mouth was pinched tight and she was wringing her hands.

Kait placed her hands over her mother's. 'It's okay, Mum. It can't be that bad. Tell me what he said.'

'He said he was going to kill us all.'

'Okay, that's bad.' Kaitlyn threw back the bedclothes, struggling to hide the fear revving inside her. 'When did this happen?'

'Just now. I had to wake you. Daniel's crying. He said the man was swearing a lot.'

'Okay, okay. I need to get that phone to Ryan.'

Julia shook her head. 'Is he caught up with something bad?'

'I'm not sure. I think he's undercover, but maybe I'm wrong. Only one way to find out.' She dragged on a pair of trackpants and a T-shirt as she spoke. 'Where is it?'

'On the table.' Julia followed her into the lounge, where Daniel was sitting, looking forlorn.

She dropped a kiss on his head and wrapped a quick hug around him. 'It's okay, baby. It's okay. You did nothing wrong. Nothing. I'll be back.' Then she ran for her car, pocketing the phone and scrunching Ryan's jacket under her arm.

She was doing twenty when she hit the road. The car's back end fishtailed as she floored the accelerator. The phone in her pocket vibrated, then rang. She ignored it. No way was she giving them any more information.

Dust flew in a cloud as she stabbed the brakes and rocked to a stop at the foot of his stairs.

'Ryan? Ryan!'

She heard footsteps. The door opened and a freshly showered Ryan stood in the opening, wearing nothing but a pair of shorts. 'Kaitie, I thought you'd never call,' he said, a glint in his eyes. God, he was gorgeous, but she pushed the thought from her mind, her anger keeping her focused.

'Missing anything?'

He stopped smiling. 'Kait, what's wrong?'

'You left your phone behind. Dan answered it.' She watched him change before her eyes. Fear, anger, panic all flittered across his face. Anger won.

'He did *what*?' He stalked across the veranda and loomed over her.

'You don't want other people to answer your phone, don't leave it lying around.' She tossed it up to him. He caught it, one-handed. 'And the man who rang apparently wants to kill us. I hope he doesn't have an address!' she yelled.

'Fuck. Don't you train your boy to leave other people's things alone?'

She almost spat the words at him as her anger shifted up a gear. 'If that phone is what I think it is, then it should never be away from your side. So don't you dare try to shift the blame to a seven-year-old boy who thought he was doing the right thing.'

The fight went out of Ryan. 'You're right. I didn't realise. My mind was elsewhere. What a cluster fuck.' He sat down on the top step and turned the phone over in his hands.

'Is this the arsonist?'

'No. Another matter.'

'Official?'

'Kait, don't; don't ask what I can't answer.'

'So, it's okay to screw me, but you can't give me a fucking honest answer when my son's just been threatened over the phone?' Her voice was hoarse. She'd let him in. It was her fault there was danger for her family. She'd let her heart rule her head.

'I can't. With your background, you know that.' He didn't react when she glared at him. His jaw was set solid.

'Thanks for your honesty,' she snarled, before spinning on her heel and wrenching the car door open. Seconds later she left him in a cloud of dust and a spray of gravel. She tossed his jacket out the window with a frustrated cry.

'Fuck him!' She refused to give in to the prickle of tears. Feeling sorry for herself had never worked. *Deal with it, girl.*

Julia was waiting by the front door. 'Is Ryan all right?'

Kait almost laughed. Did Julia not realise they could be in danger? Was Ryan all that mattered?

'He's got his phone back. He'll be fine now.'

'Was he angry?'

'*I'm* angry that he left it here.'

'But he must be in trouble.'

'And now we're caught up in it too. For heaven's sake. I slept with the man, I didn't expect threats on our lives to follow on from that.'

Julia's lips pinched tight. Sex before marriage was still a taboo in her books. 'What's done is done. What do we do now? Report this to the police?'

'He *is* the police.'

'Right.' Julia looked uncertain. 'Then we'll be fine?'

'No.' Kait couldn't give her hope. 'Not necessarily. What time is it?'

'Eight o'clock.'

'Dan's missed the bus.'

'He was too upset.'

'Of course he is.' Kait felt like smacking the side of her head. She was distracted, not thinking, off balance. She was even snapping at her mother. And she knew where the real blame lay. She went to find her son.

What the hell had she been thinking? She shouldn't have let herself believe the impossible. Love was not for her.

Dan was sitting under the rose gum, shredding leaves. He didn't look up as Kait dropped onto the grass next to him. Sticks dug into her bottom and thighs. 'I'm sorry you had to hear that, Dan.'

'But what about Ryan? The man said he'd cut him into little pieces.' His eyes still brimmed with tears and a smear of snot coated his top lip.

'*Shh, shh, shh.*' Kait wrapped her arms around him. There was no resistance in him as he leant into her. 'It's just a misunderstanding, Dan. No one's going to hurt Ryan.' *Except me, if I get a chance to kick his shins.* 'Ryan said it was just a mate being silly. Playing tricks on him.'

'Really?' Dan didn't sound convinced. He looked up at Kait's face, searching for the truth. She'd had five years to perfect the art of hiding her emotions. She summoned a grin.

'Yep. He said they were old school friends and Ryan forgot to ring him for his birthday because he was so busy yesterday.' She warmed to her lie. 'So, this was his silly mate's payback. Ryan's very sorry you were scared by it.'

Dan sniffed, his shoulders going back. He sat up straight, only tear stains left on his cheeks now. 'I wasn't scared. I was worried.' His eyes were still red. 'For Ryan. He's my friend. I like Ryan. Nana likes Ryan.' Kait felt the weight of his words settle in her stomach, dragging her lungs down. She made a conscious effort to relax her muscles. The devil was in Dan's unspoken words.

'And Ryan likes you too,' she replied.

'Right.' He swiped his nose across the back of his hand, leaving stray pieces of leaf dust on his face. Kait flicked them off, searching for more comforting words that wouldn't add to the lie.

'And do I still have to go to school?' he asked.

She looked at his hopeful face. 'No. You can stay home. We can do something together. Just you and me.'

'And Ryan?'

She shook her head, her mask in place. 'No, he's a bit busy at the moment.'

'Aww.' The disappointment on her son's face was more than she could bear. When had Ryan become so central to Dan's life? How did it happen so fast?

'Can we visit him later?' Dan asked.

'Maybe,' was the best she could manage, pushing to her feet.

'Let's get some breakfast. I'm starving, how about you?'

'You like Ryan too, don't you?' Dan left a trail of eucalyptus bits behind him as he shuffled along beside Kait. 'Mum?'

'Of course. He's a nice man. Now, what do you say we go into town and buy some croissants for breakfast?'

Dan's eyes were round now. 'Again?'

'Sure, why not?'

'Okay. ' He clattered through the door, the morning back in perspective. 'Nana, Nana! We're having croissants for breakfast.'

If only it were as easy as that, Kait thought.

Chapter 38

SPEEDY circled around the back of the pub, keeping his hat low over his eyes. It had taken two days to get the information he needed. Two long days, where he'd stayed low, gone about business just like normal – driven the bus, gone to the pub – but he'd kept an eye on Ryan and McCormack. Don Adler wasn't answering his phone. He didn't know what the hell that meant, but soon it wouldn't matter anyway. Bothered him a bit that young Daniel hadn't been catching the bus. Wasn't sure how to take that, but hopefully it wouldn't last.

He found the Harleys parked outside. No-brainer. Six of them in a shiny row.

Hard experience in jail had taught him never to approach a bikie from behind. Front on, hands on display and a smile on your face. If they drew first, you were fucked.

With a quick swallow he pushed open the door to the main bar. The change from light to dark momentarily blinded him. The noise directed him, raucous laughter and rough accents. They were grouped near the pool table, beers in raised. He made his way towards them.

'G'day.' He didn't expect a handshake. These weren't the sort of people who abided by normal civilities. 'I'm Derek Barton.' The name felt awkward on his tongue after all this time. 'Carmichael said I'd find you here.'

'Who the fuck's Carmichael?' The largest of the men lumbered to his feet. He must be the gang's enforcer.

'Greg Carmichael. Longbay.'

'Really.' The others stayed seated while the big man came and stood over him.

'Really,' Speedy replied. 'Oh-one to oh-six. C block.'

'So you read the newspapers.'

'No, but I know Carmichael did. Every day.'

'You're the bloke that torched the rock spider's house.' The smallest man spoke up. All eyes turned to him; he must be Weasel Tyson, the leader. 'What do you want?'

'I need some risk eliminated.'

Weasel laughed. 'You got to be fuckin' joking. I'm on bail. You think I'd breach that?'

'They're not.' Speedy nodded his head at the man's companions. 'It's just a beating. Nothing more. Carmichael said you'd be up for it.'

'Carmichael doesn't run my fuckin' life, mate,' Weasel said with a sneer.

'There's money involved.'

'Of course. If there wasn't, we wouldn't be having this conversation at all.'

Speedy ceded the point. 'How much?'

'Where are they?'

'Here. He's staying here somewhere.'

'Talk to Whizzer.' Weasel nodded at the big man, who loomed over Speedy.

'Outside. Walls have ears.' The giant jerked his head towards the door.

It took Speedy twenty minutes to get what he needed. Grant

fuckin' McCormack wouldn't know what hit him.

'You know someone called Ryan O'Donnell?' Whizzer asked as they clasped hands.

'Ryan O'Donnell?'

'Yeah.'

Speedy shook his head. 'Who is he?'

'Friend of ours. Moved up this way from Sydney a month back. We're looking for him.' He tapped the side of his nose.

Speedy considered it. 'Bit over average height, average build, dark brown hair? Driving a four-by-four with New South Wales plates?'

'Could be. Got a serious scar on his left upper arm?'

Speedy nodded. 'Calling himself Bradley Ryan, moved here five, six weeks ago from Sydney. Good-looking rooster with fuckin' attitude. Said he was a fireman.'

'Where's he live?'

'Place called Happy Jack Road.'

'Near here?'

'Twenty minutes on the main highway.'

'Show us.'

'I can't, mate. I've got a bus to drive this afternoon. School kids.' He knew that would resonate.

'Later, then. We'll be here.'

'Right. Before six.'

Speedy barely hid his jubilation. Maybe he wouldn't have to deal with Ryan after all. Two for the price of one. Bikies didn't tolerate rock spiders, either. Knew they were fuckin' filth.

Chapter 39

'BYE, Mum. See you this afternoon.'

Dan slapped a kiss on her cheek and bundled out the car door, slinging his bag over his shoulder, his shirt already untucked at the back.

'See you, Dan. Have a good day.'

The door swung shut and she watched him until he was inside the school gate, enjoying the rare opportunity to see him with his mates. He raised his hand in farewell before joining his group of friends. Around her, other mothers were doing the same. She smiled at a couple she knew. This rhythm of her son's life was new to her; it was Julia who usually went to parties and school functions, did the rounds of the seasonal sports. Many men must live their lives like this, Kait thought, not comfortable with that idea. Tomorrow she would be back at work, slotting into the familiar 'four days on, four days off' roster. Maybe Julia was right and something had to change.

She drove home via the supermarket, checking behind her constantly. If a threat was headed their way she wanted to see it coming.

When she got home Julia was in the kitchen, the benchtop covered in cooling cakes.

'Yungaburra markets this weekend,' she said evenly when Kait frowned. 'You know I always supply cakes for the CWA stall.'

'Right.' Kait chewed her lip. 'Do you think it's a good idea this week?'

'Kait, we have no idea if this threat is real or not. I, for one, am not changing my routine just because your boyfriend has some security issues.'

'He's not my boyfriend,' Kait retorted. 'And I didn't invite him into our home in the first place.'

Julia flushed. 'Yes, but Dan and I didn't end up between the sheets with him, either.' Her raised eyebrow was more eloquent than words.

'This is ridiculous.' Kait was angry, but now was not the time to argue with the one person she knew she could trust. 'I just want to keep us safe. I'm sorry if that annoys you.'

'But you can't, Kait.' Julia's face softened. 'And that's the one thing you've never accepted. You weren't responsible for Stephen's death or Chris's actions, whatever they were. You shouldn't hold onto that responsibility. It's crippling you.'

'It's not. We're here, we've made a new life.'

'Dan and I have, but you're still an island, keeping everyone at arm's length.'

'And look what happens when I let anyone in. They turn out to be trouble as well.'

'Not if he's a policeman. Ryan dropped by when you were out. I said you'd be home soon.'

'I don't want to see him.' Kait knew she sounded petulant, but she didn't need to face any more emotion right now.

Julia shrugged and turned back to her icing bowl. 'That's very mature of you, dear,' she said, her tone neutral.

Kait stalked off to her room and started up her computer. Admitting Julia might have a point was never easy. Several times over the last forty-eight hours Kait had dialled Morgan's number, but each time she held back. She'd deliberately made few close friends when they moved north. There were fewer lies to tell, fewer questions to answer if no one got under her carefully constructed guard. Morgan and Lauren were two exceptions. You couldn't work that closely with people and not confide in them. They knew why Kait had moved north.

What Kaitlyn had never shared was her pain. Not just the pain of the devastating fires or the guilt over her husband's suspected crimes, but the pain of losing her father, the gaping hole his death had left. The troubles of the last few weeks had dredged up that sadness, opened those old wounds. Her heart ached and she had nowhere to turn. All she could do was focus on something she could control.

Whatever it took, she would get to the bottom of the Chris Jackson mystery. The trail had become clearer, but she didn't have a definitive answer yet. Kait worked steadily through her list, hearing the garage door open and close. Julia hadn't said goodbye. She must be ticked off.

The phone rang. Rubbing her tired eyes she peered at the caller-ID. Ryan again. She picked up the receiver and disconnected the call without a word. What good could talking to him do? She slid the volume control down to silent.

Yesterday morning she'd passed on her suspicions about Speedy to her friend in the Federal Police. Bad luck if she trod on Ryan's toes. And she didn't trust the local coppers to do the right thing. Why would they believe her? Speedy was too well liked. The Feds would follow it up.

Kait checked her emails. A reply from Martin. He confirmed that the ute she'd seen at the house in Kairi was registered to Chris

Jackson. No surprises there. But Martin had gone one better and attached a copy of Chris's driver's licence. Pay dirt. Would she recognise the photo? She opened the attachment and almost cried out.

Pressing the palm of her hand against her sternum, she could feel her heart trying to force its way out of her body. It couldn't be. Could it? Dizzy with shock, she clutched at the desk.

Speedy was Chris Jackson? The man she suspected of being the arsonist was pretending to be her ex-husband? How did that happen? What was the connection? She should have realised he lived at Kairi. He'd always said he lived near the lake and she'd never asked where exactly. Now she even knew which house.

Did Ryan already know? Was that why he'd befriended them in the first place? She felt sick. How could he have done that to her? But then, he was an undercover, so why the hell not. Chances were, it had all been deliberate. Was she a suspect or an accomplice?

Her stomach rolled with a wave of nausea. Danger and liars. They followed her wherever she ran.

Her family was in jeopardy again. She stumbled to the bathroom. The water running over her wrists sent a shudder through her, but didn't ease the fierce fire in her body. She sluiced it round her neck, rinsed her mouth, cleaned her teeth. None of it could wash away the nausea of betrayal, the flush of fear.

She straightened and glared at her reflection. Her face was pale and mottled, her eyes red, but determination tightened her jaw. It was her problem and she had to fix it. Maybe she should send Julia and Dan away until she did.

Should she confront Speedy? No. She shook her head, her hair an angry cloud around her face. It might make her feel better, but it would be unwise.

Her pager beeped.

No! Not now. She looked at the message. *RFB training night tomorrow.*

The phone had five missed calls on it when she picked it up to respond to the pager.

'Sorry, but I can't make training tomorrow night,' she told Stan.

'That's okay. You know what you're doing anyway. We're hoping to get some more volunteers. Speedy wants to do a drive with the local services clubs.'

She sucked in a breath. 'Right. Good idea. Look, I've got to run. Can you cross me off the list for the rest of the week, Stan? It's a bit hectic with work right now.'

'Sure. Whatever you need, Kait. You've been busy the last month.'

Amazing. She'd managed to have a conversation concerning Speedy and sound normal. But she sure as hell couldn't cope with him – or Ryan – in person.

But there were other measures she could take. First things first. Get Julia and Dan out of harm's way. Port Douglas. She'd send them there for a week. She found a three-bedroom apartment near the beach and booked it for the following night. Not soon enough, but she knew Julia wouldn't drive there this afternoon.

She sent an email back to Martin and one to her friend in the Feds. Someone needed to take action, even if she couldn't.

The kettle had just boiled when she heard the roller door go up. She'd missed lunch altogether.

Dan spilled into the house. A sleepy Nero wriggled with delight as Dan hugged him.

'Hey, Mum, we're ready for the concert tomorrow night. I'm playing the piano by myself.'

She plastered a smile on her face. 'Really, honey? That's fantastic. When did you find this out?'

Julia came in on the tail end of the conversation. 'We knew yesterday, but we were going to surprise you, weren't we, Dan?'

He looked crestfallen. 'I forgot. Sorry, Nana.'

'No, it's better this way,' Kait assured him. 'That's wonderful. I'm so proud of you.' She wrapped her arms around him, feeling her stomach relax with the feel of her boy, safe in her arms. The most precious thing in her world. She let him go. 'Tea, Mum?'

'Sure. Ryan flagged me down at the end of the road. He thought you were out. Were you asleep?' Julia asked.

'No, busy working.' Kaitlyn kept her back to her mother as she ladled tea leaves into a pot.

'Oh, I see.'

Kait registered the tone, and knew her mother would wait until later to slip something in.

'I thought we could all do with a change and go to Port for a few days. What do you think?'

'Port? Cool, no school. Can Nero come too?'

'Maybe not with us, but he can stay with Morgan or Lauren. He can have a holiday too.'

'Really?' Julia's voice had an edge to it. 'Since when?'

'I found a special on the web. Thought it would be nice for a change. Go swimming.'

'Dan, how about you go and get out of your uniform and bring your homework through. Smoothie?'

'Banana?'

'If you like.'

'Yep. Come on, Nero, come on, boy. Let's go.' He scampered out of the room with the excited dog.

'Kaitlyn, what's going on?'

'I want you and Dan safe, Mum.'

'But Port?'

'I was sending you tomorrow and I'll drive there from work. Looks like it will have to be the day after, once Dan's done his concert.'

'But why?'

Kait straightened her back, then faced her mother. 'I think I know who killed Chris and Dad. He's here. Here in the Tablelands. He's the arsonist.'

'How can that be?'

Kait opened her computer and turned the screen to face her mother.

'Who is he, Mum? You tell me.'

Julia covered her mouth with her hands. 'Oh no. Surely not.'

'Oh yes. It's Speedy, and he's using the name Chris Jackson.'

Julia's eyes filled with tears. 'How could he do that to us?'

Chapter 40

RYAN yanked on the park brake and sat for a moment before he turned off the ignition. It had taken ten frustrating minutes to find a park on the Esplanade. He looked across at the Angsana Resort where the shrink was staying. Typical, only the best for Leila. Palm Cove reminded him of Noosa ten years ago. A little laidback, a little shabby-chic, but in the tropics. The only thing missing was surf. The Great Barrier Reef made darn sure the only waves that slid up the white, coarse sand barely managed to break.

Ryan dragged a deep lungful of salty air in through his nose. Relax, he told himself. Just get the meeting over and done with and head home again. He rolled his shoulders, his hand reflexively rubbing his upper arm. He'd kill for a surf right now. Paddling a board had been crucial in rebuilding his damaged arm and, if he was being honest, critical in getting his sanity back. He missed the power of the waves and the exhilaration of the ride. He missed the solitude of the early-morning break, the water silver in the sunrise. Missed the anonymous camaraderie of a group of surfers hooting their way down the face of a wave in the heat of the day. He missed the quiet times when he was Ryan, just a bloke on a board with no hidden agenda, no cover identity to remember, no hello phone to answer.

He shook his head as he got out of the car, flicking the remote. But his boss and Leila were wrong about his mental condition and he resented being dragged down here for a counselling session. He was pissed off they'd decided he was spending too much time at his neighbour's house and was therefore in danger of unravelling.

As far as he was concerned, he was as stable as he ever had been. Ryan understood what his boss and Leila seemed to ignore: you had to be nuts in the first place to stay undercover so long. It messed with your head in a way you couldn't understand if you hadn't done it. You were cut off from everything that was real.

He'd been crazy when he joined the Federal Police. If he walked away he'd still be crazy. And right now he'd still be crazy about a woman with red hair who was refusing to take his calls or answer her door. Kait had every right to be annoyed. He'd fucked up big-time. Let his guard down and endangered them all and now he had to fix it.

'Ryan? Are you trying to rub that arm off?'

'Leila.' Damn, she'd been watching him and her observations would be added to his file. He smiled as she walked up to him then slipped back into the role he always played with her. Cat to her wary mouse. 'You're looking as gorgeous as ever.' His voice had a husky edge and his eyes were hooded as he ran his gaze over her, knowing full well it would unsettle her. He caught the flash of annoyance and something else in her eyes before she had her professional smile back in place.

'You're late.'

'Sorry.' He was unrepentant and she knew it. He gave her a peace offering. 'There was some sort of hold-up on the Kuranda Range Road. I think they were clearing up from an earlier accident.'

'Right.' She walked ahead of him and he couldn't help but

admire her long legs and swaying hips. She really was too good-looking to be a hardnose shrink. But then he'd just turned into the sexist pig his partner kept accusing him of being.

He stifled a sigh. It probably came from having a mother who had no interest in anything except her next hair appointment, lunch engagement or charity ball. God help her if she ever noticed she had a son. Between her and his career-obsessed father, it was no wonder he was happy pretending to be someone else.

The coffee shop nestled on the corner of Williams Esplanade, next to a gallery and a row of trendy boutiques. Wooden shutters, low couches and brightly coloured cushions gave it an ambience of tropical decadence.

Surprisingly, Leila made for one of the low couches and sat on one end, patting the cushion next to her. Since he'd forced the compromise of a coffee shop rather than a meeting room in the hotel he'd expected her to ensure there was a table between them, to keep some distance. 'Coffee, or do you need food as usual?'

'Coffee and you is enough for me,' he teased, enjoying the pink that flooded her cheeks. She picked up the menu, studying it as if it were a policy document, her trademark double frown line appearing between those arching brows. A month ago, he might have tried to talk his way back to her suite. It would be sure to have a wide, soft bed, just perfect for a lazy day of delicious sex. But for once, the thought didn't pique his interest. Not even a whisper of stirring.

'Don't go there, Ryan. I'll remind you once again we have a professional relationship. I have no intention of sleeping with any of my clients. Ever.' The sweet tone didn't disguise the steel.

'Very happy to prove the exception to the rule, babe. This meeting was your idea, not mine.' He stretched an arm out along the back of the couch, his hand resting mere millimetres from her shoulder.

She snapped the menu closed and smiled at the wild-haired waiter who had appeared with notepad in hand. 'Soy latte for me, thanks, and raisin toast, lots of butter. My friend will have a double-shot flat white.' He hid his smile. Leila must detail everything in his case notes. They'd had one early meeting in a coffee shop when he'd still been physically recovering and refusing to cooperate. He'd told her some shit about strong coffee and raisin toast helping his mental state.

'Actually, I'll have a pot of Earl Grey, thanks.' Ryan winked at the man. 'Not good to become too predictable, is it? Then they take you for granted.'

The man grinned back and left with their orders.

'Tea. Hmm.' Leila leant back, studying him. 'Is that what Brad Ryan drinks?'

'No, that's what Kaitlyn Scott drinks and since you are no doubt here to discuss the charming widow, I thought I might as well have her on the table. Metaphorically speaking, of course.' He raised an eyebrow at her as he unfolded his legs and stretched them towards her.

'She's older than you.'

'Biologically, she's got eleven months on me. In life years, compared to me she's barely out of nappies.'

'I wouldn't say that. Here.' She slid a buff-coloured envelope across the table. 'Everything you should know about Kaitlyn and Daniel Scott before you get in any deeper.'

'Who said this is anything but gratuitous sex?' He didn't touch the envelope.

'I do. You know —' The waiter returning with a brightly

coloured teapot and a coffee interrupted her. Leila smiled at him, her dimple just appearing.

'The toast won't be long,' the waiter said.

'Thank you,' she replied, and he disappeared again.

'I understand you, Ryan. I know you think I don't, that I'm just a new kid out of uni and you're the seasoned professional who's been there, done that, but I understand you. Right now, you're up to your neck in doubts because this woman has got you. She's everything you've never had. And I don't doubt she cares about you. But if you think *you* have baggage, she's got a trainload hidden away and it's tied up in your current case.'

'Really,' he drawled, feigning boredom and ignoring the line of sweat in the middle of his back. He tipped sugar into his cup and topped it up with a dash of milk, pleased his hands weren't shaking. 'And you've come all this way to tell me that?'

'No, I've come all this way to have a holiday with my boyfriend. But because your boss thinks there's a situation developing I agreed to do this meeting as a one-off so they wouldn't have to knock you out and drag you down to Sydney. You should try to remember some of us have regular normal lives.' She didn't need any inflection in her voice.

'You've got a boyfriend? Since when?' He wasn't going to admit her words had hit home.

She shook her head and sipped her coffee. 'Irrelevant. The boss wants a report and he'll get one. You get the benefit of someone neutral pointing out the issues.'

'Really?' Now she had him intrigued. 'You've gone out of your way for me?'

'No, for Crusoe. He's worried about you. If he's worried, then the boss is worried, and I'm worried.'

Her toast arrived, the smell mouth-watering. He picked up a thick slice and slanted a grin at her. 'Like you're going to drink soy and eat butter? Thanks, princess.' It was gone in three large bites.

She hid her smile behind her serviette as she patted her lips. The stern look was back in place. 'You need to read the file. She's been hurt too much before. Don't waltz in and then waltz out of her life. She doesn't deserve it and she sure as hell doesn't need it.'

'You make me sound so heartless and cruel.' He clasped his hands together in mock anguish. She didn't take the bait.

The second slice of toast was even thicker than the first and he licked the butter from his fingers, waiting for her to speak again. The battle of wills went on for several moments while he chewed more slowly. She broke first.

'It's not entirely your fault you have an aversion to commitment. However, it is your choice not to face it. You could use that rather extensive brain of yours and work through your issues. Or —' She held up a dainty finger to silence him as he started to laugh. 'Or you could just admit that you like wallowing in your own self-deception and simply be well mannered enough not to prey on vulnerable women. This is out of character. It's destructive.'

'I don't prey on anyone, Leila. Kaitlyn's a consenting adult who is a long way from the "normal" women I pick up.' He waggled his fingers in the air as inverted commas. 'Besides,' he said dismissively, 'it's been one roll in the hay, all too brief, and a couple of pecks on the cheek. That's hardly preying.'

She hit him with a bland look of disbelief. 'I'm reliably informed you've had dinner there, fought fires with her, toyed with her, played with her kid, loaned her your uncle's diaries and made a great many inquiries about her. If I know you —'

He cut her off. 'Then if you know me, if you really know me, you'd understand that this is different. Maybe I've even listened to you through all those endless quiet sessions. Wouldn't that be a turn-up for the books, hey? Princess Leila just might have been right after all. Who knew you could look like a doll and still be smart enough to analyse people correctly?'

She looked up at him and he thought he caught a hint of anger. He was being rude as usual. Why would she be surprised? She'd heard it all before from him.

'You can go and tell Crusoe I don't need his dirt file to know that this woman is deeply scarred. You can also tell him that for the first time in my life I've met someone who's taken me for who I am, not what I can be or should be.' His words came out in a rush and he couldn't stop them.

'She doesn't look at me and see a project she can spend her life working on. I'm sure she sees me as a father figure for her son, but that's because I choose to be, not because she expects me to be. I have never, ever in my life met someone who gives without asking in return. You have no idea how powerful that is. And since I don't know who the hell I am any more, how can I ask her to trust me, to love me?' Leila suddenly looked out of focus and he realised his eyes were full of tears. What the hell? He stood, rocking the table and spilling her coffee. 'You can't understand that. You can't know.'

He didn't wait for a response and stumbled out into the street and across the road onto the beach.

'Fuck it.' He kicked off his leather scuffs. Where had all that come from? He never lost control. Never. His feet sank into the sand and his strides ate up the beach. Ahead of him, the coast curved around to a headline, palm trees overhanging the beach and pretty umbrellas dotting the sand. He barely noticed.

His phone beeped. He peered at the screen, struggling to read the text message in the bright sunlight. *I always knew you'd make it. You know where to find me. L.*

He exhaled and pushed the phone back into his pocket. Right now, it wasn't him he was worried about. Did Leila think everything he did was a foregone conclusion? What if Kaitlyn told him to move on? He shook his head in disgust. And that brief moment of weakness back there? Shit, he'd almost cried. For the first time in a long time, maybe forever, he'd let someone in and now there was a risk that she'd simply walk away from him. Had his lies done too much damage already?

He sat down on the sand under a wide, spreading tree. The fallen leaves littered the sand around him and he turned one of the large, flat ovals over in his hands.

And if she did walk away from him? If she didn't want to know the real Ryan?

Then there'd be no second chance for him. He wouldn't be attempting it again. If this was love, it hurt like hell and he wasn't going through it twice. It scared him. He almost laughed out loud at that: a soft, motherly woman scaring the big, bad undercover operative. What a fucking riot. But there was no certainty here, no solid footing to help keep his balance. He was no longer in complete control. For so many years he'd made damn sure he was the only one steering his ship.

How the hell had this happened?

His phone vibrated and he pulled it out. Not the hello phone.

'What?'

'You've got problems. Nemesis are in town looking for you. Seems someone's given them extra incentive with some folding stuff.'

'Really?' Ryan got to his feet.

'They're in Atherton. Your mate's involved.'

'Kaitlyn?' Ryan's heart threatened to break out of his ribs.

'No, that would be your sweetheart, you simpleton. Speedy. Speedy Jackson.'

'Speedy's tied up with Nemesis? Of course I can see that connection.' His sarcasm was wasted on Crusoe.

'Just get your arse back up the hill. Leila said the chat went well?'

'Fuck off, Crusoe, and stop being a bleeding heart.'

'Not my heart that's bleeding, bro. '

'Nor mine. So, what does the boss want?'

'Up the hill, but stay out of sight. The boys are being mobilised from Cairns. You'll have more back-up than an army battalion.'

'Great. I'm heading there now. And Crusoe?'

'Yeah, bro?' He knew Ryan hated being called that.

'Get Kaitlyn Scott and her family out of there.'

'Working on it.'

'Just do it.'

Ryan tried Kait's number as he drove. Still no answer. He'd stop by on his way past and break in if he had to. He had to talk to her before it was too late.

If it wasn't already too late.

Chapter 41

GRANT McCormack sipped his coffee and glanced over his newspaper. The wire was itching the centre of his chest. He had a good view of the main street but was relieved the undercover cops had his back. Once the private detective had informed him that Chris Jackson had been meeting with members of the Nemesis OMG, McCormack had organised his own protection. Cooperating with the authorities made dealing with Jackson a whole lot simpler. And safer.

There were currently two policemen watching his back. One, the only other occupant of the cafe in the mid-morning lull, was drinking tea at a table along the back wall and scowling at his computer screen. The other lounged on a bus stop up the street. His scruffy hair and tatty jeans blended right in with the local vagrants. Somewhere in a back street nearby was a van full of men with surveillance equipment, listening to him breathing in, breathing out.

Grant was edgy. It was seven days since Jackson had shot at him, and nothing else had happened. He'd been here for almost ten days, and had barely slept at night. He wanted to be rid of Jackson and his threat to burn down the defunct Greentrees plantation.

The block of land did have potential for gold mining. Grant was sure of that, but he was also damn sure McCormack Mines would not be going forward under his father's way of doing business.

The issue of insurance fraud at Greentrees wasn't going to go away. Now McCormack had shipped Jackson to the police, MCM as the parent company would be prosecuted. He may not have been party to his father's crimes, but once he'd taken the reins he'd been slow to act. He'd done a deal with the Feds and the tax office which meant he should escape jail, but Adler wouldn't. MCM would face massive fines. And that might well be the end of McCormack Mines. The business would be broken up, sold off.

Consequently he'd applied for the mining lease on both blocks bordering the Greentrees land in the name of his own fledgling company. If the government granted them, then he personally would negotiate with the landholders, whoever they may be.

The burble of motorbikes snapped him out of his reverie. Six of them cruised past, turned around the roundabout and crawled back up the other side of the street. The motors shut down one by one as they parked in front of the shops opposite the cafe.

He watched two men remove their helmets and walk towards the pub further up the street. The other four sauntered towards the zebra crossing. Were they coming for him? Still no sign of Jackson. He should have been here by now. He glanced around at the policeman behind him. The slight nod wasn't reassuring. Two against four? It could be bloody ugly and they needed Jackson on tape discussing the fires to make sure the accusations stuck.

The four burly men crossed the road and headed for the cafe's front door. He could see the other policeman up the street, shuffling down the footpath and looking aimless. The one at the rear of the coffee shop pushed a chair aside with his foot, the sound scraping on Grant's nerves, before moving to the front counter.

He half blocked access to the cafe, but was shouldered out the way by the first bikie through the door. A scuffle broke out. They were still arguing when the second policeman barrelled through the door, causing a pile-up.

Grant felt the sweat between his shoulderblades trickling around the tape on his back. Where the hell was Jackson? Was this about to go pear-shaped? Had Jackson been lying about the meeting all along, and had no intention of showing up?

Outside, a big ute with a bank of lights on the roof pulled up. Finally.

The first biker had made it to Grant's table. 'McCormack?'

'Who wants to know?'

'None of your fuckin' business. You're coming outside.'

'No, I'm not.' He stared back into the hard face that leered at him.

'No, you are.' The hand that grabbed him and hauled him to his feet was enormous. It felt like multi-grips had locked around his muscles.

'No. Get off.' He jabbed with his other hand into the giant's solar plexus. It almost broke his fingers and Grant couldn't stop his grunt of pain.

'Hurt something, mate?' the giant laughed at him.

Grant was dragged across the table before he realised what was happening. The coffee cup and sugar bowl smashed on the floor. He grabbed the teaspoon and this time he aimed lower, driving the handle into the man's denim-clad crotch. It worked. The big man dropped to the ground just as Jackson came through the doorway in his RFB uniform. He had to sidestep the heated argument by the front door. Grant figured the cops didn't want to pull guns on the bikies until they had Jackson on tape.

'Friends of yours, Jackson? Come to make sure they did the job right?' Grant asked, putting tables and chairs between him and the still-writhing biker. The waitresses were both cowering behind the counter and he hoped they had enough sense to stay down. He could hear one of them screeching into the phone, no doubt calling the cops. Where the hell was the Feds' back-up?

'Don't know what you mean.'

'The word on the street is you paid these arseholes to rough me up. Your mistake; I hired my own thugs.' He jerked his head at the melee. 'I'm not standing by while you burn this whole district down.'

'You were happy enough when it suited you and your fuckin' father. Don's pretty pissed with you.'

'You and Don Adler can rot in a cell together.'

'No one's going to listen to you, laddie. Your hands have just as much ash on them as your father's. It wasn't my idea to burn the pines. It was his.'

'You were the one doing the burning.'

Jackson laughed. 'No way of proving that.'

The fallen bikie was struggling to his knees, still clutching his groin. In desperation, Grant tried another tack.

'So, tell me how you lit the first one.'

Jackson blinked rapidly. Too late, Grant saw the recognition in his face as Jackson's hand flashed out and grabbed the front of his shirt, twisting the listening device off his skin. Grant swung at him, hoping it was still recording as Jackson went ballistic, screaming into his face.

'You fuckin' set me up, you fuckin' moron!' he yelled. He shoved Grant backwards into the bikie who by now was hauling himself to his feet. They went down together, sending furniture flying. 'I'm not fuckin' going back to jail. You can all fuckin' burn.'

The back-up police finally crashed out of the swinging kitchen door, but Jackson was too fast. He fled, his ute careening down the road and leaving the Feds scrambling for chase vehicles and shouting orders.

'That wasn't in the plan,' one of them muttered. 'Cross, Stoner, get these boys in cuffs. You,' he said to Grant, jerking his head towards the cafe again. 'Inside. Let's get the wire off.'

'What now?' Grant asked him as they moved indoors.

'Better hope we catch him before he does something crazy.'

Chapter 42

FUCKIN' McCormack had set him up, dobbed him in to the police. Speedy couldn't stop his hands from shaking as he hooked into another hairpin bend. He'd gone past angry. He'd filled the drums in the back of his ute with fuel instead of water. Happy Jack Road would soon be a raging, roaring inferno that would destroy McCormack Mines, Grant McCormack and Ryan. And Kaitlyn. She'd let that filthy man into her home. She deserved to lose everything too.

Dan would be all right. Dan would be at school. He'd be safe.

He saw the turn-off coming up and changed down through the gears. It took him a couple of minutes to open the fire trail gate and lock it behind him. No point making it easy for the team who'd be sent out for this one.

It was impossible to keep the smile from his face. Little Miss Snooty Scott was going to find out what it was like to start all over again for the second time. He knew what he'd seen last weekend, on the day of the Mareeba fires. She'd been kissing Ryan; she was no passive innocent. Made him sick. Filthy scum had his hands up her shirt and she'd let him.

The ute's engine blew a stream of black smoke as it laboured up the steep incline, loaded down as it was with fuel. There was enough there to light a couple of decent fire lines. If anyone cared to ask him, he was out doing some back-burning. An official uniform bluffed them every time. The wind was going to send this fire raging up Happy Jack Valley and straight through Kaitlyn Scott's place.

If it got her mother, that was a shame. She was a real lady. But then he'd be Dan's only living relative. He'd keep the boy safe. He cleared the back of his throat, tasting bile and so much more.

For thirty-five years he'd kept his secret close. He'd hated his younger half-brother Chris from the moment he was born. It was Chris's fault that his father had a filthy preference for small boys. Chris's fault that he was the man's son so he was safe, whereas Speedy, just a stepson, was fair game.

It had taken him until his twenties to kill his stepfather and his own mother. She hadn't protected Speedy, hadn't believed him. She had no right to live. It had taken another fifteen years to track down the other scum, one of his stepfather's friends, who'd preyed on young boys too. Speedy was sorry he'd only managed to burn the man's house down. He'd wanted to roast him alive, hear him scream as his hair frizzled and his skin fell from his face, but the man hadn't been home.

That was when Speedy made his mistake and got caught. But in prison they'd treated him like royalty. No one liked kiddie-fiddlers, rock spiders. He'd been a hero for having the balls to do something about it. And he'd fooled them all. He'd done a degree, cleaned up his act, played nicely in the sandpit. All the while he'd kept tabs on his half-brother. Watching, waiting for him to do something wrong. And he had.

He got married and had a child. Speedy knew where that would lead. It was better to kill him that let him do anything to that boy. He'd be just like his father. He had to be.

Another gate loomed ahead and Speedy got out, leaving the

park brake on, still lost in his memories.

His own fuckin' brother hadn't recognised him when he turned up at the house, but the bloody old man had. The arson investigator had been doing his own digging into Chris's family. Speedy hadn't meant to kill the doddery fool, but he had. Chris was more difficult so Speedy had bashed him before dousing him in so much fuel that they were never going to find any significant remains.

From there it had been easy to take his brother's identity. He knew everything about him. Just a straight name change, a bit of sleight of hand, and bingo, Speedy with a prison record was gone. Chris, who to all intents and purposes was a dead man, could reinvent himself.

And he had.

Until now.

He'd seen Ryan grooming the kid. He knew the type: loners, easy to get along with, plausible story, nice to everyone. And that gormless mother had done nothing to stop it. For Christ's sake, she'd probably even fucked Ryan. That made her as bad as Ryan. So they could all die. She was filthy trash as well.

He got to a deep vee in the hill and stopped. A heavy layer of smoke obliterated the sky, from a contained fire burning to the north in tiger country, but he thought he heard the drone of an aircraft engine. Probably one of the water bombers en route from Lake Tinaroo. By the time they saw anything through the cloud this one would be out of control.

The drip torch was on the floor of the ute and he dragged it out, resting it on the ground beside the tray. It was full of fuel already so he didn't need to lift the covers off the tray yet.

'Next stop,' he muttered, touching a match to the spout of the torch. Flame licked and wavered as the breeze caught it. He started to walk up the slope, away from the ute. Had to keep enough clearance to get himself out. He'd walked a hundred metres before he dipped it to the ground, the grass instantly blackening as it ignited. He turned back to the ute and stopped dead. The back end of the tarp was turned back.

'What the fuck?' He quickened his pace. He got to the open door of the ute. The keys were missing from the ignition. A dart of fear lanced into him and he spun around. 'Who's there?'

Chapter 43

THE pall of smoke ahead soared into the air. The wind in the upper layers spread the thick black cloud sideways, making an anvil-top that loomed over the countryside.

'You're sure the engines aren't going to be affected?' Tim asked.

'They'll be fine,' Lauren replied. 'Last time Border Watch was involved in this they had aircraft up for the best part of a week, running continuous surveillance. My mate Brett reckoned it was the worst conditions he'd ever operated in.'

'They were horrendous. And it was my first time in an aircraft this small. I was so airsick,' Kaitlyn said, grateful her voice stayed steady. She was still feeling the stress of leaving Julia and Dan alone while she headed back to work. 'I was also scared witless, wondering if I was going to die before we caught the arsonists.'

'But you did. You caught two or three, didn't you?' One of the federal police was a chatty woman. Kait thought her name was Sarah, but she'd had too much on her mind to concentrate when they'd been introduced.

'We did catch two.' Kaitlyn kept her voice light.

'Still must have been bloody hard,' Matt, the mission observer, chimed in from the station opposite her. She didn't reply, just angled her head at him in a silent thank you.

Lauren got a clearance to descend to the lowest safe altitude. In these conditions they'd need to be at the optimum height for the

FLIR to do its job. Matt had his equipment ready to go. Kaitlyn figured there was no harm in reiterating the procedure one more time for all of them, including the three visitors they had on board. With a federal policewoman, a customs observer, and an expert from Queensland Fire and Rescue, the aircraft was crowded.

'So guys, remember, we're looking for any vehicles, including cars, trucks or motorbikes, in remote locations. We record and photograph any contacts and take their details. Any sign of fire, on the other hand, we call in to the incident controller so they can get fire crews in there as fast as possible.'

'And we're using the sat phone for that, right?' Matt queried.

'Yep, but we can also get them on radio if need be. Remember, if we do find an embryonic fire then our job is to track any vehicles leaving the scene. It's vital that we don't lose contact with the vehicle or any occupants who might try to make a run for it. Our evidence may be the difference between a successful prosecution and these mongrels getting away with it. It was crucial in the Canberra fires.'

'The water bombers are up as well,' Lauren added. 'So, eyes and ears need to be everywhere, guys. They'll be operating low-level with a couple of helicopters filling in from Lake Tinaroo and Koombaloomba Dam. I believe the others will all be crop dusters out of Mareeba. These guys know what they're doing, but we can provide vital information to help pinpoint their resources and minimise the spread.'

'Conditions on the ground are forecast to be pretty crappy,' Tim said.

'Yeah.' Lauren shook her head. 'Swirling winds from the north, temperature in the mid- to high thirties, plus tinder-dry countryside. Perfect recipe for the nutcase who's lighting these things.

Your place is ready, Kaitlyn?'

'As ready as it can be. Kind of wish I was home, but Julia knows what to do. And so far, the pattern with these fires suggests they're mostly being started in remote locations. Our place is pretty close to town.'

'Right.' Tim sounded sceptical and Lauren cut in before Kaitlyn could say any more.

'Kait designed the whole place herself. Her water tanks are underground with generator-driven pumps, so when mains water or the electricity supply gets interrupted Kaitlyn's place is still good to go. If there's ever a cyclone headed our way I know I'm heading up the range. A hot shower and a flushing loo, plus Julia would cook up a storm if the only thing left in the cupboard was a can of baked beans.'

Kaitlyn managed a laugh. 'Lauren's making it sound indestructible and I hope it is, but you never know with wildfires.'

'Do you need to be there to turn the sprinklers on?'

'I can start the generators and then leave the property. That's what Julia will do if I'm away. If I'm home then it's different. I'd stay and defend.'

She steadied herself as the aircraft hit a patch of turbulence and lurched. 'The big thing we've all learnt over time is the danger of ember attacks. If there are leaves in your gutters or gaps in your roof cavity, you can have a decent-sized fire burning on your property before you're even aware of it. If you're home you can stop it taking hold.'

'Wow.' Matt looked up from his screen. 'I always figured you just stood guard with your garden hose and put out anything that came close.'

'If it was that easy we'd never lose anyone.'

Lauren interrupted and headed off any further discussion. 'So, we'll have five hours' endurance once we're there. There's always danger towards the end of the duty that we get seriously fatigued.' She paused as Tim answered a radio call. The other three were conferring in the back and Kait hoped none of them were going to get airsick. Flying in turbulence was tough on first-timers.

Lauren carried on talking. 'Tim and Matt, you know what it was like a few weeks ago, when you were stuck holding over Biboohra. Drink plenty of water and keep stocked up on food. There's no opportunity to relax on this one.'

There was silence from the rest of the team as they went about their tasks. Nothing more they could do now, except keep vigil over the Tablelands and hopefully forestall any serious outbreaks.

Kaitlyn stretched her neck from side to side. This was more confronting that she'd thought it would be. And she'd been lying when she said Julia knew what to do. Dan had a better handle on the equipment than her delicate mother. Kait could rely on Julia to drive Dan to safety in time, but the house might well have to fend for itself. There was nothing she could do – as the acknowledged specialist on fires in the Cairns base, she had no other option but to be here in the aircraft. She also knew exactly what the arsonist looked like.

Her teeth were aching from clamping them together. She knew she needed to relax or in five hours she'd have a screaming headache and the drive home would be hell.

Smoke already tainted the cabin. Matt coughed, clearing his throat.

She patted his shoulder. 'This is just the beginning. The worst part is trying to differentiate a deliberately lit blaze from something that may have been caused by a fire front 20, 30 kilometres away. We'll both have tired eyes by the end of this.'

The closer they got to the fire, the more the aircraft jolted as though they were driving over giant potholes. The intensity of the thermal activity being thrown up by the fire would eventually cause storm cells to form along the smoke trail. That just added more violence to the mix, with lightning strikes potentially setting off new fire fronts. And those storms seldom brought relieving rain for the men and women fighting the fires.

In nearly five hours, their surveillance had taken them from north of Walkamin to south of Ravenshoe. They'd crisscrossed over three fire fronts that were active with crews working to back-burn. Two of those fires were in largely inaccessible areas that could only be contained and allowed to run their course. The fleet of water bombers worked tirelessly below the Dash 8, delivering load after load of water and fire retardant. A revised weather forecast predicted a strong southerly change with isolated thunderstorms. If that continued for a day or two it would hopefully bring welcome rain as the warm moist air from the ocean hit the Great Dividing Range and dumped its precious load.

Kaitlyn glanced out the window again. If her thoughts were starting to drift then so were the rest of the crew's. Thankfully, the next aircraft was due at any moment. They all needed a break.

The sat phone beeped. The incident controller. She pressed the button to answer. The voice on the other end was garbled, and she only heard a few words. They were probably calling from deep in hill country.

'I'm sorry. Can you say all that again?' She paced her words, hoping the speaker would take the hint and slow down.

'Suspected arsonist is headed for the Greentrees block out at Happy Jack Valley. How soon can you relocate?'

'Shit.' Kaitlyn swore before she could stop herself. 'Sorry. Give me a minute.' She put the phone on hold and tapped Matt's shoulder. 'Get the topographical map. What's the straight-line distance and a heading to fly to Happy Jack Valley from here?'

'Ah, hang on.' Matt ran the scan range out on the map and located the valley. 'It's going to be ten, fifteen minutes' flying time and a course of pretty much due north.'

'Lauren, take up a heading of due north. I'll explain in a minute.'

She punched the sat phone button again. 'We'll be there in ten to fifteen minutes. Any more information you can give us?'

'We've had a phone call. Someone claims to have seen the suspect heading out of town in a heavily laden ute. We have no way of knowing whether this is a hoax or real. We're still trying to locate the caller.'

'Okay, okay.' Kaitlyn felt some of the tightness leave her muscles. 'We'll get there. Any description of the ute?'

'If it's the same one registered to the suspect, it's a white Toyota trackback with a bull bar, spotties and a gun rack. Rego is juliet oscar golf, eight five six.'

She knew that registration, knew now without a doubt they were hunting Speedy. 'Okay, copy that. We'll let you know if we find anything.'

Once the call was terminated she passed on the details to the others. Only Lauren would know the significance of the location. She wasn't surprised when she saw Lauren leave the flight deck and walk down the aisle between the long-range fuel tanks. Her friend's hand was heavy on her shoulder, the sympathy clear in her eyes.

'Ring Julia and tell her.' Lauren said, squatting down by Kaitlyn's chair. 'No one will blame you. You can't do your job like this. At least get them out of the way.' She stood up and carried on walking to the tiny galley in the back of the aircraft.

Kaitlyn knew Lauren was right. She would have a hard time staying calm if her family was in the way of a raging fire. For the first time, she regretted her hubris in thinking she could defy fire and all its might. Why had she even bothered trying when she'd lost so much already? What did she think she was proving? That she wasn't scared?

Insane.

Right now she was terrified. She couldn't go through this twice.

Lauren returned with a cup of water. 'Here. Drink. And as the captain of this ship, I'm making the decision for you. If you don't ring them, then I will.'

'Thanks.' Gratefully, she met Lauren's steady gaze.

'You can be damn certain I'll wear any repercussions for making a private phone call from the sat phone. Do it, Kait.'

Kaitlyn's fingers shook as she dialled the number. It rang and rang and rang before it finally diverted to the answering machine. 'Julia. It's me. I need you to take the plastic box with all the vital paperwork and the back-up drives and leave the house. I'm sorry to do this to you, but you have to trust me. I'm . . .' She swallowed to stop her voice cracking. 'I'm going to be home in a couple of hours, but there's been some developments with the hunt for the arsonist. Let's not take any chances with —' The machine beeped at her as it cut off the end of the message.

She dialled again, this time to Julia's mobile. It went straight to voicemail and Kaitlyn left a similar message. Had Julia left early to collect Dan from school? It was only just after lunchtime. Had the police got her out already? Kait should have stuck with her first plan and sent the two of them to Port Douglas yesterday and bugger the damn recital tonight. But she'd been swayed by Dan's excitement, by Julia's excitement. She'd caved in and she shouldn't have. Focus, she warned herself, focus on a plan.

Ryan. Maybe he was home? It was a long shot, but the volunteer fire crews were rotated out of the action to get some sleep. His phone went to voicemail as well and she left a message asking him to check on Julia. Was he ignoring her now? Possibly.

'We're almost there,' Matt said. Kaitlyn realised he'd been watching her frantic efforts in silence. 'We'll stop the bastard, Kaitie. If we get him lighting it, the crews can be on the ground in minutes. Nothing to stop us organising the water bombers ourselves.'

She nodded her thanks, grateful he turned back to his console as she brushed a lone teardrop from her cheek. The memories were trying to overrun her and it took all her concentration to keep them at bay. Her body was hyper-alert, on edge. She wanted to walk but there wasn't room. Her muscles were rigid to the point of straining.

The aircraft had flown back into a thick layer of cloud and smoke. The overlay of the weather radar showed several significant storm cells dead ahead of them. Right on cue, the turbulence hit, buffeting the aircraft and shaking loose items to the floor. Reflexively, she tightened her seatbelt and saw Matt do the same.

'This altitude work for you?' Lauren asked. 'We can go down another thousand feet if you need.'

Kaitlyn did the calculations and shook her head. 'No, this will give us maximum clarity. You agree, Matt?'

'Yep. If he's up to mischief in a 10-mile radius of Happy Jack, we'll find him.'

'Right. We're coming over the top now. Start streaming the video imaging back to base.' On the vision, Kaitlyn could see the familiar grid pattern of plantation pines. On one side was her house, squatting low and angular on the escarpment. On the other side was Ryan's place.

'No specific heat returns anywhere yet.' Matt was glued to his screen.

Kaitlyn took her range wider. 'It looks like they've put up roadblocks at either end of the main road leading into and out of Oakey Creek. They must be taking it very seriously.'

'Yeah?' Lauren sounded surprised. 'Police roadblocks?'

'From what I'm seeing, yes.'

'Then call them back and tell them to get down to your place and make sure Julia's out of there.'

'No time now,' Kaitlyn replied, even though her fingers almost itched with the urge.

'Bullshit,' Lauren swore. 'Tim, your controls. Just keep flying the pattern. Give me the number, Kaitlyn. I'll do it —'

'I've got a heat return,' Matt interrupted. 'An oversized diesel tray-back ute up a forestry trail. We've just passed over it. Turn around on a reciprocal heading.' The aircraft started to bank right as he finished speaking.

'Kaitlyn, the number,' Lauren demanded again.

'As soon as we stop this guy, Lauren. If the police leave a roadblock he might escape. Julia will already have left. Let's just do our job.'

Matt had his range zoomed in to its maximum. 'It's stationary. Definitely not moving. The FLIR's locked on the target. Strange, but I think I'm seeing two bodies as well. Could there be two of these arseholes working together? Kaitlyn, what do you think?'

'It's possible.'

'Okay, steady as we go over the top.' In tense silence, Kaitlyn and Matt tried to make sense of what they were seeing.

'That's a positive identification of the suspect vehicle,' Kaitlyn confirmed. She knew it well.

'Yeah,' Matt agreed, 'but there's no sign of fire yet.'

'Call the incident controller,' Lauren urged. 'They were the ones with the tip-off. Give them the position and they can send the police in to get them.'

'We need proof, otherwise they'll get away with it.'

'How much more bloody proof do they need?' Lauren complained.

'I hate to say it, but these two need to start a fire and we need to see them do it. And get images,' Kaitlyn added.

'No need to hesitate any longer. There's a fourth heat source and I'd say it's like a giant blow-torch. There.' Matt stabbed at the screen. 'It's moving. I've got the guy on the screen. The other one's by the back of the ute.'

'It's him.' Kait knew without a doubt she was seeing the same man she'd tracked in Canberra. His body language, his walk, his arrogance – unmistakable. This time she had a name for him. Speedy. She was shaking now, her voice ragged. 'Fire's started to spread. Keep the equipment tracking the sources you think are people and if that ute starts to move, we follow it.'

'Gotcha.'

Kaitlyn got through to the incident controller as the aircraft circled over the top. She gave them the details as she watched Speedy head back to the ute, torch in hand.

She disconnected and glanced out the window. The police would stop him at the roadblocks. There was no way out.

'We're tightening the turn and coming back over the top.' Lauren spoke from the front.

'Great,' Kaitlyn said, turning back to the FLIR. 'Hey, the ute's on the move. Get a close-up on the camera, Matt.' Kait's back was hurting with the tension. It was clear the man with the drip torch was headed up the hill on foot.

The vision zoomed in on the driver of the vehicle. He was alone in the car. Who was the low-life working with Speedy? Kaitlyn choked back a cry as the face became clear. 'No, it can't be him,' she whispered before slumping back in her seat. 'It can't be!'

Chapter 44

SPEEDY spun around, a snarl on his face, as he yelled, 'Stop playing about! Where are you?'

Ryan stood up and strode around the rear end of the ute. 'I'm here, Speedy. Surprised?' He was battered from rolling around in the back of the ute and furious with himself for being unarmed and so unprepared. He hadn't hesitated when he saw Speedy's vehicle parked at a petrol station. Hiding in the back behind the drums of fuel hadn't been the smartest thing he'd done in a while. Finding himself locked in there by the tight rubber cover had been confronting.

Still, he was here.

Speedy turned with his fists raised, contempt in his eyes. 'You.' He hawked and spat on the ground. 'You're no threat to me.'

'Afraid I am, buddy. I'm a federal policeman. You're under arrest for suspected arson.' Ryan cocked his head at the blaze that was starting to spread. 'Though I guess you could say that was proven, not suspected any more.' He stayed just out of striking distance from the still-live torch.

Speedy laughed at him, hate stamped on his face and in the rigid cord of muscle up his neck.

'You're filthy scum. Don't you dare stand judge and jury on me. I know about you.' He'd gone red in the face as he shouted at Ryan, spit flecking his lips. 'You're a fucking disgusting paedophile.'

Ryan almost choked. 'What the hell are you talking about?'

'I've watched you grooming that poor kid.' Speedy laughed again, a high, manic sound that scraped on Ryan's nerves. 'But you can't stop this now. Arrest me if you want, but by the time you take me in, your house and the bitch's place will be gone.'

'Kait and Dan's house? What the hell has she done to you?'

'I know your type. I know women will do anything for sex. Lie, cheat, turn their backs on their sons. I know!' He was screaming now.

Ryan could only shake his head, edging closer. 'Sorry, buddy. You're wrong. Kaitlyn's done nothing to hurt you. Anyway, the water bomber will be here soon, so her house will be safe.'

There was genuine amusement in Speedy's laugh this time. 'No, mate. I told the guy in charge of the bombers that I was doing some back-burning out this way. By the time they work out what's what it will be too fuckin' late.'

'No, you're wrong.' Ryan felt his jaw lock. It was going to hell. All he could do was wrap this up now and get help. 'You're under arrest, Speedy.'

'You've got to catch me first.' Speedy had his hand in his pocket. As he withdrew it he flung a fistful of change in Ryan's face. One coin clipped the corner of his eye, momentarily blinding him, and Speedy took off up the slope, waving the torch ahead of him. He was literally running through fire as it took hold.

Ryan swore, wiping the drops of blood from his face. 'Get out,' he said to himself. 'There's nothing you can do here.'

He was in the ute and driving within seconds. He judged it would be quicker to go back along the main road than try to battle his way up an unknown forestry trail. Up ahead he could see a patch of sunlight as a break in the cloud appeared. For an instant he was looking at a Dash 8 aircraft banked in a turn, then it was gone again. Maybe they would call it through. It was the best he could hope for right now.

The phone in his pocket beeped and he hauled it out. A message from his boss, asking for a report. He drove one-handed as he hit dial. The measured voice at the end of the phone did nothing to placate him.

Ryan interrupted his boss. 'Get the Scotts out now. Speedy is hell-bent on torching them and the house. He's nuts, gone psycho and he's on foot in the Greentrees block with a drip torch. Get the water bombers in!' He was yelling and didn't care. He'd never been so scared in his life. This was a family that he cared about in a way he couldn't yet comprehend and now they were in the path of a lunatic with liquid fire.

His boss's reply was succinct. For the next 10 kilometres, as Ryan came in and out of phone range, he tried every phone number he could think of to get hold of Kaitlyn or Julia. He left messages, but there was no way of knowing whether they'd get them. If he'd had the school's number he would have tracked Dan down. He pounded the steering wheel. 'Damn it, damn it, damn it.' This couldn't be happening to them. Not again.

He hit the roadblock on the main road doing 80 and almost locked up the wheels slamming to a halt. The young constable wasn't one Ryan recognised and from the look on his face it was clear he was trying to decide whether to draw his weapon or not.

'I'm a Fed, Ryan O'Donnell.' He put his hands up, not wanting to alarm the lad any more. He didn't need anything else to go wrong. 'This vehicle needs to be taken in as evidence. It's the arsonist's vehicle. Where's your partner?'

'We work single out here. Too short-staffed with everyone busy on the fires. It's just me.' He saw the constable's Adam's apple bob as he swallowed. He looked uneasy, admitting to being alone, and Ryan couldn't blame him. Not only did Ryan look like a demented criminal, he was also driving a vehicle on the wanted list.

'Can you call through on your radio for me?' Ryan said urgently. He inclined his head to the patrol car. 'Give the desk sergeant my name. We need to get those water bombers into this block now. And it would be good if forensics could pick this up.' He pointed at the ute. 'I've contaminated it enough.'

'Yes, sir.' The constable barely took his eyes off Ryan as he headed to his vehicle. Ryan followed him over and could see the young man peering through the windscreen at him as he called it through. The conversation was short and terse.

When the constable stood up, he stayed behind the door as if fearing Ryan's reaction. He had reason to.

'Sarge says, can you drive the car in? We don't have enough manpower. He says the bombers have been diverted to a block down near Carrington Road that went up about an hour ago. They should be here sometime in the next hour.'

'Fuck.' Ryan slapped the bonnet of the patrol car. 'That's not good enough. Get back on that radio. This fire is going to roar up there.' He pointed at the slopes behind them that were already starting to trickle smoke ahead of the flames. 'And God knows where Speedy's gone.' The policeman just looked at him and didn't budge.

Ryan was torn. If he left the ute, he had no transport. If he took it then he compromised evidence they'd need for a conviction. It should have been a no-brainer, but this time a woman he loved and her family were in danger.

'I need to get up the hill to Happy Jack Road. Can you call someone to pick me up?'

'No one's allowed up that road. It's got a block on it as well.'

'Yeah, that's for the punters. I'm a cop too and I live up there.'

'Sorry, sir. It won't make any difference. It's a fire risk and they've closed it off.'

'Did they get the family out first?'

He shrugged. 'Dunno. Not everyone wants to go. Miss Scott is pretty vocal about staying and defending. I doubt she'd go anyway.'

'Shit.' Ryan turned away, furiously sifting through options. If Kaitlyn was there she didn't only have fire to worry about. Speedy was headed her way and now that Ryan knew what his motivation was, he doubted Speedy would be dropping by for a cup of tea.

There was only one option and this young cop was not going to be happy.

'Mate, can you give me a hand with some stuff from the tray? We need to put it in the boot of your car. Keep it safe.' He flashed his most reassuring smile and started towards the back of the vehicle. Still looking uncomfortable, the constable ambled along behind him.

Ryan peeled the cover back. 'If we both reach in we should be able to lift the containers out. They're pretty heavy.'

As soon as the younger man was leaning forward and off balance, Ryan hit him at the base of his neck, catching him as he fell. 'Sorry, lad. I'll buy you a beer.' He checked his pulse. It was steady. The lad was already groaning. Ryan dropped the keys to the ute on the ground in front of him.

'Promise to return your gun too, buddy,' he murmured,

unclipping the holster and hefting the weapon in his hand. Handy piece of gear, but a Glock 22 was not his choice of gun. He checked the ammunition clip, then sprinted to the patrol car.

The wheels squealed as he hit the accelerator. The trail of destruction and paperwork he was leaving in his wake was going to mean nothing if he couldn't keep Kaitlyn, Dan and Julia safe.

Chapter 45

'THE other aircraft's inbound and they've got the vision on him. They'll stay with him.' Lauren said. 'We're cleared to track direct to Cairns. Do you know anyone at Mareeba Airport?'

'Why? We can't land there. We're not permitted off task.' Kaitlyn's protest was half-hearted. She was still in shock at seeing Ryan driving the ute.

'The hell we can't.' Lauren shook her head. 'They can't sack all of us, can they? So, does anyone know someone in Mareeba?'

'Gordo does stuff with the Warbirds.' Kaitlyn hesitated, wanting to believe there was a chance she'd get to her family in time. 'If he's there, he has an old four-wheel drive he might loan me.'

'Then ring him. I'll let Brisbane Centre know we're going to be asking for clearance for Cairns via Mareeba. It'll add a couple of minutes to the flight time.'

Kaitlyn hit dial on the sat phone again and sagged with relief in her seat when Gordo answered. She could see him sitting in his cramped office, poring over an aging aircraft manual. In typical Gordo fashion he didn't ask any questions. The car was there and she could borrow it. Before she'd even thanked him and hung up she could feel the Dash was on a steep descent.

'Strap in,' Lauren said. 'Five minutes to touch down. I'll shut the left engine down, throw you out and we'll be airborne again before the trackers even notice. No job is worth the lives of your family.'

'Thanks, Lauren. I appreciate what you're doing.' Kait's throat was tight and the tears she held so close were threatening to spill over. Kindness did that to her.

'Any time.'

Kaitlyn hugged her arms around her body. Her stomach was churning. Could she have misread Ryan so badly? Was he working with Speedy and not with the AFP at all? He'd never admitted to being an undercover cop. Did she so desperately want to believe in him that she'd turned him into something he wasn't?

The aircraft vibrated as the undercarriage came down and she braced against the pitch change as the flaps extended. Out the window she could see the flat, red-brown earth around Mareeba Airport.

Lauren had the aircraft stopped outside the largest hangar minutes later. 'Good luck,' she said, turning around as Matt went with Kait to open the air-stair door. 'Go get 'em. Call if you need me. I'll handle Tony.'

As Kait ran across the tarmac and into Gordo's office, the Dash had already pirouetted and was roaring down the runway. If anyone could talk their way out of this, Lauren could.

Gordo greeted her with the keys in his hand. 'Here you go, girl. It's half full. Do you need it long?'

'Can I let you know? It's a family emergency.'

'Not Julia, is it?'

'Not exactly. The fire's headed for us.'

'Oh, shit. Whenever, then.' Gordo waved her protest away. 'Go. You know which one it is?'

'The white Nissan.'

'That's it. Get outta here.'

The big diesel under the bonnet seemed to shudder as she floored it up the Walkamin jump-up. The poor old thing was used to plodding everywhere at 80. Once she pushed it over 110 the wicked vibration in the steering wheel stopped, although the directional control was pretty loose. She was gambling that none of the speed camera guys would be out and about. The fires would be draining all available resources.

She checked her phone again. Still no signal. She couldn't ring anyone, not even the police. All she could do was hope they'd already apprehended Brad Ryan and Speedy. The vicious headache tightened its grip and she ran her hand around the back of her neck, trying to relieve some of the tension. It didn't work.

In the flat country leading up to Tolga and the turning to Oakey Creek she had a clear view to the south. Columns of smoke towered above the landscape. The sky ahead was a boiling black mass with flashes of red. Hell on earth. The visibility overhead was lousy, but she could still pick out storm cells mushrooming high above the Tablelands.

In the rear-vision mirror she could see clear blue summer sky with not a care in the world. Somehow the contrast felt like the U-turn her life had just taken. And she hadn't seen it coming.

A low-flying crop duster growled past, probably headed for Mareeba to refuel. Another line of cars towing caravans loomed ahead. She hit the accelerator, winding the old car up. In the distance she could see a semitrailer heading towards her, but she figured she should make it if she overtook.

Pulling out, she realised there weren't any gaps between the three car-and-van combinations. She willed the clunky vehicle to go faster, feeling herself physically pressing into the seat as it rumbled up the road. One of the cars tooted her as she shot past. The semi flashed his lights, veering towards the hard shoulder, and she darted in front of the lead vehicle with the sound of horns blaring in her ears. Her heart felt like it was going to crack open her chest.

Until she knew her son and mother were safe, nothing was going to stop her. She had to assume they were at the house and she needed to reach them. If they weren't there then Julia had already driven to safety and that would be a blessing.

She had a mental picture scorched into her brain of where the roadblocks had been set up. Driving into Happy Jack Road wasn't possible, but a firebreak cut through the plantation at the midway point. Provided the fire wasn't spreading too quickly it was her only way in. The track came out on the escarpment halfway between her place and Ryan's. She felt her lips compress at the thought of him.

How could he have deceived her? The proof was there in the photographs, wasn't it? He was driving Speedy's ute and leaving the scene of a newly lit fire. Where was he headed now? To pick Speedy up at the top of the trail? Did they then plan to escape in Ryan's car? The pain in her temples from the stress was nothing compared to the pain in her heart. She'd let this man into their lives and now he and his actions were threatening everything she held dear.

She hit the turn-off just past Tolga and headed up into the hills. Gordo's car was going to be put to very good use. She just hoped its four-wheel drive mechanism was actually working.

It occurred to her that she had no idea if it had free-wheeling hubs or not. Knowing Gordo, it would have. She swerved onto the hard shoulder, slamming to a halt in a shower of dirt and hopped out. Yep, she was right. It took a moment to lock them in place and she grimaced when she noticed an oil stain discolouring the left-hand one. *Please, please let it be working*. The terrain up the track was going to be challenging. The last thing she needed was to get caught in a fire.

Climbing back into the big car she realised the radio was crackling with static. She hit the wrong button trying to turn it off and picked up the local ABC station. The news was on, which meant a weather report would follow. She turned up the volume and floored the accelerator again.

Just before she got to the start of the trail, the calm voice of the announcer promised a cool southerly change sometime this afternoon.

'Oh God,' she prayed aloud. 'Please let it come in time.' A southerly would push the fires back over the land already ravaged. Sure, as the initial change hit there'd be danger, but with preparation it would ultimately help the firefighters get on top of the situation.

For her house it would mean a reprieve, but until that change arrived she was going to do everything to make sure her family were safe.

Everything.

Chapter 46

HIS eyes streamed and his lungs laboured, but Speedy didn't stop. He pulled the neck of his T-shirt higher to cover his nose. The muscles in his legs quivered and the soles of his feet sported grape-sized blisters.

The terrain was impossibly steep. He'd left the pine forests behind twenty minutes ago. Between the tall native eucalypts the grass grew sharp and spindly, slashing at his legs and catching his overalls.

The ground rustled with escaping animals. Everything was trying to move to higher ground, away from the fire. He'd discarded the drip torch when it ran out of fuel, but it had done the job. Behind him, the hillside was an inferno and he needed to keep moving if he were to stay ahead of it. So far it had grown in intensity rather than spread rapidly. But a wind shift or a change in the fuel load could alter all that. Ahead, through the trees, he could see the crown of the rose gum that stood in the Scotts' yard. Not far now.

A sharp crack behind him made Speedy spin on his heels, the sudden change in direction sending him crashing to the ground. Several hundred metres below him, on the line where the plantation met the old-growth forest, a gum already dead before the fire had succumbed to the heat. The ancient giant toppled down the slope, crashing through the pines below, splintering wood and showering sparks as it fell in a gathering rush. Embers rained down around him, borne by the wind that was racing ahead of the fire.

He slapped at several smouldering patches on his clothes and pulled himself to his feet, pushing on up the slope. None of this was in his plan. By now he should have been attending the fire out at Carrington Road, well away from his latest masterpiece. He'd done everything right until that scum had followed him.

As he carried on forcing his way up the hill, he tried to make sense of Ryan's actions. If he was a Fed it might explain the lily-white record, sanitised by his masters, but that didn't excuse what Speedy had seen with the boy. Being a Fed didn't make him pure as the driven snow. Anyone could be a paedophile. His stepfather had been a bank manager, for Christ's sake. And he'd gone to confession and church on the odd occasion.

Yet Ryan's claims probably did mean the cops had finally caught up with Speedy. He was never going back inside again. Sure, he'd learnt how to do things the right way in there, shut up and survive, but he wasn't doing it again. He'd die before he let that happen.

A stupid business degree in his mid-forties wasn't useful when he had nothing else to back it up. What a friggin' joke.

He stopped for a moment to get his bearings. Another 25 metres and he'd be on flat land. It spurred him on through the stitch in his side and the pain in his feet. Once he finally pushed through the last stand of trees and onto the Scotts' property, the following wind buffeted him. At this height it was roaring. Glowing spot fires danced and flared on the short grass, leaving charcoal patches as they failed to take hold. The giant gum tossed in the frenzy, showering leaves and bark around it, but even those failed to do more than smoulder when they hit the ground.

Ahead of him, the house looked deserted. It took a moment to work out what was different about it. The house was locked up tight, with metal roller blinds covering the windows. He walked towards it, shaking his head. If Julia was home, she knew him so it would be an easy thing to talk his way inside.

The ground underfoot was wet. 'Clever. She thinks she's clever,' he murmured, his mouth turning down as his eyes darted around the property, looking for movement. He faltered when he saw the fine mist being sprayed along the roofline. The heat from the fire was evaporating much of it, but it was like a fine-mesh protection shrouding the whole building. He grunted in disbelief. She really thought she had it all figured out.

That meant she was inside. If he cut the power to the property then that would stop her pump. Was she smart enough to have her power box enclosed?

He jogged around to the right of the house. Nothing on that side, so he kept going along the roadside and to the left. Bingo. The protective metal box was bigger than your average meter box, but it wasn't locked. It opened easily and he scanned the switches.

'Shit. It can't be.' The power was already off. None of the dials were running. By now the roar of the fire was getting closer and he tried to block it out. Did she have a generator somewhere?

'Hello?' A female voice came from the front of the building and he slammed the cover closed. 'Hello?' the woman repeated. 'Do you need some help?' A muscular, compact dog shot around the corner and then slowed to a stiff-legged walk. 'Nero. Nero, come back.'

Speedy knew he'd need to keep his story straight. 'Nero, hey. Good dog.' He waggled his fingers at it, but only got bared teeth in return. He gave it a wide berth.

Julia was peering out of the half-closed doorway.

'Sorry, ma'am. I'm Speedy from the Rural Fire Brigade. I'm Dan's bus driver too. Didn't realise anyone was still here. We've evacuated the area.'

She was nodding as he spoke. 'Yes, I know who you are.' The door closed all but a crack. 'We're staying put.'

'It's a nasty fire front coming up the hill. I'd strongly suggest you leave while you still have time.'

'No, we're fine.'

'We?'

She nodded. 'Kaitlyn will be here soon.'

Speedy shook his head, his throat constricting. Was Dan home, not safe at school? 'No, ma'am, they won't be letting anyone else through. The roads are blocked off. You need to come with me.'

Daniel pushed through the narrow opening at his grandmother's side. His bright red hair was the only colour relief against the thick black clothes they were both wearing. Their faces were white, the tension in them obvious.

'We'll be fine,' Dan said as Nero shot between his legs and stopped beside him, ears pricked, hackles raised.

'Hey, Dan.' He had to get the lad away to safety. He tried again. 'It would be better not to stay, ma'am.'

'No, leave us alone. We don't need your help.' Her shoulders squared off and even Dan stood taller. Her tone was positively regal and it scraped like fingers on a chalkboard over his nerves. Who did the fuckin' cow think she was? He was risking his life telling her to get out and she knew better?

'In fact, we're calling the police.' Julia's voice rose. 'I know you're an imposter, and so does Kaitlyn. You killed my husband, Kaitlyn's husband. You're a murderer!' Suddenly she was screaming accusations at him as she tried to drag her grandson and the dog inside.

Speedy started towards them, but the stupid mongrel darted in and grabbed his ankle. The overalls protected him, but Speedy kicked out, swinging the dog through the air. Its teeth let go at the top of the arc and the dog flew up against the side of the house. It hit with a thud and a yelp then gathered itself and leapt at him again.

'No, no, Nero!' Julia screamed.

Before he could protect himself completely the dog had latched onto his thigh. He reacted the only way he knew how and punched it in the head. It dropped and lay still, but then a whirling dervish of flailing arms and legs fell on him. Daniel's kicks landed solidly on his shins. Little bastard was a fighter, he'd give him that, Speedy thought with a glimmer of admiration as he grabbed Daniel's thin arms and hauled him off the ground. His shins had endured so much on the journey to the house that they were almost impervious to pain. The kid could kick as much as he wanted.

'Put me down!'

'If you stop kicking me, you little shit,' he managed to grunt.

Julia was trying to get to Daniel, but was in danger of being kicked herself. She was shrieking at Speedy to put the boy down. He kept them positioned like that right up until he tripped over the dog and went sprawling. Daniel was on him again, his tight fists peppering Speedy's arms and stomach.

'Enough!' Speedy roared, backhanding the kid across the face and sending him flying. The lad landed awkwardly and looked winded.

'Fuckin' enough!' He hadn't counted on the old lady having any fight in her, so when she grabbed the shovel he stared in disbelief. A friggin' seven-year-old boy, a half-grown dog, and an elderly woman thought they could best him?

'Look, lady, I'm going. Okay?' He got to his feet, keeping clear of the dog this time.

'Oh no, you're not.' She nodded at the embroidered name badge on his overalls. 'You're not Speedy. You're not Chris Jackson, either. I know who you are and I know what you did.'

'Bullshit, lady. You're nuts.'

'No.' She shook her head, the fight going out of her. 'No. What you did to my family, what you took from us . . .' Tears filled her eyes. 'What do you want from us now? How much more can you do? Why did you follow us here?'

A series of sharp cracks followed by a crashing sound came from the other side of the house. The fire had arrived. He enjoyed seeing the spark of fear in Julia's eyes as he grinned at her, licking his lips. The shovel trembled in her hands and a super-heated gust of wind hit, sending a shower of sparks billowing past them.

The kid sat up, clutching his arm, but Speedy could see he wasn't beaten yet.

'Daniel, go and phone the police. Tell them we need them here. Go. Now,' she ordered.

Speedy couldn't let that happen, but when he moved to block the boy the old lady charged at him.

'Don't you touch him again!' she yelled, swinging the shovel at his legs.

She was easy pickings and he grabbed the handle with his right hand, twisting it. Gamely she hung on, even though there was no weight to her at all.

He'd had enough. Time to leave. He took two steps forwards and shoved her back through the doorway. Without stopping to look at the result he started loping towards the driveway.

'Stop, or I'll shoot!' The yell took him by surprise but he didn't slow down, even as he felt the bullet whistle past at the instant he heard the crack of a small-calibre gun.

Chapter 47

THE fire front had already moved through the dirt trail, leaving charred and broken trees smouldering in its wake. The undergrowth had been incinerated; the earth was blackened and steaming. Kaitlyn pushed on, knowing that while she skirted to the north and the west the fire was still headed straight for her house. She feared for the tyres on the vehicle. It would only take a sharp piece of burning debris and she'd be running on rims. In these conditions that would be impossible.

She changed down a gear as the incline increased. She only had one more gear to go and the heavy diesel was making hard work of it. With an impatient flick she turned the air conditioner off. She needed all the power available. The top of the trail was the steepest. By her reckoning it could only be a kilometre or so further on.

Cresting this section, she could see the hill stretching up again after another short downhill. This was it. She gave it everything. The old car lurched and bounced as it hurtled down the hill, almost shaking her hands from the wheel. She hit the rut at the bottom and got airborne before the wheels bit in again. Then she started the long slog up. Beside her, fresh flames licked the undergrowth as the fire reached the top of the escarpment. It would be on her boundary by now.

'Please, please, let Julia and Dan be somewhere else,' she pleaded. 'It's only a bloody house and my stupid pride. Please, God.'

With only a couple of hundred metres to go, the back of the car started to slip. The wheels spun as she hit soft dirt and the car almost broached. Stopping wasn't an option because she'd never get it going again on this incline. She doubled the clutch, revving the engine to keep the torque high. It worked for another 50 metres and then the engine started to shudder as it simply ran out of power.

'No,' she cried, her frustration overflowing . 'No. You can do this.'

It stalled. She realised the car was sliding backwards, and all she could do now was swing the wheel, minus the power steering, so the back end ran into the low banking. The car stopped sideways across the track. It wasn't going anywhere.

'Right. Leg it, woman.' Kaitlyn dropped open the glove box, looking for anything useful. She was shocked to find a small handgun. For an instant she hesitated. It was six years since she'd fired anything, and that had been a yearly weapons retraining she'd barely passed. 'I can do it.'

A clip of ammunition was hidden further back and she weighed the bullets in her palm as she gingerly unlatched the door. She was now on the downhill side of the car and the door flung open, rocking the vehicle on its precarious perch. She pushed the gun and bullets into the back pockets of her flight trousers.

It was a long jump down on that side of the car and she felt her knee twinge as she hit the ground. Her eyes watered and her throat closed with the choking smoke. She reached in and snagged an old shirt from the floor of the back seat. It smelt only marginally better than the smoke-filled air, but she wrapped it around her head. The Border Watch uniform was fire retardant, so she just needed to protect her nose and mouth.

Edging past the front of the car, she headed up the hill. The heat sapped her energy. Her last drink of water had been in the aircraft and right now she'd kill for a litre or three.

By the time she reached the top road, her legs were shaking and she had a painful stitch in her side. Ignoring her complaining body, she pushed on. Ahead, she could see the smoke swirling and eddying. Up this high the wind was strong, and the rain of embers and ash was continuous. She could smell her hair singeing.

Staggering along, she risked a glance behind her. Jerry's place was unscathed for now. Her lips compressed. Ryan knew what he was doing. If the wind shifted then it would be in jeopardy again, but for now it was safe.

Bastard, she thought, her anger rearing again. Ryan had helped light the bloody thing and it was her house that was in danger. It gave her renewed strength. He'd only been playing some kind of sick, sick game.

Well, no more. They had him and Speedy, one way or another, and she was not going to let them destroy anything of hers. She would stop them.

An explosion down the slope was deafening, even over the thundering rumble of the fire. She baulked and almost rolled her ankle as she hit soft dirt. She swore to herself, lurching back to the middle of the track. *Get a grip, Kaitlyn.*

She figured she only had half a kilometre to go and it was a slight downhill run from here. Her legs were currently in danger of over-running themselves and her arms were flailing to keep her balance. Swimming was her choice of exercise, not running, and she hardly got any time to do even that.

The familiar shape of her house was now visible through the trees and she squinted, sure she could see the fine mist of the sprinklers. One part of her was ecstatic that the system was on and working. The other half was crying in pain because it meant Julia and Dan were most likely inside. She did not want them here while she battled a bushfire.

Her pace picked up as she called on reserves she didn't know she had. She drew level with her boundary fence and the front of her house came into view. She slid to a stop, gasping for breath. Julia was in the doorway, brandishing a shovel, Nero was motionless on the ground, and a man was looming over Dan.

Speedy.

A tree exploded down the slope and she saw the noise distract them momentarily. She was desperate to get to them but knew she'd only get one chance with the gun. Fighting off the urge to run screaming at him she dropped to the ground, and crawled along the fence line, grateful that the grass was fairly short. The parade of animals fleeing across the road ignored her.

She got to the gateway and scrabbled to undo the flap on her pockets. She heard her mother's voice, shrill with panic, just as she rammed the ammunition into the gun, thumbing off what she thought was the safety catch.

Testing the pressure on the trigger, she decided it felt spongy, ready to shoot. She'd just have to risk it.

'Don't you touch him again!' Julia screamed. Her words brought Kaitlyn to a half crouch, the gun steady in her hand.

She almost squeezed the trigger when Speedy pushed Julia through the doorway, but the fear of hitting her son stayed her finger. The moment Speedy ran towards her, she came to her feet.

'Stop or I'll shoot!'

He didn't even hesitate, just kept running straight at her. She pulled the trigger but was unprepared for the recoil and the shot went high. Next one she aimed ahead and low. It hit mid-thigh and he dropped.

In an instant she was on him, kicking with all her might, oblivious to his cries. She knew she was out of control, but opening the tap on five years of pain had released a deluge. This man had killed her father and her husband, and she had no idea why.

'Mummy, Mummy.' Daniel's sobs got through to her. 'Nana.'

She whirled towards her son. 'Baby? Are you all right?'

'Yes, but Nana and Nero . . .' Tears were streaming down his face. Her little soldier who never cried, who hadn't called her Mummy in three years, was sobbing his heart out while she kicked the shit out of a man she'd just shot. 'Julia?' She still had the gun trained on the groaning man and risked a glance at her mother. Julia was struggling to sit up, using the doorframe.

'I'm okay,' her mother croaked, making it to a sitting position. 'I'm okay.'

Kaitlyn could only take her at her word. 'Honey,' she said to Daniel, 'I need you to get Nero's lead.' It was all she could think of.

'But, but . . . Nero can't walk. I think he's dead.' His voice broke on the last word.

'I know, Dan, I know, but we need to tie Speedy up. Then I can fix Nana and Nero. Can you get it for me? Quickly now.'

He turned and bolted inside.

Speedy lay still, but she was sure he was pretending. This wasn't going to be easy.

'Roll onto your front, arsehole, or I'll shoot your other leg.'

He didn't move. She was convinced he was bluffing. Steadying the gun, she fired a shot into the ground next to him and this time he jerked. She didn't have time for his bullshit.

'I'm not messing. Next one's for you. Now, move!'

This time he rolled over and she could see the exit wound in his overalls. It looked relatively small and the blood was a trickle rather than a flow. It wasn't going to kill him. Good. She wanted him to rot in jail for the rest of his miserable fucking life.

Dan returned, dangling the lead. She squeezed his hand hard as she took it from him. Courage, she wanted to say, courage, but she didn't.

'Hands behind your back,' she snapped at Speedy.

He obeyed her this time, but she stayed clear of his legs. Injured didn't mean incapacitated when he had as much at stake as he did. 'Dan, you remember the lessons you had with guns, last Christmas?' She was nodding at her son, her eyes wide, trying to convey her true meaning. He'd held nothing more than a water pistol that he'd used to good effect last year.

Understanding flashed across his face and he followed her lead. 'Yeah,' he said, his voice firmer, his chin up.

'You need to keep this trained on the middle of Speedy's back while I tie him up.'

Flicking the safety back on, she handed the gun to her son, who took it in both hands and pointed it as she directed, looking like he'd done it a hundred times before.

She looped the dog lead around Speedy's wrists, tying them as tight as she dared. The lead was long enough to loop it down and around his ankles as well, bending them back to his knees. She had to punch the wound on his leg twice to get him to cooperate. Every time she stole a glance at her mother, it helped her to ignore the niggling disquiet that she could be so brutal to another human being. Time was critical. She gave the leash one last, vicious tug that made him hiss through gritted teeth.

'You're not going anywhere. Not until the police get here.'

She grabbed her son's shoulder. 'Come and stand here and don't take your eyes off him. If he moves, yell for me.'

Daniel nodded, his eyes dark with fear.

Kaitlyn ran to her mother, who was half lying in the doorway, her head resting on the door jamb, eyes closed. A trickle of blood ran down her neck and she was clutching her shoulder.

'Mum? Where does it hurt?' Kaitlyn's fingers shook as she searched through Julia's fine hair for the wound on her head. It wasn't difficult to find. The gash on the left side was nasty and very close to her temple. Kaitlyn hoped she was imagining it, but the underlying bones felt compressed.

'It's nothing. I'll be fine.' Her mother opened her eyes slowly. It looked like it took a huge effort. 'Just a silly cut, and maybe my shoulder.' She was slurring her words and looked disoriented.

Kaitlyn had to use all her strength to stay gentle and calm. Julia's pulse fluttered under her fingers. She needed to get her inside. 'Do you think you can stand?'

'Mum, Mum, the fire's at the shed!' Dan yelled, backing up towards her, the gun wavering in his hands.

'Oh, fuck.' Her family was more important than keeping Speedy safe to face the law. 'Mum, I have to get you inside. I'm sorry, this is going to hurt.'

'Just do it, do what you have to,' Julia said with a shaky nod. 'Martin phoned before the lines went down. We were right about Speedy. Martin found the connection.'

Kait didn't have time to even consider it. Their lives were at risk. 'Tell me as soon as this is over. Dan, quick, give me the gun. You need to turn the sprinklers on full and get the mops and buckets ready. Can you do that, baby?'

He nodded as he ran to her side, but his glance strayed to

Nero just before he handed the gun to her.

Kaitlyn touched his hair. 'I'll bring him in too. He'll be okay. Go now.'

She turned back to her mother as Daniel's footsteps clattered down the corridor. 'Ready?'

Once Julia was standing, Kaitlyn kept an arm around her and helped her through to the lounge, reluctantly leaving her with a cold pack pressed to her head. If she didn't make sure her fire protection was working, they'd all be dead.

And Nero. She needed to bring his body inside so they could bury him later, together. So much sorrow. Too much sorrow. Again.

The waterfall over the door drowned her as she stepped through it, and for a split second she turned her face to cool water.

'Nero?' The dog was on his feet. His sides were convulsing as he threw up, but even as she ran to him, Nero shook himself, all four legs leaving the ground for an instant, before his tail began to wag. 'Nero, good boy. Come here. Good boy.' He staggered a bit then trotted over to her and leant into her knee.

She scratched his ears and frowned as she realised Speedy had managed to make some movement towards the gate. Right now he was the least of her worries. She had faith her knots would hold and if he burnt to death then he deserved it. Once she had her system all checked and operational she'd drag him into the garage. Until then, he could try rolling as much as he wanted.

Behind her, she heard the rattle of a mop bucket, but before she could shut the front door and keep her family safe she saw a flash of white hurtling through the trees. A police car.

'Thank you. Thank you!' she cried, as it turned into her driveway at full speed. It swerved violently to miss Speedy before slamming to a stop in front of her, its driver's door flying open.

A familiar face appeared over the top of the car.

'Kaitlyn, thank God you're all right.'

For an instant she wavered, then she dragged the gun from her pocket with shaking hands.

'Stop right there, or I'll shoot.'

'Kaitlyn, it's me. It's Ryan. It's okay now. I've called it through. They'll send back-up as soon as they can.' He held his hands up, the gun loose in his fingers as he walked around the bonnet.

Kaitlyn tried to steady her hands. The jerk even managed to look concerned. 'No, it's not okay. I saw you. I saw you driving that ute, lighting the fire with him.' She waved the gun at Speedy, who'd made it to a sitting position. 'I was in the Dash doing surveillance.'

He looked shocked, bewildered. 'No, Kaitlyn, you don't understand.'

'Ryan, buddy. What took you so long?' Speedy was wheezing from the smoke, but his words still carried to Kaitlyn. 'Thank Christ you're here.'

Ryan ignored him and kept walking, tucking the gun in his waistband and holding his hands up again. 'Kait, don't do this. It's not what it looks like.' His voice was low, reasoning, steady.

'Stop!'

'Don't trust her, mate, the bitch's already shot me,' Speedy called. 'Just shoot her and be done with it. We need to get outta here. They know all about us. We've got to run.'

'Kait, he's lying.' Ryan didn't even glance at Speedy, but he was closing fast on her now.

'Stop!' She aimed high at his shoulder and squeezed the trigger.

Chapter 48

THE instant he saw her finger tighten on the trigger Ryan dived for the ground, rolling himself into a ball. The shot missed him, but he heard the window of the patrol car shatter. Speedy's manic laughter was just the catalyst he needed. He kept the momentum going, not knowing if Kaitlyn was going to take another shot at him.

He tackled her around the knees and saw her gun go flying the instant before he got her in a bear hug. Lifting her off the ground, he barrelled them both through the front door. She clawed and swiped at him like a terrified cat.

'Enough, Kaitlyn. You have to trust me.'

'Trust you?' she shrieked, finally getting free. 'You stay away from my family!'

'Mum?' Daniel had emerged from the living room, looking uncertain. 'Ryan!' His face lit up, but Kaitlyn swept him up before he could run past her. Nero bounded into the mix, almost tripping her up. She panted with exhaustion, clasping her son to her. Ryan clicked his fingers and the dog rushed to his side, licking his hand. Kait swung her son behind her.

'Mum? It's Ryan.'

'No, Daniel. His name's not Ryan. He's not who he says he is.'

'No, he's a policeman. Nana said Martin phoned before. He said he's a policeman.'

'Martin said that?'

Ryan had no idea who the hell Martin was, but he could see Kaitlyn wavering. He cut in before she could protest again. 'Kait, we don't have time. You have to trust me. Right now you need to fire up every one of your defences and I need to lock Speedy somewhere secure where he won't burn to death. We need to move. Please?'

'I saw you from the aircraft as the fire started.' She wasn't going to let this go.

'I was tracking Speedy. I called it in. It's true, Kaitlyn, I was there, but I wasn't the one who lit the fire. I would never hurt you. You have to trust me.'

'I can't.' Kaitlyn chewed the inside of her cheek, looking hunted.

'You have to. You have no other choice.' He held his gun out to her. He had nothing else he could offer. Make or break. He could only keep his gaze steady, willing her to believe him.

Another series of cracks and explosions made them both start.

'Get him, then,' Kaitlyn said with a sharp nod. 'Lock him in the laundry.' She spun on her heel. 'Daniel. Get the mops on the veranda. Now.'

'Thank you,' Ryan said, before he sprinted out the door. He grabbed Kaitlyn's discarded gun and kept going. Speedy had rolled under the patrol car and looked to be fiddling with something, despite his bound hands.

'No you don't, you shit. You're coming with me.' Ryan got hold of his calves and hauled him out. The red marks on Speedy's wrists were a giveaway. 'Thought you'd burn through them on the exhaust, did you? Bad luck, buddy. It didn't work.' The lead was partly damaged. He'd need to replace it with handcuffs just to make sure.

He rummaged around in the police car and located the spare pair. 'Come on then, time to show you some hospitality.' Sliding the cuffs into his pocket, he bent down and grabbed Speedy by the legs and proceeded to drag him backwards across the grass. Speedy kept up a steady stream of curses, despite the difficulties he was having keeping his face clear of the ground. It was only when Speedy cried out with what sounded like genuine pain that Ryan noticed the bloodstain on his leg. It looked like a bullet hole in his overalls.

'She really did shoot you?'

Speedy managed a half-hearted spit sideways. 'Bitch.'

'Yeah, so you've said a couple of times. I get the picture. Doesn't look like you're bleeding to death.'

They made it to the front door, where Ryan relented and undid the loop around Speedy's ankles. 'On your feet and don't try anything. I won't hesitate to shoot you, either.'

'Fuckin' cops.' Speedy sneered at him. 'You know what happens to undercover pieces of shit eventually?' Ryan didn't answer, just prodded him in the back with his gun to move him down the corridor. 'Someone gets the family. Best way to get to scum like you: kill the little lady and the kids. Smash their heads open, but only after they've spread their legs.'

Ryan's temper was straining against his control, but he knew he couldn't afford to snap now. If he did, he'd kill Speedy. Then he'd be back to square one, knowing he was just like the criminals he helped to put away.

Speedy continued to taunt him as Ryan hauled him into the laundry. He looked around, searching for something to secure him to.

'Open the cupboard under the sink. All the pipes in this house are metal. Cuff him to those.' Kaitlyn appeared behind him. 'When you're done, put these on and go for a shower. They need to be wet. The fire's got the rose gum.'

Ryan glanced at the black woollen clothes before he forced Speedy onto the floor, clipping one cuff on his left wrist. He was wasting time with this lowlife when they were all in grave danger. Speedy's lack of resistance was making him nervous. Did he have something else up his sleeve?

'Is she any good in the sack? Bit tall for me and way too shrewish.' Speedy licked his lips, leering up at him, and Ryan's fingers itched to backhand him. Instead, he pinched a pressure point on the man's neck, then got the other cuff around Speedy's right wrist. The patting down he gave him was none too gentle, but he didn't need to find out later Speedy had a gun hidden on him.

He wasted a moment leaning in to hiss in Speedy's face. 'I bet you scream like a girl when the lads get you in the shower block. The guards will tell them you're an arsonist who burns innocent women and children. Enjoy that, buddy.'

Gathering up the woollen clothes, he strode out. A minute later he dripped a trail of water through the house, securing the balaclava over his head. The shutters made the rooms feel smaller. The glow from green emergency lights at floor level was the only reason he could find his way around. He could just make out Julia, curled up on the couch, eyes closed, covered in a throw rug.

Nero sat by the door that led outside from the kitchen. It was the only one without a closed shutter. Ryan guessed that was the way out and he pushed it open. The heat almost flattened him.

He threw his arms up in front of his face. The air was thick with smoke, falling ash and burning embers. The gum was well alight, sparks shooting from older limbs as they ignited. Pulling the balaclava down harder over his face, he headed for the other two black-clad figures by the shed. Talking was impossible over the roar of the inferno. The entire rim of the escarpment was a writhing mass of reds and yellows, flames shooting 20, 30 metres into the sky. Each new explosion showered more debris on the buildings.

Kaitlyn pointed at an oversized mop standing in a bucket. He lifted it out, running it through the rollers lightly. A curtain of water enveloped the shed as well, but any burning embers that fell to earth near it were quickly blotted out with the mops.

Ryan got close enough to Kaitlyn to yell in her ear. 'You go and look after the house, take Daniel. I'll stay here.' The further he could get her from the active fire front, the happier he'd be. So far her protection system seemed to be working, but he didn't know how long the water supply would hold out.

She shook her head. Her eyes were shielded by welding goggles but he could sense her suspicion still.

'Go. I've got this,' he said. He put a hand on her arm and squeezed, willing her to believe him. Another crash and rumble from down the slope sent a shower of sparks high above them and onto the house. He saw her wince. Nothing he could have envisaged would have been this fierce, this all-consuming. It was going to take more than good preparation if they were to survive. 'Please.'

This time she wavered. Then she whirled away and grabbed Daniel, bending down to yell instructions. The lad nodded and hefted his bucket and mop. He had to crab-walk across to the house, the wind tearing at him.

'If it gets a hold on the shed, then leave it.' Kaitlyn shouted, her voice barely audible.

Ryan nodded and turned away, resisting the temptation to watch her run across her decimated yard to the house. Injured animals and birds sought refuge in the misting water. So much suffering and devastation. It reminded him of something from Jerry's diaries.

The old man had written about the innocent victims of the Second World War being hurt by the actions of vain men, caught in a nightmare not of their making, without an escape or even a sense of hope. As yet another scorched and dying metallic starling fell at his feet, he saw parallels.

By now, the grass had virtually all been seared away; the earth was bare and blackened. Garden beds were denuded of plants. The long, slender limbs of the rose gum were naked and charred, the curling bark glowing amber as it dropped to the ground. Ryan darted in, wielding the mop, to extinguish each piece.

Without protection for his eyes, he could only squint against the fierce burn of the smoke. Tears left tracks down his cheeks. At least the woollen balaclava filtered the air enough that he could breathe. He felt a blast of hot air on the back of his head and peered in that direction.

So far, the eucalypts further around the escarpment had escaped the fire. If the predicted wind shift arrived, though, it would envelop them in the next wave, re-energising the fire, and that would leave Kaitlyn's house in the dead man's zone. Was this the first sign that the change in weather was on its way?

If it was, then all they could do was hide inside and wait it out, putting all their faith in Kaitlyn's defences. Jerry's house would definitely be cactus.

He lunged forward again to stamp out new burning patches near the rose gum. The water still ran over the shed and, while the building's cladding sported blistered paint, nothing had warped or separated.

His bucket was almost empty and he wet the mop one last time before heading to the tap. The metal was almost too hot to touch. How much longer before the washers gave out?

How much longer could they hold out? He still had no idea how big Kait's water tanks were. Surely to God the fire had devoured everything in its path by now?

Kaitlyn and Dan were still dabbing at the steady bombardment of burning debris that littered the ground around the house. Ryan frowned. It looked like there was smoke seeping from her roof. He blinked and squinted. There was. *Shit.*

Grabbing his bucket, he started to run. 'Kait, Kaitlyn!' he yelled, his voice hoarse from the smoke. 'Kait!'

She finally turned, but he couldn't see her expression. The mop was raised in guarded position, as if she expected him to attack her.

'There's smoke from your roof,' he croaked when he got to her.

'Where?' she demanded.

'Here.' He grabbed her arm and dragged her far enough back so she could see.

'Oh no. It's the laundry!' She dropped her bucket and fled towards the door, Ryan right on her heels.

Smoke poured out of the house as she pushed into the kitchen.

'The arsehole.' She started coughing as she waved her hands in front of her face. 'I'll kill him.'

'You can't. I did that already,' Julia tottered towards the couch, clutching the gun. Despite the blood on her face and her trembling hands, she looked defiant and unbowed. 'I did it. I'm sorry. I smelt burning plastic and I went to investigate. The laundry's ruined, but I used the extinguisher and then I shot him.'

'Don't touch the gun,' Ryan warned Kait as she rushed to her mother. 'We don't need your prints on it.' She ignored him, murmuring soothing words to Julia. He looked around for something to wrap it in. Plastic wrapper off a magazine. Best he could do. He was reacting instinctively. A man shot while cuffed to a sink was going to be difficult to justify no matter the provocation. They needed to preserve the evidence or Julia would have a murder charge to answer.

Julia was still talking, her voice ragged with emotion even though Kait was trying to calm her. 'He kept laughing at me, laughing like a mad man. All I could see in my mind was my beautiful Stephen, and Chris, and everything we lost.' She had tears rolling down her cheeks, but her words had steadied. She looked at her daughter, the love so clear in her eyes. 'I tried, Kait. I told him to shut up, be quiet, but he wouldn't stop. I had to end it. I'm sorry. There was no other way. I never thought I could kill but he didn't deserve to live. Not after all that he's done. Forgive me, my darling. I'm as bad as . . .'

She slumped against Kaitlyn, the gun clattering to the ground. Ryan grabbed it with a plastic-covered hand and wrapped it up. How much more could go wrong? Kaitlyn already had Julia into recovery position on the couch. As he crouched down beside them, he couldn't miss the heavy bloodstain on the light fabric.

'Julia,' Kaitlyn pleaded with her mother. 'Mum, hang in there. We've almost won.'

Ryan went to find Speedy. Julia was right. She'd shot him, straight in the face. He was most definitely dead. It didn't give Ryan any satisfaction. The law was not going to judge Julia lightly. What a fucking mess. The empty fire-extinguisher was lying on its side. At least it had done its job. All he could do was close the door and hope enough evidence survived for forensics to make sense of it.

He strode back to the lounge. Kait looked up at him and he nodded his confirmation. 'She did, she really did.'

'Oh, Mum.' There was so much sorrow in Kait's voice; all he

wanted to do was gather her tightly against him and rock her until the horror stopped. But he knew, even if she let him, it would be no use. This horror had a long way to run.

'There's a wind shift coming, Kait. What do you want to do?' Ryan had to ask. Maybe she had a plan.

She shook her head at him, the sheen of tears making her eyes bright. 'There's nothing more I can do. Get Daniel inside. If we lose the shed, so be it. Then I can divert all the water to the house. I can't leave Mum like this.'

He nodded and got to his feet. Before he could open the door, Daniel burst in.

'The fire, it's coming from over there!' He waved a frantic arm to the south-west.

Ryan grabbed him by both arms and looked into his face. 'Stay with your mum. She needs help. Don't go outside again, okay?'

Dan nodded at him, his face serious. 'Okay.'

Cautiously, Ryan opened the door enough to squeeze through. The buckets sat where they'd dropped them, and he gathered them up. Feeling the intense heat sap his energy, he piled the equipment by the door. They'd need them inside. The fire was roaring at the shed now. Angry, leaping tongues of flame attacked it through its veil of water.

In the tops of the nearby eucalypts, as the oil in their leaves vaporised, the first hints of fireballs were emerging. Bullets of fire leapt from tree to tree, spreading the frenzy in seconds.

Ryan felt despair flood through him. The only consolation, and he could hardly bear to think of it, was that he was here with Kaitlyn and her family. If dying while trying to protect them was the last thing on earth he did, then he had at last done something he was proud of.

Peering at the devastation around him, through aching and tortured eyes, he wasn't sure whether the sting was the smoke or tears. To have come so far and lose it all was heartbreaking. He couldn't face watching it happen. She deserved to win. How much longer could this rage before it ran out of fuel and exhausted itself?

As he turned, heavy-hearted, to retreat inside, a thundering roar from the front of the house made him spin in the direction of the noise. An Ag Cat burst over the roofline, dropping a load of fire retardant in a giant pink swathe.

All he could do was stand there as it poured down on the yard. Finally. The aircraft pulled up vertical, just short of the fire, and turned in for another run. He could just make out the pilot at the controls as another precious load fell on the house.

Less than a minute after the first one had vanished, a second one came hurtling through. As the wind kept veering further around, the fire was being forced back on itself. Maybe they could win this after all.

Maybe.

Chapter 49

'JULIA. Can you hear me? Mum?' Kaitlyn dabbed at the stain on her mother's cheek and neck. The blood seemed to have stopped flowing, but her mother's pulse barely fluttered.

'It's okay.' Julia's words were barely a whisper. Over the noise of the fire, Kaitlyn had to bend low to catch them. 'I'm sorry, Kaitlyn. I'm sorry.'

'*Shh*, Mum. It's all right. You did the right thing. He would have killed us all.'

'Martin . . .' Julia swallowed, clearly struggling to talk.

'*Shh*, *shh*. You'll be fine, you can tell me later.'

'No,' Julia said, clutching at her daughter's hand. Kaitlyn couldn't believe how weak her grip was, the strength in her long, elegant pianist's fingers all but gone. 'Martin found the truth. Chris had a half-brother. Speedy. He was the one who started the fire, killed Chris, Stephen, then took his brother's identity. He must have planned it all.' She eased back against the cushion and her eyes opened wide. 'I will never believe Chris did anything but defend your father. He was a good man, just damaged, not his fault . . .' Her eyes fluttered closed again. 'I love you, my darling.'

'I love you too, Mum.' Kaitlyn was making soothing circles on the back of her mother's hand, her thumb running over the paper-thin skin. Her mind was reeling, trying to absorb her mother's words. Could Martin be right about Chris? Was he Speedy's half-brother? The adrenalin load in her body was huge and her limbs trembled, her eyelids closed. She so desperately wanted Martin to be right, so desperately wanted an answer, wanted to be able to believe in Chris again. The gaping hole in her heart she refused to acknowledge would be so much easier to bear if Chris was an innocent victim.

A drumming sound thundered across the roof. Alarmed, Kaitlyn looked to the ceiling before she identified the roar of a radial engine. The water bombers had arrived. She let out a sob of relief. Maybe they could survive. She leant against her mother's hand, her tears falling. Nero pressed close against her knee, licking at her hand. She wiped her cheeks, striving for control, as Daniel held out a glass of water.

'Does Julia need a drink?'

Kaitlyn managed to summon a smile and pulled him close. Her baby was being so strong. 'Leave it on the side table, she can reach it when she wakes up.'

He put the glass down and stood beside them. 'Will Nana be all right?'

She could see the fear in his face. He'd been brave, confronting first Speedy and then the fire. But this? Seeing Julia so obviously unwell?

'I hope so.' She wrapped her arms around her precious Dan and poured her strength into the hug. If Martin was right, then this boy's father was not an arsonist, but the victim of a vicious murderer. A harsh truth, but better than the alternative.

The door opened, letting in another wave of smoke and heat.

Ryan was backlit by the glow from outside, but there was no mistaking the squared shoulders or the determined tilt of his chin. They were going to make it.

In two strides he was beside them, his arms gathering Kaitlyn and Dan against him. She felt his shuddering relief with each rise of his chest. How had she ever doubted this man, doubted his integrity, his concern for them?

His lips were hard against her temple and for the first time in so many hours, too many hours, she dared to hope. She was home, safe. The smoky, sweaty scent of him was like a familiar cloak of safety. Heat from his body seeped through the heavy woollen clothes, warming the chill of fear from her bones.

She opened her eyes. 'Thank you.'

His fatigued smile was the only answer she needed.

Daniel wriggled free and perched next to his grandmother. 'Is she really sleeping?' he asked. Dan picked up her limp hand. 'Nana?'

Kaitlyn broke free from Ryan, realising in horror that her mother's mouth was slack and open. Frantically, she searched for a pulse. 'Julia? Oh God, Ryan!'

Ryan moved to Julia's head and pressed his fingers against her throat, but Kaitlyn could see from the movement that he wasn't finding anything.

'CPR. We've got to try,' he said. He scooped Julia up and laid her on the rug, positioning her limp body flat.

Kaitlyn nodded. Her head said it was too late, but her heart refused to give up on her mother. To surrender would mean Speedy had taken one more thing she loved. Anger was the only way she knew to control the pain that had started as a tiny bubble five years ago and was now threatening to drown her. She gathered that thought to her, pushing down so hard on her sorrow she felt her stomach muscles clench. Ryan was talking to her as he scrambled to his feet.

'You start. We need an ambulance.' He shot out the front door.

Dan's wide eyes sheened with tears as Kait started CPR. 'Nana!'

She needed to keep him busy. This was too overwhelming for him. 'Dan, it's okay. Go get me a wet tea towel, with cold water. Go.'

He came back several minutes later with the tray of ice cubes and a tea towel. 'Here.'

She looked up at him, deliberately meeting his gaze, hoping she could reassure with words. 'Wrap six up in the tea towel and then you need to hold it to Nana's forehead.' She knew it wasn't going to do much, but it would give her son a purpose. He was still crying, hiccuping sobs. 'It's okay, we'll fix Julia. It's okay, baby.'

Her need to gather him up against her and shield him from this was powerful, but she couldn't stop. She had to choose between them. Dan was young and resilient; Julia was not.

All she could do was talk to Dan as she pushed down, feeling her mother's petite ribs compress and expand, compress and expand. She wouldn't stop, couldn't stop until there was no hope left.

'I remember when Nana saw you in hospital for the first time. Her baby carrot, she called you.'

Dan almost smiled. Kaitlyn was panting from the exertion of CPR, her arms starting to tire as she talked.

Ryan came through the front door, his face grim. 'They're on their way. My turn.' He took her place and Kait knelt beside Dan, touching his shoulder with hers.

'And Grandad reckoned he'd just been replaced as Nana's favourite boy. But he said that was okay, because you were such a good-looking rooster. And do you remember when Nana caught you playing the piano?' She jerked her head at the white-shrouded grand. Dan managed a tiny crooked smile this time.

'I had chocolate cake on my fingers.'

'You did, and what did she say?'

'That cake and pianos don't mix so I'd have to choose.'

'And what did you choose?'

'The piano.' The story had been told and retold so many times, Kait was sure the scene had been rewritten, but she was determined to keep dredging up wonderful memories of her mother and her son. Dan's face had relaxed a touch. He kept the tea towel on Julia's forehead, the water from the melting ice soaking into the rug. Kait kept talking.

Ten minutes later, the front door burst open. It became surreal. Kaitlyn saw only fragments of the scene. The look between the two paramedics that said more than words; the rattle of the stretcher as they rushed it out the door, Julia jolting with every bump; flashing emergency lights, eerie in the smoke and bathing her world in red; two policeman with a roll of blue tape sealing up her laundry.

Finally they were all gone. Dan clung to her side, pressing against her for comfort. Her heart felt bruised. Inside she was crying, howling for their loss. Outwardly she functioned. No time to grieve. She managed to talk, to make decisions, to answer questions. She had to. She was a mother and her boy was going to need all her strength in the days to come.

Her pounding headache had reached migraine status. When Ryan raised the shutters, the light pierced her brain.

'You did it,' he said, his voice raw and hoarse. The view was one of devastation. 'You saved your home. And the wind shift's taken the fire north.'

Silent, she came and stood beside him. Across the scorched escarpment, she could make out Jerry's house. It looked unscathed.

Dan stood between them and she looked down at him, squeezing his hand tight. 'We did it. The three of us.'

Dan looked up at her, tear tracks streaking the ash on his cheeks, his skin so pale against the bright rose-gold of his hair. 'But Nana?'

The question in his eyes was Kait's undoing, and this time there was no stopping the flood of tears. She could only shake her head as her words dried up. There were only two of them now.

Ryan hauled Dan into one arm and crushed Kait in the middle of the embrace. 'Don't go there yet. We'll face this together.'

'Don't, Ryan. Don't do this to us.' She was suddenly furious, angry with herself for her foolish pride that had put them in the path of a fire, angry with Julia for dying and leaving her alone. But mostly she was angry with herself for falling in love with a man who changed, chameleon-like, as the job dictated. 'I know you can't stay.'

'But I can stay. I will stay.' His hand tipped her face up, yet she stayed stiff, resisting the comfort he offered. Dan burrowed deeper into his arms, his body shaking with tears.

She tried to pull away, but her heart wasn't in it. The scent of Ryan, the familiar earthy smell, wasn't even masked by the smoke. His touch was light but persistent, just enough to keep her anchored to him.

'Don't,' she protested between sobs, torn between what she wanted and what she knew she couldn't risk. 'Don't offer something we can never have, Ryan. I don't know you, the real you.'

'You do. You may be the only person who does. I'm Ryan O'Donnell, Jerry O'Donnell's great-nephew. I will not let you face this alone.'

Through her tears, she saw the truth in his eyes, the sorrow in his smile and his uncertainty. Ryan was finally standing in front of her, shorn of all his defences. The real Ryan.

He looked at her, waiting, as though he knew the battle that was raging inside her. Dan dropped his head on Ryan's shoulder, hiccuping into silence, the action profound. Kaitlyn thought her heart would break. Ryan rested his chin on top of the boy's head and for an instant his eyes closed. It hurt like a kick to the guts but warmed her at the same time. She saw beneath the tough exterior a wounded man who was hanging on just as tightly as she was. Those eyes that looked both young and old were bright with unshed tears when he opened them and she couldn't miss his arm tightening around Dan.

Her fears, her guilt, her reserve, were misplaced. She loved this man in a way she'd never experienced before. She finally understood what Julia meant when she said she'd recognised Stephen by his eyes. The connection, the love, was there in Ryan's eyes, in his unwavering belief in her, in the care with which he cradled her son.

Could they find a common path?

A knock at the front door broke the moment. Police, again. The circus was just about to begin.

Chapter 50

KAITLYN opened the wide doors to the front deck. The grass outside was hazed in green as new life burst from the blackened ground. A zephyr stirred the budding khaki leaves on the rose gum's highest branches. A month was a long time in fire country.

The house was silent. She'd just dropped Dan and Nero off at his friend Wolfie's house. They were heading to Granite Gorge for a swim to escape the stifling heat. Her first thought had been to go with them, but Courtney, Wolfie's mother, had gently shooed her out the door. 'Relax,' she'd said. 'He needs to chill out with his mates. I won't let them out of my sight. Not even Nero.'

Kait knew Courtney was right, but it took a great deal of effort to drive away and leave him. Now, alone in the house, she felt restless, edgy. She turned back to the lounge and picked up Jerry's war diary, flicking through the now familiar pages.

To never know when you might be discovered and killed is a terrible waking nightmare. No one can sustain it without damage. Some will snap, some will warp beyond repair, a few will become stronger for the burden. I pray Ryan has my strength.

She'd found comfort in the old man's sparse words. Had Ryan understood that when he gave them to her?

Perhaps.

Jerry had taken her inside the life of a spy, an undercover operative. The half-truths, the isolation and the alienation from the people they loved the most. She now had a strong sense of how anyone working undercover lived on the edge, lived by their wits, and died if they made the wrong choice. It helped put Ryan into perspective.

She put the book down again and sat on the edge of the new couch. The last month had been long, the sadness a daily shadow. The anniversary of the Canberra fires had come and gone in the latest tragedy. She and Dan had only been back in their house just over a week. Being on leave from work was good, as Dan was on school holidays, but she needed to keep busy to stop thinking, analysing.

Logistically, life was going to be a whole lot more difficult. She either had to find work here on the Tablelands, or they would have to move to Cairns. That option didn't sit comfortably right now. Dan wasn't sleeping well. Last night she'd woken to find him pressed into her back, his hands in tight fists. To uproot him from his school and his friends wouldn't help, but even part-time work with Border Watch would be difficult to manage. She'd applied for leave until the end of January, but she couldn't wait that long to make the decision. She was putting it off until after Christmas, which was three days away. They'd get through that first, then she'd have to find her courage again.

Without Julia . . .

Julia's funeral had been a simple service at the Tolga Community Church. Its pretty stone facade looked like an old-fashioned theatre. It seemed appropriate. Kaitlyn was shocked at the huge crowd of people who came. It seemed her mother had made more friends on the Tablelands than Kait realised.

Martin made the journey north. It had never occurred to Kait that the elderly man may have loved Julia too, until she saw his grief at the funeral. Her relief that his report had provided enough evidence to prove Speedy had murdered Stephen and Chris was swamped by the pain of ripping open all those old wounds. Martin had painstakingly trawled through Speedy's computer until he found Speedy's own words describing the fierce joy he'd derived from killing his brother. Along with the surveillance tapes of the Canberra fires, Martin had built a compelling argument that laid the blame at Speedy's feet.

The police investigation into Speedy's recent activities was ongoing. The arson wasn't at issue – the Dash 8 footage proved that. Speedy's own records were also meticulous. He'd detailed everything in his logs, from using a bump key to break into Kaitlyn's house, to discarding her clothes in panic when Julia came home early. He was the one who'd ransacked Jerry's house and almost run Kait off the road. But the authorities were still unravelling the circumstances of Speedy's death.

So much anger, so much hatred. Speedy was a man so wronged that he thought he could right the injustices he'd suffered by killing. In his distorted logic, Speedy had thought he was protecting Daniel. His madness was beyond Kait's understanding.

So different to Chris – gentle, damaged Chris. Tears spilled down her cheeks again. Now that she'd finally cried for her husband, five years too late, she found it hard to stop. She understood why he'd shied away from being a father, had never even mentioned he had a half-brother. What sort of a childhood had he endured? Had his father really preyed on Speedy? Had his mother turned a blind eye to it? Or was it just that Speedy had hated Chris from birth and made his life hell?

She blew her nose and dabbed at her cheeks. No wonder Chris had craved the stability of the Scotts, no wonder he'd married her even though he may not have loved her any more than she loved him. It wasn't about her. It was about Stephen and Julia. But he'd given her Daniel, their accidental son.

And Ryan?

Right now she wanted nothing more than to hear his teasing laugh. He'd promised he'd be back soon. That was two weeks ago.

What would he bring? A temporary reprieve from the loneliness in her heart? A warm place to hide for a few hours? More importantly, what comfort did she have to offer him?

In the week after the fire, after Dan had fallen asleep, they'd talked long into the night, sitting side by side on Jerry's veranda. They'd talked of life and death, of truth and lies, but they'd never talked of love. Ryan had given her space to grieve, a warm shoulder to cry on, and a reason to smile.

She needed him in a way she'd never needed anyone.

Did Ryan feel anything that strong for her, for Dan?

Would she recognise it if he did?

She stood up and walked to the piano, eased down onto the polished stool, then folded the lid back. For a moment she just sat, the seat cool against her legs, the curve of it pushing her upright. It felt as though the house was holding its breath along with her.

Carefully, tentatively, she placed her fingers on the keys where Julia had played for so long. It had been five years since she'd felt the smooth ivory. Forgotten but familiar. Her fingers were rusty, the pressure uneven, the notes faltering, but the comfort of something so deeply ingrained pushed her on until the music simply swept her away. It loosened the knots that had bound her so tightly, softened the ragged edges of despair, and brought her parents, her childhood and herself closer together again. It almost, almost, filled that gaping ache.

Ryan parked at the front of the house. Christmas was three days away and the wet season was smothering everything with humidity. He opened the car door and stopped. The air was still but for the music. It surrounded him, haunting and plaintive as the notes cried and sighed. He tried the front door. It was locked so he made his way around to the other side, where the wide glass doors stood open.

Kait sat at the piano, her hair an auburn halo of curls, her eyes closed as she played. He could only lean against the doorframe and watch, seeing the tears on her cheeks and feeling her pain. So much loss, so much sorrow. Could he ever mean enough to her to chase away the sadness, give her a reason to love, to trust again?

There was no sign of Dan and Nero. The music faded away and her eyes opened.

'Kait.'

He saw the hope flare in the velvety brown of her eyes as she smiled through her tears. In that instant he knew he was foolish to doubt that she needed him, wanted him.

'Ryan. You're here.'

'I am.' He walked over and sat on the end of the polished piano stool, hip to hip, thigh to thigh. 'I missed you.' He feathered a kiss across her temple, intoxicated by the familiar hint of cinnamon and apple. He wiped the tears from her chin and she rested her head on his shoulder, her eyes closed. They sat like that for a minute, leaning into each other.

Then her eyes fluttered open again. She stood up, put distance between them. 'How long are you here for this time?'

'As long as you'll have me.'

'Sorry?' She faltered as he stood up too.

'I've resigned. The investigation was never going to let me off scot-free. It's easier if I leave quietly. I'm an ex-federal policeman now and I'm moving into Jerry's place.'

'Jerry's place?' She looked surprised.

'The shack just up the road?' he replied with a grin.

'Oh.' She held out her hand and he took it, tugging her up against him, loving the curves and warmth of her body.

He needed this as much as she did. Her lips were soft beneath his, but he felt her tremble. Was he going too fast?

He leant back, keeping her in the circle of his arms, anchoring her to him. 'Jerry's place for now. I've got some things to sort out. And then . . .'

'And then?' she prompted him. She was waiting, the sadness gone from her eyes.

'I need you, Kait, you and Daniel. I had no idea how much until I thought I'd lost you.' The importance of what he had to say made him choose his words with care.

'But Sydney, your life . . .'

'For the last four years I've had no home, no life, no stability. You were a lifeline that suddenly appeared in the middle of all those lies.'

'A lifeline.'

'You, Dan and Julia. You showed me what a family could feel like and I wanted it so much it hurt. That night of your birthday I almost broke. You made me lose my head.' And my heart, he added to himself.

She smiled then, just a hint. 'And your phone.'

'And that's something I will always regret, but it's also my reality. Someone somewhere might come for me one day. Nemesis may be locked up for now, but that won't last forever.'

'I know that.' Her voice was strong. 'It's who you are. You were right to give me Jerry's diaries. He could have been writing a manual for the partner of an undercover. I understand you a little more. The optimistic idealist with the darkness always just there. You don't scare me, Ryan.'

He almost laughed at that, relieved she accepted it so easily. 'Jerry did more for me than I ever realised. I only worked that out when I came back here. I felt like I'd come home.'

She placed a hand over his heart, her palm warm against his shirt. 'Grant McCormack came to see me. Seems there may be gold around here.'

Ryan did laugh this time. 'He told me the same thing when I saw him during the investigation. I told him Jerry had always maintained it was only alluvial gold, but he was welcome to test drill provided he was prepared to compensate the estate.'

'I told him to go to hell and I'd see him in court,' Kaitlyn said with a quick laugh. 'Did you know it was his father who hired Speedy in the first place?'

'Yeah, I found that out as part of the investigation. I kind of thought Speedy and McCormack deserved each other. Now?' He shrugged. 'Sins of the father being inflicted on the son? McCormack's going to escape prosecution, unlike the company lawyer, so maybe he deserves a chance. I'd rather it wasn't on my patch of dirt, though.'

'And they've reopened the investigation into Dad's death and Chris's. Martin is helping this time, instead of being sidelined. He thinks it's clear-cut.'

'It would mean a great deal for Dan later on.'

'Yeah, it will.'

'And to you.'

She nodded without reply.

'So what do you want, Kaitie?'

'What I want can never happen.' Kaitlyn shook her head as he started to interrupt. 'No, no. Julia is gone and I have to build new dreams, find new hope. Dan is the most precious thing in my world now so every decision comes back to him. And you. I wasn't sure you'd come back. I'm very glad you did.' She smiled at him. 'I love you, Ryan.'

There.

The weight lifted from him. He bent and kissed her, revelling in the rush of heat, the touch, the taste of her.

It freed him.

'And I love you, Kaitlyn Scott.'

Words he never thought he'd be able to say. They'd been a long time coming.

'I know you do.' And he believed her.

He ran his hand down her head, settling the silky hair against the nape of her neck. 'I know you're hurting in ways I can't begin to understand, but I'm here to stay.'

'And *your* dreams? What about them?'

He waggled his head from side to side. 'I've got some dreams of my own, but they're pretty flexible.'

Her smile was beautiful as she leant away and touched her hand to his cheek. 'Really?'

His heart picked up a beat. 'Yes, really. I have dreams of an ugly house with a huge heart filled with laughter and barking and music, lots of music. In fact, I've always dreamt of playing the piano.'

She laughed. 'Ugly house, huh? You're not above using flattery, then.' She took his hand in hers and rolled it over. 'You have potential as a musician. Long fingers, probably a bit inflexible, but there may be some hidden talent there.'

He cupped her face with those long fingers. 'There's talent there for many more things than playing the piano, but they'll have to wait. Where's Dan?'

'He'll be back later. He and Nero are swimming with friends.'

'Well then, Ms Scott, we have plenty of time to dream.'

'Really, Mr O'Donnell?' She tilted her head. 'No. You'll always be Ryan to me, just Ryan.'

'Ryan and Kait and Dan.'

'Ryan and Kait and Dan.' She sighed against his lips. 'Come and I'll show you how much I love you. I've perfected blueberry muffins. Julia would be proud.'

Epilogue

Ullswater, Cumbria, UK

THE dark lake was fringed in slushy ice. The wind howling up the slope bit through Kait's thick coat, the temperature 30 degrees lower than when they'd left Happy Jack Road three days ago. She pulled her woollen cap further over her ears as her nose threatened to drip. Ryan's arm left a warm bar across her shoulder. She pressed closer to his side, folding Dan tight against her.

His head almost reached her chin. He'd grown so much in the last twelve months. They all had, in so many ways.

The lawn of the Howtown Hotel stretched away towards the lake. Trees, bare of leaves, stretched silvery branches up to the weak sun. Winter in the Lake District was unbearably cold, yet stunningly beautiful.

'Nana must have been freezing.' Dan finally broke the silence, twisting to peer at his mother, his eyes slitted against the wind.

'Yes, but remember Julia had Stephen with her to keep her warm.' It still hurt to say their names. Kait didn't know when that would change.

'Yeah, I guess so.'

'You sure you don't want your gloves on?' Kait asked.

'Nah, I'm fine.' Dan pulled a face, looking at the box in his hands. Kait understood.

'Maybe we should get walking before *we* freeze to the spot,'

Ryan suggested, angling his head towards the lake.

Kait nodded with an inner smile. It had taken a few months of living together for Ryan to learn to compromise, to try suggesting rather than snapping out orders. To be fair, she'd had to make similar adjustments. They were a work in progress and she liked where it was taking them.

Ahead the road was empty. A few bright spots of colour on the towering hills surrounding Ullswater proved that a few hardy tourists were out hiking. The locals, on the other hand, were tucked up in the nearby pub in front of a roaring fire, celebrating the new year. Kait was looking forward to joining them later to defrost.

'What's with the sheep?' Dan asked. 'They look weird.' Shaggy white animals with black heads and impossibly skinny black legs gazed at them with unblinking eyes from the other side of sturdy dry-stone walls.

'Swaledales,' Ryan supplied.

Kait looked across at him in surprise.

He shrugged, his grin crooked. 'I did some research into the area. Can't go anywhere unprepared.'

Kait smiled, squeezing his hand tight. Old habits died hard. She knew he missed the cut and thrust of being at the forefront of crime fighting. His colleagues still phoned to pick his brains, but she noticed he brooded less with each call. He even talked sporadically to her about his work. Sharing his darker emotions was a long way off, but she knew that unconditional love would do what no therapist could. He gave her the same comfort. With Jerry's will finally settled, the earthworks had commenced to transform his property into a camp for disadvantaged boys. Ryan was a busy man, dealing with all the red tape and government departments involved in the venture.

'Swaledales, swaledales . . .' Dan let the word roll around his mouth. 'Well, they look pretty fierce.'

'Tough as old boots,' Ryan replied.

Kait let the conversation between Ryan and Dan slide over her. She was mesmerised by the landscape. The snow was piled high on the leeward side of the walls, settling in deep hollows and hiding among hardy plants. Flurries of snow blew across the ground, and eddies of white spun off the tops of the walls. The skies were leaden. More snow by nightfall, the publican had warned them.

It was exactly as Julia had described it. Kait hoped it would give Dan another strong memory of his grandparents.

It had taken almost twelve months to unravel the mess Speedy had left behind. Once that was done, the intransigent Immigration Department had finally issued Dan with a passport. Without Ryan turning each new official letter into something to laugh at she would have lost patience. Ryan's playfulness, his tendency to pull practical jokes, made her wonder some days if Dan hadn't gained a big brother rather than a father figure. Either way, her boy had blossomed, and she had learnt to laugh again without reservation.

It had been a long year. There was no way to prove whether Speedy's claims of sexual abuse by his stepfather were true or not. But what difference would it make, anyway? It had been Speedy's reality. He believed it had happened and so many of his choices were bound up in that fact. Once he'd murdered his mother and stepfather, his course had been set. And the proof in his diaries made it very clear their deaths were not accidental.

The investigation into his death had dragged on. The footage taken by Morgan's crew as they circled over Kait's house was compelling if painful viewing. It took several forensic experts to piece all the evidence inside the house together. The gun wrapped in plastic had been crucial. She was glad Ryan had been so careful at such a time. Kaitlyn felt sure his boss had applied a great deal of heat from his side, too.

With Ryan in their lives Kaitlyn had initially returned to work. It hadn't been easy. Dan had gone back to school a hero in the new year, until the day he came home in tears. Someone, in the rough and tumble of the schoolyard, had called his mother a murderer. For a week Kaitlyn had wavered, before resigning from her job. Oddly enough, Tony had then offered her part-time work in a training role. Maybe he did care about his staff after all. She'd accepted, and now drove down the range five days a fortnight. It was still a juggling act, but with Ryan around someone was always at home for Dan.

'Hey, there's a horse like Jack.' Dan tugged at her sleeve. 'Bet Nero would like him, too.'

'Probably a bit bigger than Jack, but he is brown with a white blaze and four white socks, you're quite right,' Kait replied.

'So, can I have a new saddle for my birthday?'

'We'll see.' Kait met Ryan's gaze over her son's head. Jack the pony had been a runaway success at Dan's last birthday. It would be difficult to top that this year, but a saddle was already on order. Ryan had suggested it. He'd made a lot of good suggestions. Her heart lifted at the memory of him telling her it was unlikely the dirty clothes would stage a mutiny if they festered in the laundry basket for two or three days. Without realising it, she'd taken on Julia's obsession with cleanliness, filling the washing machine with clothes that had barely been stripped from their wearer. A coping mechanism.

And now they were here, where it had all started for her parents.

Where, in many ways, it had started for the three of them.

'Careful on the wood. It might be slippery,' Kait cautioned Dan as they reached the timber jetty.

'Yeah, yeah.'

He went to hurry ahead, but Ryan's hand shot out, pulling him back between them. 'Steady. I'm not diving in after you, Danny boy.'

Dan rolled his eyes and clutched the box tighter. The wind felt warmer here, coming straight off the water.

Finally, they stood together on the platform over the lake. Kait had no idea if sprinkling ashes like this was even legal, but she had to honour her mother's wish. They'd already replanted the rose garden around the house and scattered her parents' ashes on each precious bush, but she'd saved some. This was where it had started. This was where it would end, with Stephen and Julia together.

'You do it, Mum.' Daniel handed the box to her. She took it, but held tight to his hand.

'Together?' she asked.

He nodded and she crouched down next to him, feeling the protection of Ryan's body behind her. Daniel's hair was a bright flame against the sombre sky.

The lid came off easily and she tucked it in her pocket. The fine white ash was already trying to swirl out of the box, as if it knew its way home.

She offered it to Dan, still gripping the bottom. Together, they tipped it into the lake.

The wind took the ash and spread it in a shimmering trail. It floated on the water and drifted away from them in a silver ribbon. When the box was empty, Dan let go and she felt his hand touch a teardrop on her cheek, before he let it rest on her shoulder.

'Don't be sad, Mum. They're together now. Nana will be happy.' His solemn face broke her. 'Just like we are.'

The sob caught in her throat and she brushed tears from her cheeks as she covered his hand with hers.

Ryan held out his hand and she took it, feeling the strength, the connection in it. He brought her to her feet and enveloped them both in his arms. They stood there, wrapped together, as the lightest of snowflakes dusted across Ryan's dark coat.

Ryan's warmth, Ryan's love, was shelter from the cold.

It felt so right, so real, so enduring.

She'd found a love like her parents'; a love forged in fire that grew stronger, not weaker, because of that tempering heat.

Author's Note

While *Burning Lies* is a work of fiction I have drawn on real organisations, like Border Protection Command, for the framework and inspiration. I also refer to bushfires in Canberra, but the ones in the book are not the tragic events of 2003 and I don't wish to cause offence or distress to those who lost so much through them. What is real, however, is the use of aircraft during fire events to track arsonists. Aircraft can provide incredibly effective airborne detection capabilities that are vital for the police and fire services.

I also wish to pay tribute to the volunteers who fight fires in Australia. Queensland's Rural Fire Brigade play a crucial role in this story and I have nothing but admiration for the men and women who give their time so freely in the defence of their neighbourhoods and towns.

Lastly, to the locals on the Atherton Tablelands, I've taken some liberties with the topography of your area, setting the action in and around Oakey Creek, a place that lives only in my imagination. When it came to the crunch, I couldn't bear to allow an arsonist to burn places I love so much.

Acknowledgements

Many people contributed to *Burning Lies* and I'm humbled by their generosity. I'm especially grateful to Mal and Amanda for trusting me enough to share their experiences.

Thanks to A/Chief Superintendent Alan Hogg from Queensland Fire and Rescue Services; Kym Brown and Tim Ash for generously allowing me into their world of firefighting.

Thanks once more to Glenn for all things police; thanks also to Brett, who again provided so much of the inspiration for the Coastwatch element of this book, and to Sandy for loaning him for interrogations. Any errors in procedures are mine and I'm claiming writer's prerogative!

Thanks also to Steve and Vicki Krahe for sharing their local insights over so many visits. To Peter and Anne Tubman, thanks for being such great location scouts.

My thanks to Ali Watts for believing in the story and pushing me into new territory. Thanks to Jo Rosenberg for working so hard to polish the manuscript. It's been a pleasure working with them and the team at Penguin Australia.

My wonderful agent, Clare Forster, provided great support and wise words when I needed them.

My sister was my crit partner, agony aunt and leader of the cheer squad from the other side of the world. Thanks, Bron, we'll have to do this again!

My husband washed, cooked, ironed, and even resorted to wielding a whipper snipper on the garden edges (something that is purely my domain), so I could have the luxury of writing in peace. Graham, you are a rare and wonderful man.

To the readers who've been with me on this journey, I hope you enjoyed Kaitlyn and Ryan's story.